THE ORACLES OF TROY

Glyn Iliffe studied English and Classics at Reading University, where he developed a passion for the stories of ancient Greek mythology. Well travelled, Glyn has visited nearly forty countries, trekked in the Himalayas, spent six weeks hitchhiking across North America and had his collarbone broken by a bull in Pamplona.

He is married with two daughters and lives in Leicestershire. *King of Ithaca* was his first novel, followed by *The Gates of Troy* and *The Armour of Achilles*. He is currently working on the fifth book in the series, *The Voyage of Odysseus*.

For more information visit www.glyniliffe.com

Also by Glyn Iliffe

King of Ithaca
The Gates of Troy
The Armour of Achilles

GLYN ILIFFE

THE ORACLES OF TROY

Mereo Books

1A The Wool Market Dyer Street Cirencester Gloucestershire GL7 2PR
An imprint of Memoirs Publishing www.mereobooks.com

THE ORACLES OF TROY: 978-1-86151-211-6

First published in Great Britain in 2014
by Mereo Books, an imprint of Memoirs Publishing

The address for Memoirs Publishing Group Limited can be found at
www.memoirspublishing.com

The Memoirs Publishing Group Ltd Reg. No. 7834348

The Memoirs Publishing Group supports both The Forest Stewardship Council® (FSC®) and the
PEFC® leading international forest-certification organisations. Our books carrying both the FSC
label and the PEFC® and are printed on FSC®-certified paper. FSC® is the only
forest-certification scheme supported by the leading environmental organisations including
Greenpeace. Our paper procurement policy can be found at
www.memoirspublishing.com/environment

Typeset in 9/12pt Garamond
by Wiltshire Associates Publisher Services Ltd. Printed and bound in Great Britain by
Printondemand-Worldwide, Peterborough PE2 6XD

FOR TABITHA

ACKNOWLEDGEMENTS

As ever, I am grateful to my wife, Jane, for her patience and encouragement.

My thanks also go to Steven A McKay, Richard Sheehan,
Maureen Corderoy, Deven Kanal, Jane Davies, Kevin Marlow and
Bruce Villas for their proof reading skills and improvements to the original text.

GLOSSARY

A

Achilles	– Myrmidon prince, killed by Paris
Aeneas	– Dardanian prince, the son of Anchises
Agamemnon	– king of Mycenae, leader of the Greeks
Ajax (greater)	– king of Salamis, killed himself after being sent mad by the gods
Ajax (lesser)	– king of Locris
Alybas	– home city of Eperitus, in northern Greece
Anchises	– king of the Dardanians, allies of Troy
Andromache	– wife of Hector
Antenor	– Trojan elder
Anticleia	– Odysseus's mother
Antinous	– Ithacan noble, son of Eupeithes
Antiphus	– Ithacan guardsman
Apheidas	– Trojan commander, father of Eperitus
Aphrodite	– goddess of love
Apollo	– archer god, associated with music, song and healing
Arceisius	– Ithacan soldier, murdered by Apheidas
Ares	– god of war
Artemis	– moon-goddess associated with childbirth, noted for her virginity and vengefulness
Astyanax	– infant son of Hector and Andromache
Astynome	– daughter of Chryses, a priest of Apollo
Astyoche	– daughter of Priam and mother of Eurypylus
Athena	– goddess of wisdom and warfare
Aulis	– sheltered bay in the Euboean Straits

C

Calchas	– priest of Apollo, adviser to Agamemnon
Cassandra	– Trojan princess, daughter of Priam
Clymene	– servant to Apheidas and mother of Palamedes
Clytaemnestra	– queen of Mycenae and wife of Agamemnon

D

Dardanus	– city to the north of Troy
Deidameia	– mother of Neoptolemus and widow of Achilles
Deiphobus	– Trojan prince, younger brother of Hector and Paris
Demeter	– goddess of agriculture
Diocles	– Spartan soldier
Diomedes	– king of Argos

E

Elpenor	– Ithacan soldier
Epaltes	– Argive soldier
Epeius	– Greek craftsman and notorious coward
Eperitus	– captain of Odysseus's guard
Eumaeus	– swineherd and faithful slave to Laertes
Eupeithes	– member of the Kerosia
Euryalus	– companion of Diomedes
Eurybates	– Odysseus's squire
Eurylochus	– Ithacan soldier, cousin of Odysseus
Eurypylus	– Mysian king, grandson of Priam

H

Hades	– god of the Underworld
Halitherses	– former captain of Ithacan royal guard, given joint charge of Ithaca in Odysseus's absence
Hecabe	– Trojan queen, wife of King Priam
Hector	– Trojan prince, killed by Achilles
Helen	– former queen of Sparta, now wife of Paris
Helenus	– son of Priam and Hecabe
Hephaistos	– god of fire; blacksmith to the Olympians
Heracles	– greatest of all Greek heroes
Hestia	– the goddess of the hearth
Hippodameia	– wife of Pelops

I

Idaeus	– herald to King Priam
Idomeneus	– king of Crete
Ilium	– the region of which Troy was the capital
Ilus	– founder of Troy, grandfather of Priam

Iphigenia	– daughter of Eperitus and Clytaemnestra, sacrificed by Agamemnon
Ithaca	– island in the Ionian Sea

K

Kerosia	– Ithacan council meeting

L

Laertes	– Odysseus's father
Lemnos	– island in the Aegean Sea

M

Menelaus	– king of Sparta, brother of Agamemnon and cuckolded husband of Helen
Menestheus	– king of Athens
Mentor	– close friend of Odysseus, given joint charge of Ithaca in Odysseus's absence
Mycenae	– most powerful city in Greece, situated in north-eastern Peloponnese
Myrmidons	– the followers of Achilles
Myrtilus	– King Oenomaus's charioteer
Mysia	– region to the south-east of Troy

N

Neoptolemus	– son of Achilles and Deidameia
Neriton (Mount)	– highest point on Ithaca
Nestor	– king of Pylos
Nisus	– Ithacan elder

O

Odysseus	– king of Ithaca
Oenomaus	– king of Pisa, killed in a chariot race against Pelops
Oenops	– member of the Kerosia
Omeros	– Ithacan soldier and bard

P

Palamedes	– Nauplian prince, executed for treason
Palladium	– sacred image of Athena's companion, Pallas
Pandion	– murdered king of Alybas

Paris	– Trojan prince, eldest remaining son of King Priam
Parnassus (Mount)	– mountain in central Greece and home of the Pythian oracle
Peisandros	– Myrmidon commander
Peloponnese	– southernmost landmass of Greek mainland, named after Pelops
Pelops	– grandfather of Agamemnon and Menelaus
Penelope	– queen of Ithaca and wife of Odysseus
Penthesilea	– queen of the Amazons, slain by Achilles
Pergamos	– the citadel of Troy
Philoctetes	– Malian archer, deserted by the Greeks on Lemnos
Pisa	– region in the north-western Peloponnese
Pleisthenes	– youngest son of Menelaus and Helen
Podaleirius	– famed healer, son of Asclepius
Polites	– Ithacan warrior
Polyctor	– member of the Kerosia
Poseidon	– god of the sea
Priam	– king of Troy
Pythoness	– high priestess of the Pythian oracle

S

Scamander	– river on the Trojan plain
Simöeis	– river on the Trojan plain
Sthenelaus	– companion of Diomedes

T

Talthybius	– squire to Agamemnon
Taphians	– pirate race from Taphos
Telemachus	– son of Odysseus and Penelope
Tenedos	– island off the coast of Ilium
Teucer	– famed archer, half-brother and companion to Great Ajax
Theano	– priestess of Athena and wife of Antenor
Thebes	– northern Greek city, sacked by Diomedes
Thetis	– chief of the Nereids and mother of Achilles
Trechos	– Argive soldier
Troy	– chief city of Ilium

X

xenia   – the custom of friendship towards strangers

Z

Zacynthos   – southernmost of the Ionian islands under
                              Odysseus's rule

Zeus   – the king of the gods

book

ONE

Chapter One
LEMNOS

Odysseus, king of Ithaca, stood at the stern of the galley, his short legs planted firmly apart on the deck and his muscular, top-heavy torso rolling gently with the subdued motion of the sea. His green eyes were impassive as they studied the walls of dense fog that surrounded the ship, seemingly unconcerned at the possibility they could be creeping towards their doom on a rocky shoal or drifting past their destination altogether. King Diomedes showed less patience, beseeching and cursing the gods with alternate breaths as he stood at Odysseus's left shoulder, his blue cloak swept back to reveal a gleaming breastplate and the golden pommel of a sword hanging at his side. Eperitus, captain of the Ithacan guard, was at Odysseus's other shoulder, his eyes on the crew as they pulled at the oars.

'What do your senses tell you, Eperitus?' Odysseus asked, his smooth voice amplified by the silence. 'Are we near to Lemnos?'

Eperitus stared out at the thick mist, raising his chin a little as he focussed his hearing on sounds that were beyond the gentle creaking of the long oars in their leather loops and the swish and trickle of water across the blades. As he concentrated he began to hear things the others could not, noises diminished by distance that took a few moments to understand. With them came odours and aromas, and different tastes carried on the air, all of them delicate and insubstantial, but nevertheless distinct to his raised perceptivity.

'I can hear crowds of gulls,' he began, 'squabbling and cawing like they used to on the cliffs and hillsides around Ithaca. And waves crashing against rocks. There's a stink of seaweed and wet stone, but with a hint of soil and vegetation. It's definitely land, though I can't say whether it's Lemnos or not.'

'It is,' Odysseus said confidently. 'Which way?'

Eperitus pointed at an angle to the bearing they were travelling along. Odysseus gave a satisfied smile and glanced back over his shoulder.

'North a little, Antiphus.'

The man at the helm nodded, a determined look on his face as he leaned the twin steering oars to the left.

'I'm going to the prow,' Odysseus announced. 'I remember the rocks the first time we came here, and the last thing I want is one of them popping up out of this fog and tearing a hole in the hull.'

'I'll come with you,' Eperitus said.

'No need,' Odysseus replied, placing an arresting hand on his broad chest. 'Why don't you stay here and make sure the anchor stones are ready? You can prepare the boat, too, while you're at it.'

The fact the anchor stones and the small rowing boat could be quickly readied by any of the seasoned crew made Eperitus suspicious, and when Odysseus added one of his reassuring smiles he felt sure he was hiding something. Not that there was any point in questioning him; after twenty years as the king's friend, Eperitus knew he would not reveal anything he did not have a mind to.

Odysseus bent down to pick up a bundle of fur and a wooden club that were stowed beneath one of the rowing benches.

'That's Agamemnon's lion's pelt, isn't it?' Diomedes said.

'I borrowed it from him,' Odysseus explained innocently.

'What in Athena's name do you want that for? And what's the point of the club? If you're planning to beat Philoctetes to death, don't forget Calchas said we need to bring him back to Troy alive.'

'Philoctetes probably perished years ago,' Odysseus replied, 'especially with that stinking wound of his. The important thing is to find his bow and arrows.'

Eperitus and Diomedes watched him walk down the centre of the galley, pausing halfway beside a gigantic warrior crammed onto the end of one of the benches. Odysseus leaned down and spoke close to the man's ear, then handed him the lion's pelt and the club before continuing to the prow.

'Why's he giving them to Polites?' Diomedes asked. 'He's definitely up to something.'

Eperitus nodded. 'But what?'

'Some trick or other, no doubt.'

'No, he promised me he'd act honourably, especially after the unjust way Philoctetes was marooned on Lemnos. All because the poor wretch was bitten by a snake.'

'It was a harsh decision, but perhaps the years have helped us forget the stench of the wound and how he used to groan and wail.'

'We were too harsh, my lord,' Antiphus interrupted from his position at the twin rudder. As an archer himself, he had always empathised with Philoctetes. 'With the bow and arrows Heracles gave him he could have ended the war in the first year. Hector and Paris were the backbone of the Trojan army, but two shots from Philoctetes would have brought them down in the dust and left the gates of Troy virtually undefended.'

'Then perhaps it was the will of the gods that we abandoned him on Lemnos,' Diomedes replied. 'Though if he *has* survived, I wouldn't want to fall foul of him if he still has his weapons. A good reason for us to remind Odysseus of what we agreed, don't you think Eperitus?'

Eperitus nodded.

'Omeros,' he barked, staring at a lad who was sitting with his back against the side of the ship, busily restringing a tortoiseshell lyre, 'put that damned thing away and make the boat ready. Get Elpenor to help you. And I want my breastplate, greaves and sword ready the moment we're at anchor. If I find you've been spending more time on that instrument than you have cleaning and oiling my armour then you'll only have yourself to blame for the consequences.'

Omeros leapt to his feet and called over to another young man who had been busy casting dice with his shipmates. Eperitus was certain his armour would not have been cared for nearly as well as Omeros's lyre, but he felt no anger at the fact. The truth was, since arriving at Troy only a few months before among a shipload of Ithacan replacements, he had proved himself to be a promising warrior with a propensity to learn quickly and a calm intelligence that was not flustered by the confusion of battle. That was why Eperitus had made him his squire. More than that, though, he found he liked the boy.

'And you, Eurylochus,' he continued, looking at a pot-bellied sailor who was sitting at one of the benches and gnawing on a scrap of dried beef, 'I want you to prepare the anchor stones.'

'I'm rowing,' Eurylochus replied through a mouthful of meat, refusing to look at Eperitus.

As much as Eperitus liked Omeros, he despised Eurylochus, who used the fact he was Odysseus's cousin as an excuse to be lazy and arrogant. Eperitus's dislike was more than matched by Eurylochus's own hatred for him, which was driven by jealousy and a misguided belief that the position of captain of the guard should have been his by right. But the years had taught Eperitus how to deal with Eurylochus.

'You'll be swimming if those anchor stones aren't ready by the time I return,' he said, and followed Diomedes to the prow while Eurylochus fumed behind him.

'You shouldn't embarrass my cousin in front of the crew, Eperitus,' Odysseus chided as they joined him.

Eperitus raised an eyebrow. 'You're right. I should've just stood there and let him undermine my authority.'

'The petulance of a small-minded fool won't harm the respect these men hold you in, you know that. And humiliating Eurylochus will only provoke him to acts of petty revenge – he's done it enough times in the past. Talking of disrespecting authority, didn't I ask *you* to prepare the anchor stones and the boat?'

'They're being seen to,' Diomedes answered. 'Besides, you've had your chance for a private word with Polites, so you should be grateful for two extra pairs of eyes in this fog.'

Odysseus grinned and the three men turned to stare out at the milky vapour that shifted spectrally around the galley.

'I don't know what you're up to, Odysseus,' Diomedes continued, scanning the mist, 'but you promised us no tricks, remember? Philoctetes was shamefully treated when we left him here, and if he's still alive after ten years then I doubt he'll be feeling any better disposed toward us – especially as *you* were the one who brought him here. The first sign of deceit from you and he'll shoot us all down like tethered doves.'

'I brought him here to save him from being murdered after he beat Achilles and Medon,' Odysseus retorted. 'They'd have silenced his groaning for good if it hadn't been for me. Not that I expect him to appreciate that. But I've agreed to let you do the talking and I'll keep my promise, Diomedes – unless he speaks to me, that is. He'd sooner shoot me than talk to me, though, so that's unlikely. And to make sure he doesn't recognise me, I'll keep my hood over my face and my lips sealed.'

Eperitus gave him a sceptical look. 'And if we fail to persuade him?'

4

'How can you? Assuming he's survived this long and no passing ship has offered him passage back to Greece, then he'll have been alone on this rock for ten years. Do you think he won't snatch at the chance to get back to civilisation and a bit of human company? If he *does* show hesitation, any hesitation at all, just do what I said: offer him food and drink, and tell him about Calchas's prophecy – that Troy can't fall until *he* has rejoined the army. Believe me, after ten years without a sip of wine it'll be impossible for him to refuse, and when the alcohol reaches his brain he'll be yours for the taking.'

Diomedes frowned. 'That's trickery! I won't dishonour myself by fooling the poor wretch.'

'Forget the wine, then,' Odysseus said with an exasperated wave of his hand. 'Just appeal to his sense of glory! What is it Omeros says about warriors, Eperitus? *Always to be best, and to be distinguished above the rest*. Once you tell him he's the key to the downfall of Troy, he'll have swum to the galley before we can row there – lame or not. Persuading him to rejoin the army couldn't be easier, even for a pair of oxhide shields like you.'

'And if the end of the war and your returning home to Ithaca depends on us persuading him, and we fail?' Eperitus asked. 'What will you do then?'

'You won't fail. Calchas told us a decade ago that Troy would fall in the tenth year of the siege, so if that can't happen without Philoctetes then we're fated to succeed. It's the will of the gods.'

'Then may the gods help us,' Eperitus replied, leaning forward and staring into the fog.

The three men fell silent again as they watched for black shapes amid the creeping fronds of mist ahead of them. Eperitus's thoughts drifted back to the conversation he had had with Odysseus the evening before, after they had buried Great Ajax, the king of Salamis, on a cliff top overlooking the Aegean Sea. When Achilles had been slain by an arrow fired from the walls of Troy, Ajax had demanded his cousin's god-made armour be given to him. And who could say he did not deserve it, after carrying Achilles's corpse to the safety of the Greek lines while Odysseus and Eperitus had fought off the pursuing Trojans? Then when Odysseus deceived the Council of Kings into awarding the armour to him, the disgrace and humiliation had driven Ajax insane and he had taken his own life. Racked with guilt, Odysseus had sworn by Athena that he would never again pursue false glory, act with dishonour or be distracted from his sole purpose of returning home to Ithaca. From that point on he resolved only to seek the destruction of Troy and the ending of the war. But Eperitus knew that his friend's ideas of honour and glory were different to his, and however deep his remorse over Ajax's death he was unlikely never to resort to cunning or trickery again. To expect Odysseus not to use his natural guile was like asking a bird not to use its wings.

'What's that?' hissed Diomedes, thrusting a finger towards a tall black shape emerging from the swirls of mist ahead of them.

Eperitus narrowed his eyes; there were other shapes beyond it, more rocks waiting to rip open the ship's belly and condemn its crew to the same fate as Philoctetes. And suddenly every man on board could hear the seagulls and smell the pungent seaweed piled up on the crags, though only Eperitus's nostrils could detect the underlying stench of corruption emanating from the island, a reek he had not known in such strength for ten years. They had found Philoctetes and he was still cursed by the terrible wound the gods had inflicted on him a decade before.

'Throw the anchor stones overboard,' Odysseus shouted. 'And ready the boat. We're going ashore.'

Chapter Two
PHILOCTETES

The boat bumped against the shelf of black rock and Odysseus leapt out, slipping slightly on the layered seaweed before finding a handhold and pulling himself to safety. Antiphus threw him the rope and he held the vessel fast as the others clambered free of its cramped confines. Eperitus was last behind Diomedes and seeing Polites had left the club and lion's pelt that Odysseus had given him, stooped to pick them up.

'You can leave those,' Odysseus said quietly, passing the rope to Polites and offering Eperitus his hand. 'We'll only need them if all else fails.'

Mystified, but knowing better than to ask for an explanation from his friend, Eperitus left the club and pelt in the boat and took the king's hand. He stepped ashore and looked about himself. Through the thick fog behind them he could just see the mast and cross spar of the galley, swaying gently between two sentinels of rock. The sea in-between was lost beneath the curling fronds of white mist that rose like steam from its surface, creeping inland across the stony shore to lap at the knees of the cliffs that loomed harsh and forbidding above the party of Greeks. The bluffs were dotted with seagulls, huddled into pockets in the rock for protection from the cold breeze, and Eperitus could hear many more of the creatures nestled on the invisible cliff tops above. There was little else to see or hear in this barren corner of Lemnos, but the stench he had picked up from the galley was stronger and more offensive now, forcing him to lift a corner of his cloak to cover his mouth and nose.

'What is it?' Diomedes asked.

'Can't you smell it yet?' Eperitus replied. 'It's Philoctetes's wound,

7

I'm sure of it.'

'Impossible,' Diomedes scoffed. 'There's no way he could have survived for ten years in that sort of pain. Either the wound healed itself, or it killed Philoctetes long ago and we're here to find his bones – and the weapons he left behind.'

'You forget he wasn't bitten by any ordinary snake,' Odysseus said. 'It was sent by Thetis, in answer to Achilles's calls for vengeance because Philoctetes beat him in the race to Tenedos. The wound's a curse from the goddess, and if she wanted the pain to last for ten years without killing him then you can be sure he's still alive. One thing's for certain, though: the pain and the loneliness of this place will have sent Philoctetes half-mad at the least, if not completely insane. We need to be on our guard and do nothing to frighten him – nothing at all! And that means leaving our weapons in the boat.'

Diomedes laughed, his handsome face genuinely amused as he patted the ivory pommel of his sword.

'This blade is never more than a few paces beyond my reach, old friend, and if you think I'm going to face an embittered madman like Philoctetes without it –'

'With respect, my lord,' Antiphus interrupted, 'what good will your sword be against the bow and arrows of Heracles? It's said they never miss their target and the tips are poisonous, so if Philoctetes wants to shoot us dead then our weapons aren't going to stop him.'

'I'd rather take my chances *with* my sword than *without* it, thank you Antiphus,' Diomedes replied. 'Besides, I'll keep it well hidden beneath my cloak.'

Odysseus slipped his sheathed sword from his shoulder and set it down on a pile of black seaweed.

'One careless movement of your hand'll be enough to show you're armed, Diomedes, and then you'll only have yourself to blame if Philoctetes gets the idea into his head that we're not friendly. Either leave your sword here with Polites, or stay by the boat yourself and let Polites take your place.'

Diomedes gave him a surly look, then unbuckled his baldric and placed his sword down beside Odysseus's. Antiphus's bow, arrows and dagger were next, followed by the spears and swords of Eurylochus and Eperitus.

'Good,' Odysseus said, flicking his hood up to hide his face.

'Eperitus, lead the way – just follow your sense of smell and we're bound to find him.'

Eperitus paused to sniff the foul air, then, pulling his cloak about his shoulders, began to pick his way between the seaweed-festooned rocks and the small, dark pools that hid between them. The others followed, except for Polites, who had been given the task of keeping watch over the boat and their weapons while they were away. Glancing back, Eperitus saw Odysseus reach into the boat for a skin of water, which he threw over his shoulder before turning to speak to the giant warrior. His words were too low even for Eperitus's acute hearing to pick out from the constant cawing of the gulls, and a moment later the king had turned back and was following behind Antiphus.

Eperitus moved with the cliffs to his right – an unending wall that forbade access to the rest of Lemnos and confined them to the narrow, rugged strip of land that skirted the sea. The fog, if anything, was growing thicker. It condensed on his beard and eyelashes to form little droplets of water that would occasionally merge and trickle into his eyes or down his neck. The stench of brine and seagull droppings pervaded everything, but soon even this was eclipsed by the reek Eperitus had first picked up on the galley. The others could smell it too by now and began to complain under their breath or cover their faces with their cloaks. Diomedes and Odysseus both wore scarves to keep the rims of their breastplates from rubbing against their necks, but had pulled them up over their mouths and noses to filter out the foul odour; the others had no choice but to endure it. After a while Eperitus detected a low groaning that reminded him of a battlefield after nightfall, when the fighting had stopped and the opposing armies had settled down by their campfires, only to be haunted by the cries of the wounded among the corpses in-between, calling out for their friends to find them or to the gods to claim their wretched souls. The sound grew nearer, though none of his comrades remarked on it, and he noticed there were no more seagulls on the cliff faces above them. There was something else, too, something his instincts had been aware of for a while but he had not been able until that moment to identify. He realised they were being followed.

'What's that?' Eurylochus hissed, stopping and pointing into the mist.

Eperitus traced the direction of his finger and saw a ring of small, fist-sized stones on a plateau of rock ahead of him. They were grey with ash and a pile of burnt wood lay heaped up between them. Scattered about the remains of the fire were thin white sticks of varying lengths, which Eperitus quickly realised were the bones of seagulls. He could tell the ashes were cold, but by the smell of them they were no older than the previous night. He reached instinctively for his sword and remembered he had left it with Polites.

Odysseus moved past his shoulder and gave the remains of the fire a kick with his heel. The heavier ash that had not been blown away by the sea breeze now rose up in a small cloud about his ankles.

'It's recent,' he declared, slipping his scarf momentarily down from his mouth. 'He's here somewhere.'

As he spoke Eperitus sensed a change and realised the groaning had stopped. He raised a finger to his lips, gesturing the others to silence. A number of large boulders had rolled down from the cliff countless years before, forming a clumsy ramp that led up the sheer rock face. Eperitus's gaze followed the boulders up the side of the cliff, noticing signs of smoothing here and there, as well as smaller stones that seemed to have been put in place to act as steps where the rocks were steepest. And then, as he looked higher up the fog-shrouded precipice, he saw the triangular mouth of a cave.

'He's in there,' he whispered, pointing.

The five men moved forward together, craning their heads back to stare up at the opening above them. Odysseus laid a hand on Diomedes's shoulder.

'Be careful of everything you say. He's had ten years to dwell on his hatred of the Greeks, so don't provoke him or threaten him in any way. Remember his bow and arrows.'

He covered his face again and drew back to stand behind the others. Diomedes looked up at the cave and cupped a hand to his mouth.

'Philoctetes,' he called. 'Philoctetes, son of Poeas, if you're up there then show yourself. We wish to speak with you.'

There was no reply. After a few more moments, Diomedes turned to Eperitus with a frown.

'Are you certain he's up there? I know your senses are keener than ours, but –'

'Look again,' Eperitus said, nodding at the mouth of the cave and pinching his nose against the fresh stench polluting the already bad air.

The others peered up through the mist and saw that a figure had appeared. A tall bow was clutched in its left hand and an arrow had been fitted, drawn in readiness to fire at the hooded figures below. The weapon was undoubtedly the one Heracles had given to Philoctetes, but whether the creature that held it was the Malian archer – or even a human being at all – could barely be discerned. Its skin was pale and ingrained with years of dirt; its bare limbs were so thin and wasted that they were no thicker than a small child's; the rags that covered its torso seemed to hang like the tattered remnants of a sail over a mast; and the creature's long beard and hair made its head seem much too large for its emaciated body. But Eperitus's sharp eyes were able to see the face clearly. It was a face that was as twisted and misshapen as the trees that grew on the windswept plains of Ilium, a face that had been distorted irrevocably by years of excruciating pain and cancerous hatred, but a face that had undeniably once belonged to Philoctetes.

Diomedes stepped back, groping for Eperitus's wrist and seizing it.

'Is that … is that *him*?' he hissed, unable to tear his eyes away from the savage figure aiming its bow at them from the boulders above.

'Yes, it's Philoctetes,' Eperitus replied, freeing his wrist and placing his hand on Diomedes's shoulder, urging him forward once more.

The archer lowered his weapon a fraction, revealing dark eyes as he stared down at the newcomers to his island.

'Who are you?' he croaked, the very act of speaking causing him to break out in a fit of dry coughing that took a few moments to recover from. 'Who are you and what do you want on my island?'

'Are you Philoctetes, son of Poeas?' Diomedes repeated.

'This is the body that once bore that name, though both the man and his fame have been forgotten by this world. But *this* is the bow of Heracles, whom the gods raised up to live with them on Mount Olympus, having made him immortal like themselves. Its arrows never miss and their tips are poisonous, so if you've come to mock the ghost of Philoctetes or steal the rocks and stones that are his possessions, then beware.'

'It's true you've become a pitiful figure, Philoctetes,' Diomedes replied. 'Yet you were once a prince of Malia, and custom dictates a prince should treat his visitors with decorum, even if his home is a cold and lonely rock like this. You speak of the gods with respect in your voice, so if you honour them then honour us.'

Philoctetes frowned angrily, then shifted his position with surprising speed, using the rocks for support. Diomedes and the others flinched instinctively as he raised his bow and fired into the air. A moment later there was a squawk, followed by a loud thump as a gull crashed onto the rocks before them.

'You see?' he crowed, his eyes wide as he stared at them along the shaft of a new arrow. 'Philoctetes has provided a feast to celebrate your arrival on Lemnos! But first – just to show he hasn't forgotten how to observe the rules of xenia – he must know your identities and what it is you want of him? Are you merchants, seeking the way to Ilium or Greece? He'd lead you there himself, though you aren't the first visitors to this rock and none of your predecessors ever offered Philoctetes passage on their ships. Not as soon as they caught wind of *this*!'

He raised his leg to show a foot bandaged in cloth that was black with filth. As he did so he gave out a cry of anguished despair and fell back against a boulder, beating the stone with the flat of his free hand and raising a scream to the invisible skies above, where he knew the gods remained indifferent to his pain. Eperitus caught a movement from the corner of his eye and turned to see that Eurylochus had taken a step forward. His hand was cupped over his mouth and nose to filter out some of the reek of Philoctetes's wound, and in his eyes Eperitus could see he was debating whether to leap up the rocks and take the bow and arrows by force while their owner was paralysed with agony. Then, before Eurylochus could make his decision, the screaming ended in another fit of coughing and Philoctetes slid himself back up against the boulder. He raised his bow and drew back the arrow once more, though weakly, and aimed it at the men below.

'So who are you?' he called in a tired voice. 'Do you have any lineage to speak of? And what in the name of Heracles brings you to this forsaken place?'

'As for whom I am, you know me already,' Diomedes answered, tipping back his hood. 'I am Diomedes, son of Tydeus. I have come to ask if you will rejoin the army and fight with us against Troy.'

Philoctetes did not move. His eyes narrowed slightly as they stared down the shaft of the arrow at the king of Argos, but he said nothing. Then a flicker of anger touched his twisted features. He gripped the bow tightly and drew the string back to his sneering lip.

'He prayed you would come one day,' he said, heavy tears swelling up in the corners of his eyes before rolling down his filthy cheeks and into his beard. 'Philoctetes prayed you would come back for him, snivelling like curs, pleading for him and his arrows to save your worthless skins. He prayed for this day so *hard* and so *long*, to Heracles and any god who would listen, offering the only sacrifices his kingdom of rocks could provide – birds, fish and crabs! Have you ever tried to sacrifice a crab, Diomedes? Do the gods even accept such meagre sacrifices? But of course they do, or why else have you come?'

'Indeed, why else have we come, Philoctetes, unless it was the gods who sent us? The Greeks have need of your bow and arrows and Agamemnon himself requests that you return to the army and help us secure the final victory over Priam.'

'*Agamemnon*!' Philoctetes spat. 'What does Philoctetes care for that man and his requests? What service does Philoctetes owe to him, or to any of you for that matter? How long has it been since you abandoned him here? It must be at least five years by now.'

'It's ten.'

'*Ten*!' Philoctetes reeled back, bearing his blackened teeth in a snarl and slapping repeatedly at the boulder with the flat of his hand. 'Ten years alone, with nothing but seagulls and his hatred of the Greeks to keep him company! In the name of Heracles, can it have been so long?'

'Be glad it doesn't have to be any longer,' Diomedes said, a little impatiently. 'What's more, Agamemnon realises you were wronged when we left you here and doesn't expect you to return to the army without compensation. He offers seven copper tripods and cauldrons to go with them, never touched by fire, along with ten ingots of gold and three slave women trained in all the household arts. These are fine gifts, Philoctetes, and you will bring yourself great honour by accepting them.'

Philoctetes was half lost in a sheet of fog that had rolled down from the cliff tops above, but his husky voice was clearly audible in the damp air.

'Philoctetes always liked you, Diomedes. You were one of the few kings who had a shred of decency in them. Yet you don't have Odysseus's powers of persuasion, or that honeyed voice of his; indeed, you make Agamemnon's gifts sound as exciting as roast seagull. The King of Men should have sent Odysseus instead; Philoctetes could have enjoyed the skill of his arguments, and then had the satisfaction of shooting him dead in payment for marooning him here! Now go back in your ship and tell Agamemnon to keep his offer. Philoctetes doesn't

13

need cauldrons or gold – not here – and any "honour" attached to them would be more than compensated for by the shame of serving an army that betrayed him!'

'Then forget the gifts,' Diomedes snapped, jabbing his finger at the mist-shrouded figure above. 'Forget Agamemnon, forget the army, forget the oath we took to protect Helen. If you're so twisted with hatred of your own countrymen –'

'*Curse all Greeks!*'

'Then if you hate us so much, do it for the love of the gods – or fear of them, if that's easier. Do you think Agamemnon or any of us'd give a damn about your bow and arrows, whatever their powers are claimed to be? If the spears of Achilles, Ajax and a host of others haven't defeated Troy in ten years, what difference will your weapons make? None that I can see! The only reason we came here was because Calchas, priest of Apollo, had a vision that Troy will not fall without you. Until the bow and arrows of Heracles are brought to Ilium, every drop of Greek blood will have been spilled in vain. So if you won't return for our sakes, then do it out of respect for the gods. Or do it for yourself. Isn't it payment enough that men will say the walls of Troy only succumbed to the arrows of Philoctetes? That's more than thousands of those who have already died can claim, and many of them were greater men than you are.'

There was a long silence, during which Philoctetes was lost to sight behind the drifting mist. When it cleared they saw he had descended a little and was sitting on a smooth rock with his bow and arrows at his side. A thick, twisted branch that he used as a crutch was leaning against his inner thigh.

'Perhaps you're not as clumsy with words as Philoctetes thought, Diomedes,' he said. 'At least, not when you're touched with a little passion. And the will of the gods – and the promise of everlasting glory – are not easy things to deny, especially when the alternative is to remain here, forgotten by the civilised world and left to feast on stringy gull's meat and seaweed. What Philoctetes wouldn't do for a taste of wine, or even the feel of bread in his mouth again! Not to mention a little conversation and the company of his fellow men.'

He paused and Eperitus sensed the hesitation in Philoctetes's tone.

'Go on,' Diomedes said, cautiously.

'And yet you ask too much. Can you even begin to understand what it's like to spend – what did you say it was – to spend ten years alone? To be cursed by the gods and abandoned by your comrades, nursing a desire for vengeance and longing for human companionship, only to be offered salvation by the very men whose downfall you've been praying for all that time. Yes, he wanted you to return and plead for his help, but only so he could have the satisfaction of telling you to go to the halls of Hades. But now you've come, it's not how he'd imagined it. He's not even sure whether this isn't some sort of trick, the kind of thing Odysseus would dream up; or whether, if he went with you to Ilium, Philoctetes would spend his arrows on the Trojans or turn them on the Greeks. He needs time, Diomedes.'

'Zeus's beard, haven't you had enough time?' demanded a new voice.

Eurylochus pulled back his hood and turned to Diomedes.

'He's never going to come with us, Diomedes. He's as stubborn as a mule and twice as stupid, not to mention driven out of his senses. If you'd let Odysseus do the talking we'd have been back at the galley by now, sailing for Ilium with this twisted maggot of a man hankering to get into battle and end the war.'

'Odysseus? *Odysseus* is here?' Philoctetes said, leaning down over the boulder and staring at the piglike features of Eurylochus. Eurylochus looked down at his feet, realising his slip, and Philoctetes turned his fierce eyes on the hooded figures behind him. 'Which one of you is Odysseus? Declare yourself or Philoctetes'll shoot all three of you where you stand!'

'You're a damned fool, Eurylochus,' Odysseus snarled, removing his hood and walking out in front of the others. 'Get from my sight before I cut out your tongue and feed it to the seagulls!'

Eurylochus could not meet Odysseus's angry gaze and retreated into the mist. As he slipped away, a gurgle of cold laughter spilled down from the rocks above them.

'He should have known you'd be here,' Philoctetes crowed, smiling with triumphant hatred. 'He should have guessed Agamemnon wouldn't send Diomedes for a task like this. Only the great deceiver – Odysseus himself – would do. Ha, ha! Philoctetes has prayed for this chance for so long. And now, Odysseus, your treacherous ways have finally caught up with you!'

He drew back his bow and took aim.

Chapter Three
HERACLES

Eperitus felt his heart race. If he had been allowed to bring his spear he could have launched it at the skeletal, wild-haired wretch perched among the boulders above them, but as Philoctetes drew back the feathered arrow so that its poisonous head rested against the top of his left fist there was not even enough time to throw himself in front of his king. Then, in the split moment before Philoctetes released the bowstring, Odysseus raised his hand.

'Stop!' he commanded.

His voice had such power and authority that Philoctetes was compelled to retain his pinch-hold on the arrow and lower his bow a little. He looked down the shaft at the man he had spent ten years hating – hating him still, but powerless for an instant to bring about his destruction.

'Philoctetes, I do not deny your right to kill me,' Odysseus began. 'Indeed, what man who had suffered as you have suffered would not want to kill the one he blamed for his misfortunes. If you send my spirit down to Hades then I would not begrudge you your vengeance, even though your haste will have deprived Penelope of a husband and Telemachus a father. You, after all, are the victim, the man who through no fault of his own was betrayed and abandoned to die on this forbidding rock.'

He swept his hand in a half-circle, looking up at the churning walls of mist and the dark mass of the cliff faces beyond them.

'In truth, I'm amazed you were able to survive this long in such a place. There are few, even among the greatest warriors of Greece, who could have kept themselves alive amid this desolation.'

'Philoctetes had the bow Heracles left him,' Philoctetes said. 'And his hatred of you, of course.'

Odysseus nodded as if in sympathy, though his eyes did not leave Philoctetes for one moment.

'Of course. Hatred is a powerful force among mortals. It gives a man endurance in adversity, a purpose to go on living when there is nothing else to live for. In battle it focusses his strength and gives him an urgency that is difficult for his enemies to overcome. But hate does not nourish a man, Philoctetes, nor is it something he can master. I know a warrior who, for twenty years, has been crippled by his loathing of his own father. If he could leave his hatred behind there would be few men to match him in this age of the world, but it distracts him and holds him back, preventing him from becoming what the gods meant him to be.'

Eperitus felt a flush of anger that Odysseus should dare draw parallels between himself and the wretched figure standing among the rocks above them. His father was a black-hearted murderer who had killed a king and taken his throne for himself, and when Eperitus had refused to support his vile crime or acknowledge his rule he had exiled him from the kingdom for life. Shortly afterwards he had fallen in with Odysseus and followed the new path the gods had laid before him; but he had never forgiven his father's sin or forgotten his desire to kill him and wash clean the stain from his family's name. Indeed, a man of honour could do no less, and Odysseus's comments were a stinging betrayal. Eperitus stared at the back of his head, willing him to turn so he could challenge his accusation, but the king kept his gaze stubbornly fixed on the Malian archer whose arrow was still pointed at his heart.

'No doubt the man you speak of had his choice,' Philoctetes said. 'And yet what choice did Philoctetes have? His hatred of you was the only difference between life and death. He chose life.'

'Wrong, Philoctetes. You chose death. The Philoctetes who led his fleet out from the Euboean Straits and beat Achilles in the race to Tenedos is dead. His hatred murdered him and left *you*, a living wraith, a mere husk of humanity!'

'No!' Philoctetes shouted, raising his bow and drawing the string taut. 'No! Philoctetes is alive, and when you're dead he'll be free again.'

'Kill me and any vestige of Philoctetes that remains in you will die with me,' Odysseus retorted. 'Just listen to your babbling speech. Ever since you emerged from that cave you've referred to yourself as *he* and *him*, never *I* or *me*. Whatever you are, you aren't Philoctetes. But perhaps you're right that he isn't completely dead yet. Perhaps something of the old Philoctetes, the *true* Philoctetes, is left inside you. And to him I'm as vital as that crutch you lean on. The thought of me has kept him alive all these years, and though *you* hate me, without me *he* would disappear forever. Kill me and Philoctetes will truly die. Only you will be left!'

As Philoctetes stared back down at Odysseus, it was clear the king's words had provoked a shift deep within his consciousness; a realisation that without the object of his hatred he would succumb fully to the wild, insane creature that lurked among the rocks of Lemnos, reeling between pain and hunger while it eked out an existence on the flesh of seagulls. If he killed Odysseus, the precious Philoctetes – the proud, handsome archer whose memory he guarded like cherished treasure – would be lost forever. While Eperitus watched, a sharp jolt of pain brought Philoctetes crashing down onto the rocks with a cry. His thin voice, stripped bare of any humanity, rose up into the fog-filled air and screamed to the gods for mercy. His screams broke the trance Odysseus's voice had thrown over the others and both Diomedes and Antiphus raced towards the foot of the cascade of boulders to help him. Odysseus called them back.

'Leave him! The pain will go, but let us see what it leaves behind.'

Philoctetes's shouts continued and all they could see was his hand flailing above the boulders, slapping pitifully at the stone until the pain began to ebb and, at last, he found his voice again.

'Have mercy!' he shouted, still lost from view. 'Kill this poor wretch and put an end to his pain. Kill Philoctetes and the bow and arrows are yours, that's what you came for isn't it? It's the weapons that have magical powers, not him. He'll give them to you if you'll take his life, just as Heracles gave them to Philoctetes for ending his suffering. For pity's sake, do what Philoctetes has never been able to bring himself to do!'

'For pity's sake we will not,' Odysseus replied. 'Pity and the will of Zeus. Don't you realise the gods gave you your hatred of me to keep you alive? And now they've sent me to bring you back to the world of men, Philoctetes. I may have earned your loathing for abandoning you here, but it was Achilles who wanted you dead and Medon – your own lieutenant –who had agreed to murder you. Yes it was my suggestion that you be marooned on Lemnos, but it was made to save your life.'

Philoctetes had pulled himself up onto the rock and was staring down at Odysseus again.

'Medon was going to kill … me?'

A slight lift of one eyebrow was Odysseus's only outward reaction to the fact Philoctetes had referred to himself as *me* for the first time since they had coaxed him out of his lair. He opened his mouth to reply, then abruptly shut it again. Surprised by his silence, Eperitus and Diomedes looked at Odysseus and then followed his frowning gaze to the figure scaling the boulders to Philoctetes's right, just beyond the edge of his sight. It was Eurylochus.

'Damn him,' Eperitus whispered.

'Yes, Medon,' Odysseus answered, his voice calm despite the threat posed by Eurylochus as he stole up on Philoctetes, intending to take the bow that had been left on the boulder behind him. 'But Medon is dead – slain by a woman, as befits his treacherous nature. And Achilles has also given up his spirit, which now resides in the Chambers of Decay. Nothing stands between you and a return to the army, Philoctetes. The gods have already stated that great glory awaits you – renown that will eclipse all that has passed before. If you can just surrender your bitter hatred and forgive a group of foolish men who've been made wiser by ten years of suffering and loss, then you can leave this place forever and return with us to civilisation.'

Philoctetes's restless eyes betrayed the struggle that was taking place within. And yet it was a struggle he had only moments to win, for Eurylochus had now emerged on the large boulders behind him, the hem of his cloak floating in the breeze as he looked down at the bow and arrows just a short dash away from him.

'Decide, Philoctetes,' Odysseus said, more urgently now. 'Will you come with us to everlasting glory or will you remain king of your island realm? Will it be bread and wine, or seagulls and mist? Decide!'

The scuffing of a leather sandal on stone gave Eurylochus away. With a speed that seemed impossible for such a miserable creature, Philoctetes had snatched up his bow and fitted an arrow to the string before Eurylochus could leap down onto the rock and take them for himself.

'Treachery!' he shouted, pointing the weapon at Eurylochus, who fell back over the boulder with a squeal of fear, followed by a loud cry of pain. Philoctetes turned now and aimed at Odysseus. 'Philoctetes should have known better than to trust a beguiling serpent like you. You say that if you die he will die with you, but that's just another lie; when he shoots you down he will become free.'

Philoctetes pulled back the bowstring and Odysseus dropped to his knees, throwing his hood over his face. Then, as Philoctetes let out half a breath and steadied his aim, a booming voice rolled down from the cliff tops, startling the men below as it echoed between the rocks and rebounded from precipice to precipice.

'Stay your hand, Philoctetes!'

The archer felt the strength in his arms weaken, forcing him to relax the bowstring and lower the weapon. He looked about himself, searching for the owner of the voice in the fog. Down on the rock shelf below him, Eperitus, Diomedes and Antiphus looked around in confusion, while Odysseus tipped back his hood and glanced discreetly upwards. Then Eperitus gave a shout and pointed to the cliffs above, where a giant figure stood silhouetted against the swirls of white mist.

'Who are you?' Diomedes called, feeling instinctively for the sword he had left by the boat.

'Silence!' commanded the newcomer. 'The gods speak only to those whom they choose, and I have not left the halls of Olympus to waste words with you, Diomedes, king of Argos. I have come to talk to Philoctetes.'

The archer lurched forward to lay across a boulder, from where he could scrutinise the figure in the mist.

'Heracles!' he exclaimed after a moment, his eyes growing wide with shock and wonder. 'Then you did become a god after your death, just as the priests declared. And now you've come back to save Philoctetes from these liars and cheats! See, lord: he's looked after your bow and arrows for you; everything just as when you gave them into his care.'

'Looked after them?' Heracles scoffed. His features were impossible to discern, but the outline of his famous lion's pelt was visible on his head and over his shoulders, as was the thick club that hung menacingly from his fist. 'You've no more looked after them than if I had entrusted them to one of the sheep you were tending that day you lit my funeral pyre! You've used it for nothing more than shooting down seagulls, when it should have been on the battlefields of Ilium killing Trojans. And when Odysseus and Diomedes offer you the chance to use them for your own glory – and for mine – what do you do? Complain and bemoan your lot!'

'Forgive your faithful servant!' Philoctetes groaned, burying his face in his hands. 'Command him, lord, and he will repay your trust.'

'Philoctetes,' the booming voice ordered, 'you know full well what you have to do. Take my bow and arrows to the killing fields of Ilium. Use them as the seer, Calchas, directs you and reap the glory that is rightly ours. Go with Odysseus and do not hold on to your hatred for him, but be thankful that he saved your life and returned for you.'

With that, having spoken more words than Eperitus could remember him putting together in all the ten years he had known him, Polites slipped away into the mist and headed back to the boat.

Chapter Four
RECONCILIATION & HEALING

Odysseus must have known they would fail to persuade Philoctetes to give up his hatred and return to the army. He must have known it from the moment he had heard Calchas's prophecy, hence his plan to disguise Polites as Heracles using an oversized club and Agamemnon's lion's pelt. He must have planned every detail during his whispered conversations with Polites on the voyage to Lemnos, knowing that the one man whom Philoctetes revered and respected above all others – and whose command he would obey – was Heracles. Eperitus realised all of this the moment Polites had been swallowed up by the fog, and though the deception did not sit easily on his conscience he could not deny that Odysseus's foresight had saved their lives. What was more, it had ensured Philoctetes would come back with them to Ilium and bring the end of the war one step closer.

Philoctetes was the first to speak after Polites had gone. He pulled himself up to lean against the nearest boulder, and as he turned to the men below it was no longer the face of a man half deranged by pain and loneliness that stared down at them. Suddenly his eyes seemed full of life, lifted from their despair and given purpose and meaning once more.

'Odysseus,' he began, 'will you help a cripple down from these treacherous rocks? And will one of your men fetch the rest of Philoctetes's arrows ... no, *my* arrows from the cave above? It is the god Heracles's command that *I* return with you to Troy, and it is with pleasure *I* will fulfil his wish.'

Odysseus and Diomedes ran forward to help him, followed closely by Eperitus and Antiphus. As the kings took Philoctetes by his arms, Antiphus picked up his bow and the clutch of arrows he had brought with him – handling them with reverence – while Eperitus sprang up the rocks towards the mouth of the cave. He passed Eurylochus on the way, still hiding behind the large boulder where he had fallen, though whether out of fear of Philoctetes's arrows or Odysseus's wrath Eperitus could not say. He ignored him and quickly reached the entrance to the cave. Here the stench was at its strongest, where Philoctetes had holed himself away for so many years, gnawing on his bitter memories as he waited between the bouts of pain that would paralyse him for long moments at a time. For Eperitus, whose sensitive nostrils were almost overwhelmed by the stink, he felt as if he were standing at the entrance to the Underworld, that place of deepest misery where a man's soul was condemned to spend infinity in loneliness, forgotten by the rest of the world. Indeed, that was where Philoctetes had been the last ten years of his life. How had he endured such an existence without hurling himself onto the rocks below, Eperitus wondered? And the answer had to be hope – hope of rescue and returning to the world of men. To have taken his own life would have been to have damned himself to an eternity in the halls of Hades, where even hope did not exist.

Eperitus stepped into the darkness and immediately felt something crunch beneath his sandal. Another step brought the same sensation, as if he was walking on small, brittle sticks. Looking down, he saw that the cave floor was carpeted with bones, the scattered skeletons of countless birds that Philoctetes had shot and eaten to eke out his squalid existence. It was like the lair of some ancient beast, and there was no way through except to tread on the littered bones. He carried on, one step at a time, deeper into the gloom until the ceiling of the cave forced him to stoop. Eventually he was able to pick out a pale circle on the floor ahead of him. It was Philoctetes's bed, made entirely of seagull feathers. They had been compacted down by his weight over the years and the pus from his wound had permeated them so that the stench in that confined space was now unbearable. It took all of Eperitus's self-discipline not to turn back. Finally, just when he thought he could not bear to take another step, he saw the leather quiver lying on the edge of the bed. Eperitus snatched it up and ran out of the cave.

He stood atop the cascade of boulders and took several lungfuls of the clean sea air. On a clear day he would have been able to see far across the Aegean, and the approach of the Ithacan galley would have been obvious a long time before its arrival. But the fog had shrouded everything, leaving only the tips of treacherous rocks, appearing and disappearing among the white billows like the humps of great sea monsters. Below him, barely distinguishable in the mist, were the figures of the others gathered on the rock shelf. Eperitus swung the quiver onto his shoulder and picked his way down between the tumble of boulders.

The array of expressions he met at the bottom was almost amusing, and were it not for the fact he wanted to vomit from the smell of Philoctetes's wound, Eperitus would have smiled. Eurylochus looked like a whipped child, his usually ruddy jowls now flushed crimson and his eyes fixed firmly on his sandals. Odysseus, who was normally able to prevent his feelings from spilling out into his features, wore a rigid look that was as much to do with the foul stench of Philoctetes – who he was carrying on his back – as it was his anger with Eurylochus. As for Philoctetes, the archer's face was as bright as a breastplate as he clung to Odysseus's shoulders, staring around at the dark cliffs that had been his home for a decade and beaming triumphantly. Antiphus was passing the length of Heracles's bow up and down through his fingers, his wide eyes oblivious to everything else, while Diomedes was almost green as he tried manfully to hide his nausea in such close proximity to Philoctetes's foot.

'Come on,' Odysseus said as Eperitus joined them, and set off at a jog.

With Philoctetes calling out the best path through the rocks and little pools, they would have made quick progress back to the boat had they not been stopped by the sudden screeching of their guide as a fresh wave of pain attacked him. Odysseus laid him down and the others stood by helplessly as Philoctetes thrashed about on the rock, crying out almost gull-like and cursing each of them in turn before turning his ire on the gods. When it was over, it was as if nothing had happened and Philoctetes urged Odysseus to pick him up again and press on.

As they reached the boat, Polites sprang to his feet and hauled on the rope a little too sharply, causing the small vessel to bang against the edge of the rock. Philoctetes eyed him closely, and the others could not disguise their anxiety as they turned and paused.

'I *know* you,' Philoctetes said. 'Yes, I know you. You were with these others when they abandoned me here all those years ago.'

A look of momentary relief crossed Polites's face, but was quickly replaced by shame as he lowered his eyes.

'Sorry, my lord.'

'Did you hear that?' Philoctetes crowed, turning to the others and half pulling Odysseus around with him. 'He called me "lord"! Me, the most wretched creature that has ever dwelt beneath the face of the sun. Lord Philoctetes!'

He was still laughing as they lowered him into the boat and rowed to the galley, only stopping to look back at Lemnos in a moment of contemplation. His reflections on ten years of misery did not last long though, and soon he was cackling again as he was handed up to the crew on the deck of the ship, their faces already pale from the stench of their new passenger. They fed him bread – he refused to eat anything else – and gave him wine weakened with five parts water, which quickly had him roaring drunk. Then, as the anchor stones were pulled up and the oars slipped back into the sea, he fell asleep savouring the simple texture of bread in his mouth, while Odysseus carefully – and with greater resolve than it took to charge into battle – removed the tattered dressing from his foot, bathed the wound and wrapped a new bandage about it. He was violently sick afterwards, but that single gesture of mercy earned him more respect from Eperitus than possessing the armour of Achilles could ever have done.

'You knew I'd fail, didn't you,' Diomedes said.

He was standing between Odysseus and Eperitus as the three men waited at the prow of the galley, watching the humped shape of Tenedos growing ever nearer. Its rocky flanks had been given a coppery glow by the sun as it set behind them in the west, as had the low cliffs of the mainland of Ilium that lay in a thin line beyond it. Eperitus's keen eyes could pick out goats hugging the steep hillsides, and the small white houses and olive groves of the few islanders who had clung on to their occupied homeland. A Greek warship and three merchant vessels lay at anchor in the harbour below, the same harbour that had seen Philoctetes claim victory over Achilles in the race from Aulis to Tenedos, which had provoked Achilles's jealous anger and resulted in Philoctetes's abandonment on Lemnos. The archer was sleeping in the stern, his snores still audible over the creaking of the rigging and the slapping of the waves against the hull.

'Admit it,' Diomedes insisted, turning to Odysseus. 'Before we even left Ilium you knew how everything would turn out. You knew Eperitus and I wouldn't want you to use your tricks on Philoctetes – not after the army had abandoned him so cruelly – and you knew we'd insist on doing the talking. But you *also* knew we wouldn't stand a chance of succeeding. Am I wrong? And did you guess your own turn at persuading him would come, but that even your honeyed tongue would fail? You did, didn't you?'

A glimmer of a smile crossed Odysseus's lips, but no answer. Diomedes smiled, too, and shook his head.

'Either way, you must have known we'd only get the poor cripple to come with us by tricking him.'

'You make it sound as if that's what I was hoping for all along,' Odysseus protested. 'You're wrong, though. Polites and the lion's pelt were a contingency, that's all. I'd rather Philoctetes had responded to the call of the prophecy and come with us because he recognised his chance of salvation. And when he wouldn't listen to you, I'd hoped that reason and good human logic would convince him to give up his anger. It nearly worked, too,' he added. 'As it was, I had to use the only means guaranteed to win him over – Heracles, whom Philoctetes worships above all else. You can call it a trick if you like, but without my foresight we'd all be back on Lemnos with poisoned arrows sticking up from our lifeless bodies.'

Diomedes shrugged his acknowledgement of the truth.

'I thought you agreed to conquer Troy by honourable means,' Eperitus said, his tone accusative. 'You said your guilt over Ajax's suicide was going to keep you from stooping to trickery.'

Odysseus turned his piercing green eyes on his captain.

'Ajax would still be alive today if I hadn't used deceit to win the armour of Achilles. He was my friend; I should have spoken to him rather than humiliated him, even if the gods wanted to see him humbled. Do you think with hindsight I wouldn't have found another way? Do you think your father would have murdered King Pandion and stolen his throne if he'd known it would result in the death of his eldest sons and earn him your undying hatred? Of course not. Besides, when I swore not to act with such dishonour again, Eperitus, I never said I'd stop using my cunning. It's the greatest gift the gods have given me and to reject it would be to disrespect them. It'd be like asking you to ignore your sense of honour, or Diomedes to cast aside his courage. On the contrary: I intend to use my guile at every opportunity I get, if it brings the destruction of Troy closer and opens the way for me and my friends to go home. And though I'd rather Philoctetes had chosen to come with us for his own sake, the most important thing is that he's with us now and, somehow, he is going to fulfil the will of the gods.'

'I'm sorry,' Eperitus said. 'Sometimes my principles make me a harsh judge.'

Odysseus shook his head dismissively. 'Not as severe as you used to be. I think the war has taught you a few things about the true meaning of honour, Eperitus; it's mellowed you. One day you might even reconsider your hatred towards your father.'

'That's twice you've questioned my desire to avenge his crimes, *my lord.*'

'Hate eats a man from within, *my friend*, and vengeance does not cure it.'

'Neither will mercy.'

'And his servant, Astynome?' Odysseus persisted. 'What about her?'

Eperitus did not reply, but turned his burning gaze on the flanks of Tenedos and kept them there while the island grew steadily nearer.

They did not beach the galley among the other Ithacan ships in the sprawling Greek camp, but sailed further up the coast and tossed out the anchor stones in a small cove. It was Odysseus's intention they should try to clean Philoctetes up and heal his wound before they presented him to the Council of Kings, though he did not say how he hoped to cure such a vile and persistent injury. Nevertheless, he ordered the crew ashore and by the time the sun had set, leaving a blood-red smear across the western horizon, they were already busy making fires and preparing their evening meal. In earlier years they would have been taking a reckless risk, exposing themselves to death or capture by a Trojan night patrol, but these days their enemies had had enough of war and were resigned to staying within the safety of the city walls, abandoning the plains to the Greeks.

Philoctetes was the last ashore, where they laid him still sleeping on a litter. Shortly afterwards, two Greek horsemen arrived at the top of the beach and trotted down towards the Ithacans. Odysseus, who by his constant glances in the direction of the camp appeared to have been expecting their arrival, went to meet them. They spoke briefly, then the riders pulled their horses about and galloped off.

'Agamemnon sent them,' he explained, returning to the others. 'They spotted our sail, of course, and wanted to know what we were up to. I told them to send Podaleirius; Asclepius's son will know how to treat Philoctetes's wound.'

'Neither he nor his brother could cure him ten years ago,' Diomedes said. 'Why should he succeed now?'

'Because it's the will of the gods, my friend,' Odysseus replied with a confident smile.

The smell of the wound grew in its offensiveness without the sea air to carry some of it away, but they were at least relieved of the archer's intermittent fits of pain as he remained in a deep sleep until Podaleirius arrived on horseback, his leather satchel bouncing against his hip. The healer dismounted and, after a curt nod to the others, knelt beside the sleeping form. Repeatedly sweeping his long hair from his eyes, he undressed the wound and bent low to inspect it.

'Bring me a torch,' he ordered.

Eperitus fetched a brand from one of the campfires and stood over Podaleirius, wincing in disgust as he prodded and picked at the black sludge of rotting flesh on the top of Philoctetes's foot. Podaleirius took a wooden bowl from his satchel and set it down on the sand.

'You have water?' he asked.

Antiphus knelt and filled the bowl from the skin at his hip, while the healer pulled out a cloth and unwrapped two sharp knives. He dropped the cloth into the bowl, then held up one of the knives so that it glinted in the torchlight.

'Lord Apollo, grant me the skill to heal this wound,' he whispered, then lowered the blade to the liquefied flesh.

Chapter Five
THE EYE OF APOLLO

Cassandra pulled the cloak tighter about her shoulders in an attempt to keep out the cold west wind that haunted the plains of Ilium. Looking up, she could see a circle of tall plane trees at the top of the slope, their branches silhouetted by the waxing moon. She tipped back her hood to reveal a beautiful but melancholy face, her skin pale in the thin half-light. Her dark eyes contemplated the temple of Thymbrean Apollo with unease. As a girl she had encountered a young man there who offered to teach her the art of prophecy. In her naivety – partly enticed by his noble looks and partly thrilled at the thought of reading the future – she accepted and for months he had shown her the mysterious secrets of divination. Inside the shadowy temple, where the pillars were the boles of the trees and the ceiling the interlaced fingers of their branches, he showed her how to peel back the dark layers of her mind and use her inner eye to see far and wide, into things past and things yet to come. The knowledge was fearful for one as young as she was, but it quickly enslaved her, and when the man had taught her everything she needed to know he told her his price. Her virginity. She was at once horrified and excited by his impudent demand, but in spite of the way he made her heart race and her skin flush with desire she reminded herself that she was a princess of Troy, the daughter of King Priam, and she refused him. His handsome face became dark and terrible and in that moment he revealed his divine nature to her, transforming into a being of light and glory before her eyes. But Apollo did not rape her, as she had expected, or threaten to take back the gift of prophecy; instead he cursed her, announcing that her visions would continue but her words of doom would never be believed. And so it had been ever since.

She shuddered at the memory – and at the knowledge she would soon be calling on the god again. Inside the temple she would ask him to open the future to her. Though she had refused her body to Apollo, to have his divine spirit inside her was an experience much more intense and intimate than she imagined physical intercourse could ever be. And like sex, prophecy had its dangers. When a woman allowed a man to enter her body, she risked pregnancy and death in childbirth, but when she allowed a god to enter her mind she risked insanity. Yet it was a risk she had always been ready to take, and all the more so now as she sensed the end of the war approaching. Looking back over her shoulder she saw the River Scamander in the vale below – gleaming like a line of mercury as it fed into the great bay – and the high walls and towers of Troy rising up beyond it. She loved the city with all her heart, though few within it loved her; and if, by sending her inner eye farther than she had ever dared to go before, she would discover how to keep Troy safe, then the loss of her sanity was a peril she was prepared to face.

She climbed to the top of the ridge and entered a dark gap in the circle of trees. The floor inside was laid with heavy flagstones that had been polished smooth by the feet of countless worshippers and gleamed in the filtered moonlight. Cassandra did not wait for her eyes to adjust to the deeper gloom – she could have found her way around the temple blindfolded if she needed to – but walked up to the pale monolith at the far end of the temple. She dropped to her knees before the marble altar, letting her gaze hover briefly on the carved effigy of Apollo in the shadows behind it, then lowered her forehead to the hard floor. As she bent her body, the leather satchel at her hip slipped to the flagstones and she heard the contents twisting and thrashing inside, hissing in protest before becoming still again.

'Lord Apollo,' she whispered, feeling the blood rush to her head and the coldness of the stone against her skin. 'Bringer of dreams. Receive my sacrifice.'

She pushed herself up with the palms of her hands and, still kneeling, fumbled with the tie of the satchel. It came free and she thrust her hand inside, grasping for the smooth, cord-like body of the snake. She caught it close to the neck and lifted it free, holding it at arm's length so that it danced in anguish before the rough image of the god. A small woollen bag had been tied around its head to keep it from biting or attempting to escape. Cassandra unslipped the knot and pulled the bag away to expose the thin, triangular head with its dark eyes and flickering tongue.

She had been given the creature by Apheidas in exchange for her prayers. He had been a follower of Apollo all his life, and though he bred snakes for the priests to sacrifice to the god, he was no priest himself. The Fates had made Apheidas a soldier, a powerful commander in the Trojan army, and with the deaths of Hector, Achilles and most recently – so rumour from the Greek camp had it – Great Ajax, he knew the zenith of the war had been reached. The conflict had endured for ten years because of the valour of these three men, and without them the end would come quickly for one side or the other. And so he had approached Cassandra with his gift, out of respect for her devotion to Apollo, and asked her to pray on his behalf so that the god would help him with what he had to do.

Cassandra pulled the satchel over her shoulder and let it drop to the floor. Her cloak followed, revealing white priestess's robes. The icy wind that penetrated the ring of trees took away the heat that the cloak had retained and she felt her flesh stiffen beneath the gauzy material. Gripping the snake, she held it down against the altar and drew a dagger from her belt. The blade gleamed and Cassandra's gaze hung on it for a moment before moving to the crude idol in the shadows. This had been carved from the trunk of a living tree long ago, when the temple had first been established, and the ravages of time and the weather had left it so featureless that only the horn bow and the bronze arrow that it clutched in its lumpish fists identified it as Apollo.

'Protect your follower, Apheidas, son of Polypemon,' she said. 'Watch over him in battle. And aid him in this task he has taken upon himself, about which he keeps his own counsel but which he says is for the glory and preservation of Troy.'

She lowered the blade to the neck of the snake.

'And I call on you to speak to me, lord. Enter me. Fill me with your presence and guide my inner eye. Show me the things I seek, show me how I, too, can protect Troy from the wolves at her gates. Lord of the bow and the lyre, show me and don't spare me, even if I have to cross into the realms of madness to witness these things. Let me know what must be done to save my city.'

She pressed the knife against the snake's skin, feeling the momentary tension as the scales resisted and then gave. The blade slid quickly through the flesh to the unyielding stone. Dark blood poured over the pale altar and, stopping her thumb over as much of the wound as it would cover, Cassandra hastily lifted the severed body to her raised lips. The warm liquid filled her mouth and spilled over her chin and neck to spatter her white robes. She squinted against the coppery taste and stumbled backwards, releasing the dead snake and the knife as she fell to one knee. She slumped forward onto her knuckles and her black hair fell over her face like a curtain, hiding the mixture of revulsion and fear on her features. Her heart was beating faster now, knowing from long experience that she had but moments left in the waking world, moments in which her mind remained connected to her body and could feel, smell, hear, taste and see the temple around her.

And then it came.

She was thrown onto her back. Her wide eyes stared up at the ceiling of dark leaves traced with silver. Then there was a rush of light as if the moon had expanded to a hundred times its own size, filling the temple and swamping her retinas with whiteness. At the same time, the gentle rustling of the wind grew to a roar like the sound of a monstrous wave rolling towards her. The cold night air bit into her flesh with the intensity of fire, burning her nerve endings and arching her back until, with a scream, she felt her conscious mind ripped from her body and pulled upward through the branches of the temple into the cloudless, moon-dominated sky. She continued to ascend, glimpsing the Scamander and the dark mass of Troy to her right, while away to her left was the semicircular wall of the Greek camp with the beetle-like hulls of their thousand ships blackening the shoreline. Then she was plunging forward, not by her own will but drawn inexorably on towards the great, glittering blanket of the ocean, until she was leaving Ilium behind and soaring over the waves at a height that made the islands below appear like stepping stones. Formless in her flight, as if she were a ghost rushing on its way to the eternal halls of Hades, she could neither feel the wind that herded skeins of cloud across the face of the moon, nor hear its roar filling her ears; neither could she taste the dampness in the air, nor smell the cold clarity of the night. But she could see. Like a great eye she could see far and wide, all the way back to Ilium – already in the dim distance behind her – and beyond. To the north she saw the mountainous lands of Troy's former rivals, before the Greeks had come and Priam had bought their allegiance. South, she could see the country of Egypt, even though it was many days journey by ship and several weeks on foot. Yet it was towards the west, to the never-before-seen land of her enemies, that her mind was focussed.

The gods had shrouded Greece in cloud, but beneath its tattered edges she glimpsed mountains and valleys, rugged and beautiful, dotted throughout with white-walled cities and towns that slumbered peacefully in the darkness. This was the cradle of the fleet that had brought so much destruction to her homeland, and she felt nothing but revulsion as it came rapidly closer. Then the sea was gone and she fell through the clouds to skim bird-like across the land below. Now she could see orchards and vineyards; ramshackle villages and hillside enclosures half-filled with sheep; roads left unguarded by abandoned watchtowers, from which the soldiers had long since been called to war. She passed a city nestled beneath two mountain peaks and felt a surge of black fear at the sight of it, but before it could overwhelm her she had moved on, over more mountains and plains until she saw a river below, its surface shining like glass as the moon broke momentarily free of the clouds. She followed its course and saw a high mound that she instinctively knew was the barrow of a long-dead warrior, and without any lessening of speed plunged towards it. If she had possessed hands to throw before her face, or a mouth with which she could have screamed, she would have; but there was no sense of impact as she passed into the barrow, or of having come to a stop as she found herself inside the high-ceilinged chamber beneath. Though there was no light in the tomb, she could see a sarcophagus before her with the carved figure of a horse above it. Inside was a bone, one of many that made up the giant skeleton of a man, but this single shoulder blade was starkly white – made of ivory, the work of the gods. Briefly she wondered why she had been brought here, and immediately she knew that this was one of the answers that she had sought. A voice spoke the name of the man whose tomb this was, and she understood at once that unless the Greeks took the ivory shoulder blade from the sarcophagus the walls of Troy would never fall.

Then she was free of the chamber and returning east, moving through the air at great speed until the clouds opened to reveal a large island far below her. She saw a palace on top of a hill overlooking the main harbour, and as her mind's eye descended to enter its empty halls she wondered what the significance of the island was and why Apollo had brought her here. Then a vision of a great warrior appeared, dressed in magnificent armour that she had seen once before from the walls of Troy. The helmet was gold with a red plume, the breastplate shaped in the perfect likeness of a man's torso, and the shield had seven concentric circles filled with figures that moved as if alive. The armour had been made by Hephaistos, the smith-god, for Achilles. But Achilles was dead, his ashes buried beneath a barrow on the plains of Ilium. And then she understood the meaning of the revelation. The warrior in the armour was to take Achilles's place on the battlefield; without him, the Greeks would return home defeated.

She turned from the terrible vision and found herself crossing the Aegean once more, hurtling back to Ilium and the temple of Thymbrean Apollo. But the oracles of Troy's doom were not yet over. As she hung over the circle of plane trees, expecting at any moment to be reunited with her physical self, she looked across the Scamander to the great city with its high walls and towers and its gates that had withstood the might of Agamemnon's army for ten years. And then the sloped battlements began to shake and crumble. The towers fell and the gates were torn from their mountings, while in the city behind the buildings caved in on themselves in clouds of dust. People were running everywhere, their screams unheard by her sealed ears as they were crushed by falling stones or disappeared into the chasms that were opening beneath their feet. Cassandra wanted to cry out in terror but was unable to make a sound, as the mound that Troy was built on started to rise up, like a monstrous subterranean creature waking from centuries of slumber, destroying the city on its back as it came to life. And as Troy disintegrated and was gone, all that remained was the mound – higher and blacker and smoother than Cassandra had ever known it before, and yet strangely familiar. It was then that she recognised it. The Palladium, the wooden effigy that stood in the temple of Athena in the citadel of Pergamos. Legend said that it was an image of Athena's friend, Pallas, whom the goddess had accidentally killed. It had fallen from heaven when the city was being built and had landed in the unfinished temple, a sign of the goddess's divine protection. Without it, Troy was doomed to fall.

As the meaning of the third oracle became clear to her the vision faded and the night grew suddenly dark, consuming the light of the moon and the stars until nothing was left but stifling blackness. Panic threatened for a moment, then Cassandra saw tall grey pillars emerge from the darkness on every side of her. Briefly she thought she had returned to her body in the temple of Thymbrean Apollo, but the absence of any of her other senses quickly told her she was still dreaming.

Something *was* different, though.

She could not feel the quickness in her breathing or the rapid beat of her heart, but she knew she was afraid. Something terrible had happened. She looked up and saw the figure of a woman above her, seated on a stone plinth with a spear in one hand and a shield in the other. The crude, stern features of her helmeted head were fixed in a cold gaze as Cassandra knelt at her feet with her hands raised imploringly to the statue of the goddess. She recognised the inside of the temple of Athena, but Apollo was no longer showing her the tasks the Greeks would need to perform to conquer Troy. This was the future, *her* future. Outside, though she could neither hear the flames nor smell the burning, she knew there was fire on the streets of Pergamos. People were fleeing in terror and soldiers were running among them, though whether they were Trojan or Greek she could not tell. Time blurred and she sensed herself curled up in fear at the feet of the statue, when the temple doors were flung open and the sounds of battle burst in. The once-peaceful chamber now echoed with the clash of bronze, followed by the screams of women and children in pain. Rough hands pulled at Cassandra, turning her over to stare into the eyes of a small man with a snarling, angry face. Coiled about his shoulders was a brown snake that hissed in defiance at the unfamiliar temple. The soldier's eyes fell upon Cassandra and his malicious look transformed to one of sneering lust. She looked away and he slapped her hard, before seizing her clothes and tearing them from her. She was conscious of her naked breasts and the terrifying strength of the man as she tried to fight him. Then he hit her and her resistance ceased. She fell back to the floor beneath his heavy body, his leather armour doubtless cold and hard against her soft skin. He entered her roughly and forcefully, without any reverence for the purity she had preserved for so long. Suddenly her nostrils were filled with the smell of blood and, arching her back on the rough flagstones, she screamed.

The sound shattered the silence that had enclosed her senses and tore through the temple like a blast of wind, rustling the leaves overhead and spilling silver scales of moonlight across the ground. With a rush like water filling a clay jar, she felt the physical sensations of sound, smell, touch and taste pouring back into her, trapping her consciousness once more with the clumsy heaviness of the corporeal world. Her thin, underdeveloped body felt as if it was encased in bronze armour, each small movement suddenly cumbersome and ungainly; her ears were momentarily sharp, filling her head with the sound of the wind and the roar of the sea, and the nerve endings in her skin reported every detail of the flagstoned floor, while screaming at her with the coldness of it. Her mouth was saturated with the taste of blood. The smell of it – mingled with the odour of soil and bark and the different aromas from her own body – was so overpowering she thought she must be covered in it. Then, with a shock that sank straight to the pit of her stomach, she recalled the soldier in the temple and looked down to see that her dress had indeed been ripped open and there was blood over her neck and breasts. She placed a hand between her legs, dreading that she would find more blood, and when she felt nothing remembered, finally, that it had been a dream and the blood belonged to the snake she had beheaded. She relaxed, but only until she recalled that what she had seen had also been a vision of the future. And it was then she sensed she was being watched.

Chapter Six
NISUS OF DULICHIUM

Penelope, queen of Ithaca, paced the earthen floor of the great hall. The flames from the circular hearth cast a crimson glow over the four central pillars and the circle of empty chairs where the Kerosia – the council of Ithacan elders – had sat earlier that day. The warm light pulsed against the lime-plastered walls, where it fought with the dense shadows for possession of the murals. The contest ebbed and flowed, revealing hints of the scenes depicted high up on the walls, of armoured men fighting and dying in battles of their own. Penelope, who had seen the murals almost everyday for the past twenty years, hardly even noticed them any more.

She reached an alcove in one of the walls – where a small effigy of the goddess Athena stood stiffly clutching her spear – then turned on her heel and retraced her steps towards the high-backed throne. The long wait was making her nervous. Though the palace was her home, in view of what she was planning to do she did not want to be noticed out of her own quarters so late at night. She reached the vacant throne, glanced at the double doors that led to the courtyard beyond, then turned again and headed back to the alcove. The nerves that tightened her stomach were a welcome distraction from the hole left by her loneliness. She had felt incomplete ever since Odysseus had sailed to Troy a decade before, but at least her son's presence had comforted her; now that she had sent Telemachus to safety in Sparta, though, she was completely alone. The heart that had longed so painfully for her husband's return now yearned to breaking point for her son.

And yet, as she reached the alcove again and looked down at the crudely carved face of Athena, she knew she could not afford to show weakness. She was a queen, and while her husband was away the burden of ruling Ithaca lay firmly upon her shoulders. As a woman, though, she could not rely on the strength of her arms, only the ability of her wits.

She turned and stared at the doors, willing them to open. Nothing happened and she continued pacing. She had other weapons, of course. She was tall and beautiful and could use these assets to her benefit, an art that her cousin Helen had developed to perfection – at terrible cost to the Greek and Trojan worlds. But Penelope had never been adept at playing that game. It went against her nature: as far as she was concerned men should only be flirted with for one reason, and *she* already had a husband. No, she thought, her needs would have to be dire if she were to resort to so base a method.

She reached the throne where none had sat since Odysseus's departure and ran her hand over the carved wooden back. Her husband had left her in a strong position, with the support of the Kerosia and the people behind her, but he had also left a viper in the form of Eupeithes, the power-hungry merchant who had once tried to usurp the throne. By allowing him a seat on the Kerosia, Odysseus had gambled on the hope that giving him some power might placate his greater ambitions. He had also gambled on a prompt end to the war and a quick homecoming. This was despite the oracle he had once shared with his wife, that if he went to Troy he would not return for twenty years. He had never felt restricted by prophecies, though, and had promised to return to Ithaca before anything could threaten his kingdom. So far, he had been wrong. Now the viper had raised its head and struck its first blow.

A low howl of wind shook the doors, causing her to look up. Again, they did not open and she headed back towards the alcove. Eupeithes had bided his time, of course. It was even possible he had never intended to make a bid for power, but the length of Odysseus's absence, combined with disillusionment among the nobility, had stirred his dormant ambitions. Either way, he had made his move now and suddenly, unexpectedly, the Kerosia was his to control – and only the king could overrule the council of elders. Having bought Polyctor's loyalty years before, after Phronius's accidental death – or murder, as most suspected – Eupeithes had been able to bargain for Oenops, another of his cronies, to take the old man's place. That had left Nisus, Halitherses, Mentor and Laertes – Odysseus's aged father – still loyal to the throne, but recent events had changed the balance again. While

Halitherses had secretly sailed to the Peloponnese with Telemachus, taking Odysseus's heir to safety in Sparta, an assassin had been caught in the boy's empty room. Eupeithes was the obvious one to have ordered the prince's death, but the assassin had sworn his employer was Nisus of Dulichium.

Penelope looked over her shoulder at the ring of chairs around the hearth. They were still draped with furs for the members of the Kerosia who had met that morning to discuss the allegation against Nisus. As the accused, Nisus was unable to take his own seat, and with Halitherses travelling to Sparta with Telemachus that had given the majority to Eupeithes. The verdict was almost a formality: Nisus was guilty of treason and had been sentenced to be executed the next day. What was more, Eupeithes had used the absence of Halitherses to have his own son, Antinous, voted on to the Kerosia as Nisus's replacement. At a stroke, the Kerosia was now in Eupeithes's hands and there was nothing Penelope could do about it.

The doors creaked open and a splash of weak moonlight cut a wedge across the dark floor. A cloaked figure paused in the doorway, waiting for his eyes to adjust to the gloom before slipping into the hall. A second, shorter man followed him.

'Who's that?' Penelope called, anxiously.

'Penelope, it's me.'

The tension eased from her muscles as she recognised Mentor's voice.

'You were longer than I expected,' she said, moving from the shadows into the warm firelight. 'Were you delayed?'

'A little. The guard on the gates is one of the new men that replaced the reinforcements sent to Troy. I don't know I can trust him, so Eumaeus and I found a way in over the palace wall.'

Mentor crossed the great hall and kissed Penelope on both cheeks. He was handsome with a neatly trimmed beard and hard, confident eyes. The stump where his right hand had been severed by a sword was cased in leather, and though the wound had prevented him from going to war at Odysseus's side it had at least ensured Penelope his friendship and support in trying to preserve her husband's kingdom at home. Beside him was a man with a red-brown face and a head of thick, curly hair. Eumaeus was a slave, but as loyal to Odysseus as anyone on the island.

'What about Nisus's guard?' Mentor asked.

Penelope shook her head. 'A Taphian.'

Eupeithes had a long association with the Taphians, old enemies of Ithaca, and had insisted a troop of the tall, ruthless spearmen be added to the palace guard.

'Then we have to kill him,' Mentor said, throwing his cloak aside to reveal the sword tucked into his belt. 'We'll take the body with us and dump it into the sea – at least then we can claim Nisus bought his loyalty and helped him to escape.'

'Eupeithes will never believe that.'

'It'll seem the most likely explanation, and until he can disprove it he won't be able to accuse anyone else. Are you still willing to draw the guard away from his post?'

Penelope nodded and crossed to a small door at the back of the great hall. The two men followed.

'Wait either side of the door,' she instructed. 'I'll make him follow me into the hall and then you can … do whatever is necessary.'

She pulled open the door and stepped into the long narrow passageway that skirted the great hall. It was dark but for two dying torches that hung at intervals along the walls. To her right was a corner that fed round to the rear of the palace and the stairs that led up to the sleeping quarters; to the right, the corridor stretched away into murky shadows, with several doorways on the right-hand wall that opened into storerooms. Nisus was locked in a room at the far end, where Penelope could just make out the figure of a spearman slumped against the wall. The sound of the door roused him from his slumber and he straightened up, watching Penelope as she approached.

'Come with me,' she ordered. 'I have a task for you.'

The Taphian looked at her dumbly, then slowly shook his head.

'I've given you a command,' she said, more sternly this time. 'If you wish to keep your position in the guard you will do as your queen tells you. Is that clear?'

The man simply stared at her, refusing to move. He even had the audacity to let his eyes fall to her breasts. She turned away indignantly, pulling her cloak about her, and fumed as she tried to think of how to get the brute away from the door.

'The gods are mocking me,' she hissed to herself. 'A woman's pride is her downfall, as Clytaemnestra used to say. And yet, what choice do I have?'

With a sigh, she loosened the sash about her waist so that her chiton fell open to expose her long, soft thigh. Biting her lip, she loosened it more so that the slit spread up to her naked hip. Then, forcing a smile, she pulled her cloak aside and turned to face the Taphian once more.

'When the queen asks for a man's help, she expects him to obey. Now, are you going to come with me or do I need to find someone else?'

The soldier's eyes widened a little as they regarded the bare flesh of her leg. Then, as she turned and began to walk slowly away from him, he placed his spear against the wall and followed. Penelope sensed him getting closer and quickened her pace, at the same time trying to pull her dress together so as not to expose herself to Mentor and Eumaeus. The Taphian grunted something in his crude dialect, his voice sounding as if he was directly behind her. Quickly, she slipped through the open door into the great hall, but before Mentor and Eumaeus could emerge from the shadows the man's arms slid beneath hers and his hands closed over her breasts. She gave a half scream, then Eumaeus appeared to her left holding a sack. He tried to throw it over the Taphian's head, but the man spotted him and lashed out instinctively, catching the slave in the jaw and sending him flying back into the shadows. Mentor had rushed out in the same moment, sword in hand, but had fallen back as he saw the Taphian's arm still wrapped about Penelope.

'Kill him!' she spat.

The Taphian turned to face Mentor, using Penelope as a shield. He fumbled for the dagger in his belt. Sensing what he was doing, the queen tried to grab his hand, but he was too strong for her and almost broke her wrist as he wrenched it away. Then Eumaeus appeared again, throwing the bag over the soldier's head and drawing it down to his shoulders. The man shouted and Penelope was able to pull away as he seized hold of the bag and snatched it off again. Seeing his chance, Mentor leapt forward and pushed the sword into the man's chest, forcing it through the ribs with all his strength until the point emerged out of his back. His arms ceased thrashing and his large body went limp, falling back against Eumaeus and then to the floor.

'By all the gods,' Eumaeus exclaimed. 'Why don't Taphians ever die easily?'

'Do you think anyone heard?' Penelope asked, rubbing her bruised wrist and wincing at the pain.

Mentor paused and cocked an ear, but after a moment of listening to the silence that had returned to the palace, he shook his head.

41

'Wait here,' he said. 'I'll free Nisus.'

'The farthest storeroom, down to the left,' Penelope told him as he disappeared through the doorway.

He came back moments later, followed by a grey-haired man whose rich clothes were now torn and shabby looking. One eye was black and swollen and there was blood in his nostrils and on his beard. Nisus looked down at the body of the Taphian, then at Penelope.

'Thank you, my lady,' he said. 'Mentor has told me the risks you've taken to save me.'

'A small repayment for the loyalty you've shown me over the years, Nisus. It's too dangerous for you to remain on Ithaca, though; you must leave at once and not return until you hear my husband has come back. Go to Sparta and help Halitherses to protect Telemachus until I send for him.'

Nisus nodded. Eumaeus handed him the Taphian's cloak, then bent down to heave the corpse onto his shoulder.

'Sleep well, Penelope,' Mentor said. 'We'll make sure Nisus reaches the boat, and that our friend's corpse is never seen again.'

As they were going, Nisus turned to Penelope and looked at her a last time.

'Take care, my lady,' he said. 'Things are changing rapidly now. You must play for time. In everything you do, try to buy time for Odysseus and the army to return.'

'I will,' she assured him.

And wondered how such a thing would be possible.

Chapter Seven
HELENUS

Cassandra looked up and saw the figure of a man silhouetted in the entrance to the temple. He was short, and though the shape of his body was hidden by the robe that reached down to his ankles, she sensed he was young and lightly built. He took a step towards her and a circle of moonlight fell across his pale, beardless face.

'Did you do it?' he asked.

His black eyes lingered on Cassandra's nakedness and there was a carnal fascination in them, but as the girl sat up and drew back against the altar, pulling the halves of her torn clothing together, the longing in his features faded and he took another two steps into the temple.

'I said did you *do* it?' he repeated, his soft lisp becoming more pronounced.

She pointed at the decapitated body of the snake, the blood of which was still wet on her face, neck and chest.

'Yes, Helenus, I did it.'

A smile spread across Helenus's face. He stared down at his sister, his lustful curiosity replaced by an eagerness to hear more.

'And? Did he answer? Did Apollo come to you?'

Cassandra met her younger brother's gaze. He had inherited Priam's handsome looks and piercing eyes, but there was none of his mother's kindness in them. Hecabe's only legacy to her son was her weedy, diminutive stature, which he hated because it meant he would never be a powerful warrior like his older brothers, winning honour in battle and earning the adoration of the people. Instead, he was destined to live in their shadow, privileged by his royal blood and yet overlooked because of his youth.

'Of course he came. Does he ever miss the opportunity to torture me?' she replied. 'And, yes, he gave me visions.'

'Of the future?'

Cassandra thought of the soldier in the temple of Athena, but *that* was personal. A gift from Apollo for her alone. She shook her head.

'No, something greater. He gave me three oracles, the keys to Troy's survival – or her destruction!'

'What were they?' he insisted, his voice harsh and eager.

Cassandra held her hand out to him and he helped her to her feet, his eyes dropping to her bloodied breasts again as the halves of her dress fell open.

'I'm your *sister*, Helenus,' she reminded him, standing up straight and no longer trying to hide her nakedness.

Helenus lowered his eyes to the floor. Seeing the heap of Cassandra's cloak, he picked it up and – averting his gaze – handed it to her. Cassandra threw it about her shoulders and leaned back against the altar, lightly scrutinising her brother as he stood before her. Normally his clothes were expensive and fashionable, as befitted a son of Priam, but tonight she could see he wore the white robes of a priest beneath his rich double cloak. Not that he was a priest yet, of course – most priests of Apollo had shaven heads and were at least twice Helenus's age – but he was already an initiate and had used his father's authority to become an apprentice at the temple in Pergamos. His royal blood ensured he would one day rise to the priesthood, a position of power and influence, but not for many years yet. Not unless he could show Apollo had singled him out for a higher office. And for that he had to provide proof he had received the god's blessing.

He glanced at Cassandra, saw that she was covered, and reached out to place his hands on her upper arms.

'What are these oracles, Sister? If we know the secrets of Troy's survival, given to us by the gods themselves, then the Greeks can never be victorious! Tell them to me so that I can announce them before our father's court.'

'And reap the glory for yourself.'

Helenus dropped his arms to his side and turned away again, this time in a sulk.

'It was *your* suggestion. Nobody ever believes a word *you* say, remember?'

'Yourself included, Helenus. When I asked you to tell Father that Queen Penthesilea would be killed by Achilles, you almost refused to go.'

'And I would have refused if you hadn't begged me,' he snapped. 'What if you'd been wrong? I would have looked ridiculous, claiming visions from Apollo that never came true.'

'But they *did*.'

'And who couldn't have predicted that Achilles would kill the queen of the Amazons?' he retorted. 'That arrogant bitch was asking to be sent to Hades.'

Cassandra gave a dismissive laugh. 'A lucky guess then, was it? So when I told you Achilles would die trying to storm the Scaean Gate, why were you happy to announce *your* vision in front of the whole assembly of elders?'

'Because I'm a gambler,' Helenus answered, meeting Cassandra's gaze and holding it without shame. 'I saw how they looked at me after I'd – after *you'd* – predicted the defeat of Penthesilea, and I knew that if you were right about Achilles's death they'd think I was truly blessed by Apollo. I admit I didn't believe you, but my instincts told me to risk it. And what choice did I have? I'm never going to match Paris or Deiphobus on the battlefield, and as for becoming a priest of Apollo – I barely dream when I'm asleep, let alone receive revelations from the god when I'm awake! That doesn't mean I'm not ambitious, though. I *am*,' he said, punching the palm of his hand, 'and if by telling your prophecies to a believing audience I can speed my way into the priesthood, then so be it. That's why you approached me in the first place, isn't it? Nobody would believe these visions if they came from you, but people will listen to them from me. And you know I'll never let on because I want all the glory for myself.'

'I'm sorry, Helenus,' Cassandra said. 'I didn't mean to mock you. If you'd rather not hear the oracles, I'll understand.'

'Don't play coy with me, Sister – you're as desperate to tell them to me as I am to hear them. Share the visions Apollo gave you and I promise they'll be revealed before the whole assembly. There's to be a council of war in a few days time: I overheard Father telling Paris he wants to discuss new allies.'

'Yes, I know,' Cassandra said. 'He wants to send an embassy to Eurypylus and his Mysians.'

'How could you know that?'

Cassandra closed her eyes and let out a long breath.

'I dreamed it, of course, some days ago. The Mysians are the only people in the whole of Ilium that have refused to help us, because of

Astyoche's feud with Father. But even though she hates him, she's still his daughter and Priam is prepared to offer her the last and greatest of Troy's treasures – the Golden Vine – if she'll send her son to our aid. I have foreseen that she will accept his offer.'

'And will Eurypylus rid us of the Greeks?' Helenus asked hopefully, leaning forward to study her face in the gloom.

Cassandra answered with a dark look and an almost imperceptible shake of the head. Helenus felt an instant of dismay, then frowned and pulled back from his sister.

'All the more reason to hear these oracles, then. Tell me what you saw, Cassandra.'

As he spoke, the wind outside the temple picked up, whistling between the silver trunks and rustling the branches overhead so that the spots of moonlight on the flagstones danced and whirled. In the flurry of sound and movement, Cassandra stepped forward and embraced her brother tightly, pressing her lips to his ear and whispering to him the things she had seen. His expression was momentarily void of thought and emotion as he listened intently, his gaze resting on the crude effigy of Apollo behind the altar. Then she finished speaking and kissed him on the cheek, before dropping back against the marble plinth and staring at him. He frowned back at her as he took in what she had said to him. Then his eyes narrowed questioningly.

'The god *told* you these things? You're certain of them – you're certain you understood the visions correctly?'

Cassandra sighed and shook her head, though her gaze grew more fierce at his disbelief.

'Of course I am. And you'll tell Father? You'll keep your promise?'

'Yes,' Helenus answered after a pause. 'I'll tell Priam and the whole council of war. What have I got to lose, after all? If the oracles aren't fulfilled and Troy survives, then who's to say I was wrong? If they aren't fulfilled and Troy falls anyway, who will be left alive to care?'

Chapter Eight
THE RETURN OF THE OUTCAST

O dysseus leaned against one of the laurel trees at the entrance to the temple of Thymbrean Apollo and looked down the slope to the wide bay below. Once it had been home to hundreds of vessels, from visiting merchant ships and high-sided war galleys to the small cockle boats favoured by the local fisherman. Now it was empty, its occupants either destroyed or driven away by the war. Two rivers fed the bay – the Simöeis to the north and the Scamander to the south, the latter gleaming darkly in the faint starlight. Rising up from the plain beyond the river were the pallid battlements of Troy that had defied the Greeks for so long. At the highest point of the city was Pergamos, a fortress within a fortress, its palaces and temples protected by sloping walls and lofty towers where armed guards kept an unfailing watch. Further down, sweeping southward from the citadel like a half-formed teardrop, was the lower city. Here rich, two-storey houses slowly gave way to a mass of closely packed slums where thousands of the city's inhabitants lived in squalor and near starvation. Here, also, were camped the soldiers of Troy and her allies, ready at a moment's notice to man the walls or pour out onto the plains and do battle. And though it was the Greek army that laid siege to Troy's gates and penned its citizens in like sheep, the very stubbornness of its defenders ensured that the Greeks were no less prisoners themselves, doomed never to see their homes and families again until those god-built walls could somehow be breached and the bitter war brought to its bloody conclusion.

A little way off, sitting on a boulder overlooking the slope, was Eperitus, his back turned to the temple as he looked down at the few lights that still burned in the sleeping city. Odysseus wondered whether he had sensed his presence or was too consumed by whatever thoughts had driven him away from his comrades to seek his own company among the rocks and shrubs of the ridge. Odysseus could guess what those thoughts were though, and felt it best not to disturb them.

'He's still asleep,' said a voice behind him.

'Good,' Odysseus replied, turning to face Podaleirius as he emerged from the shadows of the temple. 'It's the best thing for him.'

Podaleirius had cut away the dead flesh from Philoctetes's foot while they had been on the beach, and, after bathing the wound with a mixture of herbs from his leather satchel and binding it, had insisted on them carrying him on a stretcher all the way to the temple of Thymbrean Apollo. There they had found a trail of fresh blood leading to the headless body of a snake on the altar, but Podaleirius had said it was a good sign and set about offering prayers to Apollo for Philoctetes to be healed. The ceremony, it seemed, was over and Podaleirius had left his patient in the care of Antiphus.

He looked over to where Eperitus sat.

'Is he alright?' he asked, with the natural concern of a healer.

'He will be,' Odysseus replied, lowering his voice to a whisper. 'This isn't a good place for him.'

Podaleirius nodded, as if he understood, and looked over at the great city on the other side of the vale.

'I've heard his father is a Trojan,' he whispered back. 'A nobleman, some say.'

'A highborn commander in Priam's army, but no less a bastard for it. He was exiled to Greece many years ago, making his home in the north in a city called Alybas. There he married a Greek woman, Eperitus's mother. Then when Eperitus was barely a man, his father killed the king, who had once accepted him as a suppliant, and usurped his throne. Eperitus refused to support him and was banished – that was shortly before I met him. Sometime later, the people of Alybas rebelled against his father and he fled back here to Ilium, but Eperitus never forgave him for his treachery.'

'He chose honour over blood, then,' Podaleirius said. 'But the call of a man's ancestry is strong. Are you certain he can be trusted not to go over?'

He tipped his chin toward the city to indicate what he meant. Odysseus could have taken offence at the questioning of his captain's loyalty, but Podaleirius, it seemed, had already guessed some of the truth.

'Not to his father,' he replied. 'He has already faced that test.'

'Then he passed?'

'Barely.'

'I think I see,' Podaleirius said. 'And the test happened here, in the temple. Am I right? That's why he doesn't like the place.'

Odysseus had been regarding Eperitus's back throughout the conversation, but now turned his gaze on Podaleirius.

'You're an astute man.'

'I can gauge the moods of others, that's all. Healers learn to read things that warriors cannot. How was he tested?'

Odysseus, who had used subtle words to draw information from many men, recognised that Podaleirius was playing the same trick on him now, lulling him into letting slip the dangerous truth of what had happened in the temple of Thymbrean Apollo. He could refuse to answer, of course, and the conversation would end there and then. But he knew Podaleirius was a man of integrity and was not one of Agamemnon's many spies. He felt he could trust him with the anxieties that had been troubling him about his captain.

'His father wanted to speak with him, hold a parley on neutral ground here in the temple. Yet he knew Eperitus was too proud to listen to him. So he sent a woman to entrap him, to whisper in his ear as they shared a bed, to slowly and lovingly persuade him that he had misunderstood his father all along; that all he wanted was to offer a deal to Agamemnon that would ensure peace. And so Eperitus agreed, knowing it was treachery to meet with an enemy but in his heart hoping that the offer was genuine and the war could be brought to a close. He did it for my sake, so that I would be released from my oath and could go back home to Ithaca and my family. But he was wrong. His father did not want peace, but power. He offered to open the city gates in exchange for Priam's throne. Agamemnon would receive his fealty and he would receive a crown, with Eperitus as his heir to continue his legacy. It was nothing more than Alybas all over again and Eperitus saw straight through it.'

'Then he refused.'

Odysseus nodded. 'Though his refusal came at a price. There was a fight and Eperitus's former squire, Arceisius, was killed. He blames himself for the lad's death and now he's more determined than ever that his father should die. But this anger isn't good for him. It holds him back, gnaws away at his soul.'

Podaleirius pursed his lips and looked over at the seated figure.

'That isn't the posture of a man burning for revenge. There's something else. The woman you mentioned – his father's servant – he fell in love with her, didn't he.'

'And she with him.'

'Genuinely?'

'Yes, though that wasn't part of her mission. And now they are separated by the walls of Troy and her treachery. His sense of honour won't let go of that, though I wish it would. It's love he needs, not revenge.'

'Now you're beginning to sound like a healer,' Podaleirius said with a smile.

'Are you ready?' Odysseus asked.

He looked Philoctetes up and down, barely able to believe the change in him. The wild, half-mad wretch they had found on Lemnos looked almost human again as they stood waiting outside Agamemnon's palatial tent. After a night of fitful dreams in the temple of Thymbrean Apollo, he had woken at dawn refreshed and free from his pain. More miraculous still, when Podaleirius had changed his dressing the wound was clean and already beginning to heal – a result that Podaleirius admitted was beyond even his skill and could only be attributed to the gods. The rest of the day had been spent at the temple, awaiting the summons to the Council of Kings. While Eperitus had remained silent and reflective, Odysseus had put the time to good use. He cut Philoctetes's hair and trimmed his beard, and, after he had bathed, gave him fine new clothes. By the time the messenger from Agamemnon arrived, he was recognisable as the man who had set out with them from Aulis ten years before. The only differences were his wasted limbs and painfully thin body, and the stick that he was forced to lean on as his foot recovered. He also seemed to have put aside his animosity toward Odysseus, accepting the Ithacan's help without grudge and even asking him to carry his sacred bow and arrows – rolled up in a cloth – as they set off for the Council. Odysseus felt no qualms, though, that the change had come about because he had tricked Philoctetes into believing Heracles had ordered him to go to Ilium. If it brought the defeat of Troy closer, it was justified.

'I'm ready,' Philoctetes replied.

'Then let's enter,' said Eperitus with a nod to the guards, who pulled aside the entrance to Agamemnon's tent and ushered them in.

Though it was late in the evening, the summer sun had not yet disappeared beyond the edge of the world and its distant fire gave the flaxen walls and ceiling of the great pavilion a pink tinge. The air inside was warm and stuffy from the heat of the day, the flames of the hearth and the press of bodies that had crammed in to witness the return of the man they had left for dead. The smell of fresh sweat mingled with the sweet aroma of roast meat, spiced wine and the platters of still-warm bread that were laid out on the long tables around the hearth. Behind them, crowded thigh to thigh on the low benches, the kings, princes and commanders of the Greek army fell suddenly silent and stared at Philoctetes.

The archer shuffled forward, leaning heavily on his crutch.

'You have beef?' he asked, looking at the overlapping platters, stacked like so many pebbles on a beach. 'And red wine?'

'We have every meat you could desire, Philoctetes,' answered a voice from the hushed assembly. 'Beef, mutton, goat, ham, fish … whatever you want. And as much wine as you can drink, so long as you keep a clear head. Now, come sit before us and eat your fill. We will talk when you are ready.'

Agamemnon, dressed in his customary white tunic, blood-red cloak and the ornate breastplate King Cinyras had given to him, snapped his fingers and a swarm of slaves rushed out from the shadows to attend to the Malian prince and his companions. Within moments, Philoctetes, Odysseus and Eperitus were seated on a bench before the circular hearth, behind a long table on which the slaves set down dish after dish and basket after basket of the richest foods imaginable. Kraters of wine were pushed before them and Eperitus was forced to place a warning hand on Philoctetes's wrist as he drained his vessel and raised it for more. Meanwhile, Odysseus looked at the bearded faces beyond the heat haze of the flames, all of them watching keenly as the skeletal phantom of the man they had abandoned helped himself to handfuls of food from every platter in reach. There was fascination and not a little revulsion in their eyes, and also guilt. Though every one of these

GLYN ILIFFE

men had committed acts that were heinous even by the savage standards of warfare, something about the abandonment of a comrade-in-arms had never left them, as if they knew the wrath of the gods had been upon them ever since their betrayal. Agamemnon, in particular, regarded Philoctetes with absorption, resting his chin on his knuckles and fixing his cold blue eyes on the man in whose hands the future of the war lay. On his left sat Nestor, the old king of Pylos who acted as Agamemnon's military adviser. His grey hair and beard had turned almost white since the death of Antilochus – his favourite son – only a few weeks before, and his eyes were now deep wells of grief that had forgotten the joy of life. To Agamemnon's right was his brother, Menelaus, his red hair thinning on top and his plaited beard spread like a net across his broad chest. Though embittered by the loss of his wife to Paris, his face was kinder than his older sibling's and he watched Philoctetes with nothing but pity.

Eventually, Philoctetes leaned back, lay his hands across the bulge of his belly, and let out a rolling belch. He smacked his lips together and wiped his greasy beard on the sleeve of his tunic.

'Beats seagull,' he said, then repeated his appreciation with another belch.

'Then if you're ready, we'll begin,' Agamemnon said. 'You know why we sent Odysseus and Diomedes to bring you back to the army, of course – the prophecy that the gates of Troy will not fall without the weapons of Heracles. You have them with you?'

Philoctetes nodded and there was an almost palpable stilling of breath as Odysseus handed him the long bundle of cloth. Philoctetes whipped off the covering to reveal the tall, perfectly crafted bow and its leather quiver, tightly packed with black-feathered arrows. A murmur passed among the assembly, but was quickly stilled by Agamemnon's raised hand.

'Good. But before we speak more of the prophecy, we must first look back ten years to your wounding and our stranding you on Lemnos. You have to understand, Philoctetes, that for our part it was not personal. It may have been for Achilles, who was jealous that you beat him in the race from Aulis – and he was a hard man to defy when he was determined about something – but the rest of us can only blame our weakness. The stench of your wound and the constant wailing were enough to drive any man insane, even hardened warriors like us, and we succumbed to our moral flaws. That it was the will of the gods, too, shown by the fact Podaleirius healed you last night but could not a decade ago, does not lessen our guilt. We abandoned you to terrible deprivation and suffering and for that we are sorry.'

Grunts of approval met the apology, but Philoctetes had been reminded of the wrongs that were done to him and stared sullenly about at the circle of faces, bathed in the orange glow of the fire.

'A gracious confession of your guilt, and one which I will accept,' he grunted. 'Though only because my lord Heracles personally ordered me to put aside my anger and come to Troy. It's for his glory and mine that I am here, so let us get to the crux: why *am* I here, exactly? These arrows never miss and they kill every living thing they pierce, but they cannot knock down walls or shatter gates from their hinges. So what do you want from them?'

'This has nothing to do with what Agamemnon wants,' spoke a voice from the mouth of the tent's entrance. 'Indeed, the King of Men knows only a portion of what the gods have shown to me. And that is why he has summoned me here now – to speak the rest of the prophecy.'

A stooped figure, cloaked and hooded, moved in a shuffling hop to stand between the hearth and Agamemnon's golden throne. One pale hand dangled limply from the opening in his cloak, beneath which could be seen a white dash of his priest's robes. He raised his other hand to the lip of his hood and slipped it back, revealing a bald head and skull-like face. His dark eyes swept across the Council of Kings and came to rest on Philoctetes. One outcast facing another.

'I am Calchas,' he announced, 'one-time priest of Apollo in the city of Troy, and now a worthless wretch forgotten by most and valued by none.'

'Then we have much in common, Calchas,' Philoctetes replied. 'But if you are the reason I was brought here, speak and let us know what the gods command.'

Calchas nodded, then paused and bowed his head, as if summoning a difficult memory.

'The night Great Ajax took his life, I was asleep beyond the boundaries of the camp. It was there that Apollo visited me, telling me that Troy can only fall if certain conditions are met. What they are I don't know, for the god only showed the first of them to me: that you, Philoctetes, should be fetched from Lemnos to kill the one enduring stalwart of Troy's defences. Of all the sons that once served King Priam, only one remains of any note. His arrows have slain many great heroes and with a bow in his hand he has no match, which is why you and the weapons of Heracles are the only way we can rid ourselves of him. Philoctetes, if Troy is to fall you must first kill Paris.'

'No!' Menelaus bellowed, leaping from his chair and seizing Calchas by the front of his cloak. 'Paris is mine! He stole my wife and brought this miserable war upon us. If anyone's going to kill him, it's going to be *me*.'

Calchas shrank back in fear, but Agamemnon was quick to come to his rescue.

'Leave him, Menelaus,' he commanded. 'If the gods have said Paris will be killed by Philoctetes then that's what must happen.'

'Damn the gods and damn all prophecies! Paris is going to perish at *my* hands, not by some shepherd prince because of the words of a drunken priest. Admit it, Calchas! You'd been drinking again and this supposed prophecy was nothing more than a wine-soaked dream.'

'*I said leave him*!' Agamemnon boomed, rising from his throne and pointing at his brother. 'You had your chance weeks ago when you faced him on the battlefield, and you squandered it. Now the gods have taken it out of your hands.'

Calchas tore himself from Menelaus's grip and almost fell back into the fire.

'It's true,' he croaked. 'The gods are tired of waiting. Paris must die now, and his death will cause the Trojans to lose heart.'

'What?' scoffed a short warrior with a single, angry eyebrow that sat low over his fierce-looking eyes. A large brown snake hung from his shoulders, hissing and flicking out its pink tongue at the watching Greeks. 'The Trojans lose heart over Paris? Did they lose heart when Hector died? And he was ten times the man Paris is.'

Voices were raised in agreement, but Calchas was not cowed by them. He had seen the will of the gods and he knew he was right.

'What Little Ajax does not appreciate,' he said, looking round at the Council, 'is that with Paris dead many in Troy will demand Helen be returned to Menelaus. Others will insist she remains, and both sides will squabble over who will have her. There will be division within the walls of Troy and the Trojan people will lose their resolve to continue. If Philoctetes can kill Paris then the reason for the war – his love for Helen – will have been taken away.'

Agamemnon stepped down from the dais on which his throne sat and dragged Menelaus back in the direction of his own chair.

'The gods have spoken. Paris's death will sow dissent among our enemies and perhaps open the gates of their city from within. Philoctetes, tomorrow morning you will ride with Odysseus and Eperitus to Troy where you will challenge Paris to a duel, offering the bow of Heracles as his prize if he can defeat you. Are you ready to honour Heracles's command and cover yourself in glory?'

'Or a shroud,' Philoctetes replied. 'Whichever the immortals deem most fitting.'

'Hector, don't go. We need you here!'

Helen opened her eyes. The first light of dawn was stealing in through the eastern windows and casting its rosy glow over the muralled walls of the bedroom. The painted trees and flowers and the animals that gambolled through them never seemed so lifeless as they did at this time of the morning, when the flat, hazy light robbed them of their colour and motion.

'Hector, no. If you die, Troy will fall. I can't take on your mantle alone.'

Paris was talking in his sleep. The same old slurred anxieties that had haunted his dreams since the death of his brother, pleading – she guessed – for Hector not to go out and face Achilles. Pleading not to be left the crushing responsibility of the hopes and expectations of the whole of Ilium. Though he could feign courage and calm conviction before the people as he walked the streets in his fine armour, and though he could even fake confidence to Helen in their waking time together, his dreams betrayed his uncertainty, his fear. Had Hector been the same, she wondered? Had Andromache lain beside him at night and listened to his worry and self-doubt?

She reached out a hand and brushed the black locks of sweat-damp hair from his forehead, tracing the long pink line of the old scar that ran from above his eyebrow diagonally across his nose and cheek to end almost at his jaw. It was not a handsome face, but it had strength and endurance; and beneath the closed eyelids was a passion that showed itself as much in love as it did in war. Much more so, she thought with a smile as her long fingers drifted to the streaks of grey above his ears and began stroking him.

'Shush now, my love. I'm here. Your Helen's here.'

He turned to face her, eyes still shut firmly in sleep, and laid a rough hand on the curve of her waist. His flesh was hot, causing her to flinch. Then she heard voices echoing along the narrow corridor outside their room. Frowning, she sat up and looked at the door, the furs slipping down to expose her chest.

There was a soft knock.

'Mistress?'

The maid's voice was low but urgent.

'What is it?'

The door was pushed open and Helenus strode in, followed by the apologetic maid. The prince looked alarmed and ready to speak, but the sight of Helen's nakedness stopped the words before they left his mouth. Surprised by his unexpected entrance, Helen pulled the furs over her breasts and glared her anger. Paris woke beside her.

'What is it?' he mumbled.

Helenus blinked twice then looked at his brother.

'Paris, there are three men at the gates. Greeks.'

'Then kill the bastards!'

'But they've come asking to speak with you. One of them is demanding … well, he's demanding an archery duel.'

Paris rubbed the sleep from his eyes and sat up.

'What do you mean a duel?' he asked. 'Is it … is it Menelaus?'

'No. It's Odysseus and his captain.'

'*Odysseus*?' Paris repeated, frowning this time. 'Why in the names of all the gods would Odysseus want to challenge me to personal combat?'

'Not Odysseus,' Helenus said. His eyes kept flickering towards Helen, who was holding the furs firmly over her nudity. 'It's the third man, a stick of a figure who looks like he hasn't eaten for a year. He has a bow that must have been made by the gods – far too grand a weapon for a wretch like him.'

Paris was intrigued now. He swung his legs out of the bed and waved his younger brother back towards the door.

'Tell them I'm coming,' he snapped.

Helenus bowed, and, with a last lingering look at Helen, left. Helen laid a hand on her husband's shoulder and he turned to look into the irresistible eyes that had won so many victories over him in their ten years of marriage.

'Don't go,' she said. 'Call Helenus back and tell him to send Odysseus and his companions away.'

'I can't. I'm a prince of Troy, Priam's eldest remaining son. I should at least hear what they have to say.'

'You *know* what they have to say,' Helen replied, her dark eyebrows furrowing. She swept aside a lock of black hair that had fallen across her face. 'They want to kill you, Paris. Don't give them the chance.'

Paris looked away. His tunic and sandals lay where he had left them the previous evening, but before he could reach for them Helen threw aside the furs and took hold of his wrist. He turned to her as she raised herself on her knees before him, still retaining her grip on his hand but making sure he could see the full glory of her naked body. And just as she had known it would, the sight of her white skin and the orbs of her breasts captivated him at once. Helen knew there were many in Troy who had accused her husband of losing his manliness for her sake, who, despite his increasingly selfless – even reckless – feats on the battlefield, grumbled to each other that he was not the commander he had once been, in his years spent conquering Troy's enemies on the northern borders, before she had entered his life and brought a new war. What they meant, of course, was that he was not Hector. Since his older brother's death, Paris had felt ever more acutely the weight of expectation that had been placed on his shoulders – by his father, by his younger brothers, by the army and its allies, and by every other man, woman and child in Ilium. And with that expectation came a growing resentment towards her, whom many thought of as a barrier preventing him from devoting himself to the cause of his nation. And they were right. She would do anything in her considerable power to stop him from throwing away his life for Troy. She no longer cared whether the city was destroyed a thousand times over and every living being in the whole of Ilium put to the sword, as long as he lived and they could be together.

As he looked at the face that had pierced his heart a lifetime ago, and the flawless body that he had come to know with such intimacy, she could sense his resolve wavering. That he wanted nothing more than to climb back beneath the furs with her and enjoy the soft warmth of her body enveloping his was written in every feature of his face, but she knew he was not hers again yet. She stroked the back of her hand across his stomach and down into his pubic hair, letting her palm turn inwards so it brushed across him and came to rest on his inner thigh. He responded by reaching down to cup her breast and run his thumb over her nipple.

'Stay here with me,' she said in a half-whisper, dropping back invitingly onto the rumpled furs. 'The sun's barely in the sky and our bed is still warm. Let Odysseus and his archer friend go back to their fellow Greeks, while you and I make love.'

He knelt across her as she spoke and the dawn light gave his muscular torso a coppery tinge. Then something in his expression changed and he pulled away, almost angrily. And she knew she had lost him.

'What's wrong?'

'I can't.'

'Can't what? *Paris*!'

'I can't let them go back. Not without at least speaking to them first. Hector would have gone.'

'You're not Hector!' Helen snapped.

'No, I'm not. But Hector's dead because of me –'

'Because of *me*, you mean.'

'Because I fell in love with you and brought you back here,' Paris countered, though gently. 'Thousands are dead because of my decision. And that doesn't mean I regret taking you from Sparta, Helen. I will never regret that, whatever may happen. It does mean I have a responsibility to bear, though – to my father, to the people of Ilium, and above all to you. When Achilles slew Hector, his burden fell on me: to protect this city and its honour. If I fail to meet even the smallest challenge, then the people won't blame me so much as they'll blame you. And I won't have that.'

He snatched up his tunic and pulled it over his head, then knelt and put on his sandals. Helen, seeing that her naked body could no longer hold him, picked up the dress that lay where she had discarded it the night before. It had taken only an instant to throw off in her eagerness to make love to her husband, but long, agonising moments to put back on as Paris ignored her pleas and threw open the door of the bedroom. She hurried after him barefoot, not caring that the sides of her chiton were loose and revealed her ribcage and thighs as she ran down the corridors and out of the palace.

'Wait Paris,' she insisted, catching up with him.

'Don't try to dissuade me, Helen. I'm determined to speak with these men.'

'Then speak to them if you must, but do you have to accept the challenge? A duel between skilled archers is little more than a game of chance. Will you put your life so freely into the hands of the gods?'

He stopped and turned to her. They were standing in the middle of the wide courtyard that fronted the palace, where scores of slaves and soldiers were already going about their morning chores. Not one failed to cast a glance at Helen, whose beauty was radiant and enthralling even without the pampering of her maids. She barely noticed them, used as she was to the stares of men and women alike.

'Our lives hang by the will of the gods every day,' Paris replied. 'But I promise you I won't accept this challenge blindly. Hector knew his importance to the survival of Troy and never risked himself needlessly, unless it was when he walked out to face Achilles alone. I won't make the same mistake. And yet I will speak with Odysseus. It's my duty.'

Chapter Nine
DEATH IN THE MORNING

'Then be all the more careful,' Helen said. 'To exchange words with that man is as perilous as any duel.'

Paris smiled and kissed her forehead, then carried on walking. Helen followed a few paces behind, down the ramps that led to the walls of the citadel, through the arched gateway and out into the streets of the city. Before long they were mounting the steps to the battlements that overlooked the Scaean Gate. Helenus was waiting for them, along with a number of guards who turned to stare at Helen in her half-dressed state. A glance from Paris forced them to look away again.

'There they are,' Helenus said, pointing down to where three men stood in the shadow of the sacred oak tree outside the gates. The plains down to the River Scamander and the slopes beyond the ford were empty: they were completely alone. 'Odysseus, Eperitus and a man who calls himself Philoctetes. Who he is I don't know – I've never seen him on the battlefield before – but he's the one who dares to challenge you.'

Helen stared at the thin figure with the drawn face. Though he was unimpressive in himself, the weapons he carried inspired awe and fear: a bow of gigantic size – as tall as its owner – and an ornately decorated leather quiver stuffed with black-feathered arrows. Any one of those bronze-tipped barbs could bring death to the man she loved, and with a growing sense of dread she reached for Paris's hand. Before her fingers could entwine themselves between his, though, he pulled away and leaned over the parapet.

'I am Paris, son of Priam,' he shouted in Greek to the small party below. 'I know you, Odysseus, Laertes's famed son, and I know the face of your captain from the thick of the battles our armies have fought. But *you* I don't know. State your name and lineage, if indeed you are human at all – for you look more to me like a wraith conjured up from Hades.'

Helenus translated for the men on the walls and sneers of laughter rippled through their ranks as they forgot Helen's beauty and pressed closer against the battlements, eager to watch the spectacle unfold. Philoctetes was untroubled by their mockery and hobbled forward on his crutch.

'I am Philoctetes, son of Poeas, and these are the weapons of Heracles, which he bequeathed to me. If I appear unfamiliar and somewhat malnourished to you, it's because my fellow countrymen stranded me on the island of Lemnos shortly before the war began, where I lived on a diet of seagull and rainwater until Odysseus brought me back to the army just two days ago.'

'I've heard of you,' Paris nodded, 'though your suffering is news. Tell me, why would a man who had been left to starve by his comrades want to return and fight for them?'

'For glory, and to honour the name of Heracles,' Philoctetes answered. 'And because Heracles himself ordered me to kill you, which I must do if the gates of Troy are ever to fall to the Greeks.'

Helen heard the words and stepped forward to stand beside her husband. Unseen by any of the others – except for Helenus, whose eyes had not left Helen since her arrival – Paris slipped his arm about his wife's waist and smiled mockingly at the Greek archer.

'But *I* have no intention of fighting *you*, Philoctetes. Why should I? Who are you but a half-starved cripple whose only fame comes from an accident of place and time? That you were present when Heracles wanted to take his own life is neither here nor there. That he gave you his bow and arrows in exchange for lighting his funeral pyre does you little credit. And who have you killed of any renown? Go back to your bed and sleep off your drunken bravado; I'm going back to mine to enjoy the company of my wife.'

He turned to go, but the laughter of his soldiers as they pointed at Philoctetes could not hide the voice that now called out to him.

'Why should you meet Philoctetes's challenge?' it said, with such calm reason that Paris was compelled to stop and listen. 'Why indeed, for what man of honour would fight unless something was at stake? Something worth fighting for.'

Paris turned and looked down at the short, bulky figure of Odysseus. Despite his lack of elegance and physical beauty his voice was delightful on the ears, so much so that anyone addressed by it felt obliged to reply just so that they could hear it again. Paris had fallen into the trap and stepped up to the battlements, ignoring Helen's attempts to pull him back.

'What can you possibly offer that would tempt me away from the caresses of my wife?' he asked, slipping his hand free of Helen's fingers.

'Look for yourself,' Odysseus replied. 'The bow and arrows of Heracles. They are yours if you can defeat Philoctetes. This is no trick, Paris. As you can see, we're alone; no army will spring out from the stones or rise up from the river bed if you possess the courage to step out from behind your walls.'

'No thank you, Odysseus,' Helen answered. 'Paris has a good enough bow already, as several score of your comrades would tell you if they were still alive. Now, go back to your camp and use your powers of persuasion to make Menelaus return to Sparta without me. Or don't you want to see your beloved Penelope again?'

'Indeed I do, my lady, but with Hector dead and his place only half-filled I doubt I will have long to wait. What do you say, Paris?'

'I say damn you, Odysseus,' Paris returned, angrily. 'Is that the best your famous voice can do?'

'And is this the best *you* can do?' Odysseus replied, matching his anger. 'To let a woman fight your battles while you cringe in the shadow of your dead brother? Don't you even have the guts to fight a cripple with a weapon that's almost too big for him to wield? Hector wouldn't have refused, not with the eyes of his countrymen upon him and his reputation at stake.'

Helen saw Paris look left and right at the soldiers on either side of him. They were not laughing now, but were staring at him with expectation. His honour had been insulted; worse still, Odysseus had compared him to Hector – the one test Helen knew he dared not fail. He looked at her, into her eyes, and she sensed the struggle within him, the choice between duty and love.

'If you came to challenge my brother, Odysseus, you're too late,' he replied. 'Go home and take your scarecrow with you. I'll not fight him.'

'Then retreat to your palace and fight your battles in bed; let Helen be the only Greek you bring down, piercing her with the one weapon you've still got the courage to wield.' There was a ripple of laughter from the men on the battlements. 'But leave your bow. Give it to someone worthy of calling himself a Trojan, someone brave enough to stand in your place. Perhaps Helenus, there? Or did the greatness of Troy die when Achilles slew your brother and dragged his body behind his chariot –'

'Enough!' Paris shouted, gripping the parapet. He turned to his brother. 'Helenus, send for my armour and my bow. No man accuses me of cowardice; I'm going to kill Philoctetes, and then I'm going to put an arrow through Odysseus's black heart, too.'

'Wait!' Helen ordered, staring at Helenus. She turned to Paris. 'You're a fool if you let Odysseus provoke you into this nonsense. Why don't you stop thinking of Troy and filling Hector's place, and think of me instead – of *us*! I love you, Paris. Did you drag me halfway across the world and fight a war for ten years just to gamble everything we've built for *this*? For an accusation of cowardice, when you know you're the bravest man in Troy. In Aphrodite's name, won't you think about what you're doing?'

Paris looked into her blue eyes for a moment, then turned to his brother.

'You decide, Helenus. If I fight this man, will I win or lose?'

Helenus frowned. 'I don't understand –'

'You have the gift of prophecy, don't you? You foresaw Penthesilea's death, and the fall of Achilles. The priests talk of you with awe; they say Apollo has blessed you greatly. So tell me, will I be victorious or not? If you say yes, I will fight; if no then I will remain here with Helen and let the wind blow this straw man back to the Greek camp.'

Helenus looked at his sister-in-law and she saw his eyes fall briefly to her breasts, doubtless savouring the impression of her nipples beneath the thin white cloth. She could sense his strong desire for her in that moment, a desire she knew he had felt ever since he was a boy, before he could have understood the nature of his feelings for her. And it was then she noticed something darker than lust enter his expression, a realisation of the power that had just been given to him. With a nod to Paris, he closed his eyes and bowed his head in concentration. He stayed like that for a while, with all eyes upon him, then clapped his hand to his forehead and grimaced. Stifling a cry, he fell forward into Paris's arms.

'What did you see?' Paris urged, gently shaking Helenus's shoulder. 'Did you see me shoot Philoctetes? Is that it?'

'No,' Helenus groaned, looking groggily up at his brother. 'But I did see you holding the bow of Heracles above your head, with the straw man lying at your feet.'

'Then I will be victorious!' Paris smiled, triumphantly. 'Guard! Go fetch my bow and arrows.'

'And your armour, my lord?'

'Just my weapons.'

Helen watched the soldier run down the stone steps and up the main road towards the citadel of Pergamos. She did not trust Helenus or his vision and it was with a quickening heart that she turned to Paris. The light of the morning sun was resting fully on the city now, drawing the people out of their houses and casting long shadows behind the soldiers on the battlements. Paris was looking at her, but as their eyes met his gaze wavered guiltily for a moment before he could force himself to resist her accusative stare. Then his rugged face with its familiar scar broke into a smile.

'Don't worry,' he reassured her. 'Helenus has foreseen my victory. This will be over in moments.'

'Helenus is just a boy whose ambitions outstrip his abilities,' she countered. 'But you are a warrior, and the last hope of Troy rests on your shoulders. You don't have to fight this man, Paris.'

'I do, and the reason I have to fight him is precisely *because* the hopes of Troy rest on me. There are enough witnesses here to let the whole army know I backed down from an open challenge, even after Helenus predicted my victory. I would lose my authority, and in an army authority is everything.'

He placed his arms about Helen and drew her into an embrace. The muscles of his chest and stomach were firm beneath his tunic and yielded little to her touch, making her feel like a child.

'What about us?' she asked. 'This whole war has been about us, our love for each other. Thousands dead and maimed, thousands more widowed and orphaned. If you die it will all have been for nothing.'

Paris gave a half-laugh and stroked her hair as she lay her head on his chest.

'The war was never about us, Helen. It was about power and greed and honour and hate. We're just symbols for all the rest of them to hide behind. We're unimportant, really.'

'But you're everything to *me*, Paris. If you die, I don't want to live. I love you.'

She looked up at him but was distracted by a noise on the steps. The guard had returned and now stood awkwardly a short distance away, Paris's bow and quiver of arrows held in his hands. Paris loosened his hold on Helen and stepped back from her.

'I love you, too,' he said.

Then he took the weapons from the soldier and descended the steps to the gate.

'There's your new home,' Halitherses said. 'At least for the foreseeable future.'

The old man sat on his tired horse and looked down at the city of Sparta, a flash of white halfway across the wide plains of the Eurotas valley. Telemachus was beside him, sitting astride his pony with his hand held across his forehead to shield his eyes from the sun.

'It's big.'

'Of course it's big. Do you think a powerful king like Menelaus would rule over a little backwater like Ithaca?'

Telemachus turned his green eyes on his ageing guardian.

'Ithaca may be a backwater, but it's home and one day I'll be its king.'

'Let's hope so, lad. Let's hope so.'

Halitherses smiled down at the young boy. He had his mother's good looks and would inherit her height too, in time. His facial expressions and way of speaking, though, were reminiscent of Odysseus. It seemed strange to the old soldier that Telemachus's mannerisms should be so like those of the father he had never known, and yet it was also a comfort in dark times. To have a physical reminder of the absent king kept Halitherses hopeful that Odysseus would one day return.

He looked back at the valley stretched out below them. From the heights of the pass that had led them through the Taygetus Mountains they could see the River Eurotas sparkling in the distance as it wound its way from the great city southward to the coast. A thick heat haze shimmered over the farmlands on either side, but the distorted air could not hide the fact the crops were scanty and meagre, a patchwork of swaying stalks that held no comparison to the oceans of corn and barley Halitherses had witnessed here twenty years before. The little farmsteads that dotted the plain were ramshackle and in some cases deserted, while the city itself had lost its golden lustre, if not its size. It was typical of all he had observed on the journey from Ithaca. The whole Peloponnese had grown dull and shabby without the governance and protection of its kings, like a once-beautiful house that had fallen into disrepair. Its inhabitants had become suspicious and unfriendly, while here and there migrants had begun to drift down from the lands north of Greece, resented but not resisted as they built their homes and communities in a country that was not their own. Everything was in decline, and Halitherses doubted even the return of the armies from Troy could reverse the decay that had set in.

'Come on then, lad,' the old man said, touching his heels to the flanks of his mount. 'There's still a long way to go, and I want to get there before nightfall. The gods have kept us safe so far, but I don't want to spend another night in the open if it can be avoided.'

'Halitherses?'

Halitherses turned to see Telemachus had not moved.

'What is it, lad?'

'Is my mother safe?'

'Of course she is,' the old man answered, trying to disguise his hesitation. 'Her enemies are becoming more powerful, and they want your father's throne – I've never kept that a secret from you – but they know they can't get it without Penelope. She's the key and they need her alive, or I wouldn't have left Ithaca. And she's more than clever enough to handle Eupeithes until your father returns.'

Telemachus frowned and looked down at the ears of his pony, twitching randomly in the faint mountain breeze.

'What if my father never returns?'

Halitherses turned back and laid his large, sun-browned hand on the boy's head.

'Don't worry about that, lad. Ithaca's like a lodestone to Odysseus. He'll come home again one day. I promise you.'

'I wish I had your confidence in him,' Telemachus said, then kicked back his heels and sent his mount trotting in the direction of Sparta.

Halitherses watched him thoughtfully, then, with a click of his tongue, urged his horse forward to catch up with his young charge.

Odysseus saw Helen appear at the battlements, her perfect face stricken with concern. A moment later he heard the squeal of wooden hinges as the Scaean Gate swung open. The movement raised a thin haze of dust, through which the figure of a man could be seen striding towards them.

'He's fallen for it,' Odysseus said.

Philoctetes shifted nervously and Eperitus placed a hand on his bony shoulder.

'Don't be concerned,' he reassured him. 'You have Heracles's bow and arrows that never miss. This is why the gods gave them to you. It's time to fulfil your destiny.'

Philoctetes nodded but did not speak. Still in the shadow of the walls, Paris was removing the arrows from his quiver and pushing them point-down into the soil by his feet. When a dozen had been planted he tossed the heavy quiver to one side and stood with his legs apart. Helen sobbed quietly on the walls above, while all along the parapet a crowd of soldiers and townsfolk were gathering to watch the duel.

Philoctetes began pulling the arrows from his own quiver and setting them in the ground to his left. After the sixth he handed the leather tube to Odysseus, who replaced the lid and slipped it over his shoulder. There was a tension in the air that reminded him of the nervousness he felt before every battle, but was made oddly more acute by the knowledge he would not be fighting and could, therefore, do nothing to influence the outcome. The thought made him suddenly uncomfortable. The conclusion of the war had been compressed into a single action, to be decided between just two men. If Philoctetes failed, then the siege would drag on and it would be more long years before Odysseus saw Ithaca and his family again; if he succeeded in killing Paris, another barrier would be removed and the prospect of going home would come a little closer. But at that moment, there was little else Odysseus could do to sway his own destiny.

He slipped the thin, grubby scarf from about his neck and looked at Philoctetes.

'Are you ready?'

The archer, tight-lipped and slightly pale, nodded. Odysseus glanced at Eperitus, who moved out wide to his right. When he was well beyond the range of even the wildest shot, the king turned and walked out to the midpoint between the two opponents. He glanced at Paris, who took a deep breath, exhaled and gave a curt nod. Odysseus stepped back a few paces then held up his hand and let the scarf dangle from his fingertips.

'No arrows to be fitted before my signal,' he declared. 'When the scarf touches the ground – and *not* before – you will fit your arrows, aim and fire. After the first missile, you can continue shooting until either you or your opponent is dead or mortally wounded. There will be no other bloodshed, whatever the outcome,' he added in the Trojan tongue, staring up at the walls where several archers had appeared.

Paris waved them back and they melted into the crowd. His eyes moved to Helen, lingered on her tear-stained beauty for a heartbeat, then returned to Philoctetes. Despite the cool morning breeze, beads of sweat stood out on both men's foreheads. Their eyes squinted, reluctant to blink as the moment approached. Then Odysseus raised his hand a fraction and, suddenly, the scarf was falling.

It fluttered down onto the grass and the two men reached for their arrows. Philoctetes's fingertips grasped clumsily at one of the flights and knocked the missile to the ground. He went for a second, but Paris had already seized his first and was fitting it to his bow. He fumbled slightly, causing the crowd to gasp as he almost dropped the arrow; then he was pulling the string back to his cheek and taking aim. Philoctetes plucked up an arrow, just as Paris's missile whipped across his jaw and drew a red line through the flesh. He blinked with shock and Odysseus felt his heart thundering within his chest, wondering whether Philoctetes would falter and panic. Then the archer's instincts took over. He fitted the arrow and pulled back the string.

'Aim for the body,' Eperitus shouted, forgetting that the arrows of Heracles were magical and could not miss.

Philoctetes's hand rested against his bloody cheek. He closed his left eye and looked down the shaft at Paris, who was already fitting his second arrow. Philoctetes snatched half a breath, steadied his aim and fired.

The point hit Paris between the second and third fingers of his left hand, the bronze tip driving through the tendons and bones until it emerged spitting blood and flesh from the back of his wrist. Paris's bow dropped to the floor as he lifted his hand above his head and cried out in pain. The crowd on the battlements shouted out in horror, but by this time Philoctetes's second arrow was racing towards its target. It entered Paris's right eye and the force of the impact spun him around so that his screams echoed back at him from the walls that he had fought so hard to defend. A third arrow then tore into his ankle, as if in cruel mockery of the shot with which Paris had claimed the life of Achilles a few weeks before. It knocked his leg from beneath him and brought him crashing to the ground, where he gnawed at the dust in his agony. Philoctetes had already fitted a fourth arrow to the giant bow and, when Paris began to claw at the earth in an effort to pull himself towards the Scaean Gate, raised the weapon to his cheek once more and took aim. But before he could release the string, Odysseus appeared beside him and pushed his arm down so that the arrow thumped into the ground at his feet.

'Enough!' the king exclaimed. 'Damn it, Philoctetes, you could have killed *her*.'

They looked over to the shadow of the gates, where the radiant white figure of Helen had run out to be with her dying husband. She knelt beside him, cradling his head in her lap and hiding his disfigured face behind a veil of her black hair. Her shoulders shook and they could only imagine the tears she was shedding over her lover, from whose eye one of Philoctetes's arrows still protruded.

'Enough then,' Philoctetes agreed as Eperitus joined them. 'Let him die in peace with his wife. I've done what the gods demanded of me. Let's return to the camp.'

book

TWO

Chapter Ten
A WAY OUT

Helen could still see Paris's face in the darkness, a mass of blood with the open wound where one of his men had drawn the arrow from his eye. The other eye was a lifeless orb, finally still and dull after so much suffering. She saw it even though night had fallen and every light in the room had been extinguished. She even saw it when she closed her eyes and pressed the palms of her hands over the lids. Though ten days had passed since his death, his maimed features would not leave her.

She slid down in the fur-covered chair and flopped her arm towards the table, where the fingers groped clumsily for the krater of wine. She found it and pulled it to her lips, spilling it over her chin and slender white neck as she drank. A dark line of liquid raced down into her cleavage, but she hardly seemed to notice as she fumbled the empty krater back onto the table and drew herself heavily to her feet. The room swayed unsteadily about her as she stood, snapping back to its start point each time she blinked. But even among the uncertain blurring of furniture and darkened corners she could still see Paris's dead features staring back at her. With an effort she walked to the window and tugged at the heavy curtains clinging on to them for balance until she found the sill of the window beyond and leaned out.

Just like the room behind her, the clustered buildings in the citadel below the palace slid towards the corner of her vision, as if a Titan had escaped from Tartarus and was tilting Troy onto its side. She leaned onto her elbows and buried her face in her hands, closing her eyes and finding Paris there waiting for her.

'Enough!' she shouted, not caring less for any eyes that might be watching her from the streets and buildings below. She slapped her hand down on the cold stone and looked up at the night sky, bejewelled with a thousand stars. 'Enough. I told you not to listen to Helenus, not to leave me. Oh Paris, how long will I have to suffer like this?'

She listened to the silence, then steadied herself against the side of the window and stared down at the roof of the great hall a little below and to her right. A pool of red light marked the hole in its apex where a line of smoke from the fire below trailed out into the night sky. A murmur of voices escaped with it, competing against each other in anger or agitation. Helen looked at the red glow and closed her eyes despairingly, knowing that they were debating her fate at that very moment. Even before the ashes of Paris's funeral pyre had grown cold, both Deiphobus and Helenus had asked for her hand in marriage. Deiphobus, she knew, had loved her from the very first, always showing her the highest respect and courtesy and never allowing a word to be said against her. Nevertheless, his request had outraged her and she had let him know this in the harshness of her rebuttal. Helenus had followed shortly after, brimming with arrogant self-confidence and no doubt buoyed by her refusal of his older brother. His determination to wed Helen and use her as a stepping stone for his ambitions was not lessened by the fact he had been a playmate of her son, Pleisthenes, or that his vision of Paris's victory had led directly to his death. Consequently, Helen's dismissal of him was even more severe than it had been of Deiphobus. But both men were princes and not used to having their requests denied, even by a woman who had once been the queen of Sparta. And so they had demanded of Priam that he choose one of them to marry Helen. The old king agreed, though not because of any sympathy for his sons. He informed his daughter-in-law that she should take a new husband. His subjects, he explained, were restless after the death of Paris and many wanted to send her back to the Greeks, something which Priam was determined would not happen.

Helen groaned.

'Why did you leave me, Paris?'

And then, on the sighing of the wind, she thought she heard a voice answer her.

'Come,' it said. 'Come to me.'

She sat on the stone sill and drew her knees up beneath her chin, looking down at the long drop. Her befuddled mind tried to calculate if it was enough – enough to kill her. She thought it was; all she had to do was relax and lean sideways. That was all, and then the torment of being apart from Paris would be over. The forgetfulness of Hades would envelop her. Helen of Troy would be no more.

But not the war. That would go on regardless of her fate. Thousands more would perish. Thousands more widows and orphans would have personal reason to hate her memory. Even though she would be gone and Agamemnon and Priam's fight would become openly the struggle for power it had always been, they would still blame her as the spark that brought death to their husbands and fathers. And that was why she could not just take her own life. The only way to end the war was to find a way back to Menelaus. If she was with her first husband again, the oath taken by the other kings would no longer hold. She would not be a prisoner of Troy any more, and neither could Agamemnon use her death to call on the Greeks to avenge her. The war would have to stop.

She swung her legs off the sill and felt the smooth floor beneath her bare feet. Pulling herself up by the curtain she walked unsteadily to the chest at the foot of her bed, where she found her black travel cloak folded ready. She had always known, from the moment Paris had died in her arms, that this would be her fate – to return to Menelaus and end the war. And yet it had taken the realisation that Priam and his remaining sons were determined not to give her up to force her into action. The very thought of facing Menelaus again after so long filled her with fear and revulsion, but she could not put off her doom any longer. She pulled on her sandals, threw the cloak about her shoulders and crossed to the door.

Outside her bedroom the corridor was dark and quiet. She followed it to the left, unsteady on her feet as she took the stairs down to the lower level of the palace, the leather soles of her sandals scuffing softly over the worn steps. She wandered past several open doorways – mostly storerooms – then turned a corner into a high-ceilinged antechamber that led out to the starlit courtyard. A soldier guarded the arched doorway at the far end, where he was talking in hushed tones to a small and curvaceous slave girl, their faces lit by a torch that burned brightly in a bracket on the wall. They were too absorbed in each other to notice Helen, who slipped back into the obscurity of the shadows. The soldier had a hardened mien – all members of the royal guard were veterans of the battlefield – but he was not so tough that he could resist the bold flirting of his pretty companion, who was leaning towards him so that his eyes could not fail to miss her deep cleavage. Taking the bait, he placed a large hand on her hip and slowly slid it up to her left breast. She angled her face towards his, but before their lips could meet a gaggle of voices in the courtyard forced them to back away from each other. Helen saw torches and the glint of armour in the darkness and ran back to the last doorway she had passed, nudging the door open and slipping inside. It smelled strongly of hay and she realised it was one of the fodder rooms for the nearby stables.

A clamour of voices and the rattle of bronze filled the antechamber. Something in the urgency of the rapidly approaching footsteps told her the soldiers had come with orders to take her to the great hall, where her fate was to be announced by Priam. Leaving the door slightly ajar, she waited until they had moved down the corridor – there were four of them, all fully armoured as if she might pose some threat – then slipped out and returned to the antechamber. The sentry and the servant girl had resumed their earlier closeness, but this time she did not care whether they saw her depart: her absence was about to be discovered anyway, and if she was to leave Troy she had to act at once. She pulled her hood up and walked to the door, forcing the would-be lovers to move apart again. The flicker of annoyance on their faces quickly disappeared as they recognised her, but she cared nothing for the guard's admiring eyes or the jealousy in the girl's features as they bowed their heads before her.

The air outside was cold and stank of horses. She almost ran across the courtyard, her cloak billowing out behind her and revealing her thin dress and bare limbs to the soldiers at the top of the ramp. They stood aside as she approached, allowing her to run down to the second tier of the citadel without challenge, although she could still hear their voices discussing her as she disappeared down a narrow side street beside the temple of Athena.

In ten years of living in the city, she only knew of one way out that did not involve gates or guards. It was not easy and it was not pleasant, but it was her only choice and she was glad that the wine had given her a bravado she would not otherwise have possessed. A couple more alleyways and side streets led her to the west-facing wall of Pergamos, where broad steps led to the parapet above. Helen froze and fell back into the shadows. Two cloaked soldiers were standing at the top, their helmets gleaming silver-like in the starlight and their horsehair plumes trailing out in the wind. Fortunately their faces were fixed on the plain beyond the walls and they did not notice Helen in the darkness behind them. After a few moments, they turned and ambled northwards with their spears over their shoulders. Aware her absence would have been discovered by now, Helen sprang up the stairs, only to stumble on the top step and cry out in pain as she cut her shin. She crouched down, biting her lip and holding the wound as she looked tensely to the northeast, but the guards did not return.

She limped to the ramparts and the one place where she could escape the city without being discovered. The stench from the latrine was almost overwhelming, but she wrapped a corner of her cloak over her mouth and forced herself forward. It was little more than an alcove with a hole in the floor that opened out over the walls. There were similar openings all along the circuit of the battlements, but only here was the long drop shortened by a flat outcrop of rock a short way down. The rock also caught most of the waste from the soldiers that used the latrine and ensured that the reek at this point of the walls was particularly close and strong. Helen looked down the hole and felt her stomach turn. It was wide enough for her to pass through, but now that she saw the dark mess against the grey rock below her resolve disappeared and she was forced to step back a few paces.

A little way to the north was the Simöeis. She would be able to wash away the filth there, but even if she could stomach escaping through the latrine and make it undetected to the river, she would have wet clothes for the whole of the long, circuitous journey to the Greek camp. Why had she not thought of that before? Her ridiculous plan had been poorly thought out and now seemed utterly impossible. But she knew she had to go through with it, however disgusting and gruelling it would be. There was no other way to end the war and prevent further misery and suffering being inflicted on the people of Troy, the people for whom Paris had sacrificed his life. She wound the cloak more tightly about her body and stepped up to the gaping, malodorous hole in the floor.

'What are you doing up here?' demanded a stern voice.

Helen spun round to see the tall figure of a man at the top of the stairs. The starlight glittered on his polished armour and there was a naked sword in his hand. For a moment she was filled with fear. Then she recognised Apheidas's handsome, battle-hardened face and her fear turned to anger.

'You may be a commander in the army, Apheidas,' she snapped, 'but I am a member of the royal family. You will address me accordingly.'

'Very well, *my lady*,' he replied, sheathing his blade and stepping towards her. 'You've caused quite a fuss leaving your quarters at night without an escort. There are search parties all over the citadel looking for you.'

'I've walked these walls every night since I arrived in Troy. Is my imprisonment now so strict that I'm no longer allowed to look up at the stars?'

'A woman of your beauty can still be attacked, even in Pergamos,' he warned. 'And you had Paris to protect you before.'

Helen turned away, stung by the reminder of her husband's death, and let her gaze rest on the dark Aegean beyond the opening to the bay. Its surface shifted gently, belying the depth and power of what stirred beneath. Far on the other side lay the land of her birth; the land where three of her children had grown up without her; the land to which her instincts told her she was doomed to return.

'And what will you do with me now you've found me?' she asked, turning to face Apheidas. 'After all, you're not here purely out of concern for my safety.'

'You're required in the great hall,' he answered, taking her gently but firmly by the upper arm. 'Priam is going to announce your fate, but first he wants you to have the chance to speak.'

'Very gracious,' she laughed, ironically. 'If being allowed to voice an opinion about the method of one's own detention can be called gracious. But before you drag me away, Apheidas, I want to ask you something.'

'What is it?'

'Must you always do what Priam tells you to do? I've heard the rumours, about how your mother was raped and murdered by a member of the royal family, and how your father killed her attacker out of vengeance. They say you were forced to flee to Greece, and that Priam took all your family's wealth and land for himself. Doesn't that anger you?'

A dark look flickered over Apheidas's features before being forced away.

'You forget Priam also allowed me to *return* to Troy,' he answered.

'Out of pity and guilt! He didn't feel so bad, though, that he was moved to restore your inheritance to you, did he. Everything you have now you have won by your own strength, fighting in Priam's wars. You owe him nothing. And if you and I have never been good friends, can you say I've ever wronged you?'

'Get to the point, Helen.'

'Can't you have some pity and pretend you never saw me? There's nothing left for me in Troy now and my misery will only be a little less with Menelaus, but if you help me over the walls I can at least return to my former husband and end the war.' Helen took a step towards him and raised her face to look into his eyes, her lips tantalisingly close to his. 'I'll give you whatever you want in return.'

'If you had that much power perhaps you'd be worth listening to.'

She seized his wrist and raised his large hand to her breast. Raising herself on tiptoes, she pressed her lips to his. He kissed her back, lightly, and passed his thumb over her nipple where it pushed against the thin material of her chiton.

'I'm yours if you let me go,' she whispered.

Apheidas looked down at her with his hard, merciless eyes and shook his head.

'Those aren't my orders,' he said. 'And you've been drinking. Come on.'

He gripped her arm and pulled her forcibly toward the steps.

Chapter Eleven
A WIDOW'S FATE

The great hall was hot and stuffy, contrasting the chill air outside. The long, rectangular hearth glowed fiercely and sent thin trails of smoke up to the shadowy ceiling high above. Its scarlet light shimmered on the faces of the men who sat in rows on either side of it, all of whom fell silent and turned to look as Helen entered accompanied by Apheidas. Most were elderly – having earned their positions of rank in the wars of their youth – and the warm glow emphasised the lines on their soft, bearded faces. But not all were old: the commanders of the armies of Troy and her allies were there, along with the remnant of Priam's sons – Deiphobus and Helenus among them. These two stood on opposite sides of the hearth, staring at Helen; Deiphobus, the eldest, had a look of relief and joy on his handsome features, while Helenus watched her with expectant confidence. Priam himself sat on a dais at the back of the hall, leaning forward from his high-backed stone chair and gazing vacantly at the flames. His vanity spent with grief at the deaths of Hector and Paris, he had stopped trying to hide his age behind black wigs and face powder and now looked the tired old man he was. His hair was sparse and grey, as was his beard now that he no longer dyed it. His eyes were watery pools of sorrow, and even his great height seemed to have been taken from him as he slumped on his throne. His clothes were still colourful and richly embroidered, but like Priam they had lost their lustre.

Idaeus, the king's herald, moved out of the shadows by the entrance to announce the arrival of Helen and Apheidas. At once, Priam lifted his head and a flicker of life returned to his eyes. He pushed himself up from the arms of his throne, his forearms shaking with the effort, and stepped down from the dais. Straightening himself with a hand into the small of his back, he brushed aside Deiphobus's attempts to help him and moved towards his daughter-in-law. There had been a time before the death of his favourite sons when, however much he adored Helen, he would have considered it beneath his position to leave his throne for her sake in the presence of so many of his advisers and commanders. Now he did not care how they regarded him, so Helen, stirred by pity, ran around the hearth and past the rows of black columns to meet him, dropping to her knees and bowing before the old king. He laid his hands on her head and stroked her soft hair.

'Stand, Daughter, and let me embrace you.'

'My king,' she whispered, and for a moment the others in the hall were forgotten as they closed their arms about each other and shared their grief for the loss of Paris.

After a moment, one of the elders stood and coughed lightly.

'My lord,' he said.

Priam released Helen and looked at the man with impatience.

'What is it, Antimachus?'

'The princess has been brought here to learn her fate?'

'I haven't yet decided my daughter's fate,' Priam snapped, throwing the elder a dismissive gesture. He shuffled back to his throne, assisted by Helen, and eased himself down onto the hard stone.

'Then may I urge you again to listen to your advisers, and indeed to the people of Troy,' Antimachus continued. 'While Paris lived we were happy to fight, so that Helen could remain among us and not be taken against her will back to Sparta. Now Paris is dead there's no reason to prolong the war.'

Helen looked at Antimachus's face with its broken nose and pointed beard. It was a face she had always disliked, for it had always looked on her with aversion. Among all the elders, only Antimachus had never been afraid to voice his disapproval of her presence in Troy. Now, for once, she hoped his argument would be heard by Priam and accepted.

Priam merely grunted.

'You've always hated Helen, Antimachus, so don't try to convince me you've ever been anything but opposed to this war. And since when have the elders and people of Troy decided what the king should do?'

'Nevertheless, my lord, we should give her back to her own people –'

'We *are* her people!' Priam roared.

Helen rushed to the king's side as he slumped back into his throne, drained by his anger and fighting for breath. She was joined a moment later by Deiphobus, the prince's hand touching hers as they sought to calm the old man.

'I must insist on this point,' Antimachus continued, with a boldness he would never have dared to show before the deaths of Hector and Paris. 'Helen has brought great evil to Troy. Tens of thousands of Ilium's young men have died for her sake, leaving many thousands more widows and orphans. Your commands will always be obeyed, great king, but only so long as you have subjects to follow them. Give her back before she proves the end of us.'

'You go too far, Antimachus,' said another elder, rising from his chair. 'Destruction may have followed Helen to Troy, but the guilt is not hers alone. She's as much a victim as any of us – a victim of men's lust and the cruel gods that gave her such beauty. Let the king deal with her as his greater wisdom sees fit, and pray to the gods he doesn't deliver *you* to the Greeks instead!'

Helen looked at Antenor with gratitude. Though he had once hosted Menelaus when he had come to Troy on a mission of peace – and his sympathies for the Greek cause were well known – he had never shown her anything other than the greatest courtesy and kindness. Yet compassion of his kind was rare, and however much she was to blame for bringing war to Troy, unless she left soon its doom would be sealed.

'Whatever the cause of this war, Antimachus is right,' she said. 'If I stay here, Troy will be razed to the ground, every man, woman and child slaughtered. One way or another, the Greeks will be victorious. But now that my husband is dead, what reason is there for the war to go on? Send me back to Menelaus and save yourselves.'

'Never,' said Helenus, his high voice out of place in the presence of so many old men. 'Agamemnon doesn't give a damn about you, Helen. All he wants is Troy.'

'Helenus is right,' Apheidas agreed. He had moved unnoticed to lean against one of the broad black pillars, his battered armour gleaming in the firelight. 'This war was always about who would rule the trade routes across the Aegean – Paris and Helen were just the spark in the kindling. Agamemnon is typical of all Greeks, greedy and self-serving; he won't go home until the threat of Troy has been wiped out, now and forever.'

'*He* may not,' Helen retorted, 'but there'll be nothing to keep the other kings here. If I'm returned their oaths will be fulfilled and Agamemnon won't be able to stop them leaving. And for all the power of the Mycenaeans, they can't win this war alone.'

There were voices of agreement from the elders, many of whom looked to Priam's bowed head in anticipation. Eventually the king raised his eyes to meet Helen's.

'I will not throw you out now, Helen. Not after we have fought ten long years to keep you here. Besides, I love you as if you were my own flesh and blood, and with Hector and Paris gone it would break my old heart to lose you too. No, this much I have decided: that you will remain a princess of Troy, and that for your own protection you will marry one of my other sons.'

'For my *protection*?' Helen exclaimed. 'Surely –'

'Don't argue with me, Daughter. The widows of Troy's fallen are gleeful that you've joined their ranks and are full of mockery for you now, but the death of your husband hasn't lessened their hatred for you. Widowhood is a hard and lonely place to find yourself, and your son, Pleisthenes, won't be of much help to you with his withered hand. But if you marry one of my other sons your position will be restored, and both Deiphobus and Helenus have asked me to make you their wife.'

'I don't *want* Deiphobus, *or* Helenus!' she protested.

'So you would prefer Menelaus?' Helenus asked, his tone aloof.

'I only ever wanted Paris.'

'Paris is dead,' Apheidas reminded her. 'He can never share your bed again, or meet the intimate needs a woman like you craves. And though your love for him is still fresh, his ghost has already lost all memory of you. Helenus, on the other hand, is alive and full of youthful strength. He can fulfil you again, and in time you will learn to love him like you did Paris.'

'A boy!' Helen scoffed, shocked by the suggestion and yet mystified as to why Apheidas had taken it on himself to support Helenus. 'He's the same age as Pleisthenes. He's barely started growing a beard!'

'What you think doesn't matter,' Apheidas snapped. 'The choice belongs to your father, and what's more, Helenus has something to offer in return for your hand. Haven't you, Helenus.'

Every eye turned to the prince, who had been staring lasciviously at the outline of Helen's body beneath her dress, before realising all attention was suddenly upon him. He switched his gaze to his father, who was leaning forward from his throne to look at his son.

'And what is this thing with which you think you can buy my favour?' Priam demanded, slowly.

'A new prophecy, Father,' Helenus answered. 'One that will ensure the safety of Troy forever.'

'Then share it with us, Son. Tell me what I must do to keep my people safe.'

Helenus swallowed and glanced at Apheidas, then back at his father. The colour had drained from his face.

'Not until Helen is my wife.'

'What?'

'Not until Helen is my wife.'

'Do you *dare* defy me?'

Priam's voice was like a clap of thunder, silencing the great hall in an instant. Helenus looked at him fearfully, but something within him knew that if he revealed the oracles Cassandra had shared with him then his father would have no reason to make Helen his wife. He forced his lips shut and looked down at his sandals.

'So be it,' Priam said. 'And what about you, Deiphobus? What do you have to bribe me with?'

'Nothing, Father, except my loyalty and my courage in battle, which I have shown again and again – unlike my younger brother, who has yet to raise a weapon in anger against Troy's enemies. But there *is* one thing I can offer that is genuine and true. My love for Helen.'

He looked at his sister-in-law, who met his gaze without flinching. Both she and Paris had always known of Deiphobus's love for her and so the revelation came as no surprise. It was clear from the way his expression changed when she entered a room, and from his unfailing defence of her whenever anyone dared to question her presence in Troy. Paris had found his younger brother's infatuation amusing, though Helen had felt only sympathy for Deiphobus, knowing that his love could never be returned. Paris's death had done nothing to change that.

'I have loved you since the first moment I saw you ten years ago at the Scaean Gate, when you were standing in Paris's chariot,' he declared. 'I've never stated my feelings openly, but you must have known them. And though it isn't my intention to disrespect Paris's memory so soon after his funeral, I believe you have to marry again for your own protection. My father has said as much, and if he indeed loves you like one of his own daughters he will forget Helenus's supposed oracle and allow you to choose your own husband.'

'No!' Helenus protested. 'Are we peasants, letting our women choose their own husbands for the sake of *love*? Father, I insist that *you* decide between us, not a mere woman whose judgement will be dictated by emotion and desire.'

'If I were to choose, Helenus,' Priam asked, arching an eyebrow at his son, 'what qualities would I see in you? Indeed, you show your inexperience and ambition when you speak of Helen with such disregard. Remember this: a man cannot find happiness in marriage unless his wife is happy too. And for that reason Deiphobus is right – I will give the choice to Helen.'

There was a murmur of surprise among the assembled elders, who leaned in towards each other to share whispered opinions. Deiphobus and Helenus both looked at Helen, who waited for the hushed discussions to cease before replying to the king.

'My choice remains the same, my lord. I already have a husband, one who was chosen for me by my foster-father twenty years ago from among the best men of Greece. He is Menelaus, king of Sparta, and if you love your people you will send me back to him tonight.'

Priam slammed his palm down on the arm of his throne.

'Menelaus may have been your husband in that barbaric land, but he is not here! And we have not fought for ten years just to give you back now. If you will not choose, Daughter, then I will choose for you. Deiphobus will be your husband. What's more, you will be married this very night here in the great hall.'

'No!' Helen shouted. 'I refuse!'

'You'll do as I command,' Priam replied, sternly. 'And as for you, Helenus, you will appear before the assembly tomorrow evening and you *will* tell us the oracle that was revealed to you.'

Helen turned and looked at the tall wooden doors at the back of the great hall. As the walls and ceiling of the vast chamber seemed to close in on her from the shadows, the doors presented her last hope of escape. But before she could think to run, Deiphobus seized her by the arm and shouted for Idaeus to fetch a priest. Helen struggled against her future husband's grip, and though Deiphobus refused to meet her beautiful, accusing eyes, he held her firm.

Helenus shot his father an angry look, then turned and left with Apheidas at his shoulder.

Chapter Twelve

IN APHEIDAS'S HOUSE

E peritus looked over his shoulder at the five horsemen riding in file behind him. They were cloaked and hooded against the cold night air, and with only starlight to guide their mounts over the unpredictable terrain their progress was slow. Odysseus was nearest. He caught Eperitus's glance and nodded.

'Still here,' he muttered, without enthusiasm.

Eperitus smiled in reply and turned his eyes back to the ground before his own horse's hooves. The grass was thin and parched, dotted here and there with broken weapons and armour from the years of fighting that had taken place across it. Looking ahead, he could see the ridge line that marked the edge of the plateau – a deeper darkness rising up against the blue-black of the night sky. His supernatural eyesight could already pick out the tall ring of trees that formed the temple of Thymbrean Apollo, silhouetted against the stars as it stood on top of the ridge. The sight of it filled him with a sudden, heavy sorrow as he remembered his former squire, Arceisius, murdered in the temple by Apheidas – and all because Eperitus had been foolish enough to agree a meeting with his father. If he had trusted his long-standing hatred of Apheidas then Arceisius's death would not be on his conscience. But he had believed the woman his father had sent to draw him into his trap, and if anything her betrayal had hurt him even more than the loss of his friend. He had shed bitter tears at the passing of Arceisius, tears of grief and regret, but after a decade of war he could understand death and had learned how to accept it. What he had not learned was how to accept treachery of the heart. He wanted to be angry with Astynome, but all he felt was sadness that she was gone. It would have been much easier to hate her for making him love her, when all along she had been living a lie, sent by Apheidas to trick him into betraying the Greeks. To hate was a familiar emotion, easy to live with. And yet, when he recalled her beautiful face framed by the dark mess of her hair, or the soft fragrance of her skin in his nostrils – so wonderful to his heightened senses – he knew he could never truly hate her. Naturally, he felt surges of bitterness and anger, as much at what he had lost as at what she had done; but then he would remember the feel of her long fingers running through his hair and the warmth of her lips against his, and he could not convince himself that she did not love him back.

'Not far now,' Odysseus said, catching Eperitus unawares as he rode up beside him.

The king had tipped back his hood and was squinting in the direction of the temple, doubtless nothing more than a black smudge atop the line of the ridge to his eyes.

'I wonder whether we'll find anything when we get there,' Eperitus replied. 'How are the others?'

'Grumbling. Just as you'd expect.'

'But why? After all, who *wouldn't* want to spend the night tramping halfway across Ilium on the whim of a crazy priest?'

'Wouldn't be the first time,' Odysseus agreed. 'However, if Calchas says the secret to Troy's downfall will be found in the temple of Thymbrean Apollo tonight, then I don't mind a short horse ride to see if it's true. Besides, Agamemnon believes him and we do whatever Agamemnon commands, right?'

'Right,' Eperitus echoed indifferently. 'Though I still say this is just another wild rabbit hunt. The problem is this whole war's been like chasing rabbits – we stop up one hole and the Trojans escape out of another. And if you ask me Calchas *doesn't* have the gift of prophecy, and if he ever *did* he doused the fire with too much wine years ago.'

'He predicted the day of Achilles's death, didn't he?' Odysseus replied. 'Anyway, the rabbit holes can't go on forever. One day – maybe *this* day – the gods will show us how to defeat Troy. And then we can go home.'

'Did Troy fall the day Paris died, as Calchas predicted?'

'That was another rabbit hole. And even if there are a hundred more holes to block, what choice do we have but to stop them up, stop them *all* up? This isn't a little matter of personal fate that you and I can try to change. It's a war, the biggest war the world has ever seen, and only the gods know how it will end. So if they tell Calchas that a new oracle, maybe the last oracle, will be given in the temple of Thymbrean Apollo tonight, then I'm going to be there. I'll do whatever they tell us, Eperitus, if it means I'll be able to hold Penelope in my arms again and see my little Telemachus.'

'Not so little now,' Eperitus said, slapping Odysseus on the shoulder. 'Come on, let's get to the temple and see what the gods have in mind.'

Odysseus turned and called to the others, then spurred his horse into a trot. Eperitus followed, hoping that Calchas's latest vision would prove right and that they would soon find the final key to unlocking the gates of Troy.

Helenus stormed from the palace in a fit of rage, so incensed at Deiphobus's victory that he did not know where to go or what to do with himself. He stomped across the courtyard, cursing his brother, Priam, Helen and all the gods in turn, before bawling at the guards to move aside as he almost ran down the slope to the lower tiers of the citadel. He yelled obscenities at the few soldiers patrolling the streets of Pergamos, then threw himself down a side alley and began beating his fists against a solid wooden door until his fury was exhausted and he slid down the cold stone doorpost to sit huddled in the dirt.

After a while a shadow fell across him. He looked up and saw Apheidas towering above him, a halo of stars crowning his dark head.

'Come with me,' he ordered.

He pulled Helenus to his feet and led him through the shadowy streets to a two-storeyed house adjacent to a small temple of Apollo beneath the outer walls. They crossed the modest courtyard to a low portico at the front of the house, which was supported by two simple columns. Apheidas pushed open the double doors and stepped directly into the main hall. The large chamber was in darkness but for the circular hearth that glowed at its centre. The four columns that surrounded the fire seemed to dance as the flickering light of its flames licked across them, warping in and out of the shadows as if moving to an unheard music. The walls of the main hall were almost lost in the dense shadows, but where the blush of the firelight reached them Helenus could see scenes of fierce battles painted on the white, smoke-stained plaster, in which lines of red-skinned warriors fought furiously for mastery over each other while the dead and dying lay piled beneath them.

'They take on a life of their own in the gloom, don't you think?' Apheidas commented. 'The firelight makes them move as if they were actually fighting.'

Helenus looked at them wide-eyed and nodded, enthralled by the depictions of battle – something he had only ever witnessed at a distance from the city walls.

'It looks terrifying.'

'War is,' Apheidas agreed, 'even after all these years. But fear is the lowest price a man has to pay for immortality – most have to die, like Hector and Achilles. And Paris, of course. Have you thought any more what you will do – about Helen, I mean?'

The commander looked straight into Helenus's eyes, reinforcing the seriousness of his question. Helenus frowned in confusion, before blinking and looking away to the murals on the walls.

'What do you mean, *do* about Helen? Didn't you hear what Priam said? He gave her to Deiphobus. They're being married at this very moment, while I stand here listening to your nonsense.' A flicker of anger tightened his lips and concentrated his brow. 'And tomorrow I'll be forced to tell the oracles to Priam, despite everything. Your stupid plan didn't work, Apheidas! All you've done is made my father angry at me.'

'So it didn't work,' Apheidas said with a shrug, his tone flat and unapologetic. 'When things go wrong in battle, a good commander adapts and changes his plans. You'll have to do the same, that's all.'

'*That's all?* What are you talking about?'

Apheidas did not reply, but turned and shouted so that his voice boomed around the hall.

'Astynome? Astynome! Where are you, girl?'

A door opened to the right of the main entrance and a servant entered. Though her face was hidden in shadow, she was wiping her hands on the front of the old dress she wore and her long legs and naked feet were visible beneath the raised hem. Helenus's tongue flicked across her lips at the sight of her bare flesh.

'Yes, my lord,' Astynome said, dropping the hem from her hands as she emerged from the shadows.

The servant's face took Helenus by surprise and made him momentarily forget his anger. She had fierce, dark eyes that hid deep passions Helenus would never understand, and her black hair and suntanned face gave her a wild beauty that was both alluring and yet far beyond his reach, challenging the young prince's sense of pride and arrogance.

'Bring us wine and something to soak it up with,' Apheidas commanded, falling into one of the dozen chairs that surrounded the hearth.

He waved Helenus into its neighbour, unaware of the dark, hateful look Astynome shot him before disappearing back through the same door she had come in by.

'Now, Helenus, do you want to marry your sister-in-law or don't you?'

'You *know* I do.'

'Then what are you prepared to do to win her?'

He stared hard at the prince, who, despite his sense of royal superiority, struggled to hold the commander's challenging gaze. He was rescued by the reappearance of Astynome, who carried a small table by a leg in one hand and a basket of bread in the other. Helenus's eyes broke away from Apheidas's and turned to the servant girl, admiring the curves visible beneath her dress as she set the table down between the two men and laid the basket on it. His licentious stare followed her out of the hall and then back in again as she returned with plates of cold meat and a bowl of fruit. Finally, she fetched a skin of wine and two kraters, which she filled and passed to the men while they looked on in silence. A moment later she had retreated into the shadows, there to wait on their needs.

Apheidas stretched across and poured a slop of wine into the flames, whispering a perfunctory prayer of thanks to the gods before drinking greedily. Helenus followed with his own libation and the two men started on the food, rolling slices of meat into the flat bread and cramming them into their mouths. After their immediate hunger and thirst were satisfied, Apheidas leaned back, belched and looked at Helenus.

'So, my prince, I'll ask you again: what are you prepared to do to win Helen?'

'I fail to see what I *can* do. By now the ceremony will be over and

Deiphobus and Helen will be man and wife. Unless you're suggesting I kidnap her, as Paris did –'

'Of course not,' Apheidas said with an impatient frown. 'But there is a more effective way to end a marriage. Indeed, it has ended many thousands of marriages in the past decade.'

Helenus shifted uncomfortably in his chair, watching Apheidas as he lifted his empty krater for Astynome to refill.

'You mean death,' the prince said. 'With Hector and Paris killed and so many other losses already this year, my father isn't likely to send the army out to face the Greeks in open battle again. The chances of Deiphobus being slain by an enemy spear or arrow –'

'Don't be so naïve,' Apheidas snapped. 'I'm saying *you* need to kill Deiphobus. And don't look so shocked. You're an ambitious lad, Helenus; with your brother out of the way not only will you be able to marry Helen, you'll be next in line for the throne! And Priam is ageing quickly. Since the death of Hector his will to live has faded; it won't be long before his mighty spirit is led away to the Underworld. And what then? Would you have Deiphobus become king, with Helen as his queen? Or would you rather see yourself ruling Troy, with the most beautiful woman in Ilium at your side?'

Apheidas leaned forward as he spoke, his handsome face bathed in the orange glow of the hearth. His tone was forceful and persuasive, not in the least bit afraid as he talked of fratricide and treason. And his barbed words had snagged in Helenus's mind, feeding on his anger and exciting his pervasive lust for power. He imagined himself seated on Priam's magnificent throne with Helen beside him, while all the elders and commanders of the army prostrated themselves in obedience at his feet. Then a cough and a small movement broke the chain of his thoughts. Looking up, he saw Astynome refilling Apheidas's krater for a second time, though her gaze was fixed on Helenus. Her penetrating stare seemed accusative, pouring cold water on his fantasies. Was his resentment so strong that he was prepared to kill his brother? And if it was, would his ambition then have the patience for his father to die naturally, or would he be tempted to hasten the process himself? Indeed, once awoken, the lion of ambition was not an easy creature to put to sleep again.

'I can't,' he said.

'You can,' Apheidas countered. 'I will be at your side to help you.

Don't you *desire* Helen?'

'Of course I do, but by now she's married to Deiphobus. And I'm no warrior; what chance would I stand against him?'

Apheidas reached out and snatched his wrist, pulling him to his feet.

'Come with me.'

He led the prince to a side entrance, thrusting the panelled door open with the heel of his free hand. At once, Helenus could feel the cool night air on his skin and smell the mingled aromas of wet foliage and damp soil. They stepped out into a square courtyard, filled with fruit trees and shrubs and surrounded by a pillared cloister. It was dark, the only light coming from the few stars that winked between the tattered edges of a thin screen of cloud. At first the garden seemed silent and still, slumbering in its own gloom. Then Helenus became aware of a low hissing that hovered at the edge of his hearing, enticing his senses and focussing them as they searched for the source.

'What's that noise?' he asked.

'That way.'

Apheidas pointed to a path that led between high bushes to the centre of the garden. Helenus hesitated a moment, then followed the line of flagstones to a border of low shrubs surrounding a large, black square in the ground. From the edge of the garden he had thought it to be a pond, but as he got nearer he noticed there was no hint of reflection in its dark waters and that a flight of stone steps descended into its depths on one side. Realising he was looking at a pit, and that the strange hissing sound was emanating from its heart, he stepped closer.

'Careful,' Apheidas warned. 'Fall in there and Priam will have lost another son.'

Helenus nevertheless edged forward and looked down. The darkness was deep and all-consuming at first, as if a hole had been torn from the living world to reveal the black chasm of Tartarus below. As he stared he became aware that something at the base of the Stygian pit was catching the starlight, causing it to glisten weakly in a hundred different places. Then he saw the points of reflected light were moving – faint, slithering signs of life that seemed to intensify and spread as he watched, until the whole of the void was filled with a hideous writhing. He stepped back and shuddered.

'Snakes! So this is where you keep the sacrifices for Apollo.'

Apheidas nodded. 'My ancestors have always been devotees of the archer god. We were warriors, not priests, but one of our duties before my father was exiled from Troy was to breed snakes for the temple. He carried it on in Alybas, after he fled to Greece, and I revived the tradition when I returned to Troy. Apollo's priests place a high value on serpents as sacrifices, but they have other uses too. Their venom, for instance.'

He placed an arm around Helenus's shoulders and steered him back towards the main hall.

'You don't need to kill Deiphobus with your own hands. The right kind of snake left somewhere that only your brother will find it; a quick bite on the hand; then Helen will soon be your wife and you'll be next in line to rule Troy.'

Helenus shook off Apheidas's heavy arm as they reached the cloister.

'I don't know what you hope to gain from this, Apheidas,' he said, turning to face him, 'but you've overestimated my abilities. I'm not sure I can do what you're suggesting.'

'Have you already forgotten your anger after you were humiliated in the palace?' Apheidas said, forcefully. 'Don't you care that Priam chose Deiphobus over you, or that he just expects you to give him the oracles tomorrow evening? He and your brother treated you like a child, but it's up to *you* to prove you're a man.'

'But I'm *not* a man!' Helenus protested. 'At least, I'm not the man *you* think me to be; nor am I the sort of man Deiphobus and my father are. I hate them for humiliating me tonight, but I couldn't easily take their places. Even if I was to do all you say, murdering my brother and taking the throne when Priam dies, who am I to rule over such a great city as Troy? In peacetime it would be difficult enough, but with an army of Greeks laying siege to Ilium it'd be almost impossible. Besides, the walls aren't as impenetrable as we thought. The oracles my ... the oracles that were revealed to me predict Troy will fall if the Greeks can do three things – I told you that! If Agamemnon finds out what they are –'

'He won't,' Apheidas said through clenched teeth, his impatience becoming evident. 'And you aren't as weak as you think. With my help Helen will be yours and you will be the one to inherit your father's throne.'

'Stop pressuring me!' Helenus shouted. 'Don't you realise your words are treasonous, that I could have you killed for the things you've said tonight?'

Apheidas stared at him through narrowed eyes.

'That would depend on whom Priam believed – a defiant, ambitious son with everything to gain from his father's death, or a loyal captain claiming he was coerced into joining a plot against the throne. But let's not succumb to our tempers, Helenus. Take some time alone, here in the garden, to think on what I've said. If you want Helen, I'll be waiting by the hearth to discuss what we can do. If your anger and ambition aren't matched by your courage, then you can return to the palace and neither of us will mention this incident again – to one another or to anybody else. Do you agree?'

Helenus gave a surly nod and turned to look at the dark garden, waiting until he heard the door shut behind him before releasing a long breath and letting his shoulders slump in despair. He quickly tensed again when he saw a figure emerge from the shadows beneath one of the cloisters.

'Don't be afraid, my lord.' It was the servant girl, Astynome. 'I followed you into the garden to see if you would agree to kill Deiphobus.'

'The testament of a maid won't help Apheidas if he intends to accuse me of plotting against my father.'

'I'm not here on his orders.'

'Then why?' Helenus asked, moving further away from the door to the main hall and nearer to the girl. 'To see if I really am a traitor? And how would you feel if I'd have agreed to your master's plot?'

Astynome moved closer so that her features were clearly visible in the gloom.

'A few months ago I would have considered you vile, lower than the creatures that infest that pit over there. Now –' She shrugged her shoulders. 'Now I don't see things in such simplistic terms. After all, I'm a traitor myself. My heart betrayed Troy for the sake of a Greek, and now he thinks I've betrayed him. But I'd gladly see Troy burn if it meant I could be with him again. So, you see, I'm in no place to judge you.'

Helenus considered her for a moment and realised there was more to the servant girl than her beauty. He also felt her words were spoken in honesty and that he could entrust his problems to her.

'The truth is, I'm so angry I could do almost anything,' he began. 'When Priam awarded Helen to Deiphobus it was a deliberate humiliation, and as the gods are my witnesses I'd rather reveal the oracles to the Greeks than be forced to give them to my father and brother! I want to teach them a lesson they'll remember, Astynome, but how can a lowly priest gain revenge against a warrior prince and a king? And yet, after tonight I don't know whether I want Apheidas's help.'

'You're right not to trust him. He wants Priam's throne for himself and he's only using you to remove the obstacles in his path. With Deiphobus dead, he would ensure the demise of your younger brothers before encouraging you to take the throne from your father. And then he would kill you and claim it for himself. That's how his mind works, Helenus. What's more, if you don't agree to his proposal he'll kill you and hide your body so it looks like you've run away in a fit of jealous anger.'

Helenus felt for the slender dagger tucked away beneath his robes and immediately knew it would be no use against a seasoned fighter like Apheidas. And yet the servant girl's words rang true. He knew he would not walk out of the captain's house alive unless he agreed on his oath to kill Deiphobus, thus starting a chain of events that would ultimately lead to his own death. Even if he told Deiphobus and his father of Apheidas's plans, what proof would he have? How would he defend himself if Apheidas turned the accusation back against him? He looked again at the servant girl, and as her eyes met his he knew she understood his dilemma and had an answer in mind.

'Then what should I do?'

'Is your anger against Deiphobus and Priam genuine?'

'Yes, but not enough to become Apheidas's puppet.'

'Then you must flee the city and go to the Greeks.'

'The Greeks,' he scoffed. 'The Greeks will kill me, or just ransom me back to my father.'

Astynome shook her head.

'Not if you do as I tell you. Over there is another door. It opens on to an alley that will take you out to the neighbouring temple. Find a horse, leave Pergamos and make your way out of the city. Ride to the Greek camp and demand to see Odysseus.'

'The Ithacan? But what if he refuses to see me?'

'He won't. Not if you offer to tell him about the oracles I heard you speak of, the ones that hold the key to the destruction of Troy. Didn't you say you'd rather give them to the Greeks than be forced to reveal them to Priam and Deiphobus? And won't this give you the vengeance you were craving? Besides, Odysseus is an intelligent man, the cleverest of all the Greeks; he'll see the importance of what you have to offer and give you whatever you want in exchange.'

Helenus pondered her words, sucking in his bottom lip as he eyed the girl's dark beauty. He thought of Helen and his humiliation in the great hall, and then of the menacing figure of Apheidas, who would reappear at any moment and demand the answer to his question.

'I should go at once,' he said with a nod. 'Your master won't wait much longer.'

He moved towards the door Astynome had indicated, but she stepped in front of him and placed a hand on his chest.

'I've helped you, Helenus, and now I want you to do something for me in return.'

'What is it?'

'When you see Odysseus, ask to speak to the captain of his guard – a man named Eperitus. Make sure Eperitus knows that it was me that sent you to the Greek camp, and that I encouraged you to entrust the oracles to them. That's all.'

Helenus nodded and with a nervous glance over his shoulder ran to the door that led out to the temple of Apollo. As he reached it, he turned to look at Astynome.

'This Eperitus,' he asked. 'Is he the Greek you fell in love with?'

Astynome nodded.

'Then I will tell him you were prepared to give up Troy's secrets for his sake. May the gods protect you, Astynome.'

Chapter Thirteen

THE ORACLES OF TROY

Eperitus rode his mount up to the top of the ridge where the temple of Thymbrean Apollo stood tall and black against the stars. Odysseus joined him and together they sat staring in silence at the familiar sight of Troy below them, before dismounting and tying the reins of their horses to the trees that formed the walls of the temple. The others followed their example and Eperitus, sword drawn, led the way into the shadowy circle of laurels. Their curved trunks bent inwards like the ribcage of a rotted carcass, looming over him as he entered, while the thickly interlaced branches formed a ceiling that only the faintest trace of starlight could penetrate. The floor within had been laid over with large, even flagstones and at the far end was an altar of white marble. It was a dim grey in the gloom, its surface scattered not with the sacrifices of reverent worshippers but the curled husks of fallen leaves. In the murk behind it was a wooden effigy, carved from the stump of a dead tree into the likeness of the god Apollo. Dense fronds of ivy bound its legs and torso and from its clenched fists protruded a horn bow and a bronze arrow, the latter gleaming dully in the shadows.

'So what are we looking for?' Antiphus asked, sweeping the leaves from the altar with his forearm and leaning across it to stare at the effigy of Apollo.

'I don't see anything different,' said Eurybates, Odysseus's squire, as he stared around at the deserted temple. Having been left in charge of the Ithacan camp while the others had sailed to Lemnos, he had insisted on riding with them that evening to relieve his boredom. The expression on his face, however, was one of disappointment. 'What did Calchas say we would find?'

Eperitus stood over the place where his father had stabbed Arceisius in the back only two weeks before, looking down at the floor as if expecting to see his squire's blood still staining the flagstones.

'Perhaps we won't find anything,' he said. 'Who's to say we've not been sent here on one of Calchas's drunken whims.'

'You're too cynical, Eperitus,' Odysseus remarked, standing with his hands on his hips and looking up at the ceiling. 'If the gods want us to know how to defeat Troy, they'll find a way to tell us. Apollo may even appear to us in person.'

With the exception of Eperitus – who had encountered immortals before – the others turned to him with looks of mixed alarm and curiosity. Antiphus slipped back from the altar and stared uncertainly at the effigy of the god, while Eurybates and Omeros followed the king's gaze up to the ceiling of branches, as if expecting Apollo to appear in the air above them at that very moment. Then Eperitus cocked his head to one side and narrowed his eyes, listening intently.

'I can hear hooves,' he announced. 'A single horse, approaching from the direction of Troy. And its rider's in a hurry.'

Polites, who had remained by the entrance, threw back his cloak and made to draw his sword. Odysseus raised a cautionary hand.

'Let him come. The temple is neutral ground, respected by both sides.'

'Not by my father,' Eperitus growled.

'It won't be Apheidas,' Odysseus replied, able to hear the distant sound of hooves himself now. 'But whoever it is, he might just be the reason we were sent here. Pull up your hoods all of you and come back into the shadows.'

The others did as they were ordered, waiting in silence as they heard the hooves top the ridge not far from the temple and then come to a sharp halt. There was a pause as the rider doubtless saw the tethered horses of the Greeks and debated whether to carry on to the temple or turn back. Then they heard him dismount and lead his animal to the circle of laurel trees. The layered boles of the trees were so densely packed that only dark glimpses of the man and his horse were visible as he came closer, but Eperitus's keen ears had already noted that the telltale sounds of leather or bronze that would have indicated a fully armed warrior were absent. Whoever the rider was, he was travelling light.

He tethered his horse and entered the temple: the slight figure of a youth, dressed in a dark cloak that was thrown back over both shoulders to reveal a simple, knee-length tunic of typical Trojan style.

His beardless face was indistinguishable in the gloom, but the hesitation in his approach betrayed his unease as he walked slowly into the circle of trees. The whites of his eyes gleamed slightly as they fell on the six hooded figures.

'This temple is neutral ground,' he declared in Greek. His voice was high and tense. 'All I want is to make an offering to the god and seek his blessing. Then I'll be on my way.'

'Go ahead and make your offering, son,' Odysseus replied in the Trojan tongue. 'We won't stop you.'

Helenus's eyes lingered on the Greeks a moment longer, then he reached into a leather satchel at his hip and pulled out four or five flat, round cakes. He approached the altar and laid them on the cold marble, before falling to his knees and bowing his head. After a sidelong, self-conscious glance at the Greeks, he closed his eyes, raised his hands before the crude effigy and began to pray.

'Lord Apollo, if I've served you with any loyalty, if my past sacrifices have brought you pleasure, then I beg you to hear my prayer. Guide me safely to ... to my destination, and let me find the man I was told to seek. My offerings are small and hurried tonight, but if you give me the vengeance my anger – no, my *fury* – demands, then I promise to thank you with the thigh bones and fat of a young calf.'

'Vengeance?' Odysseus said with a tone of mock interest.

Helenus turned to see two of the hooded men standing behind him.

'You should have gone to a temple of Artemis,' Eperitus added. 'If it's revenge you want, few gods can match her.'

'I am a follower of Apollo, not his sister,' Helenus replied. 'And now I've made my prayer I will leave the temple to you.'

He made to step around the Greeks, but Odysseus raised a hand to stop him. It was then that Helenus noticed the other four men were standing by the single egress from the temple.

'You said you would let me make my offering,' he protested.

'And so we have,' Odysseus replied. 'But don't fear. We intend you no harm. Answer us a few questions and you can be on your way.'

'What sort of questions?'

'Your name, to start with.'

'Helenus, son of Priam,' Helenus confessed, after a moment's hesitation. 'But if you're thinking I'll fetch a good ransom because I'm a prince then you'll be disappointed. I'm a priest, not a warrior, and my father values me less than the dogs that feed on the scraps from his table.'

'We're not after hostages,' Eperitus countered. 'We were sent here for information. We were told we would find the secret to the downfall of Troy in this temple tonight –'

Eperitus felt Odysseus's hand on his arm and turned to see an admonishing look in the king's eye. Clearly, he had said too much. Then he saw Odysseus's gaze turn to Helenus; Eperitus followed and saw that the prince's eyes were staring at him, wide with surprise.

'*Who* sent you?' he asked.

'Calchas, the seer,' Odysseus answered. 'Do you know of him?'

Helenus nodded.

'Yes. His reputation as a traitor is well known in Troy, though I also have vague memories of him from when I was a very young boy – his shuffling walk, and those piercing eyes.'

'And are you the one he sent us to look for?' Odysseus continued.

There was a tautness to the king's tone, like a hunter who has sighted his prey and yet is afraid to launch his spear too soon for fear of startling the animal and sending it fleeing for cover. Helenus looked at the hooded men, their features indistinguishable in the gloom, and for a moment it looked as if he would tell them everything. Then he checked himself and stepped back towards the altar, his eyes narrowed suspiciously. It seemed the prey had flown.

'Let me go. If you dishonour the neutrality of this temple you dishonour the gods themselves.'

'The temple's neutrality has nothing to do with the gods,' Odysseus corrected. 'The Greeks and Trojans came to a mutual understanding early in the war that it should be left open to both sides. And in the dead of the night there'll be nobody to witness one small violation. Take him.'

At his signal Polites and Eurybates rushed forward and seized the prince by his arms.

'And I'm curious,' Odysseus continued, watching the captive struggle uselessly against their hold. 'Why would anybody want to visit the temple so late, unless they were up to something they didn't want anyone else to know about? Who's this man you're so desperate for Apollo to lead you to, and what's made you furious enough to seek vengeance? What, exactly, are you up to, Helenus?'

'I'll speak to no man but Odysseus, or Eperitus his captain!'

'Then Apollo has heard your prayer,' Odysseus said, tipping back his hood. 'I am King Odysseus of Ithaca, son of Laertes, and this is Eperitus, the captain of my guard.'

Eperitus lowered his hood and stepped forward to look at the prince, who had given up his struggles and now hung between his Ithacan captors, staring at Odysseus and Eperitus in disbelief.

'Who told you to find us?'

'A servant girl called Astynome,' Helenus answered. Eperitus's eyes widened momentarily, but he said nothing. 'After Paris was slain, Deiphobus and I laid claim to Helen. Deiphobus is the elder and has fought valiantly against the Greeks, but I am a seer and offered to tell my father the oracles that were given to me to ensure the safety of Troy – or guarantee its destruction – if he gave me Helen for my wife.'

Odysseus and Eperitus exchanged glances.

'Go on,' the king said.

Helenus looked at the ground in anger and shame.

'Priam chose Deiphobus. My brother forced Helen to marry him there and then, against her will, while I was *ordered* to give up the oracles to the council of elders tomorrow night. They humiliated me, and I want revenge.'

He looked up and there was a fierce rage burning in his eyes at the memory of what had happened in the great hall.

'Menelaus won't be happy,' said Eurybates, still holding the prince's arm. 'He was hoping the Trojans would give Helen back to him after Paris was killed.'

'I'd hoped the same,' Odysseus confessed, 'but it looks like we'll have to do things the hard way, as usual. And yet it seems Calchas was correct: the gods have disclosed the means to conquer Troy, and the one man they've given this knowledge to is right here before us. Is your unhappiness so great, Helenus, that you're prepared to betray these oracles to the enemies of your people?'

Helenus nodded and Odysseus signalled to Polites and Eurybates to release him.

'Then tell me what they are.'

'What, now? *Here?*'

'I'm a hasty man,' Odysseus answered, with a shrug. 'The sooner you tell me, the sooner we can carry out the gods' commands.'

Helenus seemed hesitant, as if wondering whether the Ithacan king and his men could be trusted.

'First you must guarantee my safety, and once I've told you the oracles I want to be given safe passage away from Ilium. This country is no longer my home and the gods have already foretold its doom.'

'You have my word,' Odysseus said.

Antiphus and Omeros had left the entrance to the temple and were now standing either side of Odysseus and Eperitus. With Eurybates and Polites, they formed a circle with Helenus at their apex.

'Then listen to what the gods have declared,' he began. 'Troy will fall this year if three conditions are met. First, the shoulder bone of Pelops must be fetched from his tomb in Greece and brought to Ilium. Second, Neoptolemus, Achilles's son, must join the Greek army, for it's his destiny to extinguish Troy's royal line. And third, you must take the Palladium from the temple of Athena in Pergamos. Do all these things and victory will be yours.'

'Rob a grave, kidnap a boy and steal a lump of burned wood,' Eperitus mused. 'Not impossible, even if I don't see the point.'

'Oh, there's a point,' Odysseus said. 'If this is the path laid out by the gods then you can be sure there's a reason behind it. And it won't be easy, either. But at least now I know what I have to do to bring an end to this war.'

He touched the small dried flower in his belt, which all the Ithacans wore to remind them of their home.

Chapter Fourteen
THE LEGEND OF PELOPS

Agamemnon's tent was bright and airy, filled with the early morning light that filtered in through its cotton and flax walls. It was essentially the same tent he had used when the fleet had gathered at Aulis so long ago, although it was enlarged in places and the canvas panels were replaced from time to time to keep it looking clean and white. From their first arrival on the shores of Ilium, Agamemnon had refused to follow the other leaders and build himself a hut, seeing it as defeatist and a signal to the army that he did not believe in a swift victory. And as the years of war had passed, his resolve had grown stronger, though the rich furnishings, the thick furs over the floor, the wide, oblong hearth at its centre and the many guards and slaves made the tent more a palace than a temporary military headquarters.

Eperitus barely noticed the familiar surroundings as he stood with his hands behind his back, lost in his own thoughts. Helenus was beside him, noticeably nervous as he waited in the quarters of Troy's chief enemy, while opposite him Odysseus was standing with his arms crossed, his green eyes keenly watching the three men seated on the other side of the hearth. Agamemnon, Menelaus and Nestor were bent in towards each other, their heads almost touching as they spoke together in hushed voices. Eperitus's gaze fell on Agamemnon, whom he hated, and moved away again. If he had wanted to, Eperitus could have heard everything they said, but he preferred to think on the words Helenus had shared with him on the slow journey back from the temple of Thymbrean Apollo. Words he should have dismissed with all his heart and mind, but which even his usually resolute spirit could not.

It began when Helenus had mentioned Astynome in the temple. Eperitus's heartbeat had quickened at the sound of her name and his

104

thoughts slid in an avalanche back to the girl whose beauty had opened up his guard, and whose treachery had then wounded him deeper than any Trojan spear could ever have done. Since he had watched her ride away from the temple that night with Apheidas, her master, he had resolved to drive her out of his mind and heart; to disregard her false promises of marriage and children and return to the warrior's creed of immortality through glory. But the passion of his younger years – when he had not known love and his only desire was to win honour and renown on the battlefield – seemed cold and lonely compared to her, a poor comforter when he wanted nothing more than to forget the woman who had conquered him. So when Helenus had ridden up beside him and repeated the words Astynome had spoken in Apheidas's garden, that she was the one who had encouraged the prince to betray Troy and reveal the oracles to the Greeks, Eperitus felt his resolve against her weaken. She was letting him know she was prepared to see her beloved Troy defeated by the hated Greeks for *his* sake; that her loyalty was not to her homeland or to Apheidas, but to him. It was a message that his anger wanted to reject, and he might have found the determination to rid her from his thoughts again if Helenus had not placed a hand on his shoulder and looked him in the eye.

'Whatever it was she did to betray your trust,' he had said, 'she's changed. I don't understand women and I know nothing about love, but that servant girl loves you. She confessed as much to me, and I believe her.'

As Eperitus turned the words over and over again in his mind, the three kings ended their discussion and sat up. Agamemnon leaned to one side of his heavy fur-draped chair and rested his chin on his fist.

'You say these visions were given to you in a dream,' he said, eyeing Helenus coldly.

'Yes, my lord. In the temple of Thymbrean Apollo.'

'And you haven't told them to your father.'

'To no-one at all. Odysseus was the first to hear them.'

'And we're supposed to believe this is because you wanted to marry my wife, but she was given to Deiphobus instead,' Menelaus said.

There was a dark look in his eyes, still furious from the news that Helen had already been married off to another of Priam's sons. Helenus was about to reply, but Odysseus spoke first.

'He was angry at Helen's treatment – being forced to marry against her will. Didn't you hear what he said, Menelaus? That she begged to be sent back to you?'

'*A lie*,' the Spartan snarled. 'If she wanted me, she'd have found a way back years ago. The truth is your little prince wanted her for himself, or – what's more likely – he's been sent here by his father to trick us. These oracles are nothing more than a distraction, to send us chasing after our own tails rather than attacking the walls of Troy in earnest!'

'A trick?' Helenus snorted, his princely arrogance getting the better of him. He stepped forward and pointed a finger at Menelaus. 'And what would such a trick achieve? At the most, one or two galleys sent to find a dead man's shoulder bone and fetch a boy from his mother's arms. If I'd been sent to fool you, wouldn't I have been better directing half your army to besiege some distant city, or leading you into a well-planned trap?'

'The lad's right, Menelaus,' Nestor added. 'Besides, some of it, at least, makes sense. The Palladium, for instance. We've long known the value the Trojans place on that.'

Menelaus gave a derisive laugh.

'And how do you propose we steal Troy's favourite ornament? Knock on the gates and ask them to let us in? It's just a lump of old wood, Nestor.'

'The Palladium is sacred,' Helenus protested. 'Athena made it in honour of her friend, Pallas, whom she killed in an accident.'

'We have enough divine trinkets of our own,' Menelaus said. He pointed at the ornate golden sceptre that lay on a table nearby. 'That rod was made by Hephaistos for Zeus himself, who in turn gave it to Hermes before *he* gave it to Pelops, my grandfather. The man whose tomb you want us to desecrate! Philoctetes has a bow that once belonged to immortalised Heracles, and Odysseus standing beside you owns a complete set of armour that Hephaistos made for Achilles at the request of his mother, Thetis. And that's just to name a few of the god-made heirlooms that *we* possess.'

'That isn't the point of the Palladium,' Odysseus said. 'The Trojans hold that it fell from heaven into the temple of Athena when it was still being built. The first king of Troy, Ilus, was told in a dream that the city would never be conquered as long as the image remained in the temple. If we could find a way to take it from them, the blow to their morale alone would be significant.'

'And Neoptolemus?' Agamemnon asked. 'Why would the gods have us fetch Achilles's son here to Ilium? He can't be much more than fifteen years old.'

'His father was only a little older when he joined the army,' Eperitus said. 'And if Neoptolemus is even half the man Achilles was, then wouldn't he be worth the voyage to Scyros?'

'Achilles had many qualities, but not all of them were good,' Agamemnon replied. 'Do you forget the Trojans broke into this camp while he sat idle and nearly torched the fleet, all because Achilles's wounded pride would not permit him to fight?'

'Achilles made the mistake of believing his whims were more important than the war itself,' Odysseus said. 'But the gods knew better, and when Achilles's pride led to the death of Patroclus, his friend and lover, he knew it too. We shouldn't fool ourselves into thinking these oracles can be ignored. As Helenus says, it'll require nothing more than a galley or two to fetch Neoptolemus from Scyros and Pelops's bone from –'

'The strangest oracle of them all, don't you think?' Agamemnon interrupted, narrowing his icy blue eyes as he focussed on Odysseus. 'I understand the Palladium, and even Neoptolemus; but my grandfather's shoulder bone?'

'Who are we to understand the commands of the gods?' said Nestor. 'This much I can say, though: Pelops's shoulder bone was no ordinary bone; it was made of ivory and –'

'Put there by the gods!' Odysseus added, his eyes alight with realisation.

'What do you mean?' Eperitus asked, confused.

'I'll explain another time,' Odysseus answered in a low voice. He returned his gaze to the Atreides brothers. 'Whatever the significance, someone has to be sent to Pisa to fetch the bone, and then to Scyros on the return journey to persuade Neoptolemus to come to Troy. We can decide what to do about the Palladium when they get back.'

'It's a waste of effort, dreamed up by this Trojan prince to buy Priam more time,' Menelaus said.

Agamemnon held up a hand to silence his brother's protests. A moment later, he stood and signalled to one of the attendant slaves, who brought him a krater of wine.

'If I've questioned the significance of these oracles, it isn't because I was ever in any doubt that we should attempt to fulfil them. After all, didn't Calchas say we would find the key to the gates of Troy in the temple of Thymbrean Apollo last night? And now, suddenly, three new oracles are revealed to us. No, we must send a ship without further delay.'

'And who will go?' Nestor asked.

Menelaus slapped the arm of his chair.

'Damn it, if we must send someone then let me go. I haven't seen Greece in ten years, and now the opportunity has arisen I'll take it.'

'Would you desecrate our grandfather's tomb?' Agamemnon said, angrily. 'No, you must remain here.'

'Let me go.'

Agamemnon looked at Odysseus for a moment, then shook his head.

'Pelops's tomb is at Pisa in the north-western Peloponnese, just a day's voyage from Ithaca. Do you think I don't know where your heart has been through all the years of this war, Odysseus? If I were to send you, the temptation to return home would be too much. You'd never come back.'

Odysseus moved around the hearth to stand opposite Agamemnon.

'You don't know that,' he implored the Mycenaean king. 'I'm here under oath until Helen is rescued from her captors, and I won't dishonour myself, my family or the gods by breaking it. Besides, if you want Neoptolemus to come to Troy then you need to send me. Lycomedes, his mother's father, won't give him up easily, and I've a feeling Neoptolemus himself won't be simple to persuade. However, if I succeeded with Achilles, I can succeed with his son.'

'That may be true,' Nestor said. 'But I agree with Agamemnon: the lure of seeing Penelope and Telemachus will be too much for you. We can send Diomedes instead.'

Eperitus saw the look of muted exasperation, giving way to disappointment, on Odysseus's face. Agamemnon and Nestor were right – a voyage to the north-western Peloponnese would take a galley within easy reach of Ithaca, and the temptation of his home and family could prove too great a test for Odysseus. But Odysseus was also right – to bring Neoptolemus to Troy would involve facing his grandfather, the perfidious King Lycomedes, and there was no-one among the Greek kings better equipped for such a task than Odysseus. And then an answer to both dilemmas suddenly occurred to Eperitus. He stepped forward and coughed.

'There is an alternative.'

The four kings looked at him in quiet surprise. Odysseus, who was not used to being out-thought by Eperitus, raised a questioning eyebrow.

'Send Odysseus and Diomedes – and me with them – but they should go in one of Diomedes's ships, with a crew of Argives. That way, Diomedes will captain the galley and can prevent Odysseus succumbing to the temptation to return home.'

There was a moment of silence as the kings pondered his suggestion. Then Agamemnon and Nestor nodded, followed by Menelaus. Odysseus just smiled.

'And if I protest,' he said, 'you can tie me to the mast until Ithaca is far behind us.'

Helenus left on a merchant ship bound for Epirus the next morning, but it was three days before the mission to fetch Pelops's shoulder bone could begin. Despite Odysseus's enthusiasm to set sail, the eighty galleys of the Argive fleet had spent too long hauled up on the shores of Ilium to be considered immediately seaworthy. A few had returned to Argos for replacements two years before, but even the best of these needed extensive work before she could be risked on the arduous voyage back to Greece. Every piece of worm-eaten or rotted wood had to be replaced; the hull wanted waterproofing with a fresh coat of tar; the ropes of leather or loosely woven fibre were old and dry and required changing; the cotton and flax sails would not hold a strong wind without repairs; the pine oars needed polishing back to a smooth finish; and the leather loops in which they were slung had to be freshly lubricated with olive oil. It would have been quicker and easier to have used one of the Ithacan galleys that had made the journey home earlier that year, but as Odysseus had been given the choice of making the voyage in an Argive ship or not making the voyage at all, he bit back his frustration and threw himself into helping Diomedes with the preparations.

After the work had been completed, the props were removed and the galley was pushed down into the waiting sea. Now the job of victualling her began. Under the watchful eye of Sthenelaus –

Diomedes's trusted comrade-in-arms – gangplanks were laid against the side and the hand-picked crew of sixty men started loading the hull with sealed jars of wine, sacks of grain for making bread and a few goats for fresh meat. They were assisted by Polites, Eurybates and Omeros, whom Odysseus had chosen to accompany him on the mission to Pelops's tomb, having left command of the Ithacan army to Antiphus and Eurylochus. Meanwhile, Diomedes and Odysseus, with the help of Eperitus, made sacrifices at the altar of Poseidon, asking him to give them calm seas and a good wind for the Peloponnese.

When the crew finally settled down to their oars and began pulling for the open sea, thousands of soldiers crowded the beach to cheer them on their way. Odysseus watched them from the stern – with Eperitus and Diomedes standing either side of him – wondering how much the army knew of their mission. Naturally, the Ithacans who had heard the oracles spoken by Helenus in the temple of Thymbrean Apollo would have told others, and those others would have sent a wave of rumours racing through the camp. How much those rumours had become distorted and exaggerated with each retelling Odysseus could not guess, and did not much care; the army would know the truth soon enough if they were successful.

It was not long before Odysseus sensed a change in the current beneath the ship and felt a wind coming down from the north. Sthenelaus, standing with a hand on each of the twin rudders, shouted an order that sent groups of sailors scurrying to the ropes. They raised the cross spar and let go the sail, which tumbled downwards and flapped a little before suddenly filling up and bellying out. As they angled the canvas into the strong breeze, a second order saw the oars drawn back into the ship and stowed. Released from the laborious pulling motion of the rowers, the galley quickly took on a life of its own, skimming southward as it adapted to the movement of wave and wind.

With little now to do, Odysseus leaned back against the bow rail and relaxed, enjoying the natural motion of the ship and looking about at the sights of land and sea revealed in glorious detail by the bright sunshine of late morning. Rarely did he feel as much at ease as when he was on the deck of a galley with a good wind in its sail. The huge weight of his kingly responsibilities was lifted from his shoulders and he could fall back into a meditative silence filled by idle thoughts. Soon the camp was behind them, marked only by the thin towers of smoke from its fires. They had slipped past the bulk of Tenedos before Diomedes spoke.

'It feels good to be on a ship again, with the freedom of the open sea before us. And to know we're heading back to Greece for the first time in ten years!'

'Better if we were heading back home for good and didn't have to return to this accursed part of the world,' Sthenelaus growled. He had stern features and hard eyes that glared out from a face overrun by curly black hair. 'I hope this mission of yours is going to bring an end to the war like you promised, Odysseus, and not turn out to be another false hope.'

Eperitus caught Odysseus's eye and raised a sympathetic eyebrow.

'I didn't make any promises, Sthenelaus,' Odysseus replied, 'and this isn't *my* mission. We're following the will of the gods, not to mention the command of Agamemnon.'

Sthenelaus's snort showed what he thought of that.

'You can't blame him,' Diomedes said with an apologetic shrug. 'The men are keen to return to Greece and do something other than sitting around in camp or fighting Trojans, but they're wondering what the point of all this is. And they're not alone. I mean, why *are* the gods sending us after an old bone?'

'I know nothing more than you do,' Odysseus answered. 'Although it's possible the clue to the oracle lies in the legend of Pelops himself.'

'There are plenty of stories about Agamemnon's grandfather,' Diomedes said. 'But I don't see how any of them can show us how to beat the Trojans.'

'Well, I know nothing about Pelops,' Eperitus said. 'Although you promised in Agamemnon's tent you'd tell me the significance of this bone.'

'That's something we'd all like to know,' Sthenelaus agreed as he watched the wave caps ahead of the galley.

'The story's familiar enough,' Odysseus answered with a sigh, 'but if you've never had the patience or inclination to listen to it then I'll recount it for you. Many have called Agamemnon ambitious and evil, and with good reason, but he is the natural product of his ancestors, a line of men cursed with wickedness. His great-grandfather was Tantalus, about whom there are numerous tales, but none so depraved as the trick he played on the Olympians. He lived in the time when the gods walked freely among men, and some men walked with the gods. Tantalus was one such man, being regularly invited to banquet with them on Mount Olympus. Unfortunately their favour didn't inspire him to worship them more, only to regard them with contempt. He saw their frivolity as a sign of childish stupidity, rather than the result of a nature free from the shadow of pain, suffering and death. And so he decided to test their power, stealing ambrosia and nectar from their feasts and sharing it with his fellow mortals, just to see if the Olympians noticed. They said nothing because they loved him, but this only made Tantalus despise them more. As a further test, he invited them to a banquet of his own, where, in his wickedness, he served the immortals a stew from an iron pot in which he had cut up and boiled the flesh of his own son.'

'He fed them his own child?' Sthenelaus exclaimed in disbelief.

'Didn't Agamemnon sacrifice his daughter at Aulis, just to appease the anger of Artemis?' Eperitus reminded him, a hint of bitterness in his voice. 'The man's a monster.'

'It was the undoing of Tantalus,' Odysseus continued. 'The gods were not as foolish as he took them to be, all but one of them realising the meat before them was human. Only Demeter, distracted by grief at the recent loss of her daughter, ate the stew. As revenge, Zeus contrived a special torment for Tantalus, condemning him to an eternity of hunger and thirst in Hades. There he stands, up to his neck in a pool of cool water and with the heavily laden boughs of a fruit tree bending over him; but whenever he lowers his lips to the water it recedes before they can touch it; and whenever he reaches for the fruit of the tree, a gust of wind blows it just beyond his grasping fingers.

'As for his son, Zeus ordered his dismembered body to be placed back in the pot in which Tantalus had boiled them. The only missing part was the shoulder blade that Demeter had eaten whole, but the goddess replaced this with one of ivory. Once inside the pot, the parts of the body reformed and took on new life, the boy emerging even more handsome than he had been before his father had murdered him. The boy's name,' Odysseus added, leaning in towards the others, 'was Pelops.'

'By all the gods,' Sthenelaus said. 'Then this bone we've been sent to find is the ivory replacement made by Demeter.'

Eperitus frowned. 'But how is the bone significant? It was made by the gods, just like Agamemnon's sceptre, Achilles's armour and dozens of other artefacts already in our possession, but I don't see how it will help us defeat the Trojans.'

'Nor I,' Odysseus said, with a melancholy nod of his head. 'And that's half the problem. The story doesn't end there, though. Legend says that Pelops was blessed by the gods and grew to a height and stature much greater than other men, with a strength and fierceness that made him invincible in combat. But like so many great warriors, it was a woman who conquered him. He fell in love with Hippodameia, the daughter of King Oenomaus, ruler of Pisa. Now, Oenomaus was a jealous father who loved his daughter more than anything else. When Pelops asked to marry Hippodameia, the old king set him the same challenge he had put before all her previous suitors: a chariot race from Pisa all the way to Corinth. Pelops would be given a head start, but he would have to drive the chariot with the beautiful Hippodameia beside him – a distraction that could only play to Oenomaus's advantage. If he won, then the girl would be his; but if Oenomaus caught up with him, he would kill him, just as he had the dozen or so other suitors who had been foolish enough to fall in love with his daughter. To emphasise the point, the king indicated the city walls where their shrivelled heads leered down from spikes.

'Undeterred, Pelops agreed to the challenge without a second thought: he was a renowned horseman and charioteer, and being almost twice the size of most men he did not fear a fight with Oenomaus. What he did not know, though, was that Oenomaus's horses were the fastest in Greece and his spear was a gift from Ares, which, if thrown by a skilled warrior, would fly straighter and truer than any mortal weapon. Pelops only learned of these things the night before the race, in a message sent by none other than Hippodameia. She had fallen deeply in love with him and told him her father's secret in the hope he would not throw away his life for her sake.

'Pelops knew then he could not win the race. But neither would his love for Hippodameia allow him to back down. So, being a resourceful man, he approached Oenomaus's charioteer, a man called Myrtilus, and offered him half the kingdom of Pisa if he would betray his master and ensure Pelops won the race. Myrtilus agreed to help, but not in exchange for wealth or power. Ever since Hippodameia had been a young girl, he had lusted after her, dreaming of nothing more than to share her bed and take her virginity: if Pelops wanted victory, he would first have to swear an oath allowing Myrtilus to be the first to sleep with her on their marriage night. Reluctantly, knowing he had little choice, Pelops took the oath.

'The following morning, the two chariots lined up at the starting point. Hippodameia stepped aboard Pelops's chariot, her face lined with tears for the man whom she believed she was accompanying to his death. But a furtive nod from Myrtilus gave Pelops all the reassurance he needed, and with a crack of his whip and a loud shout he sent his chariot shooting forward. Oenomaus waited until the dust from his opponent's wheels had died away, then sacrificed a black ram to Zeus before seizing his spear and stepping into his own chariot. Myrtilus took up the reins and began the pursuit.

'The king's horses had not won their reputation for nothing. Despite the long head start, by the time the sun was at its hottest Oenomaus could see the dust from Pelops's chariot ahead of him. He ordered Myrtilus to go faster and had soon come within range of the young suitor. Taking Ares's spear in his hand, he drew it back and took aim, not knowing that Myrtilus had removed the linchpins from the axle of his chariot and replaced them with thinner ones coated in wax. At that moment, the heat of the sun finally melted the wax and the pins came free. Myrtilus, who felt the telltale juddering beneath his feet, leapt clear into a large bush, but Oenomaus was still aiming his spear when both wheels came off, and was caught up in the wreckage of the chariot and dragged to a horrible death.'

'Nothing more than he deserved,' Sthenelaus commented.

Omeros, who had turned from the benches and come to hear the tale, shushed him, forgetting Sthenelaus's seniority in his annoyance at the interruption.

'What about Myrtilus?' he asked.

Odysseus smiled.

'Myrtilus was saved by the bush and returned to Pisa with the victorious Pelops and Hippodameia, his prize. In the preparations for the wedding Pelops forgot all about the oath he had taken, but Myrtilus, of course, had not. At the wedding feast, he whispered in Pelops's ear, reminding him of his promise that he would be the first to sleep with Hippodameia. Pelops looked across at his wife, beautiful in her wedding dress, and nodded, putting on a show of reluctance as he told Myrtilus to wait for Hippodameia by the bridge over the River Alpheius.

It was there, after night had fallen, that Pelops found him and threw him into the deep, ice-cold waters. Myrtilus, as he knew, was no swimmer, but with his dying breath he laid a curse on Pelops – a curse he never divulged, but took with him to his grave. After he had married Hippodameia and became king in the place of her father, he began a campaign of conquest that saw him take possession of many of the cities and lands around Pisa. He was so successful the whole of southern Greece – the Peloponnese – was named after him. But he was also a tyrant, displaying time and again the ruthlessness he had inherited from his father and shown against Myrtilus. Those he could not defeat by arms alone, he tricked and betrayed. One such was the king of Arcadia, whom he invited to a feast then killed and cut into pieces – an echo of how his own father had treated him when he tried to trick the gods.

'And so there you have it,' Odysseus finished, with a sigh, 'the legend of Pelops. Whether it has any bearing on our mission, I can't yet say, but there is something else I should tell you. Before we sailed, Agamemnon came to warn me about his grandfather's tomb. He says the casket containing his bones lies at the centre of a maze, which Pelops had built to deter not only robbers, but also the ghost of Myrtilus. He said Pelops lived the remainder of his life in fear of the man he had betrayed and murdered, and that fear pursued him into the afterlife. What is more, Agamemnon says the tomb itself is cursed, though he doesn't know the nature of the curse.'

'I'm not afraid of curses,' Eperitus said.

'You may not be,' Odysseus replied, 'but Agamemnon is. I could see it in his face, and that's the actual reason he wouldn't allow Menelaus to carry out the mission. He knows the curse is real, and he fears it.'

Chapter Fifteen
THE GOLDEN VINE

'Aren't you concerned, my lord?' Aeneas asked.

The Dardanian prince leaned over the large table, his hands flat on the smooth wood, and stared at Priam seated in his golden throne. The king held his gaze for a moment, then stood and approached the table.

'Concerned that I've lost another son?' he said. 'Or that he might have betrayed his father and run off to the Greeks with the oracle?'

Priam's vanity and arrogance had all but gone since the deaths of Hector and Paris, and as he faced Aeneas he looked the ghost of his former self. His hair was grey and lank now, and his skin pale and lined; his once tall figure had become sloped and bent, while his eyes were dull and stricken with the pain of his loss. But Aeneas could still see the old disdain in them that Priam had never been able to hide, a contempt that was born out of rivalry with his cousin Anchises, Aeneas's father. The king of Dardanus had once slept with the incomparable Aphrodite, whereas Priam, who had numerous wives and had always slept with whomever he pleased, had not. But instead of taking his jealousy out on Anchises – whom Zeus had already crippled for boasting about sleeping with Aphrodite – he directed his resentment instead towards Aeneas, the result of Anchises's union with the goddess. And even though Aeneas was married to one of Priam's many daughters, as a mere prince he was forced to bear it in silence.

'I refer to the prophecy that Helenus said would ensure the safety of Troy,' Aeneas replied. 'He was furious about losing Helen to Deiphobus, and one of our spies saw him enter the Greek camp under escort three nights ago. If he's revealed the oracle to them out of spite, then they may know a way to undermine our defences.'

'You're speculating,' said Deiphobus, who was standing next to Aeneas with a silver goblet of wine in his hand. 'We don't even know what this prophecy was.'

'I do,' Priam said.

He looked at Deiphobus and Aeneas before passing his watery gaze over the others around the table: Apheidas, Antenor and Idaeus, his herald.

'How do you know?' Apheidas asked, only belatedly adding, 'my lord.'

'One of my daughters, Cassandra, came to me this evening. It was she who had given Helenus these oracles – there were three of them – which he was intending to pass off as his own. And if the Greeks want to believe them, then that's their foolishness, not ours.'

'Nevertheless, shouldn't we take some precautions?' Deiphobus asked. 'Just in case there's a weakness we've overlooked.'

'Cassandra is deluded – half-mad, even,' Priam answered. 'Her tortured mind imagines the most fantastic things that she believes are visions from the gods. They aren't. And perhaps you're forgetting something, Son.'

He looked over at the wall to his left. The daylight that was normally channelled into the great hall through conduits from the high ceiling had long since disappeared, but the flames that flickered in the oblong hearth and the torches that hung about the walls spread an orange glow throughout the vast chamber. It pushed back the shadows to reveal the murals that decorated the smoke-stained plaster, though they had been drained of the colour and energy that inhabited them during the day. Sweeping his long purple cloak behind him, Priam walked up to one of the larger-than-life depictions and reached up to touch it with the palm of his hand. It showed two golden-skinned men: one dressed in a shepherd's fleece and playing a lyre as he sat on a hillside; the other stripped to the waist as he fitted enormous blocks of stone together to make a strong wall.

'You forget, Deiphobus, that our city has no weakness,' the king said. 'Its walls were made by the gods themselves, by Poseidon and Apollo. They cannot be broken down and they cannot be scaled. Let Cassandra try to draw attention to herself, and let the Greeks chase after her fantasies. We are safe.'

'Then why have you called us here, my lord, if not to discuss Helenus's treachery?' Antenor asked.

Priam left the mural and moved slowly back across the hall, the flames of the hearth casting a tall shadow over the wall behind him. As he rejoined the others, he laid his hands palm-down on the table and leaned his weight upon them. He let out a long breath and his whole body seemed to deflate with it, leaving him a thin, elderly man heavily burdened by the responsibilities of his rank. Deiphobus and Antenor, standing on either side of him, instinctively moved closer, fearing the king might suddenly collapse. Then he drew himself up again and nodded towards a large shape in the middle of the table, draped in purple cloth. It had sat there all through the meal they had shared, arousing the curiosity of the others but so pointedly ignored by Priam that they dared not mention it themselves. Now, at last, it seemed the mystery would be revealed.

'That is the reason I've asked you here. Deiphobus?'

The king looked at his son, who after a moment's hesitation reached across and slowly pulled away the purple cloth. Aeneas and Idaeus gasped, while Apheidas called on the gods in an awed whisper. With the sole exception of Priam the men around the table leaned closer, their eyes wide with wonder and their faces shining with the glittering light reflected from the object before them.

'The Golden Vine,' Priam declared. 'Zeus gave it to Tros, my great-grandfather, as compensation for abducting Ganymede, his son, and making him his cupbearer on Olympus. It was on the promise of this Vine that Poseidon and Apollo built the walls of Troy for my grandfather, Ilus, who then cheated them of their payment.'

'But I thought this was just a legend,' Deiphobus said without taking his eyes from the Vine.

'All legends are based in truth of one kind or another, Son.'

Priam reached across and gently scooped up the Vine in the palms of his hands, lifting the cluster of golden spheres before the faces of the others. As they looked at it they were able to see that each grape had been individually crafted and was linked to a stem of gold that was supple and moved with the weight of the fruit. Three golden leaves were attached to the Vine and as Priam's fingers closed lightly about them they bent to his touch as if they were real.

'The Vine has lain hidden in the deepest vault of the palace since I was a boy, jealously guarded by each of my forefathers and never brought out into the light of day. It is the last great treasure of Troy. And now it must be given up.'

There were exclamations of disbelief and denial at the announcement, but Priam shook his head.

'Hector and Paris are dead, and the faith I placed in the Amazons and Aethiopes proved unfounded. Our armies have been decimated time and again, until the rump that remains is barely capable of manning the city walls, let alone driving the Greeks from our shores. And yet there is one final hope, a last resort that my pride has always refused to acknowledge. Until now.'

Apheidas's brow furrowed.

'What is this hope, my lord?'

'Not what, but who,' Priam replied. He lay the Vine carefully back down on the purple cloth and looked about at the others. 'I mean King Eurypylus of Mysia.'

'Your grandson?' Antenor queried. 'He'll never go against his mother's wishes, and Astyoche refuses to even recognise you as her father.'

'Our parting was bitter,' Priam agreed, nodding. 'Astyoche was a female Hector – headstrong and resolute. When I forbade her to marry Telephus, Heracles's son, she slipped away at night and rode to his palace, where she married him. We haven't spoken since. And yet there was one thing she coveted above all else, but was never able to make her own. The Golden Vine.'

Apheidas snorted his disgust.

'Do you mean you're going to exchange the Vine for the help of a king who can't do anything without his mother's permission? What possible use could a man like that be on a battlefield?'

Priam stared at him, piqued that a mere captain should dare to question the judgement of a king.

'Only a fool would dismiss Eurypylus,' he said. 'His grandfather is Heracles, from whom he has inherited terrifying strength, or so it's said. What's more, he leads an army many thousands strong, all of whom would be fresh to the fight – not tired of war like we who've been battling for the past ten years. If the Mysians can be persuaded to help us while the Greeks are still recovering from their recent losses, we might be able to throw them back into the sea once and for all.'

'But would Eurypylus come to our aid, just because you placate Astyoche with the last great treasure of our city?' Deiphobus asked. 'Wouldn't he want something for himself? He's a king, after all.'

'Rumour has it Astyoche is her son's lover,' Priam said, 'and knowing how manipulative she used to be, I can fully believe it. If I offer her the Vine, she will make sure he comes. Though you're right, Eurypylus should have something too. I will offer him Cassandra in marriage.'

Priam called for wine, while the others exchanged questioning looks. As servants appeared and refilled their cups, the king leaned across the table and replaced the cloth over the Golden Vine. At his signal, four guards moved out from the shadows and placed the priceless treasure into a wooden casket, before turning and carrying it from the great hall.

'It's late,' Priam said, draining the last of his cup. He turned to his herald.

'Idaeus, tomorrow you will begin preparations to go to Mysia. Antenor will go with you. Deiphobus, tell your sister she's going to be married. That's if she doesn't already know,' he added with a small laugh. 'And as for the king, I need my bed. Good night.'

Eperitus sat on one of the benches, wet, windswept and dejected as he huddled between Eurybates on his right and the bulk of Polites on his left. Polites acted like a wall that protected him from the worst of the storm, but the rain and the waves that broke over the low sides of the ship had already soaked him to the skin, while the howling wind that burrowed through the gaps in his clothing ensured his discomfort was complete. And, unlike the Argive sailors who were busy battling the squall under the shouted directions of Sthenelaus and Diomedes, Eperitus had nothing to take his mind off the misery of his situation. All he could do was stare at Zacynthos to the north-west, a dark lump that was almost lost between the jagged seas below, the grey, oppressive clouds above and the thick veil of rain in-between. As he stared at the sparsely populated, southernmost extremity of Odysseus's kingdom, he thought back longingly to the days they had spent on the voyage from Troy, sailing on sun-blessed oceans from one headland to the next as they tracked the Asian seaboard south to Icaria, and then hopping from island to island across the Cyclades. The weather had been kind to them, too, as they crossed the Cretan Sea from Melos to Malia – the south-eastern corner of the Peloponnese – and followed the coast round, past the mouth of the River Eurotas to the tip of the Taygetus Mountains at the cape of Taenarus. By then his legs had gotten quite used to the pleasant movements of the waves beneath the hull of the galley, and the only thing that had unsettled him as they made their way up the south-west coast of the Peloponnese – a route he vaguely remembered from ten years earlier when the Ithacan fleet had sailed to war, and from ten years before that when he and Odysseus had journeyed back from Sparta after the marriage of Helen and Menelaus – had been the ramshackle and almost deserted appearance of the harbours and fishing villages they had passed. There had been no women or children to wave at them as they went by, or groups of old sailors discussing the trim of the galley or the way she was handled. Only the cluster of small fishing boats in each harbour, and the sense they were being watched by unseen eyes, suggested the villages were inhabited at all.

Then, as they pulled up the stone anchors that morning, the weather had changed. With a speed that surprised Eperitus, the wind picked up and the skies grew dark with clouds that rolled down from the heavens to press upon the rising turmoil of the sea. The easy motion of the waves that Eperitus's legs had learned to accommodate in the earlier part of the voyage now turned violent, pitching him about the deck and turning his stomach so that he was sick over Omeros's sandals. Omeros, green-faced and almost too ill to notice, returned the compliment. Sthenelaus's voice fought against the wind, ordering the crew to angle the sail so that the ship was driven diagonally across the waves. A moment later the spar was lowered halfway down the mast to reduce the pressure and steady the roll of the galley. That was as much as they could do in the face of the gale, but as the ship drifted in relative safety a new cry went up. Land had been spotted to the north.

Eperitus, who had remained astern with Omeros, was now joined by Polites and Eurybates.

'It's Zacynthos,' Polites announced, a hint of excitement in his normally deep, slow voice. 'Come on.'

He hoisted Eperitus up by his arm and dragged him to the prow, followed by Eurybates and Omeros. Odysseus was already there, not even noticing his countrymen as he grasped the bow rail and squinted hard against the squall. They joined him in silence, staring through the sheet-rain at the almost imperceptible horizon rolling from left to right before them. Eperitus saw the line of the Peloponnesian coast on the starboard side of the galley, which Sthenelaus kept them in sight of at all times, but despite his sharp vision he was unable to see the new land that had been spotted. Eventually he caught a brief glimpse of something black and indistinct, but the act of focussing on a static point in a world of constant motion forced his stomach to contract in protest. He vomited again, this time managing to reach the side of the ship before the liquid spilled from his lips, then staggered back to suffer in solitude on the benches. One by one the others sat down until only Odysseus remained, lost in his own thoughts and memories as he stared at the southernmost point of the kingdom he had not seen for ten years.

Slowly, Zacynthos grew from a small blot to something that was visibly a large, if still distant, island. The gale was already dying away and the galley would soon head towards the mainland, to seek the mouth of the River Alpheius. There they would make their final landfall of the voyage and head inland to find Pisa, and hopefully the tomb of Pelops. Knowing this, Eperitus reluctantly extracted himself from the shelter afforded by Polites and Eurybates, and staggered up the middle of the ship to join the lone figure of Odysseus at the prow. Despite his nausea, which was exaggerated by his supernaturally enhanced senses, Eperitus fought down the desire to vomit again.

'Thinking of home?' he asked, raising his voice over the roaring wind.

Odysseus nodded.

'They're so close,' he said, just loud enough for Eperitus to hear. 'It's strange, but the nearer I am to Penelope, the clearer I can recall her face. Back in Ilium I could barely picture her, but here –' He reached out with his fingertips. 'Here it's as if I can see her before me in the rain. But it's only a memory, an image of how she used to be, and what makes it worse is the real Penelope is just over there, beyond the storm. If only I could see her as she is now.'

'I'm sure she's as beautiful as the day you left her.'

'Yes,' Odysseus said. 'Ten years would barely have added a line to her face. Unlike me. I feel like the past decade has been spent in Hades, surrounded by horrors and forgetful of the beauty of the real world. It's as if the Odysseus who sailed away from Ithaca has died a thousand times since then, and all that's left is this.' He plucked dismissively at his tunic. 'I doubt she would even recognise me any more. And what would Telemachus make of me? Could he ever come to love a father he's never known? Why, Mentor and Halitherses will be more like fathers to him than I can ever be.'

'Uncles, maybe, but you're his real father, Odysseus. Nothing can replace that. And the sooner we find this bone – '

'Agamemnon and Nestor were right, you know. If this had been my own ship I'd be on my way to Ithaca now. Oh, I'd probably tell myself it was just a short visit, a day or two to see my family. But days would become weeks and weeks months, until I'd no longer care about Agamemnon's war or my oath to Menelaus. The fact Diomedes is in command prevents that, but it hasn't stopped me thinking the strangest, most desperate things, Eperitus. Before you joined me, I was even considering whether I could leap overboard and swim to Zacynthos –'

'That'd be madness,' Eperitus exclaimed.

'Madness indeed,' said another voice.

The two men turned to see an Argive sailor standing beside them. He was tall and pale, with large grey eyes and a straight nose that did not dip at the bridge. His chin was clean-shaven, unlike the rest of the crew, and he had long, fair hair that was tied back behind his neck. Even more notable than this rare feature was the fact that his stone-coloured cloak and tunic were dry, as if impervious to the lashing rain.

Eperitus frowned in confusion, sensing something was wrong. Surely he would have remembered such a man on the long voyage from Troy? Moreover, why weren't any of the other crew members looking at the striking figure standing in the prow? It was then he saw that many were leaning against each other, their heads lolling on their chests. Others had slumped forward over their knees with their arms hanging limply at their sides. Diomedes and Sthenelaus at the helm were both reclining against the bow rail, propped up by their armpits as their heads rolled back to stare with unseeing eyes at the stormy skies above. Even more strangely, the twin rudders were not swinging freely now that the unconscious Sthenelaus had released them, but were held fast by an unseen force that kept the galley on a straight course. As his mind struggled to comprehend what his eyes were telling him, his other senses were registering that the rain was no longer driving against his skin and the sickness in his stomach had gone entirely.

As ever, Odysseus was the first to recognise her. With one hand still gripping the bow rail, he dropped to his knees and bowed his head. Eperitus followed his example, finally realising the man before them was no sailor, but the goddess Athena, Odysseus's immortal patron who had appeared to them several times during their many adventures together.

Athena leaned down and took both men by the hand, sending a wave of warmth through their chilled bodies as she pulled them to their feet.

'Even a swimmer of your skill and stamina would not reach Zacynthos through these seas, Odysseus,' she said. 'You would have thrown your life away for nothing and never seen your family again.'

'If my mortal body is frail, Mistress,' he replied, 'then my mortal heart is even weaker. Why shouldn't I risk the one when the other is already dying without Penelope and Telemachus?'

Athena looked at him and there was pity in her eyes, softening the cold, hard beauty of her ageless face. There was something else, too, Eperitus thought: a sadness beneath the compassion, as if she knew of an even more terrible fate in Odysseus's future.

'You are stronger than you think,' she said. 'How else have you managed to stay true to Penelope through all these years, when every other man has taken Trojan concubines or satisfied himself with whores? No, Odysseus, you are unique among the kings of Greece and only you can deliver Troy into their hands.

'As for you,' she added, turning to Eperitus, 'I'm pleased, if surprised, that your brain has finally managed to emerge from its long slumber.'

'Mistress?'

'I mean your suggestion of making the voyage in an Argive ship, of course. Agamemnon was right not to have allowed Odysseus to sail in one of his own galleys – the temptation of returning to Ithaca would have been too great. But without Odysseus the mission was doomed to failure and the will of the gods would never have been fulfilled. We are grateful to you, Eperitus.'

Eperitus nodded uncertainly. 'Thank you, Mistress.'

'And what is the will of the gods?' Odysseus asked.

'To see Troy defeated. The war has almost fulfilled its purpose; Zeus does not want to see it prolonged unnecessarily.'

Eperitus could see Odysseus biting back whatever words had

sprung to his quick mind. Instead, the king looked questioningly into the goddess's clear eyes.

'And how will an ivory shoulder blade help us defeat Priam and conquer his city, Mistress?'

'Think of what your qualities are, Odysseus. Ask yourself why this mission will fail without you.'

Odysseus frowned and looked away into the storm. Eperitus followed his gaze and saw for the first time how the raindrops seemed to hit an invisible shield around the ship and disappear in small puffs of steam, leaving the vessel surrounded by a thin layer of fog.

'It's a riddle!' Odysseus answered, turning sharply back to the goddess. 'There's something about the shoulder bone, or maybe the tomb itself, that will tell us how to defeat Troy. And you think I'm the one who will decipher it.'

Athena answered with a smile. 'Whatever the reason for sending you, Odysseus, don't think the tomb will give up its secrets freely. You already know about the maze.'

'To keep out the ghost of Myrtilus,' Eperitus said.

'Or so Agamemnon believes,' Athena replied, enigmatically. 'And maybe that was the story its builders put about. Yet the truth is the maze was not built to keep something out, but to keep something *in*.'

'Agamemnon said the tomb was cursed –' Odysseus began.

'In that he was not wrong,' Athena said, 'as some have found out for themselves – robbers, mostly: desperate men who were either ignorant of the curse or too greedy to care. Their bones now litter the dark corridors of the maze. But though you are neither ignorant nor greedy, your need is more desperate than theirs and by the will of the gods you must enter the tomb and face the curse that haunts it. For that reason I am permitted to help you, if only with advice. In a moment I will be gone and the crew will awaken, each of them thinking they were alone in a moment's lapse of consciousness. The storm will abate and you will be able to anchor your ship by the mouth of the Alpheius. Make camp tonight and in the morning take a small force of warriors with you, while leaving enough men behind to protect the galley in your absence. Follow the banks of the river until you reach a temple of Artemis, within sight of the walls of Pisa. On the opposite side of the water is a low hill. You will know it because it is overgrown with long grass and weeds: no animal would graze on it, even if their herders allowed them to. This is the tomb of Pelops.

'The entrance is not obvious. It's on the northern flank, below the trunk of a dead olive tree, and is covered by brambles and a layer of earth. You will have to dig your way into it and knock down the wall you find beneath. Once you've done this you will find yourselves in the antechamber to the maze.'

'And how will we find the tomb?' Odysseus asked.

'That I cannot tell you. All mazes are designed to confuse, but this one will dull your senses and have you losing all track of time and place. If you succeed, it'll most likely be by chance, although you might be able to deduce a way through if you apply your intelligence, Odysseus.'

'What do you know about the curse, Mistress?' Eperitus questioned. 'How can we protect ourselves from it?'

'Protect yourselves?' she queried. 'There's no protection from what lies within the tomb – not for mortal flesh, at least. But this much I can say, and I say it to you in particular, Eperitus. The only way to overcome the curse of Pelops's tomb is for Ares's gift to complete its purpose.'

'I don't understand!'

'You will, when the time comes,' she answered.

And then she was gone, dissolving into the air as a dense spray of seawater dashed over the side of the galley, dousing Odysseus and Eperitus and waking the crew from their induced slumber.

Chapter Sixteen
PELOPS' TOMB

Eupeithes looked up at the stars glinting and glittering above the broad roof of his house. They were a fierce white, like particles of daylight burning holes in the night, and as he traced the outlines of the constellations he wondered what a man would have to do to have his own image set among them. Then he smiled and shook his head gently: a ridiculous ambition, he mocked himself, for an overweight merchant who was neither king nor warrior.

Antinous, his son, returned from the bushes at the edge of the expansive garden, where he had emptied his bladder. He dropped heavily onto the seat between Polyctor and Oenops and stared across at his father. Eupeithes had ordered chairs to be carried out to the lawn where it was less likely that eavesdropping slaves could overhear their treasonous talk and report it back to Penelope or her supporters.

'What's the point in having control of the Kerosia if you're not going to do anything with it?' Antinous asked, picking up the argument he had walked away from in anger only a few moments before. 'Once Odysseus returns he'll reappoint a new council and leave us back where we started – if he doesn't execute us all first. I didn't throw old Phronius to his death for that to happen. We have to act while we still can: appoint a new king then form an army, ready for Odysseus's return –'

'The Kerosia can't just *appoint* a king,' Oenops protested, shaking his white head firmly. 'We haven't the right or the power, not while the true king still lives.'

Polyctor, a black-haired man with soft grey eyes and a scanty beard, leaned across and patted Antinous on the back.

'You've grown up in a kingdom without a king, used to the idea the Kerosia makes all the decisions. It doesn't, Antinous. We're only a council, subordinate in everything to the power of the throne. The only time we get to make any decisions is when the king is absent.'

'Well, he's absent now –'

Eupeithes raised his long, feminine hands for silence. There was no light in the garden and his mole-speckled skin looked grey and waxy as he smiled at the others.

'You're all correct, of course. Though we control the Kerosia, we remain but a council of advisers with limited authority – and certainly not enough to elect a new king. As Oenops implies, we can only do that if the king dies and leaves no successor. What power we do have will only last until the return of Odysseus. We therefore have to be realistic: if he comes back within the next few weeks or months, accompanied by a veteran army of loyal Ithacans, there is nothing we can do.'

Antinous threw his hands up to the heavens in a despairing gesture.

'Then why go to such lengths to take control of the Kerosia? Why did we try to have Telemachus murdered? We've risked all we have for nothing.'

'Maybe,' his father replied, 'but I don't think so. I made my wealth as a merchant, not a gambler, by relying on shrewdness rather than luck. This is no different. But before I outline the solutions, let me first delineate the problems. There are three: Odysseus's return; Telemachus, his heir; and the loyalty of the Ithacan people.'

'I'd like to hear your solution to Odysseus,' Oenops sniffed. 'Didn't you just say there's nothing we can do if he comes back now?'

'I was simply putting the case, my dear Oenops. The fact is he won't *be* coming back. I've made certain of that.'

'How?' Antinous asked, sitting up.

'I placed two men among the replacements that were sent to Troy in the spring, with instructions to murder Odysseus if the war ends and he survives. Both are more than capable of carrying out the task, and they know they'll be generously rewarded if they succeed. What's more, neither knows about the other. That way, they'll act alone and if one fails the other won't be implicated. I had to make doubly certain Odysseus doesn't make it back to his beloved Ithaca. To *our* beloved Ithaca.'

There was a self-satisfied grin on Eupeithes's face as he revealed his cleverness and forethought to the others, a grin that was justified by their stunned reactions.

'However, that still leaves us with the people and Telemachus,' he continued. 'When Odysseus fails to return from Troy, his son will inherit the throne at the age of twenty-one. That still gives us eleven years to dispose of him, but first we must lure him back from Sparta.'

'Penelope won't allow him to come back home,' Polyctor said. 'She won't risk it.'

'Neither can she bear to be apart from him for that long,' Eupeithes countered. 'You've seen how much she loves him. No, she knows she is in an impossible position: she has to remain in Ithaca, guarding her husband's kingdom, and yet she can't live without Telemachus at her side. Believe me, she will look for any opportunity to bring him back, any arrangement that will ensure his safety. I intend to offer her such an arrangement, even if it is unpalatable. And if she takes it, perhaps we won't need to kill the boy anyway.'

'You're talking in riddles, father, *and* avoiding the central question,' Antinous said. 'Who will become king?'

'Maybe you will, Son,' Eupeithes answered, rising to his feet. 'But not until we've dealt with the third problem – the consent of the people. They're fiercely loyal to Laertes's line and have a deeply rooted aversion to illegitimate rulers.'

'They'll obey whoever's put over them,' Antinous insisted.

'They will *not*,' his father snapped, his control failing momentarily. 'They will not, Son, as I have found out to my own expense in the past. No, one can't merely foist a king upon the simple-minded; their masters must have authenticity – a royal connection.'

Polyctor's brow knotted with confusion.

'Then who? Odysseus's cousin, Eurylochus, might have served our purpose, but he's away with the army in Ilium. There's no-one else we could set up as king.'

Eupeithes locked his hands behind his back and looked up at the stars, as if seeking guidance from the gods. Then he turned his gaze on the others.

'If Odysseus does not return after a set time – which *we* know he will not – we will insist he is presumed dead and that a new king takes his place to restore stability and leadership to Ithaca. I intend for that new king to be you, Antinous – a projection of myself upon the throne – but not by appointment. You must be chosen, and you must have legitimacy in the eyes of the people.'

Oenops shook his head.

'Impossible. The throne will be held for Telemachus until he's of age. He has the right of succession.'

'The ancient laws of Ithaca allow one exception,' Eupeithes corrected him. 'It's an echo of the old days when kings were chosen through the female line, as they still are in some cities. If the king dies before his sons are old enough to assume the crown and the queen marries again, then her new husband will become king ahead of all other claimants.'

'You want me to marry Penelope?' Antinous exclaimed.

Oenops shook his beard dismissively. 'She's Odysseus's through and through. She'll never marry another, not even if you were to bring her Odysseus's bones in a box.'

'Don't be so sure, my old friend. Women are fickle things; given the right incentives they can be bent to anyone's will. Now, here's what I intend to do –'

The storm had passed with unnatural quickness after the departure of the goddess, allowing the galley to reach the coast of the Peloponnese in safety. Seeing a huddle of stone huts overlooking a small, natural harbour a little below the mouth of the River Alpheius, Sthenelaus had guided the ship into the pocket of calm water and ordered the anchor stones to be thrown overboard. But when Diomedes and a handful of Argives had rowed ashore, they found their joy at being back on the soil of their homeland dampened. The old fishing hamlet had been deserted long ago.

'Doesn't bode well,' he said later that evening, speaking to Odysseus and Eperitus as they sat by a fire overlooking the harbour, while the rest of the crew and the other Ithacans were busy bedding down in the abandoned houses. 'This village should have at least fifty people in it, but by the looks of it no-one's lived here for years. And yet the sea's teeming with fish, there's plenty of fresh water just a short walk to the river, and they'd have had a good crop of fruit and olives from all the trees around here. There's only one reason can explain why they left. They were afraid of something.'

Odysseus, who had been drawing strange patterns in the dust for most of the evening and studiously following them with a stick, raised his head.

'Bandits,' he said. 'With the kings and their armies away in Troy there are barely enough men left to protect the cities, let alone these small villages. I fear for what we'll find in the morning.'

They rose again at the first light of dawn, though this was nothing more than a pale suffusion among the dark clouds that covered the skies. After they had breakfasted on barley broth, flatbread and fresh olives picked from the trees that surrounded the village, Odysseus called his Ithacan comrades to him and ordered them to put on their armour. Their greaves, leather cuirasses and helmets felt heavy and awkward after so many days aboard ship, where they had only needed their tunics and cloaks, and the feel of the shields on their arms and the spears in their hands gave them all a sense of impending danger, though none knew in what form it might come. Diomedes chose twelve of his best warriors for the expedition, leaving the remainder to guard the galley under the charge of Sthenelaus. Then, with small bags of provisions and skins of fresh water hanging over their shoulders, they sloped their spears and tramped off in double-file under the silent gaze of those left behind.

The River Alpheius was but a short distance north from the harbour. It was broad and fast-flowing as it poured out into the sea, and in the distance they could see the mountains from which it harvested its waters. The low, fumbling peaks seemed to prop up the hanging canvas of cloud that brooded with dark intent in the east, but as they walked with the river on their left Eperitus's thoughts were not on the threat of rain but on the dilapidated state of the country around them. The land on both sides of the Alpheius was choked with weeds and long grass, where once it must have been filled with crops irrigated from the river. The pastureland on the hills that rose up behind was also overgrown. Though there were occasional sheepfolds, the tumbledown walls were empty and there was no sign of the flocks that had once occupied them. Even the road they were walking along was almost lost beneath a sea of knee-high grass and was only recognisable by the wheel ruts left by the farmers' carts that had trundled along it in happier times. Most notable to Eperitus's mind, though, was the lack of people. He and his companions were the only travellers on the road and there were no boats passing up or down the river. Like the fishing hamlet they had first encountered, all but one of the villages they passed through had been deserted for some time. The exception was a huddle of pitiable cottages, surrounded by narrow strips of farmed land where the heads of the barley bowed beneath a gentle west wind. The doors of all the other dwellings they passed had been thrown from their hinges to reveal lifeless and empty interiors, but here they were firmly shut against the strange soldiers who had wandered up from the direction of the coast. A doll made from wood and rags lay abandoned in the middle of the road, kept company by a single sandal that Eperitus guessed had slipped from a woman's foot as she hurriedly scooped up her child and swept it back into the house. It was a poor village – too poor, perhaps, for the bandits who had forced the other villagers to flee – and the Argives and Ithacans passed through without pausing.

At no point during the rest of the journey did Eperitus's sharp senses tell him they were being watched, even from a distance. It was eerie and unsettling and hardly a word was spoken as the band of warriors trudged through the unhappy country. For the first time they were witnessing the hidden cost of the war against Troy, and it seemed Odysseus's guess of the evening before was right. Without the protection of their kings, the people had withdrawn to the walled towns and cities for safety from the groups of armed thieves that roamed the countryside. The land had been abandoned and trade would have all but died out, to be replaced by poverty, hunger and disease. And if the war lasted for much longer, there would be no Greece to return to.

After a while they passed through a knot of trees and came to a place that Eperitus felt was vaguely familiar. The river was broken by a series of rocks and the soft sound of the water now became a roar as it crashed against them. In the centre, where the river was deepest and the current quickest, three boulders stood up like black knuckles, while a shelf of rock jutted out from the nearest bank to make the passage by boat perilous indeed.

'Recognise the place?' Odysseus asked.

Eperitus gave a laugh and nodded. 'Of course, this is where we crossed the river on our way to Sparta twenty years ago. Didn't we build a raft further upstream from here, where the waters are calmer?'

'We repaired an abandoned ferry so we could get those mules across, do you remember? Then one of them panicked and knocked old Halitherses into the river. You dived in after him, before he could be battered to death against these rocks.'

'That's right,' Eperitus said, more solemnly.

He vaguely recalled the cold, fast water and the sight of Halitherses, the former captain of the guard, being taken along by the current ahead of him.

'We pulled you both out of the water by that shelf of rock,' Odysseus added. 'We were so young then, and old Halitherses seemed like such a relic to us. Now we're not far off the same age that he was.'

They gave the rapids a final glance and then followed in the wake of the others. They passed a small, rotten jetty where boats could be moored rather than risking the peril of the rocks, and shortly after entered the shade of a wood that skirted the banks of the river. Its cool, green gloom was a pleasant relief after the growing heat of the morning, but they were soon out in the open again, trudging along the rutted, overgrown track that would eventually take them to Pisa. Their footsteps grew heavy and they felt the sweat running in rivulets beneath their close-fitting armour, but for men who could fight all day long under a Trojan sun there was no need for rest. And both Odysseus and Diomedes were determined to reach the tomb as quickly as possible.

Shortly after midday, they came upon a bend in the river where the fast-flowing water curved around the spur of a low hill. As they climbed the ridge, Eperitus spotted a flash of whitewashed walls gleaming in the distance. Shielding his eyes against the bright sunshine, he could make out a large town nestled within the fold between two hills, not far from the river. It was surrounded by modest battlements and had a single gateway that he could see, guarded by a tall tower. Two men in armour – the first signs of human life he had seen since leaving the deserted fishing village at dawn – stood watch as an ox-drawn cart struggled along the tree-lined road towards the gate. The town was still a long way off, but in-between was a small wood from which a thin trail of smoke was drifting up into the clear sky. On the opposite bank of the river a domed mound rose like a dark mole on the face of the land.

'I can see a town,' he announced. 'It's still a good way off, but it has walls and guards and there are signs of more life inside.'

'That must be Pisa,' said Diomedes, squinting in the direction Eperitus was pointing.

'Can you see a temple?' Odysseus asked.

'No, but you see the trail of smoke coming from that wood? There's a small hill on the opposite bank of the river. That could be the tomb.'

A murmur of interest spread through the group of warriors as they strained to see, but a snapped order from Diomedes silenced them again. He led them back down to the level of the river, where the hill was lost to Eperitus's sight behind the line of trees. They followed the overgrown track to the eaves of the wood. Here the air was heavy with the pungent odour of damp earth and thick foliage, through which Eperitus could faintly discern the mingled scent of woodsmoke and roasted flesh. Before long they reached a small clearing where the glimmer of the river could be seen through the trees a short distance on the other side. In the centre of the clearing was a pile of blackened, smouldering wood, upon which the burnt thighbones of a sheep or goat were gently smoking. To the left of the pyre was a rough table of stone supported by two boulders. This crude altar was covered in a dark circle of fresh blood that was still dripping onto the trampled grass below.

'Looks like we've disturbed someone in the middle of a sacrifice,' Diomedes said, entering the clearing and poking at the fire with the point of his spear. 'The gods won't be pleased.'

'This must be the temple of Artemis that Athena mentioned,' Odysseus said in a low voice to Eperitus, as they looked around at the circular clearing in the wood. 'And if that's the case then your guess was right – Pelops's tomb is just through those trees, on the other side of the river. Come on.'

Without waiting for the others, he crossed the clearing and plunged into the undergrowth. Eperitus strode after him and together they were the first to reach the edge of the wood and see the sombre-looking hill on the opposite bank of the Alpheius. It was unnaturally perfect in shape, as if a giant bowl had been upended in the middle of the level plain, and at this range Eperitus could see it was much larger than he had estimated when he had first seen it from the ridge. Its curved flanks were featureless, covered with long grass and thorn bushes, and though the sun was bright overhead the mound seemed to absorb its light and maintain a dreary dullness.

'Even a hill as big as that can't hold too large a maze,' Eperitus said, trying to quell the despair that had crept into his heart at the sight of the mound.

'The maze will be below ground,' Odysseus replied, knowingly. 'That hill is just the earth they dug out to make it. And that should give you an idea of the size of what lies beneath.'

The river was fordable between the wood and the mound and they crossed it in single file with the water rising no higher than their waists. The olive tree that marked the opening was on the other side of the hill, just as Athena had said it would be. Not wanting to let on to the others that the goddess had spoken to him, Odysseus suggested they look for something that might indicate where the entrance to the maze was. Diomedes obliged almost immediately by pointing to the dead tree. After hacking away the brambles with their swords, they scraped at the earth beneath with a combination of flat rocks and their bare hands until they exposed the top of what appeared to be a wall. The rest was soon uncovered, but before they attempted to knock it in and open the ingress to the labyrinth beyond, Odysseus ordered the men to make torches from the materials they had brought – dowels and rags that had been soaked in animal fat – while he made a small fire to light them with. Finally, after the torches were ready and two Argives had been chosen to remain guard on the outside, Polites slid down into the shallow pit they had dug and splayed his massive hands against the stone blocks of the wall. It gave way easily under his great strength, collapsing in a cloud of dust that swept over him and forced him to turn away, choking loudly as he covered his face with the crook of his arm.

The others crowded round the edge of the pit, Odysseus, Diomedes and Eperitus foremost, trying to see through the swirling brown haze into the void that had been created. But even Eperitus's eyes were unable to penetrate the thick blackness beyond the remains of the wall, and after a moment's hesitation Diomedes ordered one of his men to light a torch and hand it to him. An instant later he was shouldering past Polites and stooping beneath the low entrance to the tomb, holding the flaming brand before him.

'What do you see?' Odysseus called after him.

'It's a chamber,' Diomedes replied from the darkness, his voice flat and stifled. 'Come and see for yourselves.'

One by one, the others lit their torches and joined Diomedes in the low antechamber, where the stale air was cold and smelled of damp earth. By the light of his struggling torch, Eperitus could see that the floor and walls were of mud and had not been dressed with wood or stone. The ceiling, too, was bare and had been broken in several places by the roots of the dead olive tree on the hillside above. At the back of the chamber, directly opposite the entrance, was a deeper darkness that he knew led down into the depths of the maze. He sensed a faint current of air coming from it, like the breath of something ancient and evil, and shuddered as it touched his skin.

Odysseus approached the passageway with his torch, revealing a roughly hewn arch and a steeply sloping tunnel beyond it. He peered down into the darkness, sniffed at it, then turned to the others.

'This has to be the way to the maze. It's too narrow for spears, so bring your swords only. And that old shield of yours will never fit down there, Eperitus.'

Though the half-moon shields of the others could easily be slung across their backs, the heirloom Eperitus had inherited from his grandfather was tall and bulky and would only prove an encumbrance in such a tight space. Reluctantly, he slipped it from his shoulder and laid it with his spear against a wall of the chamber.

'Why do we need our weapons, anyway?' said one of the Argives, leaning his spear next to Eperitus's. 'It's just a tomb, after all.'

'A warrior should never be without a weapon, Trechos,' Eperitus answered. 'Even in the houses of the dead.'

'It's the curse Odysseus is worried about,' added another Argive, a veteran warrior called Epaltes who had lost an ear and two fingers during the long years of the war. 'My wife was from Pisa, and she always said how the tomb was filled with riches befitting a great king like Pelops, but that they were protected by a terrible guardian. There's someone, or some*thing,* down there and Odysseus knows it. Ain't that right, Eperitus?'

Eperitus adjusted his sword in its scabbard and said nothing. Then Odysseus signalled to him from the archway, where he was waiting with Diomedes.

'We want you to listen, Eperitus,' Odysseus said. 'See if you can hear anything.'

'Silence!' Diomedes ordered, instantly stilling the chatter among the men.

Eperitus took Odysseus's torch and entered the mouth of the passageway, taking a few steps down into the consuming darkness that neither the flaming brand nor the thin daylight from the entrance could penetrate. It reminded him of the Stygian caves of Mount Parnassus, where long ago he and Odysseus had been guided into the presence of the Pythoness, the priestess of Gaia who had prophesied to them in riddles. He shut his eyes and concentrated.

At first, all he could hear was the fizz and sputter of the torches behind him, mingled with the suppressed breathing of fifteen other men crowded into a confined space. Then the sounds faded, pocketed away in another part of his consciousness as he pushed out with his senses. He could feel the gentle breath of chilly air rising from deep below the hillside, drawn naturally towards the comparative warmth that had spilled in from outside. Then, as he reached further and further down into the darkness, he felt the soft, absorbent earth of the tunnel suddenly give way to walls of hard stone. These branched out into narrow corridors that twisted and turned and left him quickly confused. He had found the maze and his senses could penetrate no further, except to register the faint echo of scuffling and scratching coming out of the stillness.

'Do you hear anything?' Diomedes asked.

Eperitus nodded. 'I can hear rats.'

'That's all? Then there's nothing else?'

'That I can't say, Diomedes. The tunnel leads down to more tunnels, which my senses cannot follow. The only way we're going to discover what's down there is to look for ourselves.'

'Then let's not waste any more time,' Odysseus said, taking his torch from Eperitus's hand and pushing past him into the tunnel.

Chapter Seventeen
THE MAZE

Not for the first time, Odysseus wondered why the gods had led the Greeks to this half-forgotten tomb, many days sail away from Troy and with no obvious relevance to the war there. As he thrust his torch into the unyielding blackness, he tried to guess at the significance of Pelops's shoulder bone, and what other things they might find in the subterranean crypt. Eperitus, Diomedes and the others followed him in single file and soon the ground was falling away at a steep incline beneath them, forcing them to advance slowly if they were to keep their footing. As they left the daylight of the antechamber behind and plunged deeper into the earth, they were consumed by an oily darkness that their torches struggled to throw back more than an arm's length before them. Dense cobwebs caught in the flames and were incinerated, but many more – crawling with long-legged spiders – snagged on their hair, clothing and armour to hang from them like rags. The walls of the tunnel were irregular and confusing to the senses, sometimes widening beyond the reach of their groping hands and at other times suddenly narrowing so that they could barely squeeze their shoulders between them. The ceiling, too, would undulate, rising above the heads of the tallest and then plunging again so that even Omeros, the shortest among them, had to stoop. As their senses grew tired and bewildered, Eperitus shouted a warning and seized Odysseus's shoulder, pulling him back sharply. Thrusting his torch close to the ground, he showed him a hole big enough to swallow an unsuspecting man. Odysseus shuddered at the doom his captain had saved him from. Picking up a stone, he dropped it into the hole and a few moments later the bunched warriors heard a small 'plop' as it fell into unseen waters far below.

After each man had leapt the gap safely to the other side they set off again with Eperitus in the lead, his torch held before him as he probed the darkness with his superior senses. They found no more traps, but when eventually Odysseus felt the ground level out beneath his feet and saw the passage branch into two before them he had lost all sense of time.

'So this is the beginning of the labyrinth,' he said, standing beside Eperitus. 'The first challenge we must overcome if we are to discover Pelops's sarcophagus.'

'What's your plan?' Diomedes asked.

Odysseus held his torch down each branch of the fork in the tunnel, and to the surprise of all they saw the dull gleam of stone floors and walls reflecting back from the darkness.

'I don't have a plan, only an idea,' he replied. 'I spent last night drawing out different mazes and trying to see if there was a foolproof method of finding a way through. I drew circular mazes and square mazes, mazes with the object on the opposite side of the entrance, and mazes with the object at the centre of the pattern. And I think I've worked out a solution. Unless the architect of this labyrinth was more cunning than I've anticipated, then all we need to do is keep our hands on one wall – left or right – and follow every twist or turn until it leads us to our goal.'

The others looked sceptical, especially the Argives, who were less familiar with Odysseus's sharp mind.

'Theseus used a ball of twine in the Cretan Labyrinth,' said Trechos.

'That was to help him find his way out again,' Omeros replied. 'It was Ariadne who told him the correct way in, after she received instructions from Daedalus.'

'I don't see how keeping a hand on one wall is going to help,' Diomedes said. 'Not that I don't trust your wits, Odysseus – not after all these years – but it seems to me our best hope is to split up and cover as much of the maze as we can.'

There were concerned murmurs from the others, including Diomedes's own men. Their instincts had been unnerved by the dark, confining space of the tunnels and their imaginations had had too long already to contemplate the rumours that the tomb was cursed. Odysseus shook his head.

'I think we should stay together. We don't know how big this place is, and if we separate we could spend days trying to find each other again. If my suggestion proves wrong, then we can consider something else. Do you agree?'

Diomedes shrugged and drew his sword. 'Lead the way.'

Odysseus felt a hand on his arm.

'Be careful,' Eperitus warned him.

Odysseus hesitated. 'What do your senses tell you now?'

'The air isn't entirely stale. There must be other ways in and out, but only small enough for rats and bats. And there's something else. A lingering sense of malice.'

'I feel it, too,' Odysseus agreed. 'The evil things Pelops did in life still haunt his resting place. But that's all it is – a phantom of the past. The sooner we find this bone, the sooner we can return to the daylight.'

He took a few steps down the left-hand passage and paused with his torch raised before him. After a moment's contemplation, he placed his fingertips against the wall to his right and moved forward. A dozen paces further on he stopped again. There was a large, black opening ahead of him to the right, which his torch seemed barely able to penetrate. He shook his head, as if in denial of the instinctive fear he felt, and entered. At once he stepped back in alarm, covering his face with his arm as black shapes came darting out of the tunnel. A sound like wind tumbling through the leaves of a tree filled the tunnel and small bodies were caught momentarily by the light of the torches as they fled in panic, startled by the unexpected intrusion into their secluded world.

'Bats,' he said, his voice a little higher than normal. 'Just bats.'

He continued his advance and the others followed. The air seemed colder as they turned the corner and the torches struggled momentarily to throw out any light, as if the darkness itself was suffocating them. Then the flames grew again, running in ripples up the fat-soaked cloth and throwing back the shadows to reveal a flagstoned floor and stone walls. The end of this new passageway was not yet visible, but as Odysseus stared into the blackness Eperitus touched him on the shoulder and pointed. Odysseus looked again and finally saw what his captain's keen eyes had already picked out. Something was lying on the ground several paces ahead of them: a grey ball at the foot of the left-hand wall, a bundle of rags a little further back, and the glimmer of something metallic beside them. Eperitus moved past Odysseus and knelt down by the first object.

'What is it?' Odysseus asked, his voice hushed but urgent.

'A skull,' Eperitus replied, staring down at the empty eye sockets and the open jaws that were still set in a silent scream, long after life's last breath had passed between them. 'The body's over there.'

Odysseus joined him and saw the humped shape of a ragged cloak in the shadows, torn in many places and heavy with dust. Grey rib bones were half visible through the holes in the wool, while two skeletal arms reached out into the circle of light cast by their torches. A short sword lay on top of the body.

Diomedes lifted the cloak away with the point of his blade. The material crumbled with the movement, revealing the grey skeleton beneath.

'The shoulder bone's the same colour as the rest. This isn't Pelops.'

'It's the body of a grave robber,' Odysseus said.

Eurybates picked up the sword. 'These black stains are blood. But if the weapon was dropped on top of the man's cloak *after* he was decapitated, then who killed him?'

'One of his companions?' Eperitus suggested. 'They found something of value and argued over it. Typical of their kind. The victor then left the tomb with his treasure and closed the entrance behind him. Perhaps that's all this curse is: human greed in the face of untold wealth.'

'I pray to the gods you're right,' Odysseus said, though his instincts told him otherwise. 'Now, let's find the sarcophagus and hope these men didn't have a taste for ivory.'

A little beyond the remains of the robber, the tunnel turned right. With Odysseus leading again, they advanced into the blackness for a few paces until another passage opened on their left, noticeable only by a deeper darkness and the faint, cold movement of air on their cheeks. The king ignored it and, with his fingers still tracing the right-hand wall, plunged on into the depths of the maze. Almost immediately the wall bent right and then another right, leading the huddled group of warriors shortly afterwards to a dead end. Without taking his hand from the wall, Odysseus followed it left and left again, back the way they had come until it turned right twice to lead them once more to the opening they had passed only a few moments earlier. He did not hesitate, but pressed on with his torch held before him in his free hand.

The wall led him left to another choice of ways – an opening that went straight on or a passage that headed right. Knowing he must stick to the plan he had worked out the evening before, Odysseus turned right and traced the wall in a zigzag pattern until it bent sharply back to the right again. He turned the corner and stopped so suddenly that Eperitus and Diomedes almost walked into him.

'Another body,' he announced.

He raised his torch upwards so that it shed a pool of orange light over the curled up form of a second skeleton. This one wore no cloak and the remains of its short tunic were nothing more than a few lengths of rag clinging to the ribcage and the angular protuberances of the pelvic bone. Its head remained attached to the spinal column, but the handle of a knife stuck out from its back.

'If these men died because of an argument,' Diomedes began, 'why were they both killed from behind? The first could have been fleeing, and I didn't see that he was armed; but this one's holding a dagger – look.' He pointed to a dull blade lying beneath the rib cage, the bony fingers of the dead man still bent around its handle. 'Why didn't he turn and defend himself?'

'I'm not sure,' Odysseus responded. 'Something tells me this man died long before the other – see how the clothes are more decayed – but if they weren't killed by their fellow-robbers, then I don't know how they died. I'll say this much, though: they were thieves, lightly armed and with no training in how to fight. *We* are warriors, veterans of a long and bloody war. Whoever, or whatever, stalked these men through the black confusion of these tunnels won't find it so easy against sixteen of us!'

He stepped over the body and forged on into the darkness. The others followed, many of them drawing their swords and throwing uncertain glances over their shoulders. The tunnel twisted again and again, leading them deeper into the maze as the cold blackness numbed their senses and left them feeling ever more disorientated. Time was drawn out so that moments that would have passed briefly in the daylight were stretched by confusion and growing fear into long periods that offered no hope of ending. They stumbled into each other constantly as they bunched ever closer, afraid of becoming separated in the dark. Despite the light of their brands they soon felt themselves entirely reliant upon Odysseus's hand as it trailed along the stone walls to his right. Even Eperitus's senses, Odysseus guessed, must have lost their edge, deprived of the sounds and smells of the outside world and confused by the deceptive shadows cast by the clustered flames of their torches. He realised that, but for his plan to follow the right-hand wall of the maze, they would be completely lost in a place without features and seemingly without end. He only hoped he had been correct in his deduction.

After a long time, twisting and turning and meeting at least two dead ends, he stopped and raised a cautioning hand. There, ahead of them in the shadows, was another body. Like the others, it lay front-down on the flagstones, nothing more than a skeleton beneath the rags of its former clothing. Then he saw the handle of a long knife protruding from its back.

'It's the same body we passed before,' Eperitus said behind him.

'It can't be!' Diomedes declared, pushing past him and staring down at the crumpled form. He kicked at the collection of bones and sent them rattling across the floor. 'Damn it, Odysseus, your ridiculous scheme has been leading us in circles!'

His voice rose above the oppressive air that had previously dampened every sound they had made and rang out through the tunnels, echoing back on itself so that even Diomedes forgot his anger and glanced about in concern.

'This sort of thing is to be expected,' Odysseus replied firmly. 'If you'd looked before kicking it to pieces, you'd have noticed we've approached it from the opposite direction. It's the nature of a maze to lead back on itself in places and, if anything, coming here again shows my deductions were correct.'

He moved on before Diomedes could challenge him, knowing that if he was to concede his own doubts they might refuse to follow him altogether. Diomedes might even insist that they split up – something which Odysseus now felt certain would be disastrous for all of them. As it was, they followed him without question. Ever since Diomedes's outburst, they had felt an increase in the malevolent atmosphere of the maze, as if the evil that had been slumbering there was now awake and conscious of their presence. They shrank against each other as they passed openings to other passages, or baulked as their heightened hearing detected the sounds of rodents or bats ahead of or behind them. Polites, whose great bulk brought up the rear of the file, was constantly glancing back over his shoulder and even Odysseus felt compelled to draw his sword and hold it loosely in his right hand as he traced the wall with the tip of his forefinger. Then, after many turns that had them feeling as if he had descended far beyond any hope of finding a way out again, they came upon the remains of another man. The skeleton had been dismembered and its bones spread across the tunnel, and for an awful moment Odysseus thought they had returned to the body Diomedes had kicked apart in his anger. Then he realised this was a third victim of whatever had killed the other two robbers, and that its arms and legs had been torn off by force while still alive and left littered around the torso. No-one spoke as they stepped over the bones, but Odysseus knew every man was thinking the same as himself. *What terrible creature possessed the strength to tear a man limb from limb?*

More than ever he wanted the nightmare journey to end, but the maze did not oblige his desperate desire to be free of its dark, confining walls. They wandered on interminably, past more openings and into more dead ends, not knowing whether the junctions they encountered were old or new. More than once Diomedes had to order his men to silence, and when the first torch spluttered and died out the sense of desperation among the warriors of Argos and Ithaca became palpable.

'Keep your spare torch for the return journey,' Odysseus said, as the man slid the dowel from his belt.

Eventually, just as he was wishing they would find another body to break up the monotony of the maze, he detected a change in the air. He did not need Eperitus's supernatural senses to tell him they were nearing a larger space, and soon the whole party were lifting their heads and looking about as if their eyes could see what their deeper instincts had revealed to them. Then they found it. They followed the wall round to the right, then left again to face a large black void, much wider than any opening they had yet encountered. As they paused, the sounds of their feet in the dust and the knocking of their armour were no longer smothered by the close air but echoed back from the open space before them.

Odysseus let his fingers drop from the wall and, gripping his torch, forced himself forward through the opening. Eperitus followed. There was a short passage, like an antechamber, then the ceiling opened up above their heads and they found themselves in a wide, natural cavern, bigger than the great hall in the palace at Ithaca. The torches flared up to meet the richer air, and were soon joined by the flames of the others, who had forgotten the weariness of their long, subterranean journey in their eagerness to enter the heart of the maze.

The darkness was thrown back and the vastness of the chamber was revealed to them. Thick stone columns soared up into the shadows above their heads, and by the monochromatic light of their torches the warriors saw all the gathered wealth of a legendary king lying between them. To the left were two chariots: one magnificent in beaten gold that gleamed alluringly in the torchlight; the other a shattered wreck, its screen flattened, its yoke snapped and its broken wheels laid flat beside it. In an instant, Eperitus knew this was the chariot in which Oenomaus had pursued Pelops and Hippodameia, and beneath which he had been dragged to his death. His eyes moved on from this grim reminder of Pelops's victory over his father-in-law to the heaped spoils of his victories over the other cities of the Peloponnese. Spears and swords lay in piles, while beside them were stacks of shields of the same, outdated design as the one Eperitus had inherited from his grandfather. Sets of body armour sat between them, like half-formed warriors rising up from the cavern floor. They were made of layered bands of bronze that gave the wearer full protection from his chin down to his groin, but due to their weight their like had not been seen on battlefields for many decades. Resting on top of them were helmets of bronze or leather, several of which were circled with layers of boars' tusks.

More substantial wealth in the form of tripods, cauldrons, gold and copper ingots, silver goblets and other valuables lay scattered over the flagstones in no particular order. Whether they had been left like that by Pelops's fearful but unloving subjects, or had been misplaced by the greedy hands of successive grave robbers, Eperitus was unable to tell, but they were a clear measure of how rich and important Pelops must have been in his lifetime. Some of the Argives were drawn irresistibly towards these precious items – forgetful of the dead men they had seen in the tunnels – but an order from Diomedes brought them back.

'Touch nothing,' he warned them. 'We've come for one thing and one thing only!'

Odysseus hardly seemed to notice the piled treasures about him. He remained standing a few paces in from the entrance, his gaze fixed on the wooden figure of a horse at the far end of the chamber. It stood on top of an immense stone sarcophagus, which itself was set on a dais reached by three broad steps. Lying spread-eagled across the steps was another skeleton, this one on its back and staring blankly up at the high ceiling. Of all the rest of the party, only Eperitus, Diomedes and Omeros had noticed the tomb and the grim reminder of the curse that still haunted it. Odysseus turned and indicated for the others to put their torches in the empty iron brackets that were affixed to the columns. Then, with his own held high above his head, he approached the sarcophagus.

If the curse was to strike, Eperitus thought, now was the time. Diomedes snapped angrily at the others, who were still beguiled by the treasures around them, and ordered them to place their torches in the remaining brackets and ready their swords. Eperitus hung his own torch on one of the columns, snatched up a dusty shield and joined Odysseus at the foot of the dais. As the other Ithacans and the Argives formed a defensive semicircle around the sarcophagus, he stared down at the skeletal remains before him. Whether the other robbers had reached as far as Pelops's burial chamber, Eperitus did not know, but this man had made it through the maze only to die at the steps of the sarcophagus. The manner of his death was not clear, though Eperitus noticed there was an unnatural angle to his neck.

'This is it, then,' Odysseus said, staring up at the carved horse with its bowed head and rigid, wooden mane. 'Inside that sarcophagus is a riddle that will give us the key to the gates of Troy. We just have to work it out.'

'Why a horse?' Eperitus asked.

'The Pisans are great horse breeders. They love their animals and revere them like gods, honouring them in their art, their rituals, even their funeral rites.'

'Just like the Trojans.'

Odysseus did not answer, but narrowed his eyes thoughtfully as he stared at the effigy of the horse standing atop the tomb.

Diomedes joined them. 'Let's not delay any longer. This place is making my men nervous. And me too, if you want the truth.'

They took the few steps to the dais, careful not to tread on the skeleton of the grave robber, and looked down at the stone sarcophagus. It was twice the length of a normal man and twice the width, and was capped by a heavy granite lid that formed the base for the wooden horse. The horse stared down at them in disdainful silence as they laid their hands upon the rough stone and began to push. Their arm and leg muscles strained with the effort, the veins bulging as their grunts filled the chamber, but the lid would not move.

'We need something to prise it off with,' Eperitus said.

He returned to the piles of weapons stacked amid the columns and picked up a sword. But as he was about to return to the dais, his eyes fell on a spear leaning against the wall by the shattered chariot of Oenomaus. It had a long, black shaft of some unknown wood and was tipped by a broad head. Though it must have lain there for as long as all the other weapons, the bronze had not been dulled or tarnished by the years. Instead, it shone out fiercely in the torchlight, beckoning to him irresistibly. He picked it up, surprised at how light it felt in his hand despite its monstrous size. It was then he noticed the shaft had been intricately carved and inlaid with faint traces of gold and silver, only catching the torchlight as he moved it in his hands – the work of a great craftsman. The carvings began at the head of the shaft, beneath the socketed point, and seemed to depict a race between pairs of chariots. Only when Eperitus's eyes reached the base did he realise it was the same pair of chariots, repeated at intervals, and that it was not a race but a pursuit, with the last scene showing the occupant of the second chariot impaling the first from behind with his spear.

A call from Odysseus reminded him of where he was. Picking up two more spears, he ran to the line of warriors and gave one to Polites and the other to Trechos.

'Come with me,' he ordered.

As they took the steps up to the dais, Odysseus looked at the spear in Eperitus's hands.

'It's magnificent.'

'It was lying among the other weapons. I've never seen anything like it. Look at the carvings on the shaft.'

Odysseus took the weapon in his hands while the others looked on, equally fascinated. He studied the depictions with a frown, then handed it back to Eperitus.

'This is Oenomaus's spear, the one given to him by Ares. It can't be anything else.'

'How can you be so sure?'

'You said yourself you'd never seen anything like it. Just look at how the bronze still gleams, as if it were newly burnished; and feel how light it is in the hand. Only Hephaistos himself could have made such a spear. And these pictures recall Hippodameia's suitors, whom he pursued to their deaths – until Pelops, that is.'

'Put it back, Eperitus,' Diomedes insisted. 'You'll bring the curse down upon us. If we take nothing, perhaps we'll be spared.'

'What about the bone?' Eperitus countered.

'I agree with Diomedes,' Odysseus said. 'Put it back and fetch another.'

Eperitus reluctantly did as he was ordered, returning with spears for himself, Odysseus and Diomedes. Together with Polites and Trechos, they forced the bronze points into the gap between the sarcophagus and its lid and pushed upwards. The heavy granite resisted for a moment, then with a grating protest began to move. The wooden horse quivered as the five men prised the lid slowly backwards, until finally it fell with a crash on the other side of the dais. The sarcophagus shook with the impact and sent up a cloud of dust that momentarily obscured the open tomb. Squinting and beating the air with their hands, the men stepped up and looked inside.

The skeleton of Pelops lay on its back with its arms by its side and its legs close together. It was of an immense size – in life, Pelops would have been a full head taller than Polites – and even in death the empty eye sockets contained a malice that was alarming to witness. Eperitus felt a small sense of relief to see that the left shoulder blade was creamy white, nothing like the ash-coloured bones of the rest of the skeleton; but his relief was quickly stifled by the feeling of evil that emanated from the sarcophagus. Then he began to notice the strangest thing about Pelops's remains. The bones were not separated as they should have been – lying in disjointed pieces at the bottom of the stone coffin – but were fused together and retained their human shape. Arms, legs, spine, ribs, even the oversized skull remained connected to each other, as if the flesh that had once surrounded them was still there. Eperitus opened his mouth to comment on the peculiarity of it, when he thought he saw the fingers on one hand move. An icy coldness gripped him and his instincts told him to flee, but a grim fascination kept him there. Then, with a dry, grating sound, the skull began to move, rotating slowly on the spinal column to stare up at the horrified men.

Eperitus felt a rush of fear. His logical mind tried to explain away the movement as a delayed result of them shifting the heavy sarcophagus lid. Then there was a second movement, much quicker than the first, and Trechos began choking and clutching at his neck, trying desperately to throw off the skeletal hand that had seized his throat. Eperitus reeled back in shock, catching his heel on the bones of the dead grave robber and tumbling in a heap at the foot of the dais. A moment later there was a loud snap and Trechos fell back across the steps, his neck broken.

An involuntary shout of terror left Eperitus's lips. He stared wide-eyed at Trechos's upturned face, and then began to crawl backwards on his elbows, not daring to turn his back on the sarcophagus for even a moment. The others were leaping down from the dais, their cries of horror and disbelief echoing around the chamber. Odysseus appeared above Eperitus and, seizing his hand, pulled him to his feet. Over his shoulder, Eperitus saw bony fingers clutching at the granite edge of the tomb, followed slowly by the giant skull with its hateful eye sockets and death's head grin.

'How is it possible?' he gasped, stumbling back with Odysseus towards the crescent of warriors, who were shouting in dismay. 'What gives it life?'

Odysseus's hands were shaking as they clutched the black shaft of his spear.

'I don't know what makes it move, but it's not life. Perhaps *this* was the dying curse of Myrtilus – that his betrayer's bones would never find rest.'

They blundered back into the rank of Argives and Ithacans – Diomedes and Polites had already sought refuge among their comrades – and stared incredulously as the giant skeleton raised itself to its full height and stepped stiffly out of the sarcophagus, its joints rasping like blocks of stone as they moved. It turned towards the cowering warriors, looking at them with a loathing that was unfettered by human sentiment. They had violated its resting place and every last one of them would pay with their lives.

Odysseus was the first to throw off his disbelief and come back to his senses. He pulled the spear back over his shoulder and hurled it with all his might at the skeleton. The head plunged through its ribcage, raising a cheer from the others as the horror that had once been Pelops staggered back against the sarcophagus. It stared down at the shaft that protruded from its fleshless body, but instead of collapsing in a clatter of bones, closed its fingers around the weapon and, passing one hand over the other, slid it back out. Raising the spear over its head it launched it back at the waiting warriors. The bronze point narrowly missed Omeros and sparked on the stone floor behind.

Now Diomedes ran towards the dais, brandishing his sword and snarling with anger at the death of Trechos. The copper light of the torches glittered like fire across the blade as it swept down against the monster's thigh. The blow would have cut through the flesh and bone of any ordinary man, but the curse that animated Pelops's remains must also have given them supernatural protection. The sword bounced off the bone without even marking it. Skeletal hands now seized hold of Diomedes as if he were but a child, and with inhuman strength hurled him across the cavern to land with a crash in a pile of spears.

The Argives gave a furious shout and dashed forward. The colossal skeleton moved jerkily down the steps to meet them, knocking aside the first two men as they threw themselves at him. The others quickly formed a circle about it, hacking uselessly at the hard bone or thrusting the points of their swords between its empty ribs. Epaltes, the veteran warrior whose wife had told him long ago about the curse of Pelops's tomb, ran at the monster with his sword held in both hands over his head. He swung the blade against its neck, but the sharpened bronze sprang back and flew from his grip. The next instant, the skeleton had seized hold of his arm and pulled it clean from its socket, spraying the others with droplets of gore as it tossed the detached limb into a corner of the chamber and let Epaltes fall to the floor.

'By all the gods!' Omeros exclaimed.

'How do we fight *that*?' Eurybates asked, slipping his shield onto his arm and picking up a spear.

'We must try to cut off its arms and legs,' Odysseus replied, drawing his sword from its scabbard. 'Strike at the joints – it's our only hope.'

After a glance at Diomedes, who was groggily raising himself from the pile of spears, he led the Ithacans into the fray. The skeleton had picked up Epaltes's sword and was fighting the Argives, bronze against bronze. But the superior numbers of the warriors counted for nothing: the stabbing and slashing of their weapons were ineffectual, whereas a single sweep of the fiend's sword took the head clean off one man's shoulders, and a second blow – delivered with devastating speed – pierced the heart of another, killing him instantly. Eperitus rushed into the gap left by the slain man and, remembering his king's words, sliced down at the skeleton's elbow joint. It was as if he had struck stone. The impact vibrated up his arm and the sword fell from his numbed hand. The monster opened its jaws in a silent cry of hatred, but Eperitus ducked away just in time as its blade cleaved the air above his head.

He leapt back, unarmed and defenceless. Before a second blow could kill him, Diomedes dashed in with his sword and a shield he had taken from among the ancient weapons that littered the chamber, meeting the edge of the skeleton's sword with the thickly layered oxhide. Eperitus snatched up his weapon and ran to Diomedes's side as the monster turned upon them with a flurry of blows that, even with their great fighting skill and experience, they were barely able to survive. A moment later, Odysseus was beside them.

'There must be a way to stop this thing,' Diomedes shouted over the clang of bronze. 'If our weapons can't harm it, how can we hope to take the shoulder blade? Use your brains, Odysseus.'

'Perhaps we don't need the bone,' he replied.

The three men fell back, breathing heavily as the skeleton turned to fend off another attack from the Argives and Ithacans.

'What did you say?' Diomedes asked.

'Perhaps it's not the shoulder blade that's the key.'

'Whatever the gods sent us here for,' Eperitus said, 'we won't get out again until we've defeated that thing.'

Another Argive cried out and staggered back against one of the stone columns, blood gushing from a wound on his inner thigh. A moment later he slid to the floor and was still. Diomedes shouted with rage, but before the three men could rejoin the fight there was another roar. Realising bronze alone was useless, Polites cast aside his sword and threw himself against the guardian of the tomb, seizing its wrists and pushing it back against the sarcophagus. The skeleton's own weapon fell with a clatter and, throwing a foot back against the steps, it fought against the might of Polites. For a while they seemed not to move. Polites gritted his teeth and, with sweat pouring off his face and limbs, tried to impose his flesh and blood strength over his enemy. But the supernatural curse that had taken possession of Pelops's bones was greater still. The Ithacan's shoulder muscles strained in protest as, with slow inevitably, his arms were forced back. Omeros gave a shout and ran forward to hack uselessly at the hard bone of the fiend's arms. Wrenching free of Polites's grip, it swatted Omeros aside and in the same move seized Polites's shoulder. Polites threw his head back and screamed in pain as he felt the malicious power tearing at the ligaments in his arm.

And then the words Athena had spoken on the galley as they had approached the Peloponnesian shore came tumbling back into Eperitus's head.

'The only way to overcome the curse of Pelops's tomb,' he said aloud, 'is for Ares's gift to complete its purpose.'

Odysseus turned to him and in an instant they both understood.

'Oenomaus's spear!' the king cried.

Eperitus did not wait, but ran back to the wall by the broken chariot where he had reluctantly laid down the weapon. He took it in one hand, his mind recalling vividly the story Odysseus had told as they had set out on their voyage back to Greece. Oenomaus's spear was a gift from Ares, which the king had used to pursue Hippodameia's suitors to their deaths. Its aim was straight and true, as was to be expected from a weapon gifted by the gods; but there had been one occasion when it had failed in its purpose – against Pelops. Now was the time for it to complete its task.

A shout of pain rang from the walls. Eperitus looked across and saw the skeleton tearing at Polites's arm, determined on ripping the heavily muscled limb from its torso. Odysseus, Diomedes and a host of others were pulling at the monster's arms and legs in an attempt to save Polites, though forlornly.

'Stand clear!' Eperitus called.

He pulled the spear back and took aim. The skeleton seemed to sense danger and turned to look at Eperitus. The light of the torches glowed on its grey bones and cast strange, enlarged shadows on the walls behind. Suddenly, it released Polites and began running towards the captain of the Ithacan guard, at the same moment as Eperitus launched the spear. It went clean through the fleshless ribs and carried on to stick quivering in the flank of the wooden horse that had crowned the sarcophagus. But as the bronze head passed between the bones, the ancient curse that held them together was broken and the skeleton fell in pieces to the floor. The skull rolled over to rest between Odysseus's feet. The king picked it up, looked into its empty eye sockets, then threw it against a wall where it shattered into fragments.

Omeros and Eurybates ran to help Polites, who was groaning with pain, though his arm had remained in its socket by the sheer density of his muscles. Diomedes walked over to the pile of bones and picked out the ivory shoulder blade.

'So this is what five of my men died for,' he said, bitterly. 'And yet you think we don't even need the damned thing.'

He offered it to Odysseus, who took the untarnished ivory and held it up to the light of the nearest torch.

'We must take it back to Troy, of course – the others will expect it – and yet the gods didn't bring us here just for the sake of a bone. There's something else, a riddle or a clue that will give us victory over Troy. I just have to find out what it is.'

Eperitus pulled the spear out of the wooden horse and looked about at the bodies of the dead men.

'What if there is no riddle, Odysseus? What if the gods are playing with us, giving us hope where there isn't any? What if there never was anything more here than a dead king hidden beneath a wooden horse? Perhaps the Olympians want the war to go on for another ten years.'

'A king hidden beneath a wooden horse,' Odysseus repeated, to himself. 'Or inside a horse.'

Diomedes shook his head. 'No, the gods wouldn't lie to us. They sent us to find this bone and take it back to Troy. That's all there is to it. Why does there have to be something else, Odysseus?'

Odysseus ignored him and walked over to the wooden horse on its toppled granite lid. He stroked its smooth mane and frowned.

'The Trojans revere horses,' he said, quietly. Then he turned to Eperitus and smiled. 'I have it, Eperitus,' he whispered. 'I know what the riddle is, and I know the answer. I have the key to the gates of Troy.'

Chapter Nineteen
EURYPYLUS ARRIVES

Helen stood behind Cassandra as she sat on the high-backed chair, staring gloomily at her reflection in the mirror. The polished bronze surface was uneven in places and a little tarnished around the circumference, but there was no hiding the girl's natural beauty.

'White suits you,' Helen said conclusively, gathering Cassandra's thick, dark hair in her fingers and holding it behind her head to expose the long neck and slim shoulders.

Cassandra laid a modest hand across her exposed cleavage.

'Black would be more appropriate.'

'For your husband? Come now.'

'Did you want to wear white when Deiphobus forced you to marry him against your wishes?' Cassandra replied, harshly. 'Besides, Eurypylus will not be my husband until he and his army have defeated the Greeks. My father was clear on that, at least.'

Helen looked across the bright, sunny chamber to where the wind from the plains was blowing the thin curtains in from the window. The air in Cassandra's room was warm and humid, and carried with it the sound of pipes, drums and the cheering of crowds. Eurypylus's army had already entered the Scaean Gate and was marching in premature triumph through the lower city on their way up to the citadel of Pergamos. Soon thousands of soldiers would be filling the palace courtyard below, where Priam would formally greet the grandson he had never met and give him Cassandra – Eurypylus's aunt – to be his wife. And through the wine-induced fog that had obscured her thoughts and emotions almost every day since the death of Paris, Helen recalled how she had stood in her own room in Sparta, twenty years before, and listened with disdain as Agamemnon persuaded her stepfather, Tyndareus, to offer her in marriage to the best man in Greece. She shuddered at the memory and turned back to look at Cassandra.

'Nevertheless, Hecabe has asked me to make you look your best for him, and your mother's request is as good as an order.'

'They say Eurypylus is an ugly man.'

'Who says, and who would know?' Helen laughed as she gathered Cassandra's hair up at the top of her head and pinned it in place. 'After all, who in Troy has seen him? Mysians and Trojans have hardly been good friends since Astyoche's feud with Priam.'

'I have seen him in my dreams,' Cassandra insisted, 'and he has a brutal face to match his brutal character. His heart is black, too, made so by an indulgent mother who has never denied him anything.'

'Really?' Helen responded, a hint of scepticism in her voice.

She finished tying up Cassandra's thick locks and lifted her chin a little with her fingertip. The sombre face that had for so long been hidden behind drapes of black hair was now revealed in all its loveliness. She had a small but perfectly proportioned mouth, a slightly pointed chin with the merest hint of a dimple, pale, petite ears pressed forward by the volume of hair behind them, and large eyes heavily rimmed with long eyelashes. Cassandra looked at herself in the mirror and seemed surprised at what she saw, perhaps realising for the first time that she was a woman worthy of any man's attention. Behind her, Helen stared at her own reflection and saw the beauty that had never withered with the loss of her youth, or been blemished by her grief for Paris. If anything, the years and her suffering had made her more beautiful, as if the divine blood that coursed in her veins had made itself more obvious with maturity. And something inside her suddenly wanted to tell Cassandra to cover up her beauty again, to hide it from a world that would kill and maim, burn and destroy for the sake of a woman's looks.

Outside, the sound of pipes and drums was growing closer while the cheering had faded. The Mysians had left the crowds of the lower city behind and entered Pergamos itself.

'Everyone knows there's nothing Astyoche won't do for her son,' Cassandra continued. 'And in return he hangs upon her every word, doting over her like a pet puppy.'

There was a hint of disgust in her tone, and Helen laid a comforting hand on her shoulder.

'If she has spoiled him, it's exactly because she wants him as her pet – a creature that will do her bidding without question. But I don't believe she has given him everything. Not her heart. Else, why would she send him out to risk his life in battle, for the sake of a father she despises? In her pride she wanted Priam to come begging for her help – as she knew he would, one day – and that victory, symbolised by the Golden Vine, is worth more to her than Eurypylus.'

Another gust of wind blew the curtains inward again, brushing them against a small clay jar filled with perfume that Helen had brought with her for Cassandra. It fell from the table and smashed, making the two women start. As their maids had already been dismissed, Helen slipped her hand from Cassandra's shoulder and walked over to the broken pieces, picking them up one by one and placing them in her palm. Kneeling there, she heard the pulsing of the drums and the heavy tramp of marching feet coming up the last ramp to the courtyard below, followed by a loud command and then silence. She looked at Cassandra, then stood and moved to the window. Dropping the shards of clay on the table, she brushed the fluttering curtain aside with her arm and looked out.

The large courtyard below was filled with armed men. On three sides, dressed in double-ranks, were Priam's elite guard – Troy's fiercest warriors, who wore the richest armour and carried the best weapons. On the far side were the men of Mysia: a sea of soldiers with dusty armaments, all of them young and strong with faces that were keen for war, not beleaguered and desperate for peace like the Trojans and their other allies. Behind them, on the ramp that led up from the lower tier of the citadel and stretching back into the streets beyond, were the ranks of their comrades – spearmen, archers, chariots and cavalry. They numbered in the thousands, an army that could indeed turn the tide of the war against the exhausted Greeks.

In the space at the centre of the courtyard were a handful of men. The figure of Priam stood tallest, his purple robe resplendent in the sunshine and his black wig and face powder belying the age that had so rapidly caught up with him since the death of Hector. On one side of the king were his herald, Idaeus, and Antenor, the elder; while on the other were Deiphobus and Apheidas, the highest-ranking commanders in his army. Before them all was a tall, powerfully built warrior with a broad black beard and long hair that flowed from beneath his plumed helmet. A sword was slung from a scabbard under his arm and a shield hung from his back.

Helen sensed Cassandra's presence over her shoulder.

'That's Eurypylus,' she said with certainty. 'And is he not as ugly as I told you?'

Helen stared down at his broken nose and crooked teeth, and at the cruel, selfish eyes that squinted against the bright sunshine. As she watched, Eurypylus took the hand his grandfather offered him, though with deliberate hesitation and without warmth.

'Looks are not everything,' she said. 'No-one thought Paris handsome, not with that scar; but he was the noblest man in Troy – except perhaps Hector – and for a while he offered me freedom from everything that had tied me down. That's why I fell in love with him, and love him still.'

'Look at his eyes, Helen. How could Priam give his own daughter to a man with such evil eyes?'

'Priam gives the women of his household to whomever he pleases,' Helen answered, her gaze wandering to Deiphobus, whose once cheerful face was now stern and detached. 'It's the lot of a princess to be married to men not of her own choosing. Paris helped me escape from Menelaus, but now I'm married to Deiphobus against my will. And if the Greeks ever conquer these walls, I will be Menelaus's again.'

'Eurypylus will never have me.'

Helen was not listening. Her eyes were on Deiphobus and she wanted a cup of wine.

'Marriage is inescapable,' she muttered, half to herself.

'In time, another man will take me against my will. But I will not marry Astyoche's son.'

Helen caught Cassandra's last words and turned to her.

'There are worse husbands than Eurypylus. Deiphobus forced me to marry him while I was still in mourning for his brother. But if you're planning to run away –'

Cassandra shook her head. 'There's no need, Sister. Eurypylus will be killed by Achilles before he can marry me. I have seen it.'

'Achilles is dead.'

'He will return.'

Helen looked pityingly at Cassandra's sad, pretty face.

'Well, whatever may or may not happen to Eurypylus, your mother still wants you to be ready to meet him at this evening's feast. I'll find your maid and send her to clear up the rest of this mess.'

She left Cassandra looking out at her husband-to-be and found her slave waiting outside the door. As the girl rushed off to attend to her mistress, Helen felt the darkness of her grief for Paris stealing up on her again. She lowered her head into her hands and succumbed to the sinking sense of loss once more. Then, with tears in her eyes, she went to find her own room, where she would bury her face in the single tunic of his that she had kept and cry until the mood passed. And then she would drink the wine she had hidden there and ease some of her pain.

The voyage to the island of Scyros, skirting the coastline of southern Greece, had been quiet and smooth. Water, provisions and shelter had been easy to find in the many harbours and coves along the way, though the few people who dared speak to them were at best suspicious, at worst hostile. But for the men of Ithaca and Argos it was a joy to be back in Greece again, to see her mountains and islands and every evening to sleep on her beaches. The survivors had quickly forgotten the horrors of Pelops's tomb and put behind them their grief for the comrades who had been slain there; now their minds were on the end of the war and an imminent return to their families and homes. For a while, as they sailed beneath a Greek sun and ate Greek food, their spirits were bubbling with optimism, as if the defeat of Troy was now a mere formality.

It was not, of course, and none knew that more than Odysseus, Diomedes and Eperitus. In those long days, blessed by sun and wind that required them to do little between rowing out to deeper waters in the morning and finding a sheltering cove before dark, they had plenty of time to think about what now lay ahead of them. After retracing their way out of the maze – dragging the bodies of the dead Argives with them to be burned on a pyre beneath the evening stars – Odysseus had explained the significance of the bone to Eperitus and Diomedes.

'The bone itself is nothing more than a token,' he told them as they made camp by the banks of the Alpheius. 'It will be an encouragement to the army, because the oracle Helenus gave us said Troy will not fall without it. However, it isn't the reason the gods sent us to Pelops's tomb.'

'Then what is the point of it?' Diomedes had asked.

They were sitting away from the others, around a small log fire of their own. The flames cast an orange glow over their faces, distorting their features with strange shadows. Eperitus looked at Odysseus and had absolute faith in the power of his friend's mind. There was no situation he could not think his way out of, and no riddle he could not decipher. He had found a way through the maze, and he would know the meaning of the shoulder bone. That was why Athena, the goddess of wisdom, had chosen him.

'The gods were giving us a clue to conquer Troy. The walls were built by Poseidon and Apollo: they can't be smashed down or scaled, and as long as there are men to defend them the city can never be conquered from the outside. But if we could get men *inside* the walls – enough of them to capture the gates and hold them open until the rest of the army arrive –'

'As simple as that,' Diomedes said, sardonically. 'And how do we get a large force of men into the city in the first place? Turn them into birds so they fly over the walls?'

'The maze!' Eperitus exclaimed, thinking he understood. 'You mean we should dig a tunnel beneath the walls and into Troy. The gods sent you into the maze to give you inspiration!'

Odysseus shook his head.

'No tunnels, Eperitus. The ground Troy is built on is too hard. Besides, the Trojans would see what we were up to and guess our intent. You're right in one sense, though: we were sent into that tomb to see something, something that would show me how to get inside Troy. Do you remember I once said I'd been given an idea by Astynome smuggling herself into the Greek camp in the back of that farmer's cart, and by Omeros's retelling the story of how I got past those Taphian guards hidden in a pithos of wine? Well, Pelops's tomb has finally shown me how I can smuggle an army into Troy.'

'How?' Eperitus and Diomedes asked.

'You'll see in time,' Odysseus replied with a grin.

Despite having tantalised his comrades, Odysseus stubbornly refused to say any more about the inspiration he had received in Pelops's tomb, so their thoughts and discussions now focussed on the two remaining oracles: how they would steal the Palladium from the temple of Athena in Troy and, more urgently, how they would persuade

Achilles's son, Neoptolemus, to join Agamemnon's army. Eperitus remembered the small, light-haired boy he had seen in the palace gardens on Scyros the day Achilles had joined the expedition to Troy. He sympathised with the doubts of the ordinary soldiers who questioned the value of a fifteen-year-old lad who had never seen combat before, and who had been hidden away behind the skirts of his mother's chiton all his young life. But these uncertainties never bothered Odysseus or Diomedes. The two kings understood that a son of Achilles would be worth all the effort spent in bringing him to the war. The only problem that concerned them was how to prise him away from the clutches of his deceitful grandfather and – a greater problem in Odysseus's eyes – his jealous mother.

Finally, the day came when they saw the high, rugged hills overlooking the wide harbour of Scyros. The noon sun caught the copper gates of the palace halfway up the highest hill, which flashed to them like a beacon. As they slipped towards the calm, sheltered waters of the harbour, Sthenelaus called for the sail to be furled and the anchor stones to be made ready. At first, Eperitus was surprised to see the numerous fishing boats drawn up on the shingle beach and the handful of merchant vessels at anchor. A throng of people left their homes or their chores to watch the approach of the fighting galley, showing no signs of fear, only curiosity. Then he understood: Scyros had survived the depravations of the rest of Greece because its king had not been one of the oath-takers and thus had refused to send his army to the war against Troy. Scyros had remained safe and prosperous because Lycomedes had stayed at home.

Small boats came out to meet the warship, manned by fishermen or boys offering to take the crew ashore. Soon, Odysseus, Diomedes and Eperitus were leading half a dozen Argives up the cobbled road to the palace gates, while the remainder were ordered to stay on board. Odysseus knew King Lycomedes could not be trusted and had told Sthenelaus to stay alert while they were gone, ready to come to their aid if necessary. From his lofty viewpoint, Lycomedes would have known of the galley's approach long before its anchor stones were cast overboard. There was no telling what sort of reception he might give them.

The copper gates swung open to reveal two dozen well-armed soldiers and a short, officious looking herald who insisted they leave their weapons with the guards. They had expected nothing less and gave up their spears and swords with little more than a show of reluctance. They were ushered into the great hall, sombre and shadowy despite the column of dusty light that shone down through the smoke hole in the ceiling to touch on the low flames of the hearth. Eperitus remembered the chamber well from his first visit to Scyros ten years before, though then it had been evening and the hall had been filled with nobles and lit by numerous torches. Now it was empty but for an old man and a woman. The man was seated in a wooden throne draped in furs. His hair and beard were white and his skin was ashen grey. His thin nose seemed to twitch slightly as they entered, while his small, closely set eyes watched them keenly from beneath heavy eyebrows. The woman had a chair next to his, but chose to stand as the newcomers entered, placing her hand on the back of the throne. Like him she was tall, though she was many years younger. Her hair was long and dark and her natural beauty was made more aloof and alluring by the stern gaze that she fixed on the men.

Eperitus did not recognise King Lycomedes at first, so old and gaunt had he become, but he could see by the clear eyes and hawklike stare that he had lost none of his wits. The woman he knew immediately was Deidameia, Achilles's widow – though she would not know that yet – and the mother of Neoptolemus. Of Achilles's son there was no sign.

'Welcome to Scyros, my lords,' she said. 'Step forward into the light and tell us who you are and what it is that King Lycomedes can do for you.'

'I am King Diomedes of Argos, son of Tydeus. This is King Odysseus of Ithaca, son of Laertes, and these are Eperitus, captain of the Ithacan royal guard, and our companions. We have brought a message for the wife and son of the great Achilles.'

At the mention of Odysseus's name, both Lycomedes and his daughter turned to stare at the broad figure in the shadows behind Diomedes. Lycomedes's eyes were filled with sudden suspicion, remembering how Odysseus had tricked him before; but Deidameia's face had lost its austere self-assurance and turned pale, as if already guessing the news the men had brought.

'I am Deidameia, daughter of King Lycomedes and wife of the great Achilles. What is your message?'

Odysseus stepped forward and touched Diomedes's elbow, indicating he would reply.

'Our message is for Neoptolemus also,' he said. 'Where is your son?'

'I will not allow you to speak to my grandson, Odysseus,' Lycomedes answered. 'The last time you were here you fooled Achilles into joining Agamemnon's army, and we have not seen him since. What's to say you won't try to take Neoptolemus back with you this time?'

Deidameia lifted her hand to silence her father, a gesture that raised eyebrows among their guests.

'Give your message to me, Odysseus, and I shall tell my son. He can hear it just as well from my lips as yours.'

'Very well, my lady. Your husband is dead. He fell storming the gates of Troy, where he was struck down by the arrows of Prince Paris.'

The statement was spoken evenly, but the silence that followed seemed to fix the words in the air about them. Deidameia shrank a little, as if something had gone out of her. Eperitus saw her grip on Lycomedes's chair tighten slightly. Then she drew on her inner strength and pulled herself back up to her full height. Her lips became thin and pale, her eyes stony and hard.

'Achilles died ten years ago, when he left this island in your ship, Odysseus. Thank you, my lords, for coming all this way to bring me your news. I will sacrifice to Poseidon and pray that you have a safe journey back to Ilium.'

'And Neoptolemus?' Odysseus asked, showing no signs of moving. 'He will have questions. He'll want to know how his father died.'

'You've already said he was shot by Paris,' Deidameia replied. 'I will let him know.'

'It won't be enough,' Diomedes said. 'If he has anything of his father in him, he'll want to know every detail. And not just about Achilles's death, but also about the things he achieved while alive: the men he killed, the cities he conquered –'

'That is my fear, King Diomedes. He has *too much* of his father in him, and to hear of Achilles's deeds will turn his mind towards Troy at a time when his thoughts should be of home. Lycomedes is right: you have not come here to tell me of my husband's death, but to take my son away to replace Achilles on the battlefield! Part of me feared it as soon as your sail was spotted, even though I didn't know who you were. And yet he is my son, not yours. I won't stand by and allow you to take him away like you did my husband.'

'Neoptolemus is nearly a man, my lady,' Odysseus countered. 'Such decisions can only be made by him. What's more, if you send us away without giving him the chance to question us about his father – to question the men who knew Achilles best in life, and who witnessed his death – you are denying him something every man has an elementary right to: a knowledge of his sires and an understanding of his roots. Do that, Deidameia, and his love for you may turn to hatred.'

'We will take that risk,' Lycomedes said, struggling to his feet and pointing to the doors they had entered through. 'Neoptolemus will never be yours. Now, leave my island and return to Troy.'

But as Eperitus was expecting the king to have them thrown out and put an end to their hopes of ever fulfilling the oracle, Deidameia laid a hand on the old man's shoulder and gently eased him back into his throne.

'You will excuse my father. Neoptolemus is the sole heir to the kingdom and he doesn't want to see him go off to a war that has nothing to do with Scyros. But what you say is true, Odysseus. Neoptolemus deserves to hear about his father and it's not my place to deny him that. I'll allow you to speak with him tonight, if you still wish it, at a feast we will hold in your honour.'

'We do wish it,' Diomedes answered, glancing uncertainly at Odysseus beside him.

Deidameia smiled at him, something of her earlier authority and self-assurance returning.

'You see, I have faith in my son. He has his father's love of fighting, but he is less driven by passion and more inclined to follow his intelligence. He will know why you're here, but he'll not rush madly off to war. And by ill chance for you, tomorrow morning will marry Phaedra, the girl I have chosen to be his wife and bear his children. You may tempt him, Odysseus, but in the end he will choose love over glory.'

She bowed to them, then turned and walked from the great hall.

Chapter Twenty
NEOPTOLEMUS

After the audience in the great hall, Odysseus, Diomedes, Eperitus and their escort were taken to the same wing of the palace the Ithacans had been quartered in on their first visit to Scyros ten years ago. They climbed the steps to the roof and looked down at the galley in the bay below.

'It's a thin hope now,' Diomedes said. 'If the lad's getting married, the last thing on his mind will be coming with us to Troy. We couldn't have arrived at a worse time.'

Odysseus didn't share his gloom.

'I'd say the gods have brought us here at exactly the *right* moment. Tomorrow, we would have found him a married man, freshly committed to his new life as a husband. *Today* he's in that strange, fleeting place where the old has gone but the new hasn't yet come. His mind may be full of love for this girl he's due to marry, and yet it'll also be stricken with doubt. He's young, remember. He's never ventured beyond the shores of Scyros. The news of Achilles's death may open a new door – a chance to follow his father's path, away from domesticity and into adventure. I've seen it happen to others in his position. More than that, he has Achilles's blood in his veins: when Neoptolemus sees the gift I've brought him, it'll be enough to challenge even his strongest convictions about getting married.'

'We'll see,' Diomedes replied.

In the afternoon, after they had eaten a modest lunch, Eperitus was resting on the mattress in his room when a slave brought him a clean tunic and told him he was to go to the garden as soon as was convenient. He left before Eperitus could question him, so the Ithacan changed his clothes and went to answer the summons. He followed the scent of flowers and the rich aroma of well-composted earth until he found the walled gardens where he had first seen Achilles – disguised as a girl by Lycomedes to prevent him from being taken off to the coming war against Troy. He entered it through an arched gateway and saw it had not changed much since his first visit, except then it had been spring and there had been fragrant blossoms on the trees on either side, and now it was autumn and the leaves were turning an ochre colour and peeling off to form a patchy carpet on the lawn. The circular pond at the centre of the garden was filled with lilies that boasted a handful of white flowers. Dressed in a yellow chiton and seated on a stone bench at the water's edge was Deidameia, looking at him expectantly.

'I'm glad you came, Eperitus. Please, join me.'

She patted the space beside her and he sat. He could smell her perfume, potent even in a garden full of flowers. She gave him a smile and he could see the fullness of her lips and the way her skin was still soft and supple with her youth, despite the advanced maturity he could read in her eyes.

'What do you want of me, Deidameia?'

'A warrior's bluntness, I see. I just wanted to talk a little.'

'You picked the wrong man, my lady. Odysseus is the one for talking –'

'Ah, but can I trust him? I think I can trust you, though. You have an honest look about you.'

'I think you'd find my conversation a little dull, unless you want to hear about war and death.'

'But that's precisely what I want to hear about,' she replied. 'Particularly the war in Troy and my husband's death. Were you there?'

Eperitus nodded and, reluctantly at first, told her what he had witnessed on the day Achilles had died. It would have been a short account – he had none of Odysseus's ability to embellish a story – if Deidameia had not teased out every important detail from him. She showed little emotion as the full truth was laid before her, and when the story was done insisted on hearing more about Achilles's achievements before his death. Eventually, after Eperitus's clumsy retelling was done, she turned to the real reason she had summoned him.

'Do you think Neoptolemus will be a replacement for Achilles?' she asked. 'Do Odysseus and Diomedes really believe that?'

'We do. He has his father's blood in him, after all.'

'But he is not Achilles. You will know that when you see him tonight. He can't do the things his father failed to do! So why are you here? Why leave the war in Troy for the sake of one man?'

Eperitus stood.

'It's not my place to say, my lady. Odysseus and Diomedes were charged with this mission, not me. If you had hoped to trick me –'

'Of course not,' she said, her tone conciliatory. She took him by the elbow and encouraged him to retake his seat. 'I'm sorry if I've offended you, Eperitus. I'm just a mother worried for her son. You must have children of your own.'

'A daughter.'

'Then don't you miss her?'

'She died before the war.'

Deidameia faced him and laid her hand on his forearm. Her eyes were full of compassion.

'How old was she?'

'She was nine. The truth is I hardly knew her. I slept with her mother in Sparta ten years before, but I didn't learn she'd given birth to my daughter until a short while before she died.'

'And how did she die?'

Deidameia's voice was soft now. Eperitus looked down at her slim, long-fingered hand on his arm, felt the hotness of her skin against his, and wondered whether he should answer. Whether he could answer. Then he felt the old anger rising as he thought of his daughter's murder and his own inability to save her.

'She was sacrificed to appease the gods. King Agamemnon murdered her so that his fleet could sail in safety to Ilium.'

Deidameia's eyes narrowed in confusion.

'But that was his own daughter, Iphigenia, born of Clytaemnestra. Everyone knows the story.'

'They know some, but not all. Clytaemnestra was my lover in Sparta and Iphigenia was my daughter. I tried to stop Agamemnon, but –' He stood again and stepped away from the bench. 'I must go. Odysseus will be wondering where I am.'

'Tell me why they want my son, Eperitus. As a father yourself –'

'I sympathise with you, Deidameia, I do, but that's for Odysseus to say, not me. He'll tell you why we're here tonight. And as for your son, he's not a boy any more; he's old enough to be a warrior now, like his father before him. And part of him will want to follow Achilles. You say you have faith in him, that you know him, but you don't. How can a woman really know what's in a man's heart? A man lives under the shadow of his father, for good or bad, and at some point he wants to be free of it and live his own life. How Neoptolemus does that is up to him, not you.'

He held her gaze for a moment, then turned and left.

The sun had set and the first stars were beginning to prick the deep blue of the evening sky outside when torch-bearing slaves came to their quarters with a summons to the promised feast. Without armour or weapons, Odysseus, Diomedes and Eperitus followed the slaves through the palace to the copper gates, where they were awaited by Polites, Eurybates and Omeros who had come on Odysseus's orders. Polites held a great wooden chest on his shoulder, making light of the burden, while Eurybates wore Achilles's shield on his arm, its splendour hidden behind a covering of sail cloth. Omeros was struggling to even hold the huge ash spear that Achilles had wielded with such devastation in battle. At first the gate guards were reluctant to let them carry weapons into the palace, but agreed when Odysseus said they were gifts for Neoptolemus and suggested a detail of warriors could accompany them to the great hall.

'Wait here,' Odysseus told his men as they reached the tall double doors. 'I'll send for you when I need the gifts, but *do not* enter before then – whatever you may hear from inside. Do you understand?'

The muffled sound of voices and music became suddenly loud and clear as the guards threw open the doors and ushered them in. The hall was filled with the nobility of Scyros, men of all ages who had never been called to the fields of Ilium. They were seated at long tables, piled high with food and drink that was constantly being replenished by lines of slaves. These seemed to move in eddying currents through the crowded chamber, balancing platters of bread and meat on their heads, or pouring wine into the empty kraters that were waved before their faces. The hearth was ablaze with fresh logs and pumped a twisting pillar of sparks and smoke up to the ceiling. As the newcomers were led to a vacant table there was a flicker of interest from the other guests in the hall, but it passed quickly.

Odysseus glanced up see Lycomedes watching them closely from his throne. Deidameia was seated next to her father, dressed now in a sable chiton with her hair covered in black cloth. Beside her was a young girl of perhaps thirteen or fourteen. Her youthful beauty shone out like a beacon in the shadow-filled chamber, sensualised by her bright red lips and painted eyes. Deidameia leaned across to speak in her ear and the girl looked over at the battle-hardened men who had just entered the great hall.

'I'm guessing that's Phaedra, the girl Neoptolemus will marry tomorrow,' Odysseus said as they sat at the benches.

Eperitus nodded. 'And that must be Neoptolemus.'

A youth stood by the hearth, holding his krater at arms length and pouring a libation into the flames. Odysseus had not noticed him before among the movement and noise of the hall, but now that he saw the figure beyond the heat haze of the fire he could not take his eyes off him. Neoptolemus was tall and tautly muscled, and though he had short, light brown hair and was clean-shaven – Achilles had been blond with long hair and a beard – the likeness to his father was striking. It was as if the warrior who had killed Hector, Penthesilea, Memnon and countless others on the Trojan plains had been brought back from the dead. Then Neoptolemus's eyes met his and the illusion was broken. Whereas Achilles's perfect and terrifying anger was equalled by his capacity for friendship, hospitality, pride, honour and love, his son's gaze was filled only with a cold and fearsome hostility, untainted by the oceanic passions that had made his father so humanly fallible.

Odysseus took a krater of wine from the hand of a passing slave and walked to the hearth, pouring a libation to the gods. Neoptolemus continued to stare at him and Odysseus returned his gaze for several moments – long enough to show the young prince he was not afraid of him – before raising the krater to his lips and bowing his eyes to the dark liquid. Diomedes and Eperitus joined him, slopping dashes of wine into the flames as they watched Neoptolemus return to a vacant chair beside Lycomedes. He looked at Phaedra and gave her a nodding smile, then at his mother, to whom he bowed his head with reverent formality.

'He has the eyes of a born killer,' Diomedes commented. 'Very like his father, and yet lacking something. That lust for glory, perhaps?'

'He has that, I think,' Eperitus said. 'But I don't see Achilles's love of life in him, that joy you could see in his eyes whether he was feasting with friends or riding out to battle in his chariot.'

'What he lacks is compassion,' Odysseus said. 'I don't trust him, but the gods have a purpose for Neoptolemus in Troy and so we must persuade him to come with us, whether we like it or not. And more to the point, whether Deidameia likes it or not.'

As he spoke, Lycomedes rose to his feet and walked to the edge of the dais, holding his hands up for silence. The music fell away and the hubbub of voices stuttered to a halt.

'Friends, our guests have arrived. You already know the ill tidings they brought with them from Troy, calamitous news that grieves my heart and plunges it into despair. But I will not mourn the death of my son-in-law tonight. Tonight we will celebrate the greatness of his life. Eat and drink to his memory, and be thankful that the gods have saved you from a similar end on the shores of Ilium.'

There was a cheer from the crowded benches, though many of the men there would barely have remembered Achilles, let alone have known him well during his short years on Scyros.

'Be thankful?' Odysseus challenged, raising his voice above the clamour so that voices were stilled again and all eyes turned to the Ithacan king. 'If you knew anything about his glorious achievements you would consider yourselves *cursed* not to have fought at his side. And just because you baulk at the prospect of war, Lycomedes, that doesn't mean Neoptolemus shares your delicate disposition. Surely Achilles's own son will want to hear something of his father's deeds in the war against Troy? And who better to tell him than men who fought in the battle line beside him?'

'You are the guest, Odysseus, not the host,' Lycomedes warned, barely able to contain his own rage. 'If I want a story, I will call for my bard. Until then, keep your silence!'

The hall rang with his words and no man dared to break the tension between the two kings. Deidameia looked anxiously from Lycomedes to Odysseus, and finally to Neoptolemus. As her eyes fell on her son, he rose from his chair and stared at his grandfather.

'Let Odysseus speak. I want to hear what he has to say.'

Lycomedes looked at Deidameia, who gave an almost imperceptible nod.

'Very well, Odysseus,' he said. 'Tell to us of the deeds of Achilles in the years since he left us. Stand and earn your food and wine, like the beggar you are. Speak so that Neoptolemus can understand something of the man his father was, and learn from his errors.'

Lycomedes's insult had little effect on Odysseus, who stood and looked around at the faces that were now turned to him. There was the flicker of a sneer on some as they stared at the bulky Ithacan, with the faded purple cloak his wife had given him and his long red hair and unkempt beard. Balanced on his short legs, his muscular torso and arms looked ungainly and almost comical, though few would have dared laugh into his battle-hardened face or his knowing green eyes. And yet even on Scyros they had heard about the legendary voice of Odysseus, and despite his vagabond appearance they waited in silence for him to speak.

'Ten years ago, King Agamemnon charged me with the task of finding the greatest warrior in all Greece – Achilles – who was said to be here on Scyros. When we eventually found him he was disguised as a girl, hiding away from unwelcome visitors at the insistence of his mother, Thetis.' Here he looked at Deidameia, who held his gaze firmly. 'She had foreseen that her son would die if he ever went to Troy, and thought that if she could prevent him going he would live a long and prosperous life. But, goddess though she was, she could not change her son's nature. Achilles sailed with us to Troy in search of glory, and became the fiercest of all the Greeks, the bane of every Trojan who ever faced him in battle.'

He went on to describe the long years of the war, from the first skirmish on Tenedos to the great battles that had rolled back and forth across the plains of Ilium, all the time focussing on the part played by Neoptolemus's father. With far greater skill than Eperitus's stumbling efforts with Deidameia in the walled garden earlier, he recalled in detail Achilles's grief at the loss of Patroclus, his return to war in the magnificent armour presented to him by Thetis, and how he took his terrible revenge on Hector. Though he briefly mentioned Achilles's refusal to burn Hector's corpse, he made clear how his anger was ultimately tempered by compassion for Priam. He followed this with vivid accounts of his slaying of Penthesilea, queen of the Amazons, and soon after, Memnon, leader of the Aethiopes. As Odysseus described each victory he pointedly did not look at Neoptolemus, speaking instead to the rest of the crowded hall and winning the audience over to his tale, so that they shouted in anguish or triumph as he described Achilles's various trials. Indeed, he did not need to look at Neoptolemus to know that his icy expression was slowly thawing, encouraged by the crowd around him, and that a fire had been kindled in his heart that blazed in his eyes, to the exclusion of everything else in the great hall.

Finally, Odysseus came to the death of Achilles before the Scaean Gate. The room fell into a hush as he described the shadow of Apollo falling across the closely packed soldiers, and the hiss of the poisoned arrow as it found Achilles's vulnerable heel and brought him down.

'And so your father lived and died, Neoptolemus,' Odysseus said, turning at last to the young man seated beside Lycomedes. 'But as your mother and grandfather have already guessed, we did not come here solely to bring you news of Achilles's death. You'd have heard eventually, and the message didn't need two kings to carry it. No, we're here at the will of the gods: an oracle has predicted that Troy won't fall until you've taken your father's place in the army.'

At this, the hall broke into uproar. Men leapt to their feet, sending shouts of denial up to the rafters. Neoptolemus stood also, while Odysseus advanced to the hearth and pointed at him through the heat haze.

'You are your father's heir, Neoptolemus. Will you honour his memory and return to Troy with us, or will you bring shame on him and yourself and stay here?'

'Guards!' Deidameia shouted, standing and moving to the edge of the dais. Several armed men emerged from the shadowy corners of the hall and surrounded the visitors. 'I said I would not stand by and let you rob me of my son, as you did my husband. Neoptolemus will marry Phaedra tomorrow, and in time she will be the mother of his children. He will not follow his father to Troy, but stay here and inherit the throne of his grandfather. Do you understand?'

Her last words were to Neoptolemus, who remained silent, though there was rebellion in his eyes. Then Diomedes moved to Odysseus's side.

'Time to let go of your mother's chiton, lad,' he said, raising his voice over the commotion. 'The gods have said Troy cannot fall without you, and so *you* must decide between hardship and everlasting glory, or comfort and obscurity.'

Deidameia waved the guards forward. Spear points were pressed against Odysseus and Diomedes's stomachs, while the cold edge of a sword was lifted to Eperitus's throat.

'Take them back to their ship,' she ordered, 'and if they resist, kill them.'

As they were forced towards the doors of the great hall, pelted by pieces of bread and meat from the surrounding nobles, Lycomedes had to pull Neoptolemus back into his chair.

'Wait!' Odysseus cried. 'Wait! By all means send us back to Troy, but not before Neoptolemus has received the inheritance his father left him.'

Such was the power of his voice that the guards stopped and looked to Deidameia for what to do. She turned to Lycomedes with doubt in her eyes, but it was Neoptolemus who answered.

'What is this inheritance?'

'Beware the gifts of Odysseus,' Lycomedes warned. 'They snared your father, and they will snare you.'

Neoptolemus ignored the old man and stood.

'Speak, Odysseus.'

Odysseus pushed the spear point away from his stomach and looked Neoptolemus in the eye.

'There's one thing I haven't told you about, though you may have pondered it already – the fate of Achilles's splendid armour. After your father's death, Great Ajax carried his corpse back to the Greek camp, while I fought off the Trojans that pursued us. That gave us both a claim to the armour, though Ajax's was by far the greater because he was Achilles's cousin. But Ajax had also angered the gods with his arrogance, and to get their revenge they told me to stake my claim on the armour and deny it to Ajax by whatever means possible.'

Here he paused and looked at Diomedes and Eperitus. Eperitus knew that the guilt of Ajax's suicide was still upon him and must have realised what was coming next.

'And so I cheated – I bribed some prisoners to declare that I was the one the Trojans feared the most, and by their false testimony Achilles's armour was awarded to me. That evening, Ajax lost his mind and killed himself, just as the gods had known he would. Ever since then, even though I was driven to what I did by the command of the immortals, I have known the armour could never be mine. And neither could it ever have belonged to Ajax. It has only one true heir – you, Neoptolemus.'

As he finished, he called to a slave and spoke to him in a low voice. The slave ran to the doors and opened them. A moment later, Polites, Eurybates and Omeros entered, carrying their burdens. Polites laid the large wooden box on the floor and threw open the hinged lid, revealing a flash of gold that caused a stir among the onlookers. At a nod from Odysseus, he pulled out the red-plumed helmet and lifted it in one hand above his head, turning in a half-circle so the whole hall could see it. The mirror-like finish of the gold blazed in the light of the hearth and torches and earned a gasp of disbelief. After sweeping the platters and cups from a table with a crash, he placed it down and plucked out the tin greaves, holding one in each hand as he showed them to the hall in the same fashion. Laying these beside the helmet, Polites returned to the wooden chest and retrieved the bronze cuirass that the smith-god had shaped to exactly mimic the perfect torso of Achilles.

'By all the gods!' Lycomedes exclaimed as Polites raised it high above his head.

Neoptolemus brushed past his mother and moved to the edge of the dais, his mouth wide open.

'Behold, your father's famed spear,' Odysseus said, taking the weapon from Omeros's grasp and raising it in both hands above his head, before leaning it against the table where the rest of the armour sat. 'This was the spear that killed the great Hector and countless other Trojans of great renown. Yet all these things are as nothing compared to *this*.'

He beckoned Eurybates forward and untied the strings that held the sail cloth in place. It fell to the floor, revealing the great shield of Achilles in a flash gold and silver. A shout of wonder echoed through the great hall as every eye seized on the shining disc. Its boss depicted the Earth and Sea, surrounded by the Sun, Moon and stars. Four more concentric circles showed different scenes from human life, the figures within moving and dancing and fighting as they had done ever since Hephaistos had first animated them. At the sight of the shield, Neoptolemus stepped down from the dais and skirted the hearth to be near it.

'These are *mine*?' he asked, looking fleetingly at Odysseus before returning his gaze to the collection of armour.

'They were your father's, and now they're yours, regardless of whether you come to Troy or not.'

But there was no longer any question of whether Neoptolemus would take up his father's mantle and go to war. He lifted the shield from Eurybates's shoulder and slipped it onto his own arm. Odysseus fetched the helmet and lowered it slowly onto his head, while Diomedes placed the great ash spear in his hand. Neoptolemus lifted it above his shoulder with familiar ease, revelling in the feel of the heavy armaments that fitted him so well. He turned to his mother, whose tears were glistening on her cheeks as she leaned her weight against Lycomedes's throne. Phaedra had lowered her pretty face into her hands and was sobbing loudly. Then he looked back at Odysseus and the others with a smile.

'When do we leave?' he asked.

Chapter Twenty-One
THE GREEKS AT BAY

Agamemnon closed his eyes and took a deep breath. His arms and legs felt like stone and his mind was fuddled by a night without sleep, but a new morning was upon him and he was still the leader of what remained of the Greek army. The King of Men, he mocked himself with an ironic smile.

Then he forced his lids open again and pushed aside the heavy canvas flap of his tent. As he stepped out, the top of the sun was peering over the battlements to the east, framing the figures that stood watch there. Grey smoke crept across the blue skies above them, twisting up from the smouldering bonfires that had burned great holes in the blackness of the night before. Beyond the walls were more trails from the many pyres of their enemies on the plain. The morning air, though freshened by a breeze from the sea, still reeked of burnt wood and roasted flesh.

'My lord,' said Menestheus, the Athenian king, greeting him with a small bow.

King Idomeneus was beside him, but the Cretan remained standing stiffly and only acknowledged Agamemnon with a slight narrowing of his eyes. Both men were dressed in breastplate, helmet and greaves, with swords slung in scabbards beneath their left arms. Their armour-bearers stood behind them, holding their shields and spears.

'What is it?' Agamemnon asked, too tired to bother hiding his annoyance. 'Are they preparing to attack again?'

'Their camp's astir, but they're in no hurry to renew battle,' Idomeneus answered. 'Perhaps they won't need to.'

Agamemnon shot him a stern glance. 'Meaning what?'

Talthybius appeared from the tent before Idomeneus could answer, carrying Agamemnon's shield, helmet and spears. The Mycenaean king was already wearing his greaves and the cuirass gifted to him by Cinyras of Cyprus, though its bands of gold, blue enamel and tin were still dinted and spattered with gore from the previous day's battle. He took the helmet from his herald's hands and crammed it onto his head.

'If you've got something to say, then say it,' he snapped, glaring at the two kings.

'We're worried for the morale of the army,' Menestheus said, stepping toward Agamemnon and looking him in the eye. 'The Mysians are fresh and eager to fight. Their king – this Eurypylus – is like another Hector, riding across the battlefield and bringing death wherever he goes. The Trojans have taken new heart from his presence, while yesterday we were fortunate just to reach the safety of the walls with most of our force still intact. But the men won't take much more. Even if Eurypylus and Deiphobus don't breach the walls today and destroy us, there's talk that some men are planning to slip away at night – push the galleys into the sea and just sail home. They've had enough.'

Agamemnon's brow furrowed. 'We'll see about that. Where's my brother?'

'Up by the gates, with Nestor, Little Ajax and Philoctetes.'

Agamemnon tossed his blood-red cloak over his shoulder and strode up the sand towards the countless sun-bleached tents that filled the land between the shore and the sloping ridge above it. Here, the walls and gates they had built just a few weeks before were the only thing that now stood between the Greek army and annihilation. On the other side were Deiphobus's victorious Trojans, replenished by new allies under Eurypylus. For days both armies had battled each other across the plains at the cost of thousands more men killed and maimed, but once again the fickle gods had sided with Priam and brought his warriors to the very edge of the Greek camp. And this time when the assault was renewed there would be no brooding Achilles to come to Agamemnon's rescue.

The King of Men felt his anger rising. The weakness of the kings under his command had brought them to this point, and now their fools of men were threatening to desert back to Greece. It was something he had feared more and more as the years of war had dragged on, but as he walked between the grimed and bloodied soldiers who sat or stood in dispirited groups about the mouths of their tents, he could see it in their faces. Then, as Idomeneus, Menestheus and Talthybius caught up with him – their armour clanking about them – a wounded man leaned across and spat in the dust at the Mycenaean king's feet.

Agamemnon grasped the handle of his sword and the soldier drew back. His right hand had been severed above the wrist, but to Agamemnon's shock and disbelief the men around him reached for their own weapons and leapt to the protection of their comrade.

'Don't be fools,' Menestheus warned, standing between them and the King of Men.

Agamemnon felt Idomeneus's hand on his, pushing his half-drawn sword back into its scabbard.

'Now do you believe us?' he whispered, and with his other hand on Agamemnon's shoulder kept him moving forward. 'A few more outbreaks of indiscipline like that and we'll have a full blown mutiny on our hands.'

'I'll send a detachment of men and put them under guard until the fighting's over,' Menestheus said, joining them. 'If we're victorious they can be punished as an example to the rest of the army; if we're not, then I don't suppose it matters.'

Agamemnon said nothing. The shock had passed quickly and left him in no doubt that this situation was more dangerous than he had anticipated. Only one thing would save them from destruction now – the arrival of Neoptolemus and the fulfilment of the oracle – but for all he knew Diomedes and Odysseus could still be on Scyros or in the Peloponnese, or have already perished on the long voyage there or back.

They joined the main path that led up to the walls and found Menelaus waiting for them, with Nestor, Little Ajax and Philoctetes the archer at his shoulders. Huge companies of spearmen sat in ranks by the walls, awaiting the order to stand and fight, while behind them many hundreds of bowmen were busily standing their arrows point-down in the dust, ready to fire blindly over the walls into the packed Trojans when the inevitable attack came

'They're forming up,' Menelaus growled as he walked to meet them. 'Our army can hold them, but there are plenty more men still scattered among the tents whose units were destroyed in the fighting. We need to organise them and the lightly wounded into a strong reserve, just in case the –'

'Has there been any sign of Diomedes and Odysseus's sail?' Agamemnon interrupted, casting a glance over the Aegean.

Menelaus frowned and bit at his bottom lip.

'A ship has been spotted, approaching from the west. For a while we thought it was them returning, but then it changed course northward – towards Troy.'

'It could still be them. Why haven't the galleys we keep ready on Tenedos been sent to intercept it?'

'When the badly wounded were sent over yesterday I ordered every able-bodied man on the island to return to the camp. That includes the crews of the galleys –'

'You deliberately disobeyed my orders!'

'Damn your orders,' Menelaus snapped. 'Don't you realise we need all the men we can get *here*, not at sea waiting for a galley that's probably still on the other side of the world? The sail belongs to a merchantman and nothing more. And if you'd kept your mind on the battle, rather than this fantasy over Achilles's son, perhaps the Trojans would have been pushed back behind *their* walls again, not us behind *ours*!'

'Are you suggesting *I've* led us into this situation?' Agamemnon hissed, drawing up to his brother.

Every eye was now turned to watch the argument.

'I'm saying Helenus led us all into a fool's trap. The oracles he fed us were a lie, designed to have us looking back homeward while all the time Troy was being reinforced by thousands of Mysians. Thanks to him, two of our best fighters are off on a wild rabbit hunt across Greece and we're pinning all our hopes on a mere boy – whatever his ancestry – rather than believing in our own prowess in battle.'

'Helenus wasn't lying,' Agamemnon retorted. 'But if you want to assemble your reserve of cowards and cripples, then go ahead. I'm going to the walls.'

Leaving Menelaus fuming with rage behind him, Agamemnon marched over to the gate. Nestor followed him up the wooden steps to the ramparts and together they looked out into the morning sun at their amassed foes. There was a stretch of empty grassland that had been cleansed of the dead during the truce of the previous evening; beyond this, little more than a bowshot from the battlements, stood the ranks of the Trojans and their allies. Thousands upon thousands of infantry waited with their spears and helmets glinting in the sunlight. Before them were dense lines of archers, their bows fitted with arrows and held in readiness, while behind were scores of chariots and row upon row of cavalry.

It was reminiscent of the scene only weeks before, when Hector's army had laid siege to the Greek camp. Shortly afterwards, they had succeeded in scaling the walls and throwing down the gates before pouring through the Greek tents to threaten the beached galleys. For the first time, Agamemnon wondered at how fruitless the loss of life had been between then and now: thousands of lives expended just to come full circle. The only difference, perhaps, was that the awe-inspiring figures of Hector and Sarpedon had been replaced by Eurypylus and Deiphobus. Agamemnon looked over at the Mysian king standing boldly in the front rank and saw the confidence in his grim face, a confidence justified by his fighting ability. He had brought down many Greek champions in the terrible battles of the preceding days, and none of the surviving kings were able to overcome him. If the oracles were true and not the fantasy that Menelaus claimed them to be, then Neoptolemus would have to be more than a mere shadow of his father to defeat such a warrior. But unless the gods delivered Achilles's son on to the shores of Ilium before the day was out, it would be too late anyway. For the war would likely be over, and the Greek army slain or taken into captivity.

Then a flash of white on the Aegean caught his eye. He looked westward across the waves and saw the smudge of a sail shining against the blue waters as it steered towards land. For a moment his heart leapt with joy. Then he saw the ship was not heading towards the Greek camp, but north to Troy – the same galley Menelaus had already spoken of. Almost certainly a merchant, as his brother had guessed, chancing the blockade of the city to bring much needed luxuries at extortionate prices. And with every Greek now waiting behind their walls, the daring captain was sure to make his destination and reap a rich reward.

There was a movement on the plain and Agamemnon watched Eurypylus raise his hand and motion towards the camp. With a great shout, the swarm of archers surged forward to within range of the walls. Behind them, the spearmen began to advance and the tramp of their sandalled feet shook the air. Eurypylus's voice called out a command and hundreds of bows sang out in reply. Agamemnon and Nestor dived down beneath the parapet as arrows whistled overhead, followed by cries of anguish and despair from the men behind the walls.

The battle had begun.

Chapter Twenty-Two
THE SHADOW OF ACHILLES

What does it mean?' Omeros asked, leaning against the bow rail and staring at the thin columns of smoke twisting up from the shores of Ilium.

'There's been another battle,' Diomedes answered.

'Is it Troy?' Neoptolemus said, shouldering through the crowd of men gathering at the prow of the galley. 'Are we too late?'

He seized hold of the bow rail and glared at the dark crust of land, his face filled with concern that the war might be over and his chance of emulating his father gone.

'Perhaps we are,' Diomedes said, 'but not because Troy has fallen. That smoke's coming from the Greek camp.'

Eperitus put a hand against one of the leather ropes that threaded down from the mast, steadying himself against the roll of the ship. They had sailed through the night, with Odysseus and Sthenelaus navigating their course by the stars as they hurried back to Ilium, and the early morning sun was now rising full in their faces as they forged east across the waves. He shielded his eyes against its glare and tried to make out what the source of the smoke was. Unlike his comrades, to whom the far shore was but a strip of grey cresting the blue of the Aegean, he could see the walls and towers that guarded the Greek camp and the hundreds of black-hulled ships drawn up on the beach behind them. He could see the mounds of burnt wood on the upper reaches of the ridge that hemmed in the camp, from which the dark spires of smoke were rising. And he could see that more columns drifted up from the plain beyond the defences of the Greeks.

'The camp hasn't been destroyed. There's been a battle, though; the smoke is from the funeral pyres of the dead. Some are inside the walls, but some are outside, and that can only mean the camp is under siege.'

182

Odysseus, who had been at the helm with Sthenelaus, now joined them.

'You're right, though where Priam found enough soldiers to launch another attack at this late stage in the war I don't know. But if the Trojans are laying siege to the walls, then we'll be of more use landing further up the coast, beyond the camp, and seeing what we can do from there.'

Diomedes gave him a questioning look.

'With sixty Argives? We'd be better landing in the camp and bolstering the defences.'

'You seem to forget I am with you,' Neoptolemus said. 'The son of Achilles is worth more than sixty Argives, or even six hundred. If there's a Trojan army before the walls of the camp, we should attack them from behind and drive them in panic and slaughter back to their own city.'

Diomedes looked at him for a moment, but despite his greater rank, age and experience decided to concede the point.

'The gods themselves chose you, Neoptolemus,' he said, giving him a slight bow, 'and who am I to question their judgement? If you're ready to stand in your father's footprints, then it will be a pleasure to fight beside you.'

Neoptolemus smiled and gripped Diomedes's hand.

'Then let's arm for battle.'

He set off towards the helm, where his splendid armour was kept hidden beneath drapes of sailcloth. Eperitus looked at Odysseus, who shrugged and turned on his heel, shouting orders for a change of course away from the camp and towards Troy.

As the ship's crew burst into a brief period of high activity, Eperitus went to the bench where his armour was stowed and pulled on his breastplate. Omeros joined him, helping him with the buckles that held the two halves together. Eperitus glanced across at Neoptolemus, who was struggling to fit the bronze cuirass that Hephaistos had crafted in exact mimicry of Achilles's muscular torso. An Argive offered his help – doubtless keen to lay his hands on the beautiful armour – but Neoptolemus refused sharply and struggled on. Not for the first time, Eperitus found himself wondering how Neoptolemus would perform in battle, whether he had inherited Achilles's prowess, pride and thirst for glory, or whether he would wither beneath the great shadow of his father. The only thing Eperitus felt certain of was that Neoptolemus would be a lone warrior, suited more to the heroic duels between champions than the close press of the battle lines, in which each man's life depended as much on his neighbour as himself.

By the time the crew were armed and ready to face whatever lay waiting on the plains of Ilium, the shoreline was close enough for them all to see the beached galleys of the Greek fleet to the south-east, the sprawl of tents beyond them and the defensive walls that had been erected on the ridge above. Long trails of smoke still fed upwards from the pyres of the dead, leaning at diagonals with the prevailing westerly wind. But of a besieging army there was no sign, until the moment the galley began its approach towards a small cove a short march north of the Greek camp. Then they heard the familiar hum of massed arrows and saw the sky above the cliffs to the south-east darken as thousands of missiles filled the air. A sense of haste took hold of the galley as the sail was lowered and the oars thrust through their leather loops into the water. The crew rowed the vessel silently into the cove and the anchor stones were cast into the shallow sea. Then they leapt overboard and splashed towards the narrow semicircle of sand.

Neoptolemus was first to reach the shore and left deep footprints behind him as he sprinted up the beach. He gained the shelf of black rock at the edge of the sand and stopped, waiting, it seemed, for the others to join him. But as Eperitus reached him he realised Neoptolemus's hesitation had been nothing to do with his comrades. He stood with his feet at the lip of a shallow rock pool, staring down at his reflection on its still surface. Eperitus saw the image in the circle of water and frowned in disbelief. The figure was not Neoptolemus but Achilles, with his distinctive golden hair and beard and the unforgettable face that was both terrifying and wonderful to look upon. As the others gathered around, an awed silence fell over them.

'It's the ghost of your father,' Odysseus announced, standing beside Neoptolemus. 'The gods have placed his image in the pool as a sign to you. You must complete the destiny they denied him, Neoptolemus, and bring about the end of Troy.'

'I have no memory of what he looked like,' Neoptolemus said. 'He was just a shadow, flitting about in the furthest corners of my past. And yet I've never been able to escape that shadow. My mother, my aunts and my grandfather were always encouraging me to be like him. And now even the immortals want me to replace the man whom they destroyed.' He set the toe of his sandal against a smooth black pebble and flicked it into the pool, shattering the image in the water. 'Well, we shall see whether I'm worthy of his legacy or not, and whether I can also make a name for *myself*. And the place to begin is atop that ridge.'

He sprang across the pool, seemingly heedless of the weight of his armour or the great ash spear that most men could barely lift, and ran towards the grassy ridge that led to the plains beyond. The others followed, spreading out into a line as they topped the ridge and looking across at the sun-bleached walls of the Greek camp and the dark mass of the Trojan army that lapped about them. They were still some way to the north-west of the raging battle, but they could hear the roar of thousands of voices and the ringing of weapons. Hundreds of ladders were visible against the battlements, where indistinct figures struggled for mastery over each other.

Neoptolemus, who had instinctively knelt down in the high grass to observe the battle, turned as Odysseus, Diomedes and Eperitus joined him. His young eyes were alive with excitement.

'The Trojans are already on the walls. It'll be a fair sprint if you're up to it, but we haven't a moment to lose.'

Diomedes shook his head and pointed at the crowds of Trojan cavalry waiting impatiently behind the mass of attacking spearmen. 'They'd spot us before we could cover half the distance. We'd be cut to pieces on the open plain.'

'We'll follow the gulley,' Odysseus said, indicating the dried up stream that fed down into the cove from the plateau. It curved eastward in a thin line that swept behind the waiting cavalry, reaching to within a spear's throw of them before veering off to the north. Though the water had disappeared with the summer sun, the tall grasses that marked its course would provide them with reasonable cover if they kept their heads low.

Neoptolemus clearly disliked the notion of sneaking into a fight, but gave a reluctant nod and followed Odysseus at a stoop along the shallow gulley. The rest trailed after them, over sixty in all, and the clatter of their armour and weapons earned stern rebukes from Diomedes and Sthenelaus as they brought up the rear. Last of all was Eperitus, who had lingered as long as possible while his sharp eyes swept the ranks of restless horsemen in search of Apheidas. His father was the commander of the Trojan cavalry, and though Eperitus knew he had to be somewhere on the battlefield, he was unable to pick out the hated figure from among the multitude of the enemy. Clutching his spears in his hand, he followed Sthenelaus into the narrow defile.

Fortunately, the din of the battle covered the sound of their approach and the hundreds of horsemen did not spot them through the tall brown grass as they traced the course of the dead stream to a point behind the nearest squadron. As the line of spearmen halted and lay down in the grass, Eperitus could see the backs of their enemies' helmeted heads as they watched the battle raging on the walls. Then there was a shout of excitement and the Trojan cavalry followed it with a cheer. Eperitus dared to raise his head above the cover of the grass and saw the dust shaking from the timbers of one of the gates as it opened from within. But no force of Greeks came sallying forth. As the horsemen had guessed, the gates had been captured by the spearmen who had scaled the walls and now a flood of their comrades were pouring in through the breached defences.

Neoptolemus chose that moment to rise to his feet. Despite the dust, his armour gleamed in the morning sun and Eperitus could see the figures moving within the concentric circles of his shield. The red plume of the helmet was like a river of blood flowing over the nape of his neck and down the back of his bronze cuirass. As he stood the other Greeks joined him, climbing awkwardly to their feet beneath their unwieldy armour. The line of warriors moved their shields onto their arms and readied their spears. Odysseus strode forward through the grass, raising his hand high above his head, and still the Greeks had not been noticed. Eperitus pressed his fingers to the picture of a white hart on the inside of his shield, a reminder of his daughter Iphigenia, the first victim of the war against Troy. Cupping a spear in his right hand, he took aim at a horseman who was unnervingly close now that he had emerged from the protection of the gulley.

It was then that one of the Trojans turned and saw the newcomers. Confused as to why a group of spearmen were behind the cavalry and not in the thick of the fighting, he reined his horse about and trotted towards them for a closer look. An expression of alarm spread across his features and he pulled up sharply, turning his mount to the left. He shouted a warning to his countrymen, just as Neoptolemus ran forward and hurled his father's spear at him. The bronze point drove clean through his leather cuirass and pulled him bodily from his horse, sending him crashing to the ground. Neoptolemus yelled in triumph and ran to retrieve his spear from his first kill. Several cavalrymen turned at the commotion behind them, their faces instantly transformed with fear at the sight of the enemy warriors. Then Odysseus dropped his hand and sixty spears flew through the air towards the startled Trojans.

Chapter Twenty-Three

NEOPTOLEMUS & EURYPYLUS

The volley of spears was followed by the anguished cries of men and the whinnies of dying horses. Panic tore through the orderly ranks of the Trojans as mounts crashed to the ground in clouds of dust and riders struggled to control their startled beasts. Eperitus's weapon had hit the base of his target's spine, sending him twisting in bloody agony from the back of his horse. Gripping his remaining spear, he joined the Argives and Ithacans as they rushed the confused cavalrymen. Odysseus and Diomedes led the charging Greeks, but ahead of them all was Neoptolemus, his father's spear retrieved and held out before him. A Trojan noble, resplendent in his cuirass of overlapping bronze scales and his boars' tusk helmet, dug his heels into his horse's flanks and came out to meet him. Neoptolemus's spear found his chest with stunning speed and the man toppled back from his horse, a look of shock on his face. In a single, fluid movement, Neoptolemus drew out his sword and hewed the man's head from his shoulders. Then the line of advancing Greeks swept past him and smashed into the frightened mass of their enemies.

Eperitus's weapon found the throat of an ageing rider, dyeing his white beard red as the blood gushed out over his chest. He sensed a looming presence to his left and turned with his shield to meet the jabbing spear point of another horseman. The man's thrust lacked the momentum of a full charge, though, and was easily brushed aside as Eperitus's spear simultaneously found his attacker's upper arm, tearing through the unprotected muscle. Dropping his weapon with a cry of pain, the Trojan flicked back his heels and sent his mount galloping out of the melee and away to safety across the plain.

Others were not so fortunate. The ruin of dead horses and riders was all about, but the worst of the destruction was piled around

Neoptolemus. Standing amid the corpses of men and beasts, he dealt out death with a speed and ferocity that reminded Eperitus of Achilles. He wielded the great shield as if it were a wooden toy, parrying every blow that his attackers dared aim at him, while his sword found their flesh again and again until it was running with gore. Then, as Eperitus watched in silent admiration, someone pointed at the god-made armour that had so awed and terrified the Trojans in earlier battles. A cry of dismay went up and Neoptolemus's enemies fell back, leaving a ring of annihilation around him. The shout was repeated, spreading quickly through the hundreds of closely packed horsemen, and though they outnumbered their foes several times over they began to withdraw from the fight, some of the horses rearing and flailing the air in panic as they retreated. The shouts were in the Trojan tongue, but Eperitus understood them and smiled.

'Achilles! Achilles has returned from the dead!'

Now the mauled cavalry were streaming away, fleeing in horror at the return of the man they feared more than any other – a man who had seemingly defeated death itself and come back from the halls of Hades. The infantry and archers that still seethed about the walls like boiling water now glanced uncertainly over their shoulders, seeing hundreds of horsemen break and flee with the name of Achilles on their lips. And then, out of the dust of battle strode the very image of the dread warrior, his armour gleaming as he tugged his spear from the chest of one of his victims. A line of warriors followed in his wake, their number exaggerated by fear and the swirling dust, so that the Trojans began to feel uncertain of the victory that for a moment they thought they had won. All this Eperitus could see in the faces that were now turned towards them, and in an instant he understood the value of Neoptolemus – this second Achilles – and why he would be so important to the final destruction of Troy.

But they had gained only a minor success, temporarily driving away a company of cavalry and dinting the confidence of their enemies; the greater battle was far from over. As the rear ranks of the Trojan foot soldiers turned their shields, spears and bows towards the newcomers, a second unit of cavalry began forming up to charge. Eperitus glanced across at Odysseus, flanked on either side by Polites, Eurybates and Omeros, their spears tipped with dark blood. The king caught his gaze and raised an eyebrow in typically understated fashion at their dilemma.

As Neoptolemus saw the forces gathering against them he laughed aloud, his veins flowing with reckless confidence, as if he had not only inherited his father's armour but his indestructibility also. Levelling his great ash spear above his shoulder, he cast it at the line of cavalry and plucked a rider from his mount, sending him tumbling to his ruin in the dust.

A shout of anger erupted from the Trojans. A single horseman burst from the mass of beasts and men and galloped at the lone figure of Neoptolemus, a long spear couched beneath his arm and aimed at the warrior's chest. Eperitus saw him and cursed: it was Apheidas. For a moment he was at a loss, wanting to see his father dead and yet not by the hand of Neoptolemus, or anyone other than himself. The Trojan cavalry were charging in the wake of their commander and Eperitus heard the voice of Diomedes calling for his men to close ranks. On the walls, Trojans and Greeks cried out the name of Achilles – the former in dismay and the latter as a rallying cry – and the fighting broke out again with renewed vigour. Then, as Eperitus seized his spear and resolved to run out to face his father, Odysseus grabbed him and pulled him back. Eperitus tried to release himself, but the king held him tight and pressed the whiskers of his beard close to his ear, so that he would be heard over the din of battle.

'It's too late,' he said, guessing what was on his captain's mind. 'Run out there now and you'll be killed for certain. All you can do is ask the gods to save him for you, if that's what you want.'

Eperitus watched Apheidas galloping down on Neoptolemus, the wind trailing his hair and cloak behind him, and knew Odysseus spoke the truth. With a bitter scowl, he called on Athena to protect the man whose death he had craved all his adult life, promising her the sacrifice of an unblemished lamb if she saved him from Achilles's son. No sooner had he spat the words from his mouth than the terrifying hum of hundreds of bowstrings filled the air. The Greeks instinctively ducked behind their shields, but their caution was unnecessary: the Trojan archers had loosed their arrows at the reincarnation of Achilles, whose unexpected appearance had filled them with dread and a determination to send him back to the Underworld. The murderous shafts poured towards the splendidly armoured figure, forcing Apheidas to break off his charge and steer his mount away from the fall of shot. Neoptolemus crouched low behind his shield, which no earthly arrow could pierce, then rose to his feet again in defiance of the archers and the fast-approaching cavalry. An instant later, he was swallowed up by the wall of charging horses.

Apheidas – still ignorant of his son's presence – now sent his black stallion galloping towards the knot of enemy spearmen. The rest of his command followed, intent on wiping the small band of Greeks out of existence. While the Argives and Ithacans instinctively closed ranks to form a circular buttress against the fast-approaching cavalry, Eperitus rushed out to meet his father, determined to avenge the deaths of King Pandion and Arceisius. More than ever now he regretted that the spear of Ares had been left back in Pelops's tomb. Its unerring accuracy would have brought Apheidas down in the dust, even at that distance, but Agamemnon had given strict orders that his ancestor's crypt was not to be plundered. And so Eperitus pulled his spear behind his shoulder, aimed at his father's chest and waited for him to come nearer.

The second volley of arrows hit the Greeks with a silent whisper. Diomedes and Odysseus had shouted warnings, but Eperitus – aware of nothing but the charging figure of his father – did not realise his danger until the bronze tip of an arrow tore into the muscle of his right thigh. It was as if his leg had been knocked from beneath him by a giant hammer, toppling him backwards so that his armoured body met the ground with a thud. He lay there like a stricken titan, momentarily paralysed by the pain of his wound and the approach of unconsciousness. His vision began to fade, like a funnel into which a dark liquid was being poured, and he was dimly aware of the thunder of hooves rising up through the ground and into his ribs. There was a mingled odour of dust, sweat and horses, too, and he knew he only had moments now to live.

Then a strong hand seized the back of his breastplate – the thick knuckles digging into the nape of his neck – and began dragging him at speed through the long grass. His vision cleared again, and he almost shouted in terror as he saw the Trojan cavalry bearing down on him less than a spear's cast away, their well-bred mounts steaming and snorting as their riders drove them madly on into battle. More hands were hooked beneath Eperitus's shoulders and he was hauled rapidly through a gap in the Greek line, before being dropped hastily into the grass. He caught a brief sight of Eurybates and Omeros standing over him, and then Polites – whose vast strength had pulled him to safety –

before the Ithacans were turning and rejoining the double-ranked ring of Argives, ready to meet the Trojan onslaught.

Grimacing with pain, Eperitus drew himself up on one elbow and placed a hand on the sword slung beneath his left arm. The Greeks had one hope if they were to survive the charge – to stand firm and not flee, whatever their impulses might scream at them to do. It was rare that a horse would ride into an unbroken barrier of shields and spears; instead, its instincts would drive it around the sides with the rest of the herd, losing the impact of the charge and compelling its rider to attack his enemy side-on. But if one man in the shield wall lost his courage and ran, the gap he left would be like an open gate, inviting the cavalry to surge in and tear the Greeks apart from within. Eperitus had seen it happen on many occasions, and the memory of those massacres made him tense as the din of hooves reached its climax.

The Greeks held their nerve. The vast body of horses rushed past and around them, accompanied by the shouts and curses of their riders. A spear thudded into the ground beside Eperitus and he felt a body crash down behind him, though whether Greek or Trojan he could not tell in the confusion. A mounted warrior appeared, framed in the circle of blue sky above the heads of Omeros and Polites, but Eurybates pierced his throat with his spear. Suddenly there were horsemen on every side, hacking at the shields and spear points of the Greeks. The clang of bronze filled the air and for a while Eperitus feared his comrades would be overwhelmed by the sheer number of Trojans. But the horsemen were disadvantaged by having to present their unshielded flanks to the Greeks in order to wield their spears and swords, and many were brought down. After a brief but fierce fight, Eperitus heard the unmistakeable voice of his father calling out from behind them. The Trojans began to pull away.

Now a shadow fell across him and he looked up to see the outline of Odysseus, black against the slowly rising sun. He knelt down without a word and inspected his friend's leg. The arrow was still buried in the muscle at the back of his thigh, and Odysseus probed the area gently with his fingertips, causing Eperitus to wince.

'Despite your best efforts to kill yourself,' the king commented, still studiously examining the wound, 'it seems the gods have taken mercy on you. The arrow appears to have missed the bone and the main arteries, but we're in the middle of a battle and we can't just leave it in there.'

'What about the horsemen?'

'They've more important things than us to worry about, now. The Greeks have fought their way back out of the gates and are counter-attacking, led by Agamemnon and Menelaus.'

'And my father?'

Odysseus took out his dagger and sliced the flight from the back of the arrow, before cutting off a strip of cloth from a dead man's cloak. He called to Polites and nodded towards Eperitus. Then, as Polites pinned Eperitus's arms irresistibly to his sides, Odysseus seized the shaft of the arrow and pushed it through the other side of his thigh. Eperitus cried out as a surge of fresh pain racked his body, and then blackness took him. He was woken again by the slap of cold water on his face and the sight of Odysseus holding the bloodied dart before his eyes. Polites was busily wrapping the strip of cloth about his thigh.

'It would have caused more damage pulling it out,' Odysseus said apologetically, tapping the barbed arrowhead with his finger. 'And now we have to get that wound cleaned and treated, before it gets infected. Can you ride a horse?'

As he spoke, Eurybates appeared leading a tall brown mare, a survivor of the Trojan cavalry charge. Its neck was crimson with blood, but the animal seemed unhurt.

'Yes – and fight from it, too,' Eperitus answered, sitting up with a grimace. 'Where're my spear and shield?'

'We'll find them for you, when the battle's over,' Odysseus said. 'First you need to get into the camp and have that leg properly cared for.'

Polites lifted him easily onto the back of the horse and passed him the reins. Looking quickly about, Eperitus could see the Argives had lost a few men to the attack but were standing firm beneath the command of Diomedes. Meanwhile, the battle around the walls of the camp had grown in fury. The parapet had been cleansed of Trojans and was now manned by Greek archers – led by Philoctetes – who were exchanging fire with the Trojan skirmishers on the plain below. Between them, the Greeks under Agamemnon and Menelaus had temporarily regained the gates, but had been pushed back by the cavalry while Eurypylus and Deiphobus – two figures in flashing armour at the forefront of the Trojan army – rallied their spearmen for another attack. Apheidas was nowhere to be seen, but to Eperitus's amazement he saw a figure rise from a pile of dead horses and men further back on the battlefield. He was covered in blood and dust, and staggered drunkenly as he searched for something among the bodies around him, but the red plume of his helmet and the gleam of his great shield – despite its covering of filth and gore – put the man's identity beyond doubt. Somehow Neoptolemus had survived the wall of Trojan cavalry. He plucked his father's great ash spear from the body of a dead horse and turned to face the struggle before the walls. As he did so, a soldier on the battlements spotted him and called out the name of Achilles. Others joined in the cry and the spearmen under Eurypylus and Deiphobus looked over their shoulders in awe, unable to believe that the man who had struck fear into their hearts earlier had risen yet again from the dead.

The shock did not last long. Hundreds of archers turned their arrows away from the walls of the camp and aimed them instead at Neoptolemus. Before they could loose their lethal darts, though, Eurypylus shouted a deep-voiced command and every bow was lowered. Behind him, the Trojan cavalry broke off their attack on the Greeks and withdrew. The clash of weapons ceased altogether and men fell silent as Eurypylus walked towards the lone warrior. Deiphobus followed him and took him by the arm, speaking quietly but urgently in his ear. Eurypylus shrugged him off with an irritated gesture then strode out onto the empty plain, raising his spear above his head.

'I am Eurypylus, son of Telephus, of the line of Heracles,' he announced in Greek. 'If the voices on the walls are to be believed, you are Achilles, son of Peleus. But Achilles fell to the arrows of Paris and his ghost is condemned to eternity in the Chambers of Decay, so who are you? Declare your name and lineage, so I can know whether you're worthy of that armour you wear, which I will soon be claiming for myself.'

'I've heard your name spoken back home on Scyros,' Neoptolemus replied. 'There they say you are a coward, watching from behind your mother's skirts as your grandfather's kingdom is slowly strangled to death. Well, I see the rumours aren't entirely true: you've found the stomach to fight at least, though whether it was your decision or your mother's I cannot tell.

'As for me, I am Neoptolemus, son of Achilles. This armour you covet once belonged to him, but now it is mine. Vain words alone will not change that, Eurypylus, so let's see how well your mother taught you to fight.'

Eurypylus gave a sneering laugh. 'Better than your father taught you, boy.'

Tossing his spear into the air and catching it, he drew it back and launched it with a single, easy motion. Neoptolemus raised his shield just in time, deflecting the great bronze point so that it skipped over his head and clattered through the parched grass behind. Neoptolemus lowered his shield again and stared hard at Eurypylus, as if the Mysian king had thrown nothing more than an insult. Then, with a cry of pure hatred, he charged.

Eurypylus slid his sword from its scabbard and advanced to meet his opponent. Neoptolemus lunged at him with his father's monstrous spear, ripping the shield from the Mysian's shoulder and almost pulling his arm out of its socket. Eurypylus gave a roar of pain, which quickly turned to anger as he swung his sword at the younger warrior's head. Neoptolemus caught the blow on his shield and the clang of bronze echoed back from the walls of the camp. He stabbed out with the point of his spear, missing Eurypylus's abdomen by a fraction as the king twisted aside and backed away.

The watching armies, which for a few moments had been awed into silence, now shouted encouragement and cheered as the two men circled each other, seeking opportunities to attack. A Mysian soldier tossed his shield out into the long grass and Eurypylus ran towards it, pursued by Neoptolemus. He snatched up the leather and wicker disc just in time to push aside the thrust of the Greek's spear, then leapt forward with the tip of his sword. It beat Neoptolemus's guard, slipping inside the edge of his shield and finding his bronze cuirass. But the armour that Neoptolemus wore had not been forged by men in the fires of an earthly smithy. It was the work of the smith-god, Hephaistos, and had never been pierced by any weapon. It turned the point of Eurypylus's sword with a flash of sparks and the king stepped away in dismay and wonder. Neoptolemus, too, fell back a few paces, looking down at himself as if expecting to see his life's blood pouring from him. When he realised the invulnerability of his armour, his shock quickly turned to triumph. Gripping the shaft of his father's spear with both hands, he lunged at Eurypylus. The Mysian raised his shield in

defence, but the layered oxhide was no match for the cruel bronze
point or the ruthless strength behind it. The spear punched through
the shield and found the base of Eurypylus's throat, passing through
the spinal cord with such force that his head was almost torn from his
shoulders. The onlookers fell suddenly silent, and as Neoptolemus
withdrew his spear and his victim's body slumped lifeless to the ground
the Trojans cried out in grief, while the Greeks shouted to the skies in
exultation. Achilles's son drew his sword and straddled the body of
Eurypylus, taking three blows to hack off the head before lifting it by
the plume of its helmet so that everyone could witness his victory.

Now the battle recommenced with a fury. A hum of bowstrings
drove away the groans and cheers of the two sides and the air above
the Greek walls was momentarily dark with arrows, before the deadly
rain fell down among the unprepared ranks of Trojans and Mysians.
Many fell, the dead in silence and the wounded in shrieks of pain.
Other voices followed, but these were the roars of the Greeks as they
charged into their shocked enemies. The Trojan archers released a
hurried volley, felling several, but not enough to stop the terrifying
assault. Moments later the spearmen of Mycenae, Sparta, Corinth and
a dozen other nations were driving the centre of the Trojan line back
with great slaughter. From his vantage point, Eperitus could see
Agamemnon and Menelaus in the forefront of the attack, with
Idomeneus the Cretan and Menestheus the Athenian leading the fight
on each flank. Neoptolemus abandoned the armour he had been
stripping from Eurypylus, unable to resist launching his own onslaught
against the rear of the enemy line. Deiphobus, alone now in command
of the Trojans and their allies, could do nothing to halt the inevitable
disintegration of his army. At first, small groups broke and fled; then,
as the Greeks poured through the rents in their enemies' ranks, the rest
took flight.

'Go now,' Odysseus shouted to Eperitus over the din of battle. 'Find
Podaleirius or another healer. I don't want to lose you to a mere flesh
wound.'

He slapped the hind quarters of the horse and sent it leaping
forward. Eperitus, who had ridden horses since childhood in Alybas,
took charge of the frightened animal and directed it towards the gates
where the Greeks were still pouring thick and furious from their camp.
Then, as he rode between fleeing Trojans and their pursuers, a single

horn blew a long note that rose above the clamour of war and turned many heads towards its source. Eperitus glanced to his left and saw the ranks of the Trojan cavalry, who had been pulled from the chaos of battle and reformed into a controlled fighting unit. The great mass of horses and men sprang forward, building up momentum as they rode with gathering speed towards the battle. At their head was Apheidas, charging to the rescue of his retreating countrymen as he had done so many times before. And as Eperitus's eyes fell upon his father, he cast aside any thought of returning to the Greek camp. Drawing his sword, he pressed his heels back into the flanks of his mount and sent it galloping at the wall of approaching cavalry.

Apheidas saw him almost immediately. Abandoning all consideration for the rest of the battle, he steered his black stallion towards his son and leaned across its neck with his sword held at arm's length before him. While the mass of horsemen behind him raced on towards the Greek spearmen – whose flank had been left exposed by Agamemnon's headlong pursuit of the enemy infantry – a group of half a dozen riders broke off to follow their leader.

Eperitus cared little for the fact he was now facing seven horsemen, or that his chances of survival were small. With his sword outstretched before him, he focussed on his father and kicked back hard. But he had forgotten the wound in his thigh, which had been rapidly draining his strength since Odysseus had pushed the arrow out of the flesh. His blood-soaked leg now gave beneath the effort and a great stab of pain surged up through his body, weakening his hold on his horse. The last thing he saw before his vision went black and he slid from the galloping mount was Apheidas's snarling grin and the gleam of sunlight flashing from his blade.

book

THREE

Chapter Twenty-Four
THE KEROSIA

L aertes spat on the ground and shook a gnarled fist at Eupeithes. 'My son *will* return, and when he finds out what you've been up to in his absence he'll make sure you and all these cronies of yours are kicked off the Kerosia for good. That's if he doesn't just have you executed, like he should have done twenty years ago!'

'Sit back down you old fool!' Antinous growled, half rising from his chair.

'Watch what comes out of your mouth, lad,' warned Oenops, laying a hand on the youngest member of the Kerosia's shoulder and easing him back into his seat. 'Remember Laertes was once our king.'

'What does his generation care for rightful kings?' Laertes said dismissively. 'And least of all a son of Eupeithes.'

'My friends,' Penelope interjected, 'be calm and respect the rules of this council.'

She looked at the two old enemies who were staring at each other with open animosity. Eupeithes stood to her left with the speaker's staff clutched in his hand as if it were a king's sceptre, his usually pallid complexion warm and flushed from the heat of the central hearth. On the other side of the flames was the bent form of Laertes, glaring with fierce hatred at the man who had once tried to usurp his throne when he had been king of Ithaca. When Penelope had first seen her father-in-law he had been pale-skinned with spindly legs and a bloated stomach, more like an upended frog than a king. Since ceding power to his son, though, he had retired to his farm with Anticleia, his wife, and thrown himself into the hard labour of growing crops and keeping livestock. Now his distended belly had shrunk to a paunch and his flaccid muscles had become as firm as knotted rope. With his sunburnt skin he looked like the root of an old tree standing in the middle of the great hall, tough and immovable.

'Father,' Penelope said, 'Eupeithes has the speaker's staff. You must return to your seat. Please.'

Laertes sat back down with a show of reluctance and Eupeithes stepped forward into the space he had vacated.

'Whatever foolish hopes some of us may be clinging on to, it's clear to me that we cannot wait forever for Odysseus to return. The world beyond our little group of islands is changing rapidly. Outsiders are beginning to enter Greece from the distant north. They are allowed to settle and establish themselves because the mainland kingdoms are too weak to throw them out. It won't be long before they find their way here. Ithaca needs strong, singular leadership if it is to survive.'

'Perhaps you should claim the throne for yourself,' Laertes sneered, 'bringing in Taphians like you did before.'

Eupeithes ignored him and looked at Penelope. 'I have a proposal, my lady, and Oenops, Polyctor and Antinous are in full agreement with me. We feel that if Odysseus does not return within two years, he must be assumed to have perished and you must remarry for the good of Ithaca. According to our ancient laws, your new husband will then become king in Odysseus's place.'

'Never!' Laertes barked.

Even Mentor, who had sat listening uneasily to Eupeithes's slow build-up throughout the morning, rose from his chair with a look of fierce disapproval on his handsome features.

'That's preposterous! What about Telemachus, Odysseus's rightful heir? The law you quote depends on the queen *agreeing* to remarry, and Penelope would never deny her son his birthright.'

'Telemachus is still a boy,' Eupeithes retorted. 'He won't come of age for another eleven years, and Ithaca can't wait that long for a king. If Penelope's new husband – our new king – dies before then and leaves no offspring of his own, *then* Telemachus can inherit the throne.'

'You have a nerve, Eupeithes, suggesting such a thing before *me*,' Penelope said, rising from her seat. 'You act as if Odysseus is dead already! How can you expect me to marry another man when my husband is still alive? You certainly can't *force* me to do such a thing!'

Eupeithes smiled patiently at the queen.

'If I'm blunt, then it's because something needs to be done to protect the kingdom from spiralling into chaos. We can't wait forever for Odysseus to return. You must know the nobility are growing restless. They want proper leadership.'

'Are you *threatening* me, Eupeithes?' Penelope asked. 'If you want proper leadership, why don't you introduce a law that simply allows the Kerosia to elect a new king? If you're so determined to seize power, why do you need me anyway?'

'The Kerosia doesn't have that power and Eupeithes knows it,' said Mentor. 'He needs you for legitimacy, my lady. The people won't support an elected king, only one with a lawful connection to the royal line – one chosen by you. And after what happened the last time he tried to take the throne by force, he wouldn't dare seize power again without the support of the people.'

'He wants to put his own son on the throne,' Laertes said, looking at Penelope. 'It's obvious he'll insist you marry Antinous. Don't let him, Daughter.'

'Don't be ridiculous,' Eupeithes defended himself. 'Penelope will choose her own husband. I will not stand accused of forcing my own son onto the throne. Any Ithacan would be able to plead for Penelope's hand.'

'And if I refused?' she asked, tartly. 'If I decided never to remarry, regardless of whether my husband is *assumed to have perished* or not?'

'Then I cannot be answerable for the consequences. If that meant civil war and the shedding of innocent blood, then you would only have yourself to blame.'

Penelope sat down and stared at Eupeithes, but his face was so full of false concern that she could not bear to look at him any longer and turned her eyes to the open doors of the great hall, through which she could see the bright sunlight filling the courtyard. She thought of Odysseus, far away in Troy. She wondered what he would think of the way she had allowed the Kerosia to slip from her control, and of her decision to send Telemachus into virtual exile in Sparta. One thing she could be sure of, though, was that he would expect her not to give up. Things were darker now than they had been in all the years since her husband's departure, but she still had the upper hand. The people of Ithaca supported Odysseus, and sooner or later the king would return. Until then, it was her duty to buy time and delay Eupeithes's sudden push for power. And at all costs, she had to avoid forcing the old traitor into resorting to arms. If *he* knew the consequences of usurping power, there were plenty around him who did *not*. They would demand a show of strength if Eupeithes could not promise them a clear route to the throne. And she was the only one who could offer him that.

'You leave me no choice, Eupeithes. I agree to your proposal.'

A wide smile spread across the merchant's face, while behind him Antinous, Polyctor and Oenops congratulated each other openly with handshakes and pats on the back. Mentor kept his silence out of respect for the queen, though his frown spoke of his disapproval. Laertes simply shook his head.

'This is folly, Daughter. I'm not so old and bitter that I don't know what you're thinking. I was king myself not so long ago, and I haven't forgotten what it's like to have the threat of civil war hanging over my people. But to just give in to these pretenders? There are better ways to prevent bloodshed.'

'But you didn't find them when you were king, did you Father. And as long as I am queen, I will not sit by and watch Ithaca fall back into division and war.'

'Then I hope you know what you're doing, Penelope,' he said

'I hope so too.'

'More wine,' Eupeithes commanded the servants waiting in the shadows beyond the circle of chairs. 'We must seal your agreement with an oath before it is announced to the people.'

The members of the Kerosia raised their cups to be refilled. As one of the maids poured wine into Antinous's krater, Penelope saw their eyes meet and the flicker of a smile cross the young girl's lips. Melantho was only recently married – to Arceisius, Eperitus's squire, before his return to Troy – and yet the queen knew in an instant she was sleeping with Eupeithes's son. The thought made her sad for Arceisius, and even angrier with the war that had brought so evil a legacy upon Greece.

After her own cup had been refilled, she watched Eupeithes pour a libation into the flames and lift his krater into the air. Oenops, Polyctor and Antinous did the same and were reluctantly followed by Mentor and Laertes. Penelope remained in her chair, holding her krater firmly in her lap.

'If I'm to agree to marry another man,' she said, 'it can only be on one condition.'

'It's too late for that now,' Eupeithes said.

'Not until this wine touches my lips.'

'Then what is it?' he snapped. 'What condition must I agree to to obtain your promise?'

'You suggest we should presume Odysseus is dead after two years. That's too vague. I say we consult the oracle at Mount Parnassus, to ask the Pythoness when my husband will return. If he has not returned by the predicted date, then I will willingly remarry.'

'And if the oracle says he will never return?'

'Then I will choose a new husband within the year.'

Antinous stood up angrily.

'I protest. She's trying to delay –'

'Shut up and sit down,' his father ordered.

Penelope saw the doubt in Eupeithes's eyes and held out her hands imploringly towards him.

'Think about what I'm saying. If any new king is to hold power, he must have unassailable legitimacy. If I remarry in two years' time, the people might accept my husband for a while, but won't their eyes always be gazing towards the distant horizon, wondering when the true king will return? But if we consult the Pythoness and she says Odysseus will *never* return, or if he doesn't come back by the prophesied date, then everyone will know the new king has the approval of the gods. They'll accept Odysseus is never coming home and will welcome my new husband openly.'

Eupeithes's eyes narrowed as he pondered Penelope's words, but he did not have to think for long.

'You speak wisely, my queen, and I accept your condition. Antinous and Mentor will go to Mount Parnassus, escorted by an armed guard. That way, there will be plenty of witnesses to the oracle and no-one can change the Pythoness's prophetic words to suit their own ends. Agreed?'

Penelope nodded and sat down again, hoping her gamble would pay off.

Chapter Twenty-Five
PRISONER OF APHEIDAS

Eperitus woke slowly, drawn out of his dream by the mingled aromas of woodsmoke and the scent of flowers. He heard the crackle and spit of a fire and beneath it the whisper of soft voices. His eyelids were heavy – too heavy yet to open – and he could detect little or no light through the thin layers of skin. There was a throbbing ache inside his head that seemed to be faintly echoed by every muscle in his body, and as he felt the warm furs across his naked chest and the pliant mattress beneath him he wondered whether he was back in his hut in the Greek camp. But as his confused mind began to read and order the signals his senses were feeding it, a deeper instinct informed him that he was not in his hut or anywhere else he recognised. Then the lazy fumbling of his senses was trumped by the recollection of his father's face, charging at him with his sword drawn. His eyes flashed open and he tried to sit up.

It was as if a strong man was holding each of his limbs, pinning them to the table and defeating every effort he made to rise. As he fought his weakness for a second time, the figure of a woman appeared above him. She laid a gentle hand upon his chest, easing him back down to the mattress, and with her other hand placed a damp cloth on his temple.

'Be still,' she said firmly in accented Greek. 'Your wounds have weakened you. There is no point in fighting them.'

Her face was old and soft, though lined with concern, and her grey hair was tied up in a bun at the back of her head. She was kneeling beside him and high above her he could see a shadowy ceiling, where faded murals of the moon and stars were barely visible through a fine haze of smoke. He could also see the tops of the four wooden pillars that supported the roof, as well as the upper reaches of plastered walls where paintings of tall, indistinct figures twitched in the firelight. It was a hall of some kind, confirming to him that he was not back in the Greek camp. The woman's accent, he noted, was Trojan, but that meant little when almost all the slaves owned by the Greeks were from Ilium.

'Where am I?'

'You are in Troy, in the house of my master.'

Troy. The word had a crushing effect on his spirit. Somehow, he had been captured and taken back to the city of his enemies. For all he knew, the battle could have ended in a Trojan victory and his countrymen might all be slain, prisoners like himself, or sailing back across the Aegean to Greece in defeat. If that was the case, he hoped that Odysseus and the rest of the Ithacans had been able to slip away in time.

'Then the battle was lost and the Trojans were victorious?'

The old woman shook her head.

'It ended in the same way as all its predecessors – the plain full of dead men and both armies licking their wounds behind the safety of their respective walls. And don't ask me to tell you what happened,' she said, intercepting his next question. 'I don't know and I don't much care.'

'Then tell me your name.'

'I am Clymene,' the woman said.

The name was common enough, but Eperitus followed his instincts.

'Palamedes's mother?'

'Yes,' she answered, a little surprised that he knew of her. Then her attitude stiffened. 'You Greeks stoned him to death.'

Eperitus felt a pang of guilt as he recalled how Odysseus had brought about Palamedes's execution, after discovering the Nauplian prince was secretly passing Agamemnon's strategies to the Trojans. Only as Eperitus had escorted him to his death did he reveal that his mother was a servant woman in Troy – a Trojan herself – and that Apheidas had threatened to kill her if Palamedes did not betray his fellow Greeks. As the offspring of Greek and Trojan parents himself, Eperitus had sympathised with Palamedes, despite his treachery.

'I had no part in his stoning,' he said, 'though I was the one who escorted him to his execution. It was then he told me about you and how he had been forced to betray Agamemnon for your sake. I pitied him and he made me promise to protect you if the Greeks ever sacked Troy.'

'Then his last thoughts were of me,' Clymene said. There were already tears in her eyes at the mention of her dead son. 'Tell me, was his death –'

'It was quick,' he said, recalling how the rocks hurled by the Greek kings had split his skin and cracked his bones until he was no longer recognisable as a human being. They were silent for a while before Eperitus spoke again. 'Tell me something, Clymene: are you still Apheidas's servant?'

She looked away uncomfortably and nodded. 'Yes, my lord, and you are a prisoner in your father's house. He brought you back from the battlefield, even while his horsemen were still covering the long retreat to Troy. You had many cuts and bruises, gained falling from a horse – or so he told us – though by the blessing of some god your bones were not broken. You also had an arrow wound in your leg, and that was more serious. He gave you into our care and threatened us both with death if we did not save you; so we have tended your wounds for two days and a night while you slept, and you are already making a quick recovery.'

'Then you have my thanks, Clymene. But you say there were two of you.'

'Mine was the knowledge that healed your wounds, but the care – the love – that tended to them without resting was –'

'Was mine.'

Eperitus recognised the voice, and this time as he struggled to sit up Clymene helped to lift him onto one elbow. He looked around the shadowy hall – by the darkness he knew it had to be late evening of the day after the battle – seeing the fire blazing in the hearth and noting the armed guard standing at a nearby doorway. And then he saw her.

Astynome stood in the shadows a few paces behind Clymene, dressed in a simple white chiton that did little to hide the outline of the tall, slim body he knew so intimately. Her hair hung down over her shoulders in broad black tangles, framing the fine features of the face he had fallen in love with: the full lips that had declared her love for him in words and kisses; the small nose and smooth cheekbones he had once touched with such affection; and the dark eyes that had looked into his with real longing, but had kept from him the secrets of her traitor's heart. As they looked at him now he felt his veins flush with bitterness at the memory of her betrayal. Yet his anger could not completely conquer his desire to reach out and touch her, to hold her again and pretend nothing had ever come between them. For though she had been sent as a snare to draw him into his father's clutches, she had instead caught him up in her own plans – plans for a home and a family, away from the wars and politics of more powerful men. For a while he had glimpsed an alternative to the violent and glorious, but ultimately lonely, life of a warrior, only to find that the woman who had sold it to him was a liar.

'I have been at your side ever since Apheidas brought you wounded and unconscious from the battlefield,' Astynome said, leaving the shadows and walking to his side. As she knelt beside him, Clymene stood and moved back. 'I haven't left you for a moment, unless it was to fetch water or clean bandages. I even slept beside you last night, Eperitus, with my head against your shoulder and my arm across your chest.'

She smiled as she spoke, almost forgetting he was now awake as she reached out to touch his muscular arm. He grabbed her wrist, making her gasp as she felt the anger in his grip.

'Save me the mock affection. Whatever care you have administered was given on the orders of your master, not out of concern for me. If you had loved me, Astynome, you would have let me die; better that than to live as a prisoner of my father.'

'Let you die? Not while it was in my power to save you. Besides, Apheidas may have commanded me to keep you alive on pain of death, but the prayers I've given for your life and the offerings that I sent to the temple of Athena were my own. I love you, Eperitus, even if you have learned to hate me.'

'You were sent by my father to lead me into a trap!'

'I didn't know you then. When we first met, I was a loyal Trojan doing my lord's bidding, under the illusion it would bring about the end of the war.' She slipped her wrist from his grip and took his hand. 'And then I fell in love with you.'

Eperitus sensed the walls of his fury bend beneath the touch of her warm fingers. He felt a powerful urge to take her in his arms and kiss her, healing the wounds she had inflicted on him. But his warrior's caution maintained its defences against her, knowing she had deceived him once before. He took his hand from hers.

'If you loved me, why did you continue your deceit? You could have told me the truth, but you chose to carry out my father's commands to the very end.'

'Weren't you listening, that night at the temple of Thymbrean Apollo?' she asked, her tone sharp with reciprocal anger. 'Did you not hear, or did you not *want* to hear? I didn't know he was planning to betray Troy to the Greeks in return for Priam's throne, or that you were to be a pawn in his ambitions. When he told me he could make you join the Trojans and put an end to the war I trusted him, and that's why I carried on with his plan. And what choice did I have? He is my master: if I had refused to do what he told me, he would never have allowed me to see you again.'

Eperitus looked into Astynome's eyes and knew she was right. He had not considered the difficulties she had faced before, and now that he did he saw that she had never been given any option but to see out Apheidas's orders. But as the hardness in his heart began to soften, so the memory of how much he had suffered because of her stopped him from taking her hand and confessing that he still loved her. Besides, he reminded himself, he was still a prisoner in his father's house.

'And where is Apheidas now? Has he sent you to soften me up – to persuade me to join him again?'

Astynome closed her eyes and turned her head away with a sigh, and Eperitus knew he had allowed his bitterness too much rein.

'I'm sorry,' he said, taking her hand. 'I shouldn't have said that. You must know why I'm here, though, why he's permitted me to live instead of killing me on the battlefield? Does he think he can appeal to the Trojan blood in my veins again? If so, you can tell him I'm loyal to my Greek ancestry, not to some foreign culture I'm more intent than ever on seeing destroyed.'

'Do you think he would tell his plans to me, a mere servant? All I know is that he was in a jubilant mood after the battle. Along with Cassandra, he's the only person in Troy who seems pleased at the death of King Eurypylus – as if Trojan victory in battle doesn't suit his ambitions. The only other thing I know is that he's keen for you to regain consciousness.'

'So he either wants to kill me while I'm wide awake, or he has other designs for me.'

'Then we will stop him. Together. You remember how you used to tell me about him in your hut, about the kind of man he is? To my shame I did not believe you, because the Apheidas I knew had shown me nothing but kindness after my husband's death. Now I know you were right, and –' she looked at the guard and Clymene, and lowered her voice, 'and I will help you to kill him if you still desire revenge.'

'Revenge?' Eperitus replied, feeling suddenly tired once more. 'Yes, I've wanted it more than ever since you and I were last together – vengeance for King Pandion, and now for Arceisius too. But how will you help me?'

'I don't know yet, but a chance will arrive. I will pray to the gods for one.'

Eperitus's tiredness was deepening rapidly, weakening his desire to continue his show of resistance to Astynome. He knew in his heart he loved her as much as he had ever done, and before he slipped back into unconsciousness he wanted to tell her that. Weakly, he pulled his other arm free of the blanket and placed his hand on her thigh, moving it around to her hip. For a moment he felt as if his eyes would fill with tears, so happy was he to feel her warm skin beneath his fingertips and have her back at his side.

'I won't allow you to put yourself at risk, my love,' he said, fighting now just to speak. 'If I escape and he ever finds out you helped me – '

Her face, which had been concerned by his failing strength, now broke into a smile. She squeezed his hand and bent down, placing her lips on his.

'Then take me with you. My loyalty is to you now, Eperitus, not to Troy. I can return to my father on Chryse and wait for you there until the war ends. But now you must sleep. We will make our plans when you awake.'

Chapter Twenty-Six
AN UNWELCOME VISITOR

The old beggar opened his eyes to the first light of day and the smell of cooked breakfast. It awoke the gnawing hunger in his stomach and for a moment he thought of rising and petitioning the nearby Myrmidons for their leftovers. But the air beyond his dew-damp cloak was chilly with the approach of autumn, and his bed of hay was still snug and soft – a luxury for a man in his unfortunate position. Daring to stretch out an arm from his protective cocoon, he grabbed a pile of the hay and pulled it closer, stuffing it into a gap that was letting in the cold. Then his nostrils twitched at the pungent reek of horse manure and he saw that one of his bedfellows had risen early and left a heap of fresh dung close to his head. The beggar contemplated the steaming cluster for a moment, then snatched a few handfuls and pushed them into the hay beneath his back. They were like hot coals to his chilled body, and the stench and the disdainful look he received from the white mare that had produced them were a small price to pay for a little heat.

For a while after, he struggled between a reluctance to leave his cosy bed and the need to find something for his nagging stomach. His last meal had been a mixture of grain, rye and barley picked from the hay, where they had fallen from the feedbags of the horses as they ate. Then his decision was made for him: two men were approaching the pens where he lay, talking in the harsh accent of the Myrmidons. The beggar's first instinct was to cover himself in more hay and hope they did not see him, but his common sense told him a man of his heavy build would need more than a few strands of dry grass to hide behind. So he stood, brushed off some of the dung, and stooped between the wooden bars that kept the four horses from escaping.

'Who in Ares's name are you?' one of the Myrmidons snarled. 'And what're you doing in with the horses?'

'Sleeping,' the beggar replied haughtily, taking his gnarled staff from the fence post where he had left it the night before and leaning his weight upon it. 'A man's entitled to sleep, ain't he – even if he's gotta lay his head down with beasts!'

The Myrmidons closed on him angrily, only stopping as they caught the stench of manure and wrinkling their noses up at him in disgust. His appearance matched his aroma. His tunic and cloak were so ragged and torn that large patches of grimy brown skin were visible through the rents. His belt was a long piece of rope – wound several times about his waist – and he wore no sandals, leaving his bare feet caked in manure and dust. His face was almost black with dirt, while his hair and beard were matted with filth and stuck all over with pieces of hay and other accumulated vegetation. And though once a thickset man – a farmer or fisherman, possibly, by his physique – his back was now curved and his knees bent outward so that he seemed a hunched, shuffling creature to their eyes.

'Two of those "beasts", as you call them, are immortal,' the first Myrmidon sneered. 'And if their *master* had caught you in with them, rather than *us*, he'd have lopped off your head by now and thrown your corpse into the sea for the fish to feed on.'

'Immortal, you say? Then surely they're the horses of Achilles – Balius and Xanthus.'

'Not any more,' the second Myrmidon corrected. 'Achilles is dead and now they belong to his son, Neoptolemus. And unless you want him to find you here then you'd better get on your way.'

The beggar glanced over towards the huts and tents where the Myrmidon army had been camped for ten years, then looked back at the two men and nodded. But as he turned to go he saw the bags of feed hanging from each of their arms and pointed at the pile of small, red apples on top.

'Will you spare an old man an apple? I can't remember the last time I had a whole apple just to meself.'

'Get on with you!' one of the men shouted, kicking his behind and sending him sprawling into the dry grass.

The beggar watched the Myrmidons walk away laughing, then slowly picked himself up and began shuffling towards the mass of tents that constituted the rest of the Greek camp. Though the army had routed the Trojans and their Mysian allies several days before, the mood in the camp had become sullen again. Until the arrival of Neoptolemus the Greeks had suffered many casualties, and though they had repaid their enemies in great slaughter, the glory of victory had quickly grown stale and lost its appeal. The survivors mourned their fallen comrades, but even more now they longed for the final conquest of Troy that would release them from their oaths and allow them to return home. As the beggar passed between them, he saw the emptiness in their dark-ringed eyes and knew that they were at the last ebb of their strength. The coming of Neoptolemus – who had taken Achilles's position at the head of the Myrmidons and now lived in his father's hut – and his defeat of King Eurypylus had stretched their hope a little further, but it would not endure forever. The beggar could sense the war's end was close now, just as surely as the last days of summer were passing and the autumn was waiting to take its place.

He saw a banner fluttering in the wind ahead of him. It was green with a golden fox leaping across its centre, and though the material was faded and its edges tattered it remained a symbol of pride to the men who followed it into battle. The beggar watched it for a moment, then began shuffling towards it. Men looked up at the sound of his staff and quickly moved out of his way as they caught his stench and saw his filthy clothing. Eventually he found the hut beneath which the banner flickered and snapped. Three men were seated before it in tall chairs draped with rich furs – the sort of pelts, he noted with greedy eyes, that could make a beggar's life so much warmer and happier. They were clearly warriors of high rank and renown, sitting with their legs thrust out before them and kraters of wine in their laps as they regarded him with a mixture of distaste and cautious interest.

'Go warm yourself by the flames, father,' one of them said, nodding towards the circular fire before their feet.

A black pot hung over it, bathing the beggar's senses with the delicious smell of porridge while provoking his stomach into a series of groans.

'My thanks to you, King Diomedes,' he said, settling cross-legged before the campfire and holding out his blackened hands towards its warmth.

Diomedes gave him a half smile and nodded to a male slave, who walked over to the pot and doled out a ladleful of porridge into a wooden bowl. He passed it with disdain to the beggar, who cackled with joy as he raised the steaming broth to his lips.

'He stinks like the lowest pit of Hades,' Sthenelaus said, leaning slightly towards Diomedes.

Euryalus, seated on the other side of Sthenelaus, could barely conceal the sneer on his lips as the beggar slurped noisily at the contents of the bowl.

'You shouldn't encourage these vagabonds, Diomedes. Show kindness to one and before you know it you'll have an army of them at the door of your hut.'

Diomedes smiled. 'Let the man eat. Isn't there enough suffering in this world without denying a poor wretch a morsel of food?'

'There speaks a true king,' said the beggar, casting the empty bowl aside and rising to his feet. 'I knew you was Diomedes, as soon as I set eyes on you. Tydeus's son, yet greater than he.'

'It isn't your place to make that judgement,' Euryalus admonished him.

The beggar flicked his hands up in a dismissive gesture.

'Who said it were my judgement? A beggar may lack wisdom, but he ain't deaf. I'm only repeating what I've heard others say: that Tydeus was a great man who killed Melanippus at the first siege of Thebes, though he died later of his wounds. But they also say he dishonoured himself by devouring Melanippus's brains – something his son wouldn't ever stoop to.'

'You can't deny he's a well-informed vagabond,' Sthenelaus commented with a grin.

'As for *your* father, Sthenelaus,' the beggar added, 'they say he were killed by a thunderbolt, for boasting that even Zeus couldn't stop him scaling the walls of Thebes.'

'Who do you think you are!' Sthenelaus snapped, rising from his chair.

Diomedes laid a hand on his wrist and pulled him back down to his seat.

'Whoever he is, he's neither as ignorant nor as foolish as he looks. For all we know he could be a god in disguise. Do you have a bag, father?'

The beggar pulled aside his cloak to reveal a battered leather purse, hung across his shoulder by an old cord. Diomedes stood and walked to his hut, signalling for the beggar to follow. As the bent figure entered behind him, he passed him a basket of bread and another of meat.

'Here, fill your bag for your onward journey. And if a king can advise a pauper in his trade, I suggest in future you don't insult the fathers of the men you're begging from.'

The old man smiled and took both baskets, somehow managing to cram the entire contents into his purse.

'If I insult you,' he asked, 'why repay me with such generosity?'

'Because there's something about you. A presence that marks you out from the rest of your kind. You may be a god, or you may just be a good man fallen on hard times, but I know better than to turn you away with nothing more than scorn.'

'Then perhaps I'm worth a cup of wine, too,' the beggar grinned.

Diomedes raised his eyebrows a little at the man's audacity, then pointed to a table by the back wall, beneath the racks of armour and weapons he had stripped from his enemies, and told him to help himself. The beggar shuffled over and found a bowl of mixed wine surrounded by half a dozen silver goblets. After clattering about among them for a few moments, he turned with a cup in each hand, one of which he passed to Diomedes. The king took it at arm's length, holding back from the stink that clung to his guest. Then the beggar poured a meagre libation onto the fleece at his feet and raised the goblet to his lips, drinking greedily so that the dark liquid spilled down over his beard and neck.

'Zeus's blessing on you, m'lord,' he said, and with a fleeting bow pulled aside the curtain door and left the hut.

Outside, the sun was beginning to climb and the cold air and dew that had marked the dawn were swiftly forgotten. The beggar nodded to Sthenelaus and Euryalus as they stared at him with disdain, then shuffled off in the direction of the camp walls. But as soon as he was out of sight of Diomedes's hut, he placed less weight on his staff and quickened his pace, until a short while later he had climbed the slope and was approaching one of the gates. It was then he heard the sound he had been listening out for: a series of shouts and the clamour of men running some way behind him. He was barely feigning a shuffle now as he passed between the open gates and across the causeway, the guards keeping as far back from the shabby, foul-smelling old man as they could. But he had taken no more than a few paces on to the plain when a voice commanded him to stop. He turned to see Diomedes striding towards him, with Sthenelaus and Euryalus at each shoulder. A horse whip was in the king's hand and his handsome face was creased with wrath.

'Where is it?' he demanded.

The beggar backed away, instinctively covering his head with his forearms.

'Where's what? I ain't got nothing but what you gave me, m'lord.'

Diomedes reached across with a snarl and pulled open the beggar's robes. The man fell unceremoniously onto his backside, causing a ripple of laughter from the gate guards. As he hit the ground, a silver goblet tumbled from his mess of rags and rolled in a semicircle towards Diomedes's sandalled foot.

'Call this nothing?' he said, stooping to retrieve the cup.

'You said to help meself,' the beggar protested.

Diomedes raised his whip and brought it down smartly over the beggar's shoulder, causing him to howl with pain. As the whip was raised for a second strike, the beggar threw his arms about Diomedes's knees and pleaded for mercy.

'A man shouldn't beat his guests, not for nothing!' he sobbed. 'It's an offence to the gods.'

'And you're an offence to me, thief,' Diomedes replied, kicking him away and lashing his back as he scrambled through the long grass on his hands and knees.

His whimpering yelp was met by more laughter from the guards, who had now been joined by other men from the camp. As they watched, Diomedes whipped the beggar again, slashing open his filthy robes and leaving a red line on the brown skin beneath. Euryalus swung at the man's stomach with his foot, knocking him onto his back, but as Sthenelaus stepped up to follow with a kick at the man's head, Diomedes seized his arm and pulled him back.

'Enough now. He's learned his lesson.'

'It's *you* what needs to learn a lesson,' the beggar groaned, clutching at his stomach. 'Odysseus didn't attack me when I was in his hut last night; he's a proper host and knows the rules of xenia.'

Diomedes shook his head in disgust. 'So you're a liar as well as a thief. Odysseus retired to his hut last night with orders not to let anyone in. Agamemnon himself would have been turned away, so the chances of a beggar –'

'But I *was* there,' the beggar countered. 'Fact is, he invited me in to help him with a little problem he was having. Something about finding a way into Troy to pinch a statue.'

'The Palladium!' Sthenelaus exclaimed.

Diomedes rebuked him with a warning glance, then turned to the beggar.

'So you've overheard a bit of campfire gossip you think you can twist to your advantage. Perhaps you believe I'm a fool? Well, I'll show you I'm not.'

He raised the whip again and the beggar threw his hands up before his face.

'Agamemnon ordered you and Odysseus to steal the Palladium from the temple of Athena,' he said quickly and urgently, though in a low voice that would not be heard by the gate guards. 'It's the last of the oracles given by Helenus, for the defeat of Troy.'

Diomedes's arm froze above his head and he stared at the beggar incredulously.

'How could you possibly know that?'

The beggar dropped his hands away from his face and sat up, the sluggishness now gone from his movements. There was a smile on his lips and a roguish gleam in his eyes.

'Because I *am* Odysseus, of course.'

Euryalus snorted derisively.

'Such arrogance in one so low. Do you think we've never set eyes on Odysseus before? Do you *really* think we're going to believe you're the king of Ithaca?'

'This man's asking for more than a whipping now,' Sthenelaus hissed, his voice an angry whisper.

The beggar did not take his eyes from Diomedes.

'Then how would a simple beggar know that Trechos was the first Argive to be killed in Pelops's tomb, his neck snapped by Pelops's skeleton as he removed the lid of the sarcophagus?'

'No-one could know that unless they were there,' Diomedes answered. He scrutinised the beggar closely for a moment, then smiled and offered him his hand. 'By all the gods, Odysseus, even your own mother wouldn't recognise you in that state.'

Odysseus refused his friend's hand and, retrieving his stick, pulled himself slowly and stiffly to his feet.

'No Greek will ever be allowed through the Scaean Gate, but

beggars come and go as they please. These rags are how I'll get past the guards, and once I'm in I'll lower a rope over the walls so you can join me, Diomedes.'

'We'll come, too,' Euryalus declared.

Odysseus shook his head.

'Agamemnon gave the task to Diomedes and myself. Besides, the more there are of us the more risk there is we'll get caught.' He turned his green eyes on Diomedes. 'Hide yourself on the banks of the Simöeis until dark. I'll wave a light from the walls – five times from left to right and back again – to show where I've tied the rope.'

'What rope?'

Odysseus pulled back his robes and the folds of his baggy tunic to reveal the rope he had wound several times around his waist.

'The walls on the far side of the city are lightly guarded,' he continued, 'and once you're over them you'll be inside Pergamos itself. We can find our way to the temple of Athena, steal the Palladium and be back out before dawn.'

'Zeus's beard, I think it might even work,' Diomedes said with a grin, excited by the prospect of danger and the glory that came with it.

'There's one other thing I need to do while we're there, though,' Odysseus said. 'I need to find out whether Eperitus was taken prisoner.'

The others looked at each other doubtfully.

'He charged a company of Trojan cavalry alone,' Sthenelaus said. 'He's dead.'

'I spent the whole day searching for his body among the slain,' Odysseus replied sternly. 'He wasn't there! And though some say they saw him shot by an archer as he rode at Apheidas, until I see his corpse and know his ghost has departed for the Underworld I won't give up looking for him. He's my friend, and he would have done the same for me.'

'There's a chance the Trojans took him,' Diomedes said, though sceptically. 'And if they did, they'll accept a ransom for his release – or we can set him free when we take the city. But that won't happen until we've stolen the Palladium. That has to be our priority, Odysseus, especially if we ever want to see our wives and families again.'

Odysseus did not need to be told the urgency of their mission.

'Then we should go now. Take the whip and strike me again.'

Diomedes frowned.

'We've given you enough rough treatment already, for which I'm sorry.'

'Don't be. I provoked you to it, and it was necessary to make people believe my disguise; but the Trojans have eyes in the Greek camp and unless you want to arouse suspicion then you must continue to treat me as a vagabond and thief. Once you've made a display of driving me off you can return to your tent, but make sure you leave unnoticed again after sunset. And don't forget to bring my sword with you.'

Diomedes hesitated for a moment, then raised the whip over his head and struck Odysseus on the shoulders. He yelped with pain and loudly accused the Argive king of being a whore's son, earning himself another lash across the lower back. And so it continued until the beggar was out of sight and the guards at the gate had already forgotten his existence.

Chapter Twenty-Seven
AN ULTIMATUM

'Wake up.'

Eperitus opened his eyes a fraction before the palm of a hand struck him across his cheek, whipping his head to one side. Snatched from a dream about the Greek camp, in which Astynome was once more his lover, his senses struggled to grasp hold of something that would bring him back to reality and tell him where he was. The stench of burning fat pricked at his nostrils and he could hear the hiss of a single torch. By its wavering light he could see he was in a small, unfamiliar room, the corners of which were piled up with large sacks – probably of barley, judging by the smell. He was seated in a hard wooden chair, but when he tried to move he discovered he was bound by several cords of flax that wrapped around his abdomen and pinned his arms uselessly at his sides. He blinked and stared at the face of the man who had hit him – a face he did not know – then suddenly remembered he was a prisoner in Troy, alone and far away from the help of his friends.

'Who in Hades are you?' he demanded, reviving quickly from his slumber and looking around at what appeared to be a windowless storeroom.

The man did not answer, but beckoned impatiently to two armed warriors standing by the door.

'Untie him.'

The men knelt either side of him and picked at the cords holding him to the chair, while the first man drew his sword and waved the point menacingly at his stomach.

'Don't even think about trying to escape,' he warned.

'What do you want with me?'

No answer. The two men pulled away his bonds and lifted him

bodily from the chair, pulling his arms roughly about their shoulders. As they made themselves comfortable with his weight, he placed his feet on the ground and tried to stand. A bolt of pain shot up from his wounded leg. If he had not been supported he would have collapsed to the floor. Then the first man opened the door to reveal two more guards waiting outside, who followed behind the others as they carried Eperitus through a confusion of half-lit corridors, up steps, through more corridors and into the great hall of his father's house, which he recognised from when Astynome had been tending his wound. He looked for her in the shadows cast by the flaming hearth, but saw no-one in the fleeting moments before he was dragged to another door and out into bright, blinding sunlight. His eyes had become accustomed to darkness and he was forced to squeeze them shut while he was taken through what smelled like a garden filled with shrubs and strongly scented flowers. He tried blinking, but caught only confused snatches of his surroundings. More baffling was the faint hissing he could hear in the background. Then he felt himself dumped into another chair, while his arms were pinned painfully behind its hard wooden back and bound tightly with more flax cords.

'Stay close and keep your weapons to hand,' a familiar voice ordered the guards.

Eperitus's eyes stuttered open again. The dark, blurry form before him quickly gained focus and became his father, who had planted himself legs apart before his son's chair. Eperitus tested his arms against the ropes, but was unable to move them.

'Where am I?'

'In my garden,' Apheidas answered with a sweep of his hand, indicating the bushes and fruit trees that provided a cheerful green backdrop in the morning sunshine. He spoke in Greek to prevent the guards from understanding their conversation. 'You *were* locked up in one of my storerooms – your wound's healing fast and I didn't want to risk leaving you in the great hall – but I thought this would be a much more pleasant place to talk.'

'I have nothing to say to you. You should've just killed me on the battlefield and have been done with it.'

'That was my first thought,' Apheidas admitted, his voice hardening. 'After all, you've made your desire to kill *me* very clear. But I don't suffer from the same crippling lust for vengeance that you do. Revenge is a meaningless, empty passion that achieves nothing – you of all people should know that. No; when I saw you lying in the dust it struck me the gods had delivered you into my hands for a reason. So, not for the first time, I decided to spare your life.'

'What do you want?' Eperitus sneered. 'My *gratitude*?'

'Don't be obtuse. I want … I *expect* your help.'

'After what happened at the temple of Thymbrean Apollo? After you murdered Arceisius? After you used Astynome to fool me into thinking you'd changed?'

He spat at his father's feet, who replied by striking him hard across the cheek, almost toppling him from the chair. A silence followed, filled only by the sinister hissing that seemed to be coming not from the garden, but from beneath it. Eperitus sniffed at the blood trickling down the inside of his nostril.

'Nevertheless, you are going to help me,' Apheidas assured him. 'If not, *then* I will kill you in the worst way you could imagine.'

He knelt down beside a wooden box, on top of which was a pair of heavy gauntlets. He forced his hands into the stiff leather, then lifted the lid. A low sibilating put Eperitus on edge, and as Apheidas pulled out a thin brown snake from the box he felt every muscle in his body stiffen. He strained against the ropes that held him, but was unable to move.

'Still have the old fear then?' his father mocked, stepping closer and holding the snake level with his son's face.

Eperitus felt his hands shaking as he stared at the scaled, lipless creature with its thin tongue slipping in and out of its mouth. He pressed his head as far back as it would go into the hard, unyielding wood of the chair.

'Take the damned thing away! Take it away!'

'As you wish.' Apheidas stood up straight and held the snake to his own cheek, so that its forked tongue flickered against his jaw. 'You never did master your fear of my pets, did you? I've been keeping them again, you know, since I left Greece.'

'That hissing sound I can hear –'

'You don't even want to think about *that*,' Apheidas told him with a knowing grin. 'But I wonder if your tortured mind has regained any memory of *why* you fear snakes so much.'

'What do you mean?'

'You don't fear them for nothing, Son. It happened when you were very young, perhaps three years old. I'd bred snakes since before you were born, to provide sacrifices for worshippers at Apollo's temple in Alybas. I kept them in a pit in our courtyard, a courtyard much like this.'

'I remember it.'

'Do you remember falling in?' Apheidas asked, fixing his son's gaze. 'Your mother and I thought we'd lost you then. I hurried down the ladder and saw you lying on the wooden platform at the bottom, which I used to stand on to keep me safe from the snakes. If you'd landed anywhere else you would have perished in an instant, but Apollo must have been protecting you that day. Then I saw your leg was dangling over the side, waving about above all those angry snakes. Before I could reach you, a viper sprang up and bit you behind your knee. The mark'll still be there, if you care to look.'

'If it bit me, then how did I survive?'

'It was a dry bite. No venom was released. You were lucky.'

The story did not bring back any latent memories, but neither did Eperitus have any reason to think his father was lying. It certainly explained why he despised the creatures so much.

'But you won't be so lucky next time,' Apheidas added with a sudden snarl.

He threw the snake onto Eperitus's lap, causing him to jerk backwards in fear. The chair toppled over with a crash, but instead of hitting his head against the ground as he had expected Eperitus sensed a void opening up beneath him. The surprise lasted only a moment as he remembered the snake and lifted his head to stare down at its thin, curling body on his chest. A wave of nausea and dread surged through him. Then a gloved hand plucked it up and tossed it away.

His father's sneering face appeared above him.

'That's nothing to what you'll get if you don't listen to me.'

Standing now, Apheidas tipped Eperitus on his side. A black void opened up by his left ear, from which the terrible hissing he had heard earlier rose up like a living entity to consume his senses. Not daring to look, but unable to stop himself, he turned his head to see that he was balanced over the edge of a pit, and in the darkness at the bottom he could see daylight glistening on the bodies of hundreds of snakes. His stomach tightened, pushing its contents back up through his body and out into the hole below.

Then his chair was being pulled up again by four of Apheidas's men, away from the pit and back to safety in the broad sunlight.

'*Now* are you ready to listen to my proposal?' his father demanded.

'I'll listen,' Eperitus gasped, 'but you already know my answer. In the end you'll still have to kill me!'

Apheidas sighed and raised himself to his full height. He turned and picked up a leather water-skin.

'Here,' he said, holding it to his son's lips.

For the first time, Eperitus realised how dry his throat was and how much his body craved liquid. He opened his mouth and Apheidas squeezed a splash of cool water into it.

'You shouldn't be so hasty to welcome death, Son. You've plenty to live for, after all. Astynome, for instance.'

Eperitus was almost taken by surprise, but the hint of uncertainty in Apheidas's voice gave him away. His father was no fool: he knew Astynome hated him and loved Eperitus, despite all that had happened. He must also have suspected his son had forgiven her for betraying him. For a brief instant Eperitus was tempted to admit as much, if only to show Apheidas that his feelings for Astynome transcended the schemes of his father that had divided them. Then he heard a voice in his head – not unlike Odysseus's – warning him not to give Apheidas anything to bargain with. His love of the girl could be used against him; by threatening Astynome, Apheidas could force him to agree to whatever he wanted, just as he had used Clymene to bribe Palamedes to treachery.

'Don't mock me,' Eperitus said, narrowing his eyes and trying to sound angered. 'If all you can offer is that treacherous bitch then save your breath.'

'So you'll be glad to know you won't be seeing her again?'

Eperitus felt sudden anxiety clawing at his chest, but kept his silence.

'Now she's nursed you back to health, I've assigned her to other duties,' Apheidas continued. 'I don't trust her around you, and the last thing I want is for her to smuggle you a weapon of some sort. Clymene will change your bandage later and after that you'll not need any more tending to, because you'll either have agreed to help me or I'll have thrown you to my pets.'

Eperitus opened his mouth to speak, but Apheidas raised a hand to silence him.

'Before you tell me to go ahead and kill you, listen to what I have to say. Snakes are a good way to get your attention, but they won't force you into doing what I want. Neither will threatening you with death, or even, it seems, threatening Astynome. You may still love her and you may not, but I'm not going to send you back to the Greek camp with that uncertainty.'

'The Greek camp?'

'As a messenger, of course. My ambitions haven't changed from when I laid them out before you in the temple of Thymbrean Apollo – I need you to tell Agamemnon I will give him Troy in exchange for Priam's throne. The King of Men will have his victory, Menelaus his wife, and *I* will become ruler of all Ilium!'

Eperitus threw his head back and laughed.

'Still hankering to be a king? Even one subservient to the Greeks you hate so much? Well, things have changed since we last met. There's a new oracle and Troy won't fall until it's fulfilled, not even if you throw the gates wide open and let the whole Greek army inside.'

Now it was Apheidas's turn to be amused, and he looked at his son with a broad smile.

'Obviously you're referring to Helenus's visions,' he said.

Eperitus's laughter ceased and he stared at his father.

'How could you know about that? Helenus said he hadn't revealed the oracles to anyone in Troy.'

'He hadn't – except to me. Now, let me think: I already know you've found Achilles's son, Neoptolemus, and I guess you must have retrieved Pelops's shoulder bone by now. Which just leaves the Palladium, doesn't it. The last key to Troy.'

Eperitus watched as his father raised the water-skin to his lips and took a mouthful of liquid. There was something triumphal about the movement, and this time he did not offer a drink to his son.

'So, are you ready to listen yet? Threats only work on cowards, and you're no coward, but maybe I can offer you something we will all profit by: the choice between certain victory for the Greeks or war without end. Would you prefer to return home with your friends before the end of the year, or to remain in that squalid camp until you die of old age, while the kingdoms of Greece succumb to bandits and invaders?'

'I won't help you fulfil your vile ambitions, Father,' Eperitus replied, obstinately. 'The only thing you can offer me in exchange for the dishonour and pain you've brought me is your life. Give me that and I'll gladly take your message to Agamemnon.'

'You have the stubbornness of a mule and wits to match, but here's the choice anyway: help me and I'll give you the Palladium to take to Agamemnon; refuse and I will not only throw you into that pit behind you, but I will tell Priam the Greeks are planning to steal Troy's most precious lump of wood. After that, the Palladium will be so well hidden no Greek will ever be able to steal it, and then the walls of Troy will never succumb.'

Eperitus stared at his father and knew he meant what he said. The choice he had given him was stark: being cast into a pit of snakes with any hope of the Greeks stealing the Palladium gone forever; or receiving his freedom and seeing the final oracle fulfilled with a speed and ease that none could have hoped for, leading the way to victory and an end to the war. But his father would also succeed in his ambition, sealing for eternity Eperitus's shame and dishonour. He closed his eyes in despair and let his chin sink onto his chest. He could not have known that Priam had already heard the oracle from Cassandra's lips and had not believed a word of it. Neither could he have guessed that Apheidas was bluffing, else he might have felt less despondent.

'Even if you say no, Son,' his father said, 'I won't reveal your plans to Priam until I have no other option. Perhaps Astynome would be a better messenger; I understand Agamemnon wanted her for himself when she first visited the Greek camp, so if I offered her as a gift it might convince him my offer is genuine. Either way, the choice is yours: death for you and defeat for the Greeks, or life, victory and a swift journey back home. I'll return for your answer tomorrow morning.'

The Scaean Gate, which had witnessed the deaths of Hector, Achilles and Paris, was firmly shut and no amount of pounding or calling for the guards would open it. When a soldier stood on top of the battlements and urinated on him, Odysseus realised he was wasting his time and followed the circuit of the walls eastward to the Dardanian Gate, praying to Athena as he walked. He reached Troy's second great entrance and beat the flat of his hand against its sun-baked beams. Again there was no answer. Eventually, and after all his attempts to gain the attention of the guards had proven futile, he sat down beneath the cooling shade of its walls and looked out over the plain at the blue, distant mountains, trying to think how he might enter. Though he was widely credited as the most intelligent and cunning of the Greeks, especially by those who were closest to him, Odysseus's schemes were rarely thought out in any detail. Often he would begin with a good idea then rely on his wits – and the help of the gods – to see it through to a successful conclusion. This was destined to be one of those occasions.

Before long, the answer to his prayers arrived. A trail of dust appeared above the heat haze on the horizon, where the well-worn road to the Dardanian Gate issued out of the foothills. It moved slowly across the plain towards the city, eventually revealing the distant figures of a troop of cavalry, followed by a line of ox-drawn waggons laden with supplies. Shortly, the gates opened and the mounted escort – some fifty horses and riders – began filing through. The waggons followed, the sluggish beasts that drew them taking little notice of the shouts or sticks of their drivers. The final waggon was piled high with sacks of grain that made the heavy axle and solid wooden wheels squeal in protest. With an agility that belied his powerful bulk, Odysseus darted out from the shadows beneath the wall and hopped up onto the rear of the waggon. A moment later he could hear the sound of cloven feet on flagstones echoing back from the interior of the gate, and watched with a quiet smile of satisfaction – mixed with a pang of nervous anticipation – as the wooden portals were swung shut behind him.

He lay back in the sacks and tried to look as if he belonged there. Then a short guard with an angry, self-important face pointed at him and called out. Odysseus jumped down and immediately assumed a beggar's pose: back bent, eyes wide with fearful humility, hands cupped and thrust out in a gesture of supplication. The guard shouted something in Trojan that was too fast for Odysseus to understand, then brought the shaft of his spear down on his bowed spine with a whack that gave the other soldiers great amusement. Odysseus hardly felt the blow on his hardened muscles. Moving quickly, he grabbed the hem of the soldier's cloak.

'Got any food, captain?' he croaked, thickening his voice to disguise his accent.

The guard wrinkled his nose up and blinked as the mixed stench of manure, urine and stale sweat washed over him. Yanking his cloak from Odysseus's clutching fingertips, he stumbled backwards and waved the beggar away.

'Go on, you filthy swine. Get out of my sight.'

Odysseus turned and shuffled off into the narrow streets before the guard could change his mind and have him thrown back out of the gate. It was ten years since he had last entered Troy, when he had been part of an embassy sent to petition for the return of Helen. Then the population had been openly hostile to the foreign warriors who had dared to bring threats of violence to their peaceful city. Now they were less naïve, their lives changed forever by the war that had claimed so many of Troy's sons and so much of its wealth. Half of the women seemed to be widows, dressed in the black of mourning, while almost as many were prostitutes, with painted faces and brightly coloured dresses. Their wretched, hungry children scurried through the streets like rats, following the slow-moving waggons and trying to steal whatever they could lay their hands on, indifferent to the frequent cuffs of the escorts. And everywhere Odysseus looked there were soldiers, drawn from all the towns and cities of Ilium. Some were beardless boys barely old enough to carry a shield and spear; others were grey-bearded old men, ordered to fill the numerous gaps left by the dead on the plains between the Scaean Gate and the Greek camp; but most were professional warriors or mercenaries, stalking the streets with their battle-hardened faces in search of wine or women with which to pass away their boredom.

Few paid any attention to Odysseus, unless it was to avoid the odour that emanated from his wretched form. Looking up, he saw the battlements of Pergamos rising a short distance beyond the houses to his right. The temple of Athena – and the Palladium – lay within the citadel walls, and guessing that was where the supplies would be taken for safe storage, he quickened his pace to catch up with the rearmost of the waggons. After a while, the convoy turned right onto a broader thoroughfare that sloped gradually up towards Pergamos. Despite the years since he had last been there, Odysseus recognised the tall tower that guarded the main entrance. Each of its smooth, well-fitted blocks was half the height of a man, and at its base were six statues depicting different gods from the Trojan pantheon. Though these were ostensibly the same gods that were worshipped by the Greeks, the identities of the crudely imagined figures had been a mystery to Odysseus ten years before and remained so now as he followed the trudging convoy to the foot of the tower. The gates opened and the cavalry escort trotted through first, ducking beneath the short, echoing tunnel that led to the highest part of Troy. Odysseus closed the gap between himself and the last waggon, praying silently to Athena that he would not be noticed by the guards.

'Where d'you think you're going?'

The harsh words were followed by the smack of a spear across his arm. Odysseus, bent double once more, glanced up and saw the soldier who had hit him. He also noticed two others leaning their weight upon the heavy timbers of the gates as they pushed them inward behind the last waggon. Ignoring his assailant, he shuffled rapidly towards the men on the doors.

'Spare some food for an old pilgrim? Drop of water, perhaps? How about a swallow of wine?'

He clutched at their cloaks, forcing them to abandon the gates and withdraw with groans of protest from the terrible smell.

'Never mind,' Odysseus said, glancing behind as he slipped through the gap they had left. 'I'll find something at the temple of Athena. Bless you, sirs.'

He hurried forward, the rap of his stick on the flagstones repeating rapidly from the walls. Then a heavy hand seized hold of his shoulder.

'No beggars in the citadel!' the third soldier grunted, throwing him back out into the street. For good measure, he swung his foot hard into Odysseus's stomach as he lay in a pile of horse manure. 'Now, piss off and don't let me see your ugly face here again.'

Chapter Twenty-Eight
ODYSSEUS UNMASKED

Odysseus lay still for a moment, clutching his stomach and gasping for breath as the gates slammed shut behind him. Slowly, using his stick, he pulled himself back onto his feet. Looking around, he could see that the guards had retreated inside the gates and he was left almost alone on the street. Up here, as the lower city lapped about the walls of Pergamos, the houses were wealthier and boasted two storeys, which cast long, dark shadows as the sun began dipping towards the west. Odysseus withdrew to the shade of the nearest wall and sat down, wondering what to do next. By necessity, his plan to enter the city and find his way to the temple of Athena was always going to have to rely on good fortune, but it seemed the gods had turned their backs on him at the final hurdle. And yet he could not give up. If he was to lower the rope for Diomedes and steal the Palladium he had to discover a way into the citadel before nightfall. He also had to discover whether Eperitus had been brought into the city as a prisoner, though how he would glean such information was beyond even his imagination. He leaned his head back against the cold stone and closed his eyes in silent prayer. A few moments later he heard voices.

'I'll give you two days ration of wine.'

'No.'

'Three days.'

'Not for a whole week. Beside, you drew the western parapet a fortnight ago, whereas I haven't even seen her for a month.'

Odysseus opened his eyes again and saw two soldiers walking up the main thoroughfare from the lower city. They wore the same armour and plumed helmets he had seen on the men who had just thrown him into the gutter – members of the elite guard that defended Pergamos – and as they approached a desperate idea struck him. He looked around at the empty street, then sat on his haunches with his back to the wall and held his hands out before him.

'A bit of food, my lords?'

The nearest paused as he noticed the beggar for the first time, then reached into a satchel beneath his cloak.

'Here,' he said, passing him a piece of bread. 'The gods have smiled on me today, so why not you?'

Odysseus took the bread, noting the dagger in the man's belt.

'And what good fortune's worth three days wine ration to your friend?' he asked.

The man grinned.

'I drew the evening watch for the western wall, of course.'

'You'll have to forgive me, sir, I'm new to the city. Where I come from the soldiers'd rather be drinking wine and throwing dice than be out on duty.'

He no longer made any effort to disguise his accent, but instead employed his most calming tone, hoping to lull the minds of the two soldiers. He instinctively calculated how he would take the dagger and kill them both. Then, after hiding the bodies and swapping his beggars outfit for one of their uniforms, he could try and bluff his way through the gates.

'Surely you've heard about Helen of Troy?'

Odysseus hesitated and gave a slight nod.

'Every evening at sunset she walks along the western parapet, looking towards Greece,' said the other soldier. 'Pining for the children she left behind, or so they say.'

'And I'll be guarding the same stretch of wall,' declared the first, glancing triumphantly at his friend. 'Whatever people say or think about that woman, she's a beauty beyond the measure of mortal minds. There's something of the gods in her, or I'm a Greek.'

'And can she be seen from the lower city, my lord?'

'Go to where the outer wall meets the western wall of Pergamos and you'll see her. If you ask me, I think she makes sure she *can* be seen: to remind us of what we're fighting for – something much greater than mere wealth or power.'

'He's loved her since the first day he saw her,' the other soldier explained to Odysseus. 'If you go there, you'll understand why.'

'But don't get too close,' added the first. 'If she catches a whiff of your perfume, old man, she'll be back inside faster than a rabbit in its hole.'

The men laughed and walked up to the gate, rapping loudly on the panels and calling for entry. Before the doors could be opened, Odysseus was back on his feet and walking as quick as his feigned stoop would allow. He passed the tower with its row of idols and followed the curve of the walls beyond. The thought of Helen had filled his fertile mind with the germ of an idea, an idea that had saved the lives of the two Trojans. It powered him along until he saw the crenellated lip of the city wall rising to meet the battlements of Pergamos ahead of him. Already the light was fading on the streets, as the sun slid towards the ocean and was lost behind the two-storeyed houses and the high fortifications. Then the walls of the citadel bent sharply to the north-west and converged in a dark triangle with the defences of the lower city. Here Odysseus sat down with his back to a small house, looking up at the dark, saw-toothed outline of the ramparts where he hoped to see Helen.

As the clear sky slowly began to turn to a darker blue, Odysseus noticed others gathering around him. Three women in black were the first, their lined and ageing faces stern and silent as they stood together by the corner of the small house. They were followed by the angry stumping of a crutch on the cobbled street as another beggar – his left leg missing below the knee and his right eye an empty pit – entered the sombre triangle. A young mother was next, holding a small infant in the folds of her widow's robes, and behind her were three Mysian warriors, their young eyes fixed hopefully on the parapet above. A few more arrived, until at last a score of people were waiting in the shade, all of them, in one way or another, victims of Helen's beauty. Then, as one, the small crowd fell still and stared up at the walls. Odysseus followed their collective gaze and felt his own heart suddenly beating faster. Helen had come.

It was as if a final beam of the sun's radiance had alighted on the grey stone of the battlements. She wore no black to symbolise the mourning in her heart, but was instead dressed in a white chiton and robe that blushed pink in the dying daylight. Her sad and lovely face, chin raised, stared out at the sunset beyond the city walls, pained by memories of things that had passed. Like a goddess among mortals, she seemed aloof to the dark, shuffling figures below. And that was how it should be, Odysseus thought: she was too beautiful, too perfect, to be soiled with the misery and torment of a sinful universe. Its filth could not stick to her nor weigh her down, and though the widows, the maimed and the awestruck looked up at her in demanding silence, even they must surely know she was not of their world.

And yet she had offered herself to Odysseus when he had been a young suitor in Sparta twenty years before, promising to marry him if he would help her escape the claustrophobic life of her father's court. By then he had already fallen in love with Penelope, but the memory of Helen's submission gave him the courage to stand and shuffle forward. Ignoring the shocked whispers of the onlookers, he raised his face to the battlements and called out in the Trojan tongue.

'What is it you look for in the setting sun, my lady?'

Helen turned to face him and the whisperers on either side fell quiet. Her blue eyes fixed momentarily on the ragged, filthy creature that had dared call out to her, then with the slightest narrowing of disgust turned back to the horizon.

'Perhaps a winged horse to carry you away from this prison? Or maybe your own death, so your spirit can follow Paris's and share with him in the forgetfulness of Hades?'

'How dare you!' Helen replied, seizing the edge of the wall and staring down at him. 'How *dare* you foul my husband's name with your rank breath?'

'He ain't your husband no more,' cackled one of the widows.

The others joined her laughter, suddenly released from the spell of Helen's beauty and delighting in her discomfort. One of the Mysians ordered them to be silent, while on the battlements the sound of sandals on the stonework announced the hurried arrival of a guard. Odysseus immediately recognised one of the soldiers he had spoken to by the gate to Pergamos.

'My breath may indeed be rank, mistress,' he continued, 'but it can barely make worse the name of a wife-stealer and family breaker. Such a man deserved to die!'

Unused to facing effrontery, Helen's face fell blank and she stepped away from the parapet in confusion. Eager to win her favour – a word or even a glance – the guard rushed forward in her defence.

'Silence, you insolent … By all the gods, it's *you*!'

'I'm here, like you told me,' came Odysseus's jaunty reply. 'And she's just as beautiful as you said.'

The guard's mouth fell open in confusion for a brief moment, then snapping shut he pointed at the three Mysians and ordered them to seize hold of the beggar.

'Take him to the guard house. We'll soon teach him to hold his tongue before a lady.'

He turned to Helen, hoping for some recognition or approval. She was too shocked to even notice him, and with her hand on her chest was trying to steady her breathing. Below them, the Mysians were struggling to contain the beggar's surprising strength.

'You can teach me whatever you like,' Odysseus shouted out, this time risking Greek. 'But the lady might want to hear my news, first. Of Aethiolas, Maraphius and Hermione.'

One of the Mysians drew his sword and raised the pommel above Odysseus's head, but before he could strike a command rang out from the walls.

'Leave him alone!'

The three men released the beggar at once and stepped back as if burned. Odysseus looked up to see Helen leaning stiffly on the parapet, her eyes staring fiercely at him. He met her gaze and held it, knowing the mention of her children – whom she had last seen twenty years ago in Sparta – could not have failed to gain her attention. Then he saw the faintest twinge of recognition cross her features and lowered his face to the ground. He turned away, as if eager to make his escape.

'Stay where you are!' she called.

The Mysians blocked his path and he looked back over his shoulder to see Helen giving instructions to the guard on the walls. The man frowned in consternation, then turned and ran to the nearest steps. Helen followed him, pausing briefly to throw one last glance at the mysterious beggar before disappearing from sight.

The score of onlookers now surrounded Odysseus, a few of them angry but most of them intrigued as they stared at the bedraggled creature who had somehow won Helen's interest, where their own presences had never so much as received a look. Then they moved aside as orders were barked out and the guard from the walls appeared, accompanied by two others.

'What was that you said to her?' the guard snapped. 'Greek, was it? A spy, are you?'

'Just a traveller, nothing more.'

'Whatever you are, and whatever you said, you've gained her attention. She wants to see you at once.'

He signalled to his companions, who reluctantly seized the stinking beggar by his elbows and pulled him along between them. They passed through the gate and the cool, echoing archway into Pergamos, where Helen was waiting at the foot of the ramp that led to the upper tiers of the citadel. Despite his foul stench as the guards brought Odysseus before her, she remained where she was and regarded him with suspicious eyes.

'Who are you?' she asked, in Greek so that the others would not understand their conversation.

Odysseus caught the smell of wine on her breath, though there were no other signs to tell him she had been drinking.

'A sailor, my lady, fallen on hard times.'

'A beggar, cursed by the gods it seems. How do you know the names of my children? Did Pleisthenes tell you?'

'I've never met your youngest son, though I know you brought him with you when Paris abducted you.'

'He did not abduct me. I came here willingly.'

'Though not without sacrifice, leaving behind your daughter and other sons whom Menelaus had taken with him to Crete.'

Helen's eyes narrowed again, subtly changing the emphasis of her beauty.

'Not many would know that. Perhaps there's more to you than rags and a terrible smell. Perhaps you're a god in disguise – such things happen, or so my old nursemaid used to say. At the very least you're a Greek.'

'I'm no god, my lady, but I am a Greek – once an Athenian merchant from Piraeus. And for a meal and a sup of wine I can tell you about the children you left behind. They still long for their mother, or so I've heard.'

Odysseus saw the look of longing enter her expression and was glad that he would not need to lie to her. Menelaus sent ships back to Sparta every two years for replacements, and when they returned the first thing he would ask about was news of Aethiolas, Maraphius and Hermione, news which he would then share with the other kings to show his pride in his children – and assuage some of his guilt for not being present as they grew up. Something of that same guilt was in Helen's eyes as she looked at Odysseus now.

'Then they're still alive,' she said, as if to herself. Suddenly, Odysseus was aware of her eyes on his again, though this time there was a new intensity to them as they searched his face. 'Thank you, friend. I agree to your offer – a meal and wine in exchange for everything you know about my children – especially Hermione. But not before the filth has been washed from your body and you're clothed in a fresh tunic and cloak.

'Guards,' she said, talking to them in their own tongue as she turned to go, 'take this man to the palace and tell my maids to bathe him.'

'That's not necessary, my lady,' Odysseus protested, reluctant to give up his disguise. 'Food and wine will do for me.'

'Nonsense,' she replied, looking back over her shoulder. 'They bathe in Athens, don't they? And Ithaca, too, by all accounts.'

Chapter Twenty-Nine
TEMPTATIONS OF THE FLESH

Odysseus closed his eyes and laid his head back against the rim of the bath, enjoying the feel of the warm water covering his naked body. He had not had a proper bath in ten years, and never to this degree of luxury. His bath on Ithaca had been in a high-sided ceramic trough, just long enough to sit in with his legs outstretched; the one in Helen's quarters was a large oval tub set in the floor at the centre of the room, decorated with murals of dolphins, shells and other marine creatures bordered by wavy lines that represented the sea. The strong smells of manure, urine and sweat had been replaced by the subtle perfumes that Helen's maids had added to the steaming water, and as he filled his nostrils with their aroma he could almost forget that he was lying undisguised and unarmed in the heart of Priam's citadel. Naturally, though, his busy mind would not allow him to forget his present danger, for not only had he been deprived of his beggar's mask but the astute Helen had also guessed his true identity. The thought had plagued him all the way to the palace, and had he not been escorted by three armed guards he might have taken the opportunity to escape. And yet Helen had not given him away at the very time when he was most vulnerable, and the more he pondered this the more he believed she would not surrender him to his enemies – at least, not until she had had her chance to talk with him first.

And so he had allowed her reluctant maids to undress him and bathe him, pouring water over his head and shoulders until the heat drove the weariness from his limbs and he began to feel more at ease. In a short while, they would return with olive oil to rub into his skin and hair, and fresh clothes so that he would be in a fit state to be presented to their mistress. Then, of course, he would have to make an explanation of his presence in Troy and hope Helen would not give him up to the guards, who would certainly be close at hand. But he doubted the gods had placed him at Helen's mercy just so he could be surrendered to Priam. Rather, he thought, they were giving him an opportunity.

The door opened behind him, announcing the return of the maids. Instead of the hurried scuff of three or four pairs of sandalled feet, though, he heard only a single pair of bare feet walking softly and slowly across the stone floor.

'How many years since we last met, Odysseus?'

Odysseus's eyes snapped open to see Helen standing at the opposite end of the bath. She was dressed in a white chiton of a thin, revealing material, through which the points of her nipples were clearly visible. Her black hair was no longer pinned behind her head, but hung down over her shoulders so that her pale face was framed in a perfect oval. Her cheeks were touched with pink and her full lips were red; not due to any false colouration, but rather because of the empty krater that dangled from her fingertips. Her large blue eyes were heavily lidded and looked lazily down at Odysseus's nakedness. The maids had left a stool close to the edge of the bath, which Helen hooked with her toes and drew closer. She dropped onto it with a heavy motion, letting the krater roll from her fingers onto the floor beside her, and leaned her elbows onto her knees.

'Must be twenty years,' he answered.

'And now here you are, in my bath. My maids treated you well?'

Odysseus nodded.

'I'm sure they didn't enjoy it,' she said with a laugh. 'Not with those rags and that *awful* smell. Couldn't you have picked a better disguise to come spying on us in?'

'It worked well enough, though I admit I didn't expect to find myself in your bathroom.'

'But here you are, completely at my mercy.' The smile left her lips and her eyes grew dark. 'You realise I could call the guards at any moment and have you dragged before Priam? Or have you forgotten that we are enemies, Odysseus? I'm a Trojan princess, married to the heir to the throne! It's my duty to have you arrested, and my pleasure to watch you executed.'

'Your duty, yes, but not your pleasure, I think. Else why didn't you reveal who I was by the gates, when I was surrounded by armed soldiers? And why are you here with me, alone? Isn't it the truth that you don't consider yourself a Trojan at all – no more than those widows below the battlements think of you as one of them – and since the death of Paris you have no reason to want to stay here?'

'Whether I want to stay here or not isn't my decision, as well you know,' she replied sternly. Then she sighed and brushed away the locks of hair that had fallen across her face. 'But you're right: if I'd intended to give you up I would have done so by now. And I may yet, but not until you've told me about my children. I hope that wasn't just another of your lies to gain entry to the palace.'

'If it was, what's to stop me making up more lies to keep you happy?'

She smiled and shrugged lazily. 'Nothing, I suppose, but if you must lie make it good and make it convincing. I've thought about them every day for the last ten years, and more so since Paris died. I often wonder what they look like now, or whether they're married and have children. By Aphrodite, Odysseus, I could be a *grandmother*!'

They laughed together at the thought of it, and while the smile was still on her face Odysseus began to tell her all he knew about her children. When he had finished Helen did not press him with questions as he had expected, but fell silent for a while and looked down at her painted toenails.

'And what about you, Odysseus? Why did you risk your life to enter Troy? Have the Greeks accepted they'll never conquer our walls and sent you to kidnap me instead?'

'That would be a hopeless task, Helen. Getting into Troy alone is one thing, but to take you against your will and try to leave again would be impossible.'

'And if I was willing?' she teased.

There was a pause as their eyes met, then Odysseus gave a dismissive shake of his head.

'Even if you were, you're too beautiful by far to smuggle out of the Scaean Gate without being noticed.'

'Then why *are* you here?'

Odysseus looked at her again, his eyes questioning and firm.

'If I told you that, and you betrayed me, it would be a mortal blow to our hopes of conquering Troy.'

'I won't betray your mission to anyone, Odysseus. You have my solemn oath, as Aphrodite is my witness.'

'Then I've come to steal the Palladium.'

'The Palladium?' Helen gave a short, incredulous laugh, but when she saw that Odysseus was serious the smile fell from her lips and she leaned her elbows on her knees again. 'You *really* want to steal the Palladium? There're too many guards for a single warrior to overcome – and you haven't even brought a sword.'

'I'll find one.'

'But why risk everything for a lump of wood? Is it because of that old myth?' She shook her head. 'Even if you *did* manage to take the Palladium and escape with your life, the walls wouldn't just come tumbling down, you know.'

'No they wouldn't. And yet Agamemnon has ordered me to steal it, so you can either give me some clothes and send me on my way, or you can break your oath and call the guard. Which will it be?'

He rose to his feet, letting the water stream down his heavy bulk. Helen stood, too, and raised a hand towards him.

'Wait a moment,' she said. 'You can't just charge through the palace naked and unarmed. Sit down and let's give this some thought. Maybe I can help you.'

Odysseus eased himself back into the water.

'Why would you help me, Helen? If the Greeks are victorious, you'll just be returned to Menelaus and dragged back home to Sparta, to be detested until the end of your days for bringing about a war that has killed thousands.'

'Can Menelaus be any worse than Deiphobus, who forced me to marry him after Paris was killed? Can anyone who isn't Paris bring me the joy and happiness he did? And can Sparta be any worse a prison than Troy is? For that's all I am now, Odysseus – a prisoner, kept here against my will while men continue to die in their thousands for my sake. I'd rather be reunited with Menelaus than remain stuck inside these walls. At least he was always kind to me when we were together, which is more than I will say for Deiphobus. Besides, if I returned to Sparta I would see my children again. I know it was my choice to leave them, but I'm not the person I was then. I've suffered just as much as any warrior on the plains of Troy, and all I want now is for the war to end – whoever wins. Do you understand?'

She sat back down on the stool, her cheeks flushed with a mixture of wine and anger. But if the wine had released her emotions, it was the anger that drove her on now. She jabbed a finger accusingly at Odysseus.

'You have to take me with you, Odysseus. Forget the damned Palladium; the walls of Troy won't need to be conquered if the Greeks have me. Take me back to Menelaus and the war will end. All I ask is a little time to fetch Pleisthenes –'

'I'll never be able to get you and your son out of Troy.'

'I won't abandon another child, Odysseus,' she snapped. 'And think about it: if you take us back to Menelaus, then the fighting will be over and you can return to Ithaca. Surely you want to see Penelope again?'

'There's nothing I want more,' he answered, 'but this isn't the way to do it. Even if Pleisthenes agrees to come, you'll be too much of a burden – escape would be impossible. And haven't you realised yet, Helen? This war isn't about you any more. It stopped being about you the moment Agamemnon had brought the Greek kings under his command and set sail for Ilium. You're just the figurehead, something for Agamemnon to point at while he ensures the destruction of the greatest obstacle to his own power. If you return to Menelaus the war would still go on – only Agamemnon would probably have you assassinated and blame it on the Trojans, turning the war from a matter of honour to a matter of revenge.'

'So you won't help me?'

'I can't.'

'Not for anything?'

She stood and unfastened the brooch at her shoulder. The chiton slipped down to her feet and she stepped free of it, brushing it aside with her toes. Odysseus swallowed and raised himself onto his elbows, transfixed by the sight of Helen's naked body. Her oiled skin was a matchless white, broken only by the pink ovals of her nipples and the black triangle of her pubic hair. Then, before he could even think to force his gaze away, she crouched down and slid into the bath. For an agonising moment her nakedness was lost below the water, then she moved towards him and pressed her body against his.

'I'll give myself to you, Odysseus,' she whispered, her face so close he could smell the wine on her breath. 'Promise to take me away from here and I'll be yours, right now. Deiphobus is at a feast to honour the visit of King Anchises, Aeneas's father, from Dardanus; we won't be disturbed.'

'No,' he said, turning his face away.

Helen kissed his cheek and slid her fingers into his hair. The soft weight of her chest pressed down on his and he wavered, looking into her eyes and seeing the promise that was in them. The blood was in her lips and cheeks and he could feel the hardness of her nipples, craving for his touch. The wine in her veins and the grief in her heart had filled her with a reckless desire that cared nothing for what might happen if they were discovered. And her passion was infectious, spreading through the heat of her naked skin into Odysseus so that his arms slipped around her and trapped her body against his. He had not felt the touch of a woman since leaving Ithaca; now, suddenly, the long years of loneliness and need rose up like a great wave that threatened to sweep him away. But as his eyes looked into hers another instinct – deeper than his lust – told him the woman in his arms was not *his* woman. He seized her by the waist and pushed her away.

'No!' he repeated, more firmly this time. 'I will not betray Penelope.'

'Don't be a fool!' she replied hotly, rising to her feet so that the water streamed from her shoulders and breasts. 'You want me, I can feel it. And *I* want you!'

'You don't want me, Helen. All you want is for someone to make love to you and help you forget your own misery.'

'And what of it? Don't you have the same need? You haven't seen Penelope in ten years – and surely you haven't been faithful to her in all that time? Even if you have, what does it matter anyway? Take me now, Odysseus, while you still have the chance – or deny your instincts and continue in the vain, pathetic hope you might one day be reunited with your wife! Can you risk more years without a lover's touch – a touch that for all your faithfulness you might never know again?'

Odysseus thought of the oracle he had been given under Mount Parnassus, which had solemnly announced that if he went to Troy he would not see his home again for twenty years. One decade had already passed; could he bear to wait another? And then he remembered the old oracles that had said the war would end in the tenth year, and the new ones that promised Troy would fall if the Palladium could be stolen from the city. No, he insisted to himself, he would bring the war to a finish and sail back to his wife – and the pleasure of a few moments would not mar that homecoming for him. He pulled himself up onto the edge of the bath.

'I'm sorry, Helen. You're not in your right mind, and even if you were I could never become your lover. Nor can I help you escape from Troy – with or without Pleisthenes.'

Her eyes were ablaze now.

'If you refuse to help me get out then I'll make sure you share my imprisonment. All it would take is a single scream.'

Odysseus swung his legs out of the water and stood. A stack of folded towels waited on a nearby stool; he took one and began drying himself.

'Then call the guard.'

She glared at him from the bath, provoked to rage by his rejection and tempted to accept his challenge. Then she lowered her face into her hands and sobbed. Odysseus stopped rubbing his hair and looked on helplessly for a moment, before throwing the towel about his waist and kneeling at the water's edge.

'Here,' he said, offering her his hand.

'I have to be free of these walls, Odysseus,' she replied, keeping her face in her hands. 'I don't care if Agamemnon and Priam want to keep on fighting. I just want to get out, get away; be anywhere but here.'

He took her hands in his and slowly drew them back. The unconquerable walls of Helen's beauty had fallen to expose the red eyes and damp cheeks of a broken human being – the same frightened young girl he had occasionally glimpsed in the great hall at Sparta, during the feasts held in her honour so many years before.

'I can't take you with me,' he said, 'but I can give you hope. The end of the war is in sight. There's a new oracle that says Troy will fall this year if the Palladium can be taken from the temple of Athena. Diomedes is by the banks of the Simöeis, waiting for me to lower a rope to him. Together we will fulfil the oracle and seal Troy's doom, and if you want an end to your imprisonment, Helen, then you have to help us.'

She looked at him and smiled, the power of her beauty returning like the light of the sun that has been briefly concealed behind a cloud.

'I'll help,' she said with a sniff. 'I can take you to the place where the walls are easiest to climb. There are still guards, but I can distract them while you signal to Diomedes. Even then you'll be hard pressed to enter the temple and escape with the Palladium alive.'

'It's a risk we'll have to take.'

Helen moved to the edge of the bath and Odysseus helped her out. She quickly covered her nakedness with one of the towels, then turned to him with a strange expression on her face.

'There are other ways I can help you,' she said. 'My sister, Clytaemnestra, taught me how to make sleeping draughts when we were children. It's a skill I've found use for here in Troy – to sooth Paris when he struggled to sleep, and also for Deiphobus on the nights when I can't bear his touch. I can have my maids take a skin of wine for the guards at the temple, if you wish.' She met Odysseus's grin with a smile of her own. 'And there's something else – someone who can help you if you're forced to fight your way out.'

'Who?'

'A captured Greek – a nobleman, from the rumours my maids have heard. It's curious, and I don't know whether it's true, but they say he's being held in Apheidas's own house rather than the usual rooms in the barracks, so it'll be much easier to get him out – '

'Eperitus!' Odysseus exclaimed, suddenly filled with excitement. 'It's Eperitus! By all the gods, I knew he wasn't dead. Fetch me some clothes, Helen – I have to get to Apheidas's house now.'

Helen reached across and took his hand.

'Diomedes first,' she said, then turned and called for her maids.

Chapter Thirty
UNEXPECTED HELP

The streets of Pergamos were cloaked in thick darkness as Helen led Odysseus towards the battlements. The flames of their torch left an orange glow on the walls of the buildings they passed, but at that time of night there was no-one to see them as they slipped out of a servants' side entrance and between the narrow thoroughfares of the citadel. The greatest danger was from the guards patrolling the parapet, but Helen had sent two of her maids to keep them distracted while she and Odysseus signalled to Diomedes.

'Any Greek soldier who deserted his duties for the sake of a woman would be flogged,' Odysseus commented as they waited in the shadows of a house, looking up at the ramparts. 'I don't expect it's any different for Trojans.'

Helen raised a dismissive eyebrow at him before returning her gaze to the stone steps that led up to the walls.

'I hand-picked my servants for their beauty and sexual charm, and there isn't a soldier alive who could resist their advances. You've seen them, Odysseus, you know I'm right.'

Odysseus recalled the girls who had undressed him and washed him clean, and even though their faces had been screwed up into expressions of severe disapproval there could be no denying their beauty.

'So what are we waiting for?'

'No harm in being certain,' Helen replied.

After she had waited a short while longer – long enough to be sure the guards' regular tours of the battlements had been disrupted – she moved to the steps as swiftly as her long chiton would allow and ascended. Odysseus followed. His Trojan tunic hugged his knees and restricted his movement on the steps, but it was soft, warm and clean and a thousand times better than the beggar's rags he had thrown onto the hearth in Helen's house. Soon he was beside her on the wide walkway, looking beyond the parapet to the pale line of the Simöeis, lit by the sliver of moon above. The meandering ribbon of grey was interrupted in places where the banks were higher, or where clumps of trees or shrubs rose up from the river's edge.

'The walls are easier to climb here,' Helen said. 'The rock that Pergamos was built on rises up from the plain and makes the drop shorter. More importantly, when you make your escape you can't risk leaving a rope tied around the battlements. If the guards find it they'll be alerted to your presence and will raise the alarm, and as soon as they realise the Palladium has gone they'll send out cavalry patrols to block your escape across the fords of the Scamander.'

Odysseus had not thought that far ahead, but did not admit as much to Helen.

'So are you suggesting we jump?'

Helen pointed to an alcove in the walls. A deeper darkness indicated a gap in the floor and from the smell that drifted up from it Odysseus guessed it was a latrine.

'There's a rock shelf a short way below that hole. It isn't pleasant, but you can drop down to it without too much danger and nobody will even realise you were here. Until morning, that is.'

Odysseus grimaced slightly and nodded. Then he gave the torch to Helen and, with a glance either side of him along the empty walkways, began to unwind the rope tied around his waist.

'I told Diomedes to look out for a light waved five times, left to right, from the battlements.'

As he looped one end of the rope about his back and shoulders and tossed the other to the rocks below, Helen leaned over the ramparts and, stretching as low as she could reach, swung the torch in a wide arc five times. After several long, nervous moments they heard a hissed warning from below, followed by a tug on the rope. Odysseus quickly braced himself against Diomedes's weight and before long the Argive king was clambering through a gap in the crenellated walls.

'You smell a lot better,' he greeted Odysseus. 'Where'd you get the clothes from?'

Then he noticed Helen and nearly fell back through the gap by which he had just arrived.

'My lady,' he said, recovering with a low bow. 'But how –?'

'Odysseus can tell you later,' Helen said. 'Have you brought weapons?'

Diomedes, who had loved Helen ever since he had been among her suitors at Sparta in their youth, could barely take his eyes from her as he pulled aside his cloak and revealed the two blades tucked into his belt. He drew one and handed it to Odysseus.

'You're here to help us?'

'Of course she is,' Odysseus answered.

Diomedes turned to him. 'Then if we can persuade her to leave with us now, we could put an end to the war!'

'Odysseus and I have already discussed that,' Helen explained, with a slightly embarrassed glance at the king of Ithaca, 'but I refused to leave without Pleisthenes.'

'There are other complications, too,' Odysseus added, 'but Helen is ready to shorten the war by at least helping us steal the Palladium.'

'Then let's find this temple of Athena,' Diomedes said, turning back to Helen, 'so you won't have to wait any longer than necessary, my lady.'

Diomedes moved to the top of the steps, but Odysseus placed an arresting hand on his upper arm.

'There's something we have to do first. Eperitus is being held prisoner here in the citadel. We release him first and then we take the effigy.'

Diomedes looked at him with surprise, then seeing the determination in his friend's eyes gave a silent nod.

'Good,' Odysseus said.

He wound the rope around his waist again, took the torch and led the way back down the steps, entering the dark streets once more. They had not gone far when they saw two figures silhouetted against the end of a short thoroughfare. Odysseus and Diomedes raised their swords, ready to defend themselves.

'Don't be concerned,' Helen said, stepping out ahead of them and lowering their blades. 'I sent one of my maids to fetch a servant girl from Apheidas's house. I've heard it said she's befriended the Greek prisoner, so if the rumours are true and the prisoner *is* Eperitus then she'll help you find him.'

'And if she refuses?'

'Then you will have to kill her,' Helen replied.

The two figures entered the circle of light cast by the torch.

Odysseus's gaze widened at the sight of Astynome, who stared back at him with equal surprise.

'Odysseus!'

She moved towards him with a smile, then stopped as she remembered the circumstances under which they had last met. Her eyes fell to the ground.

'Is he still alive?' the king asked.

'Yes,' Astynome answered, her happiness unmistakeable. 'He was badly wounded in the battle, but I've nursed him back to health. He has remarkable powers of recovery.'

'And have you spoken with him? About the temple of Thymbrean Apollo – your betrayal?'

Astynome's gaze fell again. 'A little. I believe he has forgiven me.'

'Then I forgive you, too,' Odysseus said.

He stepped forward and folded her into his chest, holding her gently despite the immense power in his arms.

'Astynome will be your guide now,' Helen announced, looking from the girl to Diomedes and finally to Odysseus, 'but I must return to the palace before I'm missed. Perhaps we will meet again, Odysseus, at the war's end, when the flames of destruction are blowing through this fair city. And if we do, I pray you will remember my kindness to you this evening – and make sure Menelaus knows of it. I fear how he will react when he sees me again, after all that's passed between us. But until then, may the gods go with you.'

She took the torch from his hand and retreated back up the narrow street, closely followed by her maid. Odysseus and Diomedes watched her until she disappeared behind the corner of a large house, then turned to look at Astynome.

'Eperitus is locked in a storeroom in his father's house,' she said in a low voice. 'I can show you the way, but two of Apheidas's men have been posted at the door to make sure he doesn't escape.'

Diomedes gave her a dark grin.

'Oh, I think we can deal with them.'

Eperitus's arms were numb from lack of movement and he could no longer feel any sensation at all in his buttocks. The hard chair had done for them a long time ago. His senses, too, had been suffocated by the constant darkness, the cool, stagnant air and the smell of barley from the sacks piled in the corner. Time had passed at such a crawl in this unconscious void that he felt a day or more at least had elapsed since his father's ultimatum, though by the fact Apheidas had not yet come to hear his decision must mean that it was not even the morning of the next day. Indeed, if he were left there any longer – with nothing more than the faint glow of a torch lining the bottom of the door and the occasional mutterings of the guards outside – he was certain he would go insane.

But that would not happen. Inevitably, his father would return and he would be given the choice between instant death or a worthless life lived in dishonour and ignominy. Even these grim options, though, seemed unimportant compared to the consequences of his decision for those whom he cared about. For Odysseus, it meant a swift return home to his wife and the son he had barely known, or many more years on the shores of Ilium, held by an oath that could never be fulfilled. For Astynome, it could mean being sent to Agamemnon as a gift, to become his plaything. And whatever his choice, Apheidas would strike his deal with the King of Men and declare himself the new ruler of Troy.

With nothing else to distract him, the same arguments passed through his mind again and again, following a monotonous loop that he could not convert to a decision. For though his logic told him he had no choice but to agree to his father's proposal, his deeply rooted hatred for the man and his stubborn desire not to dishonour himself refused to acquiesce. It was a nightmare from which he could see no escape.

Then a twitching in his senses told him something had changed. He looked down at the flickering thread of gold beneath the door and somehow knew the guards outside were no longer alone. *Had morning arrived at last?* he wondered. *Had his father come for his decision?* If so, the guards seemed unconscious of his presence: there were no slight sounds of sudden alertness, just the continued heavy breathing and occasional scratching of one, mingled with the light snores of the other. Was it Clymene again? She had already changed his bandages, shortly after he had been brought back from the garden.

Maybe Astynome? The thought delighted him, but his delight turned quickly to fear as he realised she might have come to fulfil her final promise to him, desperately thinking she could overcome the guards herself.

As tension gripped him, there was an abrupt clatter of noise beyond the door of his prison. One of the guards – who must have been sitting – jumped up with a metallic clang of armour and spoke in a sharp tone. His words became suddenly fearful and were cut off by a grunt and a bloody gurgle, followed by the thump of a body hitting the floor. A muffled groan indicated the last waking moment of the other guard. In the silence that was left, Eperitus's keen hearing could discern laboured breathing and small, hurried movements. Then the heavy wooden bar was removed from the other side of the door and Eperitus sat up with wary expectancy.

The door swung inwards and rebounded from the jamb, only to be knocked back again by the shoulder of a heavily built man as he burst into the room. He was followed by a second figure, both armed as they stood silhouetted by the shock of bright torchlight from the corridor beyond.

'Who's that?' Eperitus called in the Trojan tongue.

'Eperitus!'

'*Odysseus?*'

'Not just Odysseus,' Diomedes added, stepping over and cautiously slicing through Eperitus's bonds with his dagger. 'And Astynome's with us, too, keeping watch at the far end of the corridor.'

The flax cords fell away and Eperitus stood. The next moment he was in a heap on the floor.

'Steady,' said Odysseus, hauling him back to his feet. 'How long have you been tied to that chair?'

'Longer than I can remember.'

'And your wound?'

'More or less healed,' Eperitus replied. He looked into the king's eyes, then broke into a smile and embraced him. 'Zeus's beard, you're the last person I expected to see. And Diomedes, too! How did you get into Troy?'

'It's a long tale, and one we'll give in full when we've got you safely back to the Greek camp.'

'So you came here to save me?'

'Don't flatter yourself,' Diomedes scoffed, slapping him on the shoulder. 'We're here to steal the Palladium and *you're* going to help us. Try leaning on this.'

He handed him one of the dead guards' spears. Eperitus moved his legs, felt some of the life come back into them, and attempted to stand. Odysseus caught him again, while Diomedes knelt down and began vigorously rubbing his calves and thighs to restore the flow of blood, though he was careful to avoid the bandaged wound.

'Everyone had taken you for dead after the battle,' Odysseus said, 'but not me. And when I heard you were being held prisoner here, I insisted on rescuing you before stealing the Palladium.'

'Try again,' Diomedes instructed, rising to his feet.

This time, with the help of the spear, he found his legs had the strength to stand once more. He took a couple of tentative steps towards the door and came face-to-face with Astynome. Without a moment's hesitation she threw her arms about him, almost knocking him back to the floor. Odysseus and Diomedes quickly busied themselves dragging the bodies of the guards into the storeroom, while Astynome drew back and looked into Eperitus's eyes. The doubt in her dark, attractive features was clear to see.

'Say you forgive me,' she whispered.

For an instant he remembered again Apheidas's cruel revelation at the temple of Thymbrean Apollo, that the woman he had fallen in love with had been sent to lure him into a trap – a trap that had resulted in the death of his friend, Arceisius. Then he recalled the look of remorse on Astynome's face as Apheidas dragged her away at knifepoint, and her confession that her love for him was genuine. And he knew, despite her treachery, that she had spoken the truth.

'There's nothing to forgive. Apheidas is manipulative and evil; we're both his victims.'

'In Zeus's name, will you just say you forgive me?'

'I forgive you. Of course I forgive you. And now you have to come back with me to the camp.'

Astynome kissed him and shook her head as she withdrew.

'Impossible. You know what'll happen if Agamemnon discovers me. Besides, I'll only burden your escape from Troy.'

'We can deceive Agamemnon and I can carry you back to the camp, if I need to.'

'Not on those legs you won't. Anyway, I'll be more use to you inside Troy. Odysseus has already asked me to do something for him.'

Eperitus narrowed his eyes and looked across at the king, who was dragging the second guard's body into a gap behind the sacks of barley in the far corner of the room.

'What?'

'I can't say I really understand it, but even if I did I couldn't tell you. He's sworn me to secrecy.'

'Time to go,' Diomedes announced, standing in the doorway with a torch in his hand. 'The night's old already and we've still to find the temple of Athena.'

'I've already told Odysseus the quickest way there,' Astynome said. 'The difficulty will be in stealing the Palladium itself.'

'And in that you can't help us, Astynome,' Odysseus said. 'You have to get back to the servants' quarters and hope you've not been missed. Eperitus, how are your legs?'

Eperitus could feel the strength returning and gave his friend a nod. He looked again at Astynome and kissed her on the lips.

'When the city falls, wait for me here, in Apheidas's house. I'll come and find you.'

She nodded silently and watched him out of the storeroom, following Odysseus and Diomedes as quickly as his numb legs would carry him.

Chapter Thirty-One
THE PALLADIUM

D iomedes followed at Odysseus and Eperitus's heels, staring in awe at the great mansions and temples of Pergamos. If the mighty walls of Troy were intended to impress visitors with her power and invulnerability, her inner buildings were built to astonish them with her wealth, piety and culture. The well-laid stones and the ornate architecture far exceeded anything the citadels of Argos, Sparta or even Mycenae could offer in competition, and Diomedes – like many before him – was being made to feel like a common barbarian as he stole through the empty streets.

Eperitus could still remember the wonder he had felt during his first visit to the city a decade before, though he no longer looked on the achievements of the Trojans with the same reverence. Now he saw Troy as nothing more than a hateful bastion that had to be conquered – razed to the ground, if necessary – so that he and his comrades could return to Greece. In that desire he had grown very similar to Odysseus, wanting only to see his homeland again. And now, having forgiven her treachery, he was determined to take Astynome with him. The thought of sharing a house on Ithaca with her pleased him greatly, and he had to force himself to stop smiling at his restored dreams and concentrate on the difficulties that lay ahead.

They turned a corner onto a wide stone road. At the eastern end a walled ramp climbed gradually up to the second tier of the citadel. It was flanked by tall poplar trees that were silhouetted black against the dark blue of the night sky, their branches sighing with the faint breeze.

'Quiet now,' Odysseus warned, turning and placing his finger against his lips. 'The temple should be to the left at the top of the ramp.'

He slid his sword from his belt and advanced at a crouch, followed by the others. Reaching the corner of the last building before the ramp, he peered cautiously around the edge. Eperitus and Diomedes joined him. There were no guards on the ramp, and at Odysseus's signal they dashed up to the second level and hid behind the wall at the top. A short way off was a stone plinth topped by a larger-than-life statue of Athena. By day, its brightly painted wood would catch the sunlight, impressing passers-by with a sense of the goddess's divine glory; but in the tarry blackness of the night it was a dull, unimpressive grey, its only authority lying in the stern features of its face. Beyond the statue was a tall, square building, footed by broad steps that led up to a pillared portico. This was the imposing entrance to the goddess's temple, and in the shadows before its high doors were the huddled figures of a dozen men.

'Eperitus!' Odysseus hissed. 'Can you see if they're moving?'

Eperitus strained his eyes against the darkness. The guards were lying in a variety of strange poses, like a collection of toy dolls that had been abandoned halfway through play. Some had managed to pull their cloaks about their shoulders before succumbing to sleep, while others just lay where they had fallen. Their spears and shields were still propped against the marble pillars of the portico and the only sound was the chorus of their mingled snores.

'They're asleep,' he announced.

As if to prove the point, he rose to his full height and strolled boldly towards the temple. Taking the steps two at a time as the others watched, he walked through the circle of slumbering soldiers and turned to face his companions. It was then he noticed another detail: each guard held a cup, or had let one fall from his fingertips, and there were small stains of dark liquid where the wine had spilled on the flagged floor.

'They've been drugged,' he informed Odysseus and Diomedes as they climbed the steps to join him.

'Of course they have,' Odysseus said, glancing nonchalantly at the scattered men. 'Helen's maids did their work well. Perhaps too well – I only hope they don't draw suspicion down on their mistress. Now, let's do what we came here for.'

They pushed one of the doors open and slipped inside. The smell of dank stone and incense was laced with the reek of burning fat from a single torch that hung on a nearby pillar. It gave off a sinister hiss that was magnified by the enclosed space, but its failing light was little more than a ball of orange in the thick gloom and did nothing to illuminate the features of the temple, which remained lost among the shadows. Seeing two unused torches lying at the base of the pillar – ready for the priestess to light when she returned at dawn – Diomedes picked them up and held them to the dying flame. They caught quickly and he handed one to Eperitus.

The twin circles of pulsing light grew in strength, pushing the darkness back to reveal high, muralled walls – the pictures too faded and smoke-stained to be discernible among the shadows – and an inner square formed by twelve stone columns. Stepping between two of the pillars, the Greeks entered a broad, flagstoned space in the centre of the temple. From here the light of their torches fell on a gigantic but illusive silhouette against the rear wall, a figure half lost in shadow as it soared up to the ceiling. They stepped closer and saw it was another statue of Athena, but larger and more impressive than any they had ever seen before. Odysseus fell to his knees and bowed his head, while the others looked on in astonished silence. Like the one on the plinth before the temple, the figure was depicted wearing only a simple chiton; her familiar spear, helmet and aegis were absent, giving her a distinctly foreign, Trojan feel. Unlike the other figure, though, this one was seated on an equally oversized throne, and set between her feet was a dull black shape that seemed more like a shadow, somehow absorbing and deadening the effect of the torchlight.

'Is that it?' asked Diomedes.

Odysseus raised his head and fixed his eyes on the Palladium.

'It must be.'

Diomedes advanced towards it with his torch raised at an angle before him. Odysseus followed, but Eperitus gripped his spear and stole a glance at the rear of the temple. His hackles were up and he had a sense of foreboding, but he could see or hear nothing in the darkness. Reluctantly, he turned and joined the others.

Eperitus had first heard a description of the Palladium from Antenor, the Trojan elder whose wife was the chief priestess of the temple. He had been their host before the war, when Eperitus had accompanied Odysseus and Menelaus on a peace embassy to seek the return of Helen. But even Antenor's matter-of-fact account had overstated the dull ordinariness of the object they had come to steal. Had it not been placed on the plinth that supported the statue of Athena, it would have reached no higher than Eperitus's thigh. As for form, as far as Eperitus could see it barely had any: there were two uneven bumps in the black wood that might have been breasts, while the lopsided knob on top could have optimistically passed as a head – devoid of neck and with nothing more than a misshapen nose for a facial feature. Two stumps on either side qualified as arms, and with no legs whatsoever its only support was the metal cradle on which it was sat.

'It's even less impressive than I'd expected,' he commented.

'And the Trojans think *this* came from the gods?' Diomedes added. 'Such fools deserve to lose the war.'

Odysseus undid the green cloak Helen had given him.

'We'll be the fools if they catch us talking here. Let's take the thing and get back to the walls – this place is making me feel uneasy.'

He threw the cloak around the Palladium, as if afraid to touch it with his bare hands, and lifted it from its stand. With deft movements, he knotted the corners of the garment together and slung the parcel under his arm. Just then, Eperitus's senses reacted to a presence. Whether a small sound or a new smell, he was not aware of the trigger that told him they were no longer alone, but he spun round with his spear held rigidly before him. The others turned in alarm, knowing Eperitus's instincts were never wrong, and snatched out their swords.

'How dare you desecrate this temple?'

It was a woman's voice, speaking in the Trojan tongue, that broke the silence. Eperitus's eyes picked out the diminutive figure of its owner in a corner of the vast chamber, dressed in the white robes of a priestess. She must have been sleeping in the temple, as many priestesses did, and been woken by their voices. Now she was approaching the three warriors with short, fearless steps that quickly brought her into the circle of light from their torches.

'Don't you know what that *is*? Put it back at once. At once!'

She was an old woman, but she had such confidence in the power of her own authority that she had not even thought to shout for the guards. Either that, or she was too shocked by their sacrilege to do anything other than follow her own outrage. She advanced again, pointing at the bag under Odysseus's arm and spluttering angrily for him to give it to her. Then her eyes fell on his face and she stopped.

'Who are you?' she demanded, narrowing her eyes. 'I know your face. Who's your commander?'

'If I have a commander,' Odysseus answered in her own language, 'it's Agamemnon, king of Mycenae.'

'Greeks!' the priestess exclaimed, throwing her hands up to her cheeks. 'How did you ...? By all the gods, I must call the guards.'

The point of Odysseus's sword was at her throat in an instant.

'You'll say nothing, Theano. Yes, I know you and you know me. I am Odysseus, king of Ithaca. These are my comrades, Diomedes of Argos and Eperitus, captain of my guard. Eperitus and I were guests of your husband before the war started.'

'Yes, I remember you now. You were welcome then, especially by Antenor, who has always loved the Greeks. For his sake, I would gladly let you return by whatever way you came into our sacred city, even giving you my sworn oath not to raise the alarm until you were far enough away. Though not with the effigy you have under your arm, Odysseus, not even under the threat of death. Athena is my mistress and the Palladium is sacred to her; if you try to take it I promise you my dying scream will awake the guards outside.'

'The guards are all dead,' Odysseus lied. 'I have no wish that you should join them, but if you try to prevent me taking the Palladium I will not hesitate to cut open your throat. Am I clear? Now, promise me your silence while we escape and I'll let you live. Make your choice, Theano.'

He raised the point of the blade a fraction so that it pressed against the soft flesh beneath the old woman's chin, causing her to draw breath sharply. The next moment, the weapon fell from Odysseus's hand with a loud clang and he stepped back, clutching his hand beneath his armpit and wincing with pain. Eperitus and Diomedes looked at him in confusion, then down at the sword on the flagstones. It was glowing red.

Something else had changed. Sensing danger, Eperitus stepped back and lowered the head of his spear towards the old woman. By now she was standing rigid with her shoulders pulled back and her fingers splayed at her sides. Bright, silvery light was spilling from her eyes and nostrils, filling Eperitus with terror and forcing him to retreat. Out of the corner of his eye he saw Diomedes's face, his eyes wide with disbelief and shock as he raised his sword over his head and made to bring it down on the priestess. Before the edged metal could touch her, it burst into flames and leapt from the Argive king's hand to skitter across the floor in blazing circles.

Odysseus and Eperitus dropped their torches and fell back to the plinth where the great statue of Athena stood. Theano had stopped shaking now, but the light continued to pour from her eyes and nostrils so that the three men could only glance at her from behind their raised hands.

'You know me, Odysseus,' she said, light streaming from her mouth. But it was no longer the voice of Theano that spoke now. It was the goddess herself. 'Have I ever failed you or betrayed your trust in me?'

Athena's anger sent tremors through the floor beneath their feet, and led by Odysseus the warriors fell to their knees before her.

'And is this how you repay my help? To steal the image of Pallas, my friend, in whose beloved memory it was created?'

Eperitus gave a sidelong glance at the king. Odysseus's head was hung low, not daring to look at the goddess, but Eperitus could see the guilt and anguish written on his face.

'I command you to return the statue to its rightful place. If you love and honour me – indeed, if you value my continued patronage and protection, Odysseus – you will do my bidding.'

Odysseus closed his eyes tightly and drew back his lips in an agony of indecision. But the effigy remained beneath his arm, wrapped in the cloak.

'*Answer me!*'

'I cannot, Mistress. I mean, I cannot return the Palladium.'

There was a moment of silence, filled only by the hiss and splutter of the torches. Then Athena spoke again, this time her voice calmer and more gentle.

'Odysseus, my child. I have watched you and loved you all your life – few mortals have been as precious to me as you are. However, if you leave this temple with the effigy of my friend, that is an affront that I cannot permit to go unpunished. You know that.'

'My orders come from Agamemnon, my lady, to fulfil an oracle given to us by Helenus. He said that Troy will not fall as long as the Palladium remains in the city.'

'Curse your stubborn beard, Odysseus. Who do you put your faith in, Apollo or me? How often have prophecies given in his name sown trouble for Greeks and Trojans alike? But my path is wisdom; it is straight and even, and though narrow it leads a man ultimately to his goal. Will you abandon me now?'

'If the oracle isn't fulfilled, I might never return to Ithaca. I might never see Penelope or Telemachus again!'

'You might and you might not, but if you insist on fulfilling this oracle then won't all other oracles concerning you come true? Will you not doom yourself to a further ten years away from home and family, as the Pythoness predicted when you were a young man? What's more, persist in this and not only will you lose my protection, Odysseus, you will also risk my *wrath*! And yet I cannot make your choice for you, so decide now and be damned.'

Theano's eyes and mouth closed and the light was extinguished as swiftly as it had come, leaving them with only the dull glow of the struggling torches. A moment later, the priestess's legs buckled and she slumped unconscious to the floor. Diomedes and Eperitus retrieved the torches they had dropped and turned to face Odysseus.

'Was that –?' Diomedes began.

'Athena,' Eperitus finished. He turned to Odysseus. 'What are you going to do?'

The king raised his head wearily and looked at them with a tortured expression and eyes that were wracked with pain. He picked up his sword, which was now cold to the touch, and stood. Diomedes's weapon was nearby and he kicked this over to the king of Argos.

'I can't bear the thought of this war going on any longer, so I've made my decision. We take the Palladium. And now we should go. We have a long journey back to the camp and the Trojans will be close on our trail as soon as they see their talisman is missing.'

'First we must tie up Theano,' Eperitus said. 'If we don't, she'll raise the alarm the moment she wakes.'

With compunction – remembering the hospitality the priestess and her husband had shown them on their first visit to Troy – Odysseus and Eperitus tied her hands behind her back and gagged her, before hiding her still unconscious body behind the immense statue of Athena. As they laid her down, Eperitus caught Odysseus's eye. He wanted to ask his friend whether they had done the right thing, to steal the Palladium in spite of Athena's direct command that it should remain in the temple, but Odysseus saw the question coming and looked away, indicating it was not a matter he wished to discuss. He was not quick enough to disguise the doubt and regret written in his features, though, an expression Eperitus was not used to seeing on the king's face.

Silently, they crossed the floor of the temple to where Diomedes was standing guard at the door. The Palladium was tucked under his arm and his sword was held tightly in his other hand.

'Hurry up,' he hissed anxiously. 'Do you *want* to be caught?'

The guards were still fast asleep on the portico and they were able to make their way back to the city walls without hindrance. Then, as they climbed the steps and approached the stinking hole in the battlements through which they were to escape, they were met by a stern challenge.

'What's your business here at this time of night? Who are you?'

A figure came striding along the ramparts towards them, the faint starlight glinting off his scaled armour and the tip of his levelled spear. Realising that all the guard had to do was call out, Eperitus raised the point of his own weapon and charged. The Trojan sprang forward to meet him, punching the boss of his shield into Eperitus's face and knocking him back against the parapet. Seeing Odysseus and Diomedes draw their swords, he ran on and thrust his spear into the Ithacan's flank. Odysseus was torn sideways and fell to the flagstones. But before the guard could think to shout for help, Diomedes's sword had sliced through his neck and sent his head over the battlements and into the darkness below.

Eperitus had regained his feet before the Trojan's torso crumpled to the floor, and in a single bound was at Odysseus's side. The king lay on his back, his eyes squeezed shut with pain. A dark, wet patch was spreading through the wool of his tunic, just below his ribs.

'Odysseus? *Odysseus!*'

He opened his eyes.

'It's nothing. A flesh wound to the side, that's all.'

Diomedes joined them and delicately peeled back the torn material to reveal a deep cut.

'It'll bleed a lot, but nothing worse than that. The gods are with you tonight, my friend.'

'On the contrary,' Odysseus replied, sitting up. 'This is Athena's way of telling me I'm on my own now. She's not going to protect me any more.'

'More work for me then,' Eperitus commented, helping him to his feet. 'Now, if you can still walk we need to get going.'

'I can walk,' Odysseus grunted, tearing a strip from the Trojan's cloak and winding it about his wound.

They tossed the corpse over the battlements, and, after dropping through the latrine hole onto the stinking shelf of rock below, carried it the short distance to the Simöeis. Here they washed as much of the filth as they could from their bodies, then with the skies growing less dark in the east – revealing the outline of the mountains – they set off towards the Greek camp with the Palladium strapped to Diomedes's broad back.

Chapter Thirty-Two
THE INSANITY OF KINGS

Eperitus folded a cut of cold goat's meat in a slice of bread and crammed it into his mouth. As a captive he had been left in a constant state of hunger and the hastened march back to the camp had made him even more ravenous. Now, though, he was surrounded by the luxury of Agamemnon's vast tent and all the food and drink he could want. A passing slave saw the empty cup before him and refilled it with wine – heavily watered down, as it was still early morning – and such was Eperitus's thirst that he emptied it at a single draught.

As the liquid sluiced down his throat he blinked the tiredness from his eyes and stared round himself. The flax sails that formed the roof of the tent allowed the rosy sunlight to filter in and give the interior a warm, bright feel, at the same time allowing the breeze from the Aegean to blow through and keep the air fresh and clean. The walls were lined with the trophies Agamemnon had won on the battlefield, while the floor was covered with expensive, thickly layered pelts as a sign of his wealth. The commanders of the army were already streaming in through the tent's different entrances and gathering around the edges of the table where the King of Men planned his battle strategies. But this morning they were not staring at the customary mock ups of the plain between the Greek camp and Troy, but at the large, black lump of wood that lay unceremoniously in its centre. The sight of the Palladium – the reason Agamemnon had summoned the Council of Kings – caused a stir of conversation that must have been heard for some distance. Normally by now Agamemnon would have called for silence so that the council could begin, but today as he stood with Nestor at his side he seemed content to allow the hubbub to continue. Pleased, perhaps, to let his commanders savour the fulfilment of the final oracle and what it meant for them all.

The noisiest were crowded around Diomedes and Odysseus, congratulating them on their success. Diomedes was revelling in the glory, recounting their exploits with unashamed embellishment, while Odysseus accepted the flood of handshakes and pats on the back with quiet dignity. He was content to allow the bloody bandage wrapped about his midriff to speak of his own part in the adventure. A few recognised Eperitus's contribution and welcomed him back from captivity, most notably Peisandros, the barrel-chested Myrmidon captain who had once helped save him from execution in Sparta. The old soldier insulted him roundly, then embraced him and told him how glad he was to learn he had not died on the battlefield. Mostly, though, Eperitus was happy just to stand back and sup his wine while his two comrades received the praise and honour they were due. After all, had they not rescued him from imprisonment? And was it not their cunning, courage and good fortune that had stolen the Palladium? Then, with a shout of triumphant joy, Menelaus entered the tent and approached the men who had sealed the fate of Troy.

'By all the gods on Olympus, why didn't you tell anyone what you were up to?' His balding auburn hair and wiry beard, both thick with grey, gave him a fearsome appearance, but his brown eyes were damp with emotion and as his strong hands enclasped each of theirs in turn they could feel the warmth of his gratitude. 'I've been wracking my brains for a way to get hold of the Palladium, and you three just walk right in and steal it from under their noses. Incredible! And there it is.'

He raised his hands toward the deformed effigy on the table and stared at it with a mixture of awe and revulsion.

'Not much to look at, is it?' Diomedes commented wryly.

'Not to our eyes maybe, but can you imagine what they're saying in Troy right now? Just think how they must feel, knowing their protection is gone and that our very next attack will be their defeat. By Ares's sword, Diomedes! At long last, everything's in place for victory. I can hardly believe that all I have to do is reach out and Helen will be mine again.'

'The same walls that have held us for ten years are still there, my lord,' Eperitus reminded the Spartan king. 'Not to mention the walls of armoured flesh that stand behind them.'

Menelaus was not listening. Though his eyes remained on the Palladium, in his thoughts he was already striding through the ruins of Troy in search of his wife.

'And yet,' he muttered, 'I don't know what I'll do when I see her. After all these years, after chasing her to the other side of the world and laying siege to her kidnappers for so long, suddenly I can't imagine what it'll be like to set eyes on her beauty again. Even to be in the same room as her! Some say she wasn't kidnapped at all, that she ran away with Paris because she had fallen in love with him.' His brow furrowed and his hands balled up into fists on the table top. 'And may Aphrodite help her if it's true, because I don't know whether I'll embrace her or run her through with my sword!'

Menelaus spat the last words out with vengeful malice, as if Helen was already standing captive before him. Eperitus briefly debated the wisdom of telling him that his wife had helped them steal the Palladium; or that, according to Odysseus's account, she had helped him enter Pergamos and told him where to find the sacred statue, even going so far as sending her maids to drug the temple guards. But he also knew it was not his place to reveal these things; it was Odysseus's. He stared at the king of Ithaca, silently urging him to speak up in Helen's defence, but Odysseus said nothing.

The other conversations had stopped dead at the bitterness in Menelaus's words, prompting Agamemnon to lean forward with his hands flat on the table.

'You'll embrace her, of course, Brother,' he said in a commanding tone. 'The kings of Greece haven't fought for ten years so that you can kill the woman they all swore to protect.'

Menelaus looked round at the circle of faces. 'Of course not,' he conceded, though without conviction.

'So,' Agamemnon continued, 'let us congratulate Odysseus and Diomedes for their guile and courage in entering Troy and stealing the Palladium. The full story can wait until we're all sat around a blazing fire with meat in our bellies and wine in our veins, and doubtless Odysseus will be the man to tell it. But now, with the third of the oracles given to us by Helenus fulfilled, we must decide on our next move. That, my noble lords, is why I've called you here.'

'I'd have thought our next move was obvious.'

The speaker's tone was matter-of-fact, but the hint of criticism caused every eye to turn to the corner of the table where the words had come from. Neoptolemus, who as commander of the Myrmidons had taken his father's place on the Council, stood with his hands behind his back staring at the King of Men. Peisandros was at his shoulder, his arms crossed over his broad chest and his wild beard thrust out defiantly. Agamemnon frowned a little, but quickly regained his usual coolness.

'Younger minds don't suffer the hindrance of greater experience,' he replied. 'What would the son of Achilles have us do?'

'Attack.'

Nestor's white beard opened with a smile. 'Of course we'll attack.'

'Attack *now*,' Neoptolemus said, punching his hand. 'You've become too used to sitting in your precious camp and letting the years roll by. And where's it got you? I say muster your armies before the walls and march on Troy. You've fulfilled all the oracles the gods laid down, so what are you waiting for? Attack now and Troy will fall.'

There were nods of agreement among the commanders and a notable growl of approval from Peisandros, but there were also a few shaken heads. The remainder of the assembly kept their opinions to themselves and turned their gaze to Agamemnon, who was equally silent as he looked at Neoptolemus.

'I say the son of Achilles is right,' said Menelaus beside him. 'We've become too comfortable in our tents and huts – or maybe we've just grown afraid of the Trojans! Let's turn our minds back to the palaces we left behind, to our wives and children. I'm sick of Ilium. Now we have the blessing of the gods, what's stopping us from marching up to the Scaean Gate and finally taking what we came here for?'

The passion in his voice roused others and the murmurs of agreements grew louder. Some contested the rashness of an immediate attack, causing the tent to fill rapidly with the sound of arguing voices, until eventually Agamemnon was forced to raise his arms for silence.

'And what do the men whose bravery gained us the Palladium say?'

Diomedes was quick to answer. 'I've always been the first to join an attack and my Argives are in the forefront of every battle, but I can't agree with Neoptolemus and Menelaus. I've seen the walls of Troy from outside *and* inside and believe me, my friends, when I tell you they won't blow away with a puff of youthful ardour. By taking the Palladium we have undermined Trojan self-confidence, but we haven't removed the hinges from their gates or knocked even one stone from their battlements. Their defences are as strong now as they ever were. No, if we're to take Troy we need to think about it, use the same intelligence that Odysseus showed when he thought up his plan to enter the city.'

Eperitus was among a handful who voiced their agreement, though he noticed Odysseus was silent. Then Neoptolemus thumped his fist down on the table and glared round at the Council in anger.

'What are you, warriors or women? If you haven't the stomach to fight then we Myrmidons will scale the walls alone and claim all the glory for ourselves!'

Opposing choruses for and against the plan broke out again, and this time it was Nestor who silenced them.

'I want to hear what Odysseus thinks,' the old man said. 'Are you with Diomedes or Neoptolemus?'

Eperitus looked expectantly at Odysseus, whom he felt must surely speak out against the recklessness of an immediate attack. As for himself, he agreed with Diomedes's call for a more thoughtful approach: the fulfilment of the oracles did not mean the walls would come tumbling down, but that a marker had been passed and the gods would somehow or other present the Greeks with an opportunity for victory. Repeatedly beating their heads against the walls of Troy, in his opinion, could only lead to one conclusion – a broken skull.

'If Neoptolemus and Menelaus want to attack Troy, I cannot go with them,' Odysseus declared. Eperitus and Diomedes exchanged satisfied glances, while others grumbled their dissatisfaction. But Odysseus had not yet finished and raised his hands for silence. 'I am wounded and tired and I need to rest, but I *won't* discourage any man who believes the time to end the war has come. It seems to me the gods have finally tipped the scales in our favour and Priam's city is ripe for the taking. So if the King of Men decides to send the whole army into battle, then I will not speak against him. I will even keep my Ithacans here to guard the ships, denying them and myself the glory of victory.'

The assembly exploded with a sudden call to arms, a call that Agamemnon was ready to embrace and encourage.

'So be it. Muster your armies on the plain. Summon every man capable of bearing arms. Troy falls today!'

Eperitus watched the kings exit the tent, all of them eager to be in the forefront of the coming battle. Even Diomedes went with them, leaving Eperitus suddenly doubtful of his own conviction that the attack would fail. He wondered whether, after being in the thick of the fighting for ten years, he and the rest of the Ithacans were about to miss the final defeat of their enemies. Then he shook his head, as if to rid himself of the ridiculous notion, and turned to the king.

'Why didn't you speak up, Odysseus? You know this is madness – do they really think another assault on the walls is going to make any difference?'

Odysseus hooked his large hand around Eperitus's elbow and pulled him through the crowded tent to one of the exits. Men were fighting each other to be the first out and back to their armies, so drunk were they with the thought that the gods were about to give them victory. Eperitus watched them in disgust, as if he stood alone on an island of reason while the rest of the Greeks crashed about him in a storm of insanity. He followed Odysseus through the crush and soon felt the soft sand giving way beneath his sandals, hearing once more the liberating sound of the waves rolling against the shore and the cry of the seagulls hovering overhead.

'Odysseus, why don't you call them to their senses?' he implored, casting a glance over his shoulder at the running figures spreading through the camp like a fire. 'Climb up on the prow of one of these galleys and shout out. Tell them this is folly. Do you want the blood of hundreds of men on your hands?'

At this, Odysseus stopped and turned to face his captain.

'Eperitus, I know as well as you do that these men are going to certain defeat. And maybe I could stop them if I tried – maybe. But I have a plan to conquer Troy now, a plan given to me by the gods, and if that plan is to succeed then the Greeks must taste defeat one last time. I'll explain everything in my hut, but first we have to find Omeros.'

Chapter Thirty-Three
HOPE OUT OF DEFEAT

Penelope rarely felt happier than when she was visiting the pig farm at the southern end of Ithaca. The sight of the fat swine trotting through the mud in the wide pens, their tiny eyes half hidden by their flapping ears, always brought a smile to her face. Even better was to be free from the confines of the small palace and out in the open air, where the sky seemed to go on forever and she could gaze south-east towards the horizon – the direction Odysseus would return by when the war in Troy eventually ended. But as she leaned against the wooden timbers that kept the noisy beasts from wandering off, she felt ever more sharply the absence of her son.

She looked down at Argus, sitting faithfully at her side with his ears pricked up and his tail wagging. He was looking expectantly towards the road that came down from the north, passing through fields of gnarled and windswept olive trees.

'What is it, boy?'

The boarhound gave a bark and stood on all fours. Penelope followed his gaze and saw a horseman approaching along the road, leaving a trail of dust behind him.

'Looks like Mentor, my lady,' said Eumaeus, the swineherd, who was standing among his pigs and throwing out handfuls of wild nuts and berries from a leather satchel at his hip.

Moments later the horseman had reached Eumaeus's hut and was tying the reins of his mount to a post. A tall black dog came out of the hut and advanced growling towards him, followed by four black puppies yapping noisily in high voices. Then, when their mother recognised Mentor and allowed him to run a hand over her ears, the puppies turned on each other and began fighting among themselves.

'Good morning!' Mentor called.

Eumaeus threw a last handful of feed to the grunting pigs, then climbed the fence and went to meet him. Penelope propped her elbow on a timber post and watched them embrace. Eumaeus said something she did not catch then disappeared inside his hut. Mentor spotted his queen and strode toward her.

'So here you are, my lady,' he said, greeting her with a smile and a kiss on the cheek. 'You've been avoiding me since the Kerosia, I think.'

'You've been away.'

'A few days in Samos, looking after the king's business. But every time I've called at the palace you've been busy or absent.'

She shrugged apologetically, conceding the point. 'I just knew you'd have some awkward questions, which I didn't want to have to answer with so many servants around.'

'Don't you trust them?'

'Some, but not all. And too many of them are inclined to gossip.'

'So what don't you want them gossiping about?'

'My reasons for agreeing to Eupeithes's proposal,' she answered, turning and leaning her forearms on the fence. 'That's why you've come out here to find me, isn't it?'

'Of course,' he admitted, joining her. 'Well, are you going to tell me?'

She sighed. 'For one thing, I want my son back here. At my side. While Telemachus stands to inherit the throne he's in danger, but under Eupeithes's proposal that danger is gone.'

'Don't you think Eupeithes might have been offering you a reason to bring him back so he could try to kill him again? With Telemachus dead there'll be no other challengers to the throne.'

'No, he won't risk upsetting the balance of things. At the least he'll wait until I remarry. And I would have thought *you*'d be pleased to have him back under your tutelage. You've taught him all he knows, Mentor, and he loves you like a –'

She faltered.

'Like a father?'

Penelope smiled wanly. 'Yes, I suppose so. That's what you've been to him in Odysseus's absence.'

'Odysseus will return soon,' Mentor said. 'The oracle will confirm that. Antinous and I depart in the morning, you know.'

'I know.'

Eumaeus reappeared from the hut with a cup of water in his hand. His guard dog and her puppies came leaping after him and Argus trotted out to meet them. The swineherd handed the small wooden bowl to Mentor, who drained the cool liquid in one draught and placed the cup down on top of a flat-headed fencepost. Eumaeus swung himself over the low barrier and resumed feeding his pigs, while Penelope hooked her arm through Mentor's and led him in the opposite direction.

'Have you already forgotten the oracle that was given to Odysseus twenty years ago? If he went to Troy, he'd be doomed not to come home again for twenty years.'

'You *know* about that?' Mentor asked, surprised.

'He told me before he left,' she replied. 'It wasn't easy to take, but he also insisted a man has the power to change his destiny if he really wants to. And I believe him.'

'So what are you saying? You agreed to Eupeithes's proposal on the grounds of an oracle you don't think will come true?'

Penelope shook her head. 'If I'd refused altogether, Eupeithes might have been tempted to force his way into power again, especially in his current mood and with that pack of wolves growling away behind him. We can't allow that to happen. But you're missing my point about the oracle. I don't believe Odysseus is bound by the Pythoness's words – I can't afford to believe it, even though the war has already lasted ten years – but if she predicted *then* that he wouldn't return for twenty years, surely she will *now* say he'll be gone for another decade? By the oath we all took at the Kerosia, and which was announced publicly, that means Eupeithes can't force me to do anything for ten more years. Not without civil war, and I'm gambling he hasn't the courage for that if there's a peaceful alternative.'

Mentor looked at her admiringly.

'Odysseus chose well when he married you, Penelope. Your cunning may have bought him ten more years, and the war will never go on for that long.'

'Find a daughter of Lacedaemon and she will keep the thieves from your house,' she said, quoting the second half of the Pythoness's riddle. 'That's one part of the oracle I'm determined will come true. And the best way I can defend Odysseus's kingdom is to keep gaining us time until he returns.'

Eperitus, Odysseus and Omeros leaned against the bow rail of the beached galley, watching the defeated army return to their tents. Filthy and exhausted, many of them wounded, they trudged down the slope from the gates with their heads low, dejected by the betrayal of the gods who had promised them victory. For all their faith in the oracles, the walls of Troy stood as strong as ever and the bodies of hundreds more Greeks lay littered in their shade, carrion for the gluttonous birds and dogs.

The appalling aftermath of another defeat left Eperitus feeling cold. More men sent needlessly down to Hades's halls, where it was said the joys of the living world were stripped away and the soul was left with nothing more than the idea they had once been alive. In that dark place there was no memory of the events or emotions they had experienced in their bodies of flesh, only a sense that something wonderful was lost to them for eternity. And yet, if Odysseus was right, their sacrifice was a necessary one so that thousands more could keep their places at life's feast. Eperitus gave the king a sidelong glance. He had changed since their encounter with Athena in the temple, become more grim with the loss of the goddess's patronage. Though whether it was despair or a determination to end the war without her, he could not tell.

'Go and prepare the wine, Omeros,' Odysseus said. 'They'll be here soon.'

The squire nodded and went to the galley's stern, where skins of wine and water hung from the twin steering oars. A short while later, they heard the sound they had been expecting – heavy footsteps on the gangplank leading up from the beach. Agamemnon stepped down onto the deck, his breastplate spattered with gore and the pure white tunic beneath filthy with dust. His red cloak was ripped and one of the cheek guards of his helmet had been torn away to reveal a fresh cut across his jaw. Behind him came Menelaus, Nestor and Diomedes, all similarly begrimed. Further footsteps announced the arrival of Idomeneus of Crete, Menestheus of Athens and Little Ajax. Last of all came Neoptolemus, whose divine armour gleamed as if newly made, though his face and limbs were smeared with blood and dirt. His eyes stared out from the unnatural mask, angered by the reversal but not dispirited.

'You sent us knowingly to defeat,' Agamemnon said, pulling the helmet from his head and throwing it onto the deck at Odysseus's feet. His blue eyes were fierce with suppressed rage.

'I said I would not oppose any who chose to go. Not that my opinion for or against would have made any difference.'

Odysseus nodded to Omeros, who took kraters of wine to each of the battle-weary warriors.

'You underestimate yourself, Odysseus,' Nestor said, taking his cup and easing his old body down onto one of the benches. 'Your intelligence is widely respected, from the lowest levy to the highest king. An opinion from you carries as much weight as a command from Agamemnon himself.'

'Nestor's right,' Menelaus growled. 'If you'd spoken up when Diomedes did, perhaps we wouldn't have ran headlong into another reverse – especially one so costly to what was left of the army's morale. When warriors have been promised victory by the gods themselves, defeat is twice as crushing. On my way back I heard men openly talking about returning to Greece, not caring that I was within earshot of them.'

'Then tell them that's what we're going to do.'

The others looked questioningly at Odysseus, as if they had misheard him. The momentary silence was broken by a sneering grunt from Little Ajax.

'Is that why you let us march off in the first place? To snap the army's will to fight? To end the war, just so you can skulk off home to your precious family?'

'You're not listening,' Odysseus replied. 'I said *tell* the army we're going to leave for Greece, not *do* it.'

'And what's the point in that?' Idomeneus asked, sitting beside Nestor and removing his helmet. 'Give them hope, only to order them back into battle again?'

Odysseus shook his head. 'Of course not. I've an idea for conquering Troy, but we have to convince the Trojans we've given up and gone home. And to do that our own men have to believe that's what we intend to do.'

Neoptolemus spat on the deck. 'Another of your famous tricks, Odysseus? Just like the theft of the Palladium? Devoid of glory and doomed to failure.'

'Perhaps you'd have us attack the walls again?' Eperitus said. 'That idea didn't exactly cover you in honour or bring about a famous victory, did it!'

Neoptolemus stepped forward, his face reddening with fury and his fingertips unconsciously touching the hilt of his sword. Diomedes quickly slapped a hand on his armoured shoulder and forced him down to one of the benches.

'If Odysseus has an idea, I suppose we'd better hear it.'

'I agree,' Nestor said. 'It doesn't take the wisdom of my great years to realise the walls of Troy aren't going to fall to force alone. But that doesn't mean the oracles were wrong or the gods were deceiving us. What *is* this plan of yours?'

Odysseus looked at Agamemnon, who gave a small nod.

'I sent messengers asking you to come here so that we wouldn't be overheard, and if you agree to my plan then you must take an oath not to share it with anyone – even your most trusted captains. I've had the inklings of a strategy for some time now, but until I went to Pelops's tomb and saw his sarcophagus I didn't know how to carry it out. That's why the gods sent me there – not to obtain a simple bone, but to reveal the one way in which my plan could succeed.'

'You're talking in riddles,' Little Ajax interrupted. 'How can a tomb help us take Troy?'

'Eperitus, do you remember what was placed on top of the sarcophagus?'

Eperitus nodded, smiling as he saw the link with the idea Odysseus had already outlined to him.

'It was a horse.'

'A horse,' Odysseus repeated. 'Because Pelops's people were renowned horse-lovers, just like the Trojans. That gave me the inspiration to build a great wooden horse, taller than the Scaean Gate, which we will dedicate to Athena in atonement for desecrating her temple, and in the hope she will then give us a safe journey back to Greece. The Trojans won't be able to resist taking it into their city as a token of their victory.'

'Victory!' Menelaus sputtered. '*Victory?*'

The others shared doubtful looks, but remained silent. Agamemnon's fixed gaze grew colder than ever, but Odysseus just smiled.

'Naturally. The defeat we've just suffered was the final stone on the mound. Didn't you say the men are openly talking about ending the war and returning to Greece? Now all we need is a good westerly wind and we can strike this camp and board our galleys for home. Or at least, that's what the Trojans will think when they find it abandoned.'

'Should we get the men to start the preparations now?' Nestor asked. He looked bemused – doubtful as to the reason for abandoning their camp after so long, but intrigued at how such a move would bring about the end of the war. 'After all, there's hardly been a puff of air over the Aegean for days now – we can't sail until the winds pick up again.'

'No,' Odysseus replied. 'When we go, it has to look like we've left in a hurry – leave the tents and everything that'll slow us down. In fact, we should burn them. What we *can* do is get the ships seaworthy and begin the construction of the horse. For that we'll need Epeius, a man who can work wood better than any of us.'

Agamemnon had had enough. He stood and folded his arms across his breastplate.

'You seem to assume I'm going to agree to your plan, but nothing I've heard so far has shown me how it will bring us victory. Why should we sail home empty handed, after so much strife and bloodshed? And why should we build the Trojans a trophy with which to celebrate our supposed defeat?'

'It's as I said: first we must convince our enemies they've won. Then, out of apparent defeat will come the victory we have sought for so long. The horse is the key, and if you'll all sit down I'll tell you what I have in mind.'

'And what about him?' Little Ajax asked, indicating Omeros. 'If we're forbidden from saying anything to our own men, why's this lad allowed to overhear this fabulous scheme of yours?'

Odysseus stared at Eperitus's squire and gave a self-satisfied grin.

'Because Omeros is essential to the plan. You see, after Agamemnon has announced we're returning to Greece, Calchas is going to prophesy that the gods will deny us even a breath of wind unless we offer them a human sacrifice. And since I've discovered that Omeros has been plotting against me, I've decided *he* will be that sacrifice.'

book
FOUR

FOUR

Chapter Thirty-Four
THE WOODEN HORSE

Helen awoke with a feeling of expectancy. The dawn light was barely filtering through the curtains when she threw aside her blankets and called for her maids. Sitting at the edge of her bed, she wondered what it was that felt so different. There were no new sounds drifting in through the window, nor could she smell anything out of the ordinary that might be warning her senses. If something had altered in the world, then she had sensed it from within: a gut feeling that told her the day was going to be unlike any other.

She yawned and ran her toes through the thick fur. Where were her maids? For as long as she had lived in Troy, her maids had slept at the threshold to her room ready to answer the mere sound of her voice. Suddenly, she clutched a hand to her chest and wondered whether they had been taken. It was a fear that had stalked her ever since she had sent them to drug the guards at the temple of Athena, the night the Palladium had been stolen. In using them so recklessly to help Odysseus she had risked implicating herself in the theft, a treacherous act punishable by execution – and an outcome which even her beauty and status could not have saved her from. Instead the temple guards had paid that price, slaughtered without hesitation on Deiphobus's orders for failing in their duty. Their quick deaths meant they had not had time to consider their wine might have been drugged, or add to this the fact the wine had been brought to them by Helen's maids. And yet Helen still lived in dread, not that her maids would betray her but that other eyes may have seen them visiting the guards.

She stood and quickly dressed herself. Glancing back across the room, she saw that Deiphobus's half of the large bed – the same bed she had once shared with his brother, and which held such sweet memories for her – had not been slept in. This was not unusual, as the prince would often sleep in his old quarters after a late night discussing the war with his father and the other commanders. He also knew Helen did not love him, though the knowledge did not prevent him coming to her when his lust urged. The thought deepened the frown already on her brow, and throwing her cloak around her shoulders she hurried out of the room.

She found all four of her maids on the walls of the citadel, pressed against the battlements and talking excitedly as they looked southwards.

'So, here you are!' Helen snapped, climbing the stone steps. 'I have to dress *myself* because *you*'d rather be on the walls gossiping among yourselves.'

'But my lady,' one of the maids began.

'My lady nothing. Get back inside, at once!'

The girls exchanged guilty looks, then after a last glance over the ramparts fled down the steps and in the direction of the palace.

Helen waited until they were out of sight, then her curiosity gaining the better of her she ran up the last few steps to see for herself what had dragged her maids away from their duties. Reaching the parapet, she looked first to the large bay lying a bowshot from the city walls. Empty, as was the sea beyond the jaws of its entrance. But she had already glimpsed the thing that had brought the four girls to the walls, and as she turned her head south she realised this was the source of the strange feeling that had woken her from her dreams. On top of the ridge that frowned over the weaving line of the Scamander, a short distance west of the temple of Thymbrean Apollo, was the gigantic figure of a horse. It stood higher than the plane trees that formed the temple – much higher – and as the light of the rising sun fell on its motionless flanks, she could see that it was made entirely of wood. Each of its long limbs was as tall as two men, and together they supported a barrel-like torso that had been skilfully crafted to follow the lines and curves of a horse's body. From its hind quarters a shower of leather strips cascaded down to the ground in mimicry of a tail, while rising up from its shoulders was a broad neck crested by a dense mane of leather bands that twisted in the wind. The head was large with a wide forehead that tapered down to its flared nostrils and bared teeth. Its chin rested on its chest and its stern eyes glowered at the walls of Troy, as if willing them to crumble and fall. The whole impressive edifice stood upon a broad platform with four solid wheels on either side, each wheel twice as big as those of a chariot or farmer's cart.

Helen leaned against the cold stone parapet and stared in disbelief. In the distance behind the horse, columns of black smoke spiralled up into the skies over the Greek camp, forming scars against the blue firmament that spoke of change and a doom yet to be revealed. As she watched, wondering what the appearance of the horse might mean and where it had come from, she saw a troop of cavalry moving out from the city and galloping across the plain. Perhaps twenty men in all, they trotted over the fords of the Scamander and dashed up the slope towards the great structure above. At last, Helen began to hear shouts from the city, spreading with rapid inevitability towards Pergamos. More people – slaves and soldiers, artisans and nobles – were running up to the walls to look out at the strange new monument. At that moment Helen knew she had to see the horse for herself, not from the battlements but where it stood on the ridge.

She ran down the steps and back to the open space before the palace. As she had expected, horses and chariots were being prepared for the journey to the ridge. Priam's golden chariot was standing ready with Idaeus at the rail, his whip in his hand as he waited for the king to arrive. There, too, was Deiphobus's chariot. The prince stood in front of the horses, patting their necks and talking to them.

'Take me with you,' Helen said, running across the trampled dirt of the courtyard and laying her arms around her husband's neck. 'I want to see this magnificent horse.'

Deiphobus looked at her a moment, then shook his head.

'It could be dangerous.'

She smiled playfully, surprising him. 'Do you think it'll *bite* me?'

'I mean it could be a lure – the bait to draw us into a trap.'

'Am I any more important than Priam? If the king is going, then surely it's safe enough for me to go too? Besides, there's already a troop of cavalry up there – they would have spotted any immediate danger.' Seeing the doubt in his eyes, she leaned across and kissed him. 'I promise I'll stay close to you.'

His gaze wandered over her again. Although she had not received the usual attentions of her maids that morning, her natural beauty was more than powerful enough to break down his resistance. He nodded and helped her up into the chariot.

By the time Priam's chariot trundled out of the Scaean Gate, followed by two dozen cavalrymen and a collection of other chariots bearing his eldest sons and the commanders of his army, ropes had already been lashed around the hind legs of the wooden horse and hundreds of men were easing it carefully down the slope towards the flat plain before the ford. Here, scores of logs were being laid across the river bed so that the great beast could be pulled across as quickly and safely as possible. The royal procession passed either side of the wooden carpet, sending up sprays of water that shone in the morning sunlight. Helen, who was so rarely permitted beyond the city walls, was revelling in the feel of the unfettered wind on her face and the sense of openness all about her. It was a hint of the freedom she would enjoy if the war ended, and in her heart she called out to Aphrodite to lead one side or the other to victory soon. She cared little whether it was the Greeks or the Trojans, so long as it allowed her to escape the claustrophobia of city life and gain the liberty she had been denied for ten years.

As they crossed the wide meadows that were still bruised and trampled from the battles of the early summer, a series of commands echoed over the plain and the men on the ropes eased the great horse to a halt. It had reached level ground and would need to be pulled the rest of the way to the ford, but the officer in charge had seen the approaching chariots and ordered his teams to rest and regain their strength. As they came closer, Helen saw that the mounted officer was Apheidas.

'My lord,' he said, dipping his head a little as Priam's chariot pulled up.

The king stepped down and walked past Apheidas towards the wooden horse, stopping a few paces short of the towering structure. The other chariots clattered to a halt and the cavalry formed a crescent behind them, while the assortment of princes and nobles dismounted and gathered behind Priam, their mouths open and eyes staring up in bewilderment and wonder. Deiphobus took Helen's hand and shouldered his way through the others to stand at his father's side.

'What in Zeus's name is it?' Priam asked.

Apheidas nodded towards the opposite flank of the horse.

'There's an inscription.'

Priam moved in a wide circle to the other side of the structure, as if afraid to come too close to it. At the same time he held the palm of his hand up to the others, forbidding them to follow. Helen watched him as he fell beneath the long shadow of the horse on the western side, his old eyes narrowing as they searched for the inscription, found it and struggled to read what it said.

'It's in Greek,' he announced with a hint of frustration. 'I can speak the damned language, to a degree, but it's a long time since I've read it. Helen, come here girl and decipher it for me.'

'Go on,' Deiphobus urged, sensing her reluctance. He released her hand and nudged her in the back. 'It won't *bite* you.'

Helen passed under the high head of the horse, not daring to take her eyes from it as she crossed to stand beside Priam. The inscription was carved in sizeable letters from the front shoulder to the hind leg. Silently, she mouthed the words to herself as she read the once-familiar characters of her mother tongue. Then their meaning became clear and she felt a cold chill brush down her spine. She glanced at Apheidas, the only other person present who had read the words and understood them. His expression was inscrutable.

'What does it *say*?' Priam urged. 'Read it out.'

Helen read it in Greek first, then translated into the Trojan tongue.

'A gift from the Greeks to the goddess Athena, dedicated in grateful anticipation of a safe journey home.'

She felt Priam's hand take her elbow, his bony fingers gripping the flesh tightly for support. Reacting quickly, she put her arm about his waist and bore his weight as he slumped against her. Nobody seemed to notice. Eyes that had been staring in awe at the wooden horse were now frozen with doubt, understanding the words of the inscription but unable to accept what they implied.

'Then is it over?' Priam asked in a frail voice.

Helen took his hand in hers and squeezed it.

'I don't know.'

Deiphobus wiped his palm over his face and staggered across the grass to stand beside his wife. He looked at the carved words, reassured himself that Helen had not lied, and allowed a smile to touch the corners of his mouth.

'They've gone home. The Greeks have given up.' Turning to the teams of men sitting by their ropes, he raised his arms in the air and lifted his face to the heavens. 'Praise the gods, we've *won*!'

Slowly, the lines of soldiers climbed to their feet and stared at the horse. A single voice cheered. Others joined it, then more, until the morning air was filled with their shouting. The crowd of princes and nobles followed with wild cries of jubilation, forgetting the differences in their ranks and openly embracing each other. A handful of cavalrymen defied discipline and galloped off in the direction of the Scaean Gate, yelling with joy as they went to spread the news to the city. Helen laid her hand on her chest, which was rising and falling rapidly. She could hardly believe it. A feeling of elation flooded through her body and again she felt the shock of what it meant chilling her flesh and bringing her skin out in goosebumps. Then her gaze fell on Deiphobus and the knowledge that she would be his forever checked her excitement, darkening her thoughts and turning her limbs to stone. Now it was Priam's turn to catch her as the sudden heaviness in her muscles threatened to pull her to the ground.

'Deiphobus, look to your wife,' he commanded. Then, as his son passed his arm beneath Helen's shoulder, the king turned to Apheidas and lowered his voice. 'Send a patrol to the Greek camp, at once.'

'Aeneas is already there, my lord. We rode out to inspect this thing at dawn and as soon as we read the inscription he insisted on taking a troop of cavalry to see for himself. He should be returning at any moment.'

'What about our spies in their camp? Have we heard anything from them?'

'Nothing for several days, which is strange in itself. They're mostly slaves, though; if the Greeks really have left, they might have taken our spies with them.'

Priam nodded and turned back to Helen.

'Can you stand? I'll have Idaeus take you back to the city in my chariot.'

'No, thank you Father. I was just ... taken aback.'

Helen forced herself upright and stepped free of Deiphobus's arms. The prince gave her a questioning look, as if guessing her thoughts, but she turned her eyes away and stared up at the horse. At that angle, its blank eyes seemed mocking and its bared teeth appeared to be smiling, laughing even.

'Father, the war's over,' Deiphobus declared. 'We should parade the horse through the streets of the city, show the people the siege has ended and Troy has won.'

'We don't know the siege has ended,' Apheidas countered. 'Besides, Deiphobus, how do you plan on getting it through the gates when the damned thing is taller than the city walls?'

'We'll knock them down if we have to!'

'Silence!' Priam ordered. 'As long as I'm still king, *I* will decide what we do with the horse. And we won't do anything until I know what's happened to the Greeks.'

Apheidas commanded his soldiers to sit down again and the snap in his tone brought a sudden end to the euphoric atmosphere. Priam's sons and the commanders of Troy's army moved round the horse to see its inscription for themselves, discussing it in quiet tones while Priam, Apheidas and Deiphobus strolled out of earshot to carry on their debate. Helen walked over to the horse and laid a hand on one of its forelegs. The wood had been carefully crafted to a smooth finish and was strangely warm to the touch. She pulled her hand back in surprise, then turned in response to a clamour rising up from the city. The Scaean Gate had swung open and hundreds of people were issuing out of it. But unlike the exoduses of the past ten years, this was not an army going forth to battle but a crowd of ordinary citizens. Word had reached the men, women and children of the city and now, with triumphant songs and shouts of delight, they were coming to see the wooden horse for themselves.

Before the vanguard had crossed the ford, though, Idaeus gave a shout and pointed in the opposite direction. Approaching across the plain, pursued by a small cloud of dust, were two horsemen, galloping as fast as their mounts could carry them.

'How many men did Aeneas take with him?' Helen heard Priam's voice asking behind her, his tone urgent.

'At least twenty,' Apheidas answered.

Then the Greeks are still here, Helen thought. The patrol was massacred and these riders are all that remain of them!

The two horses reached them within moments, drawing up sharply in the shadow of the great wooden horse. Both men leapt from the saddle and ran towards Apheidas. Then, seeing Priam standing beside their commander, they knelt and lowered their heads before the king.

'What news?' Priam demanded. 'Were you ambushed? Did that fool Aeneas lead you into a trap?'

The riders exchanged glances.

'No, my lord. Aeneas sent us back to tell you the Greek camp has been abandoned. Their ships have all gone and they've burned their huts. Aeneas has remained with the rest of the patrol to carry out a search of what's left.'

Priam trembled and Helen stepped forward, fearing he would faint again. To her surprise, he waved her back and reached down to the rider who had spoken, pulling him to his feet and embracing him. He kissed the surprised cavalryman on both cheeks, then held him at arm's length and looked into his eyes.

'What's your name, man?'

'Peteos, my lord.'

'Peteos, I declare you a messenger of the gods. And for bringing me this news I promote you here and now to the royal guard. Long may you serve me and my successors.'

The astonished soldier bowed low and backed away to rejoin his envious comrade, while the king turned to look up at the horse.

'Apheidas,' he shouted, cheerfully, 'get your men back on those ropes and tell them to drag this monstrosity to the walls. Deiphobus, take some horsemen and ride to the city. I want the battlements over the Scaean Gate knocked down so we can bring it inside. We'll honour the inscription and dedicate it to Athena, as a replacement for the Palladium that was stolen. It will stand forever as a monument to the brave men of Ilium, and above all to the courage of Hector, the stalwart of Troy!'

And what of Paris? Helen thought. Had he given his life for nothing? Worse still, would the people of Troy forget his bravery, remembering him only for bringing the curse of war down upon them? Such a legacy had been his greatest fear, and the sadness of it was deepened by the fact that victory had come so soon after his death. If he had survived a little longer – been less reckless in his desire to overcome his guilt – they would have been free to spend the rest of their days together, their love unfettered by the ambitions of power-hungry men. But the jealous gods had preferred to deny them their happiness, condemning Paris to the forgetfulness of Hades and leaving Helen with little more than a fading memory of the man for whom she had sacrificed everything.

Deiphobus mounted a horse and led a handful of riders in the direction of the ford, keen to carry out his father's instructions. As Helen watched him leave, Priam called to her from his chariot.

'Helen, come up here with me. I'm going to announce our victory to my people and I want you at my side. Let them see what they've been fighting for, and let them know that you were worth every sacrifice.'

His moment of elation had passed and she knew he was being earnest. And if she, like the wooden horse, was to be paraded as a trophy of war, then so be it. She walked over and accepted his outstretched hand, stepping up beside him. With a flick of his whip, Idaeus sent the horses forward at a gentle trot. Behind them they could hear the grunts of the men at the ropes as they took the strain once more and began to pull the giant horse towards the ford.

The chariot had only travelled a short distance across the meadows before it slowed to a halt in front of the crowd coming up from the city. As one, they fell to their knees and bowed low before their king. Only one figure remained standing in their midst, a girl dressed all in black. Priam stared at Cassandra for a moment, but chose to ignore her impertinence and signalled for the rest to stand.

'Behold the symbol of your victory!' he declared. 'At last, my people, the day has come. The Greeks have gone! The war is over! We have won!'

His words were met with cheers and ecstatic screams, which did not die down until the wooden horse had been brought so close that the rapturous crowd were forced into silence by its grim presence. Then, as they stared at it in awe, a shriek of despair rang out and Cassandra pushed her way through the mass until she stood alone before her father.

'Fools! The gods have left you blind, stumbling towards your doom with shouts of joy on your lips.'

With tears rolling down her white cheeks and her eyes wide with terror, she seized hold of her robe and pulled at the material until it tore, revealing her pale breasts. Apheidas unclasped his cloak and threw it about the girl's shoulders, hiding her nakedness.

'Control yourself,' the king ordered his daughter. 'If your gloom must drive you to hysterics, then do it in private and don't dampen everyone else's happiness on this great day.'

'Great day?' Cassandra echoed. 'For whom? Not for Troy. Not for *your* house, Father! This symbol of victory you boast about is a harbinger of *death*. It carries with it the doom of Troy. Burn it! Burn it now, while you still can!'

Chapter Thirty-Five
CASSANDRA'S WOE

A stynome looked up at the wooden horse, still reeling from the news that the Greeks had left – that Eperitus had abandoned her. Why would they suddenly strike their camp and head home? Had they given up, or did they intend to return in greater numbers, perhaps to pursue a different strategy? Either way, surely Eperitus would have found some means to let her know? If they were returning to Greece, would he not have smuggled her a message, imploring her to sail with him? Or had his anger at her betrayal turned him against her again? As doubts clouded her mind, she looked again at the horse and recalled Odysseus's words to her, spoken in confidence on the night he, Diomedes and Eperitus had stolen the Palladium.

'One day soon,' he had warned, 'a wooden horse will appear within clear sight of the city walls. Some will welcome it, but others will call for its destruction. Don't let them succeed, Astynome! By whatever means you can, make sure the horse is preserved. If it's brought inside the city walls, the war will end and you will be reunited with Eperitus; if it's destroyed, you will never see him again.'

She had not understood the meaning of his words at the time, only their urgency. And as she pondered them again they did not seem to suggest an ignominious defeat and a return to Greece, and that gave her heart. But one thing was now clear: as she heard Cassandra's call for the horse to be burned she knew what Odysseus had wanted her to do, and that both he and Eperitus were relying on her. Leaving the crowd she had followed from the city, she walked up to the horse and laid a hand on one of its oversized wheels.

'Cassandra lies. This is no herald of doom, but a gift from the Greeks acknowledging *our* victory. It should stand forever as a monument to the glory of those who fought for Troy, so that generations to come can look at it and speak their names with pride. Burn it and you will diminish their honour! Indeed, burn it and you will bring a curse down on the city.'

Hundreds of voices were raised in agreement, but Cassandra cut them short with an angry scream.

'This is madness! Will you invite your own deaths? I tell you, this horse will not become a monument to the sacrifices of the fallen – rather, it will render their sacrifices worthless!'

Her words were met with jeers and calls for her to be silent.

'Why should we listen to you?' Astynome countered. 'You're nothing but a storm crow, Cassandra, always wailing about the destruction of Troy and the death of its people. But we're still here, aren't we? The walls of Troy still stand and its warriors still man the battlements, don't they? Why should anyone believe you?'

'Because you have to!' Cassandra pleaded. 'Father, listen to me, I implore you! This thing reeks of death. If its shadow falls within the walls of Troy, then your city and everything in it will be destroyed.'

Priam looked at her with uncertainty in his eyes, but the taunts and insults from the crowd behind her grew louder. Cassandra turned on them in frustration, and seeing a soldier among her mockers ran at him and wrenched the spear from his surprised hands. The crowd fell back, shouting now with fear as they saw the dangerous rage in her dark eyes.

'Damn you all!' she cried, then turned on her heel and hurled the spear at the horse's side.

It struck with a hollow thud, and in that instant it seemed to many that they heard a second sound, a movement from within the body of the horse itself. The clamour of the crowd fell away and in the silence that followed everyone looked up at the spear, still quivering from the impact of the blow. Astynome looked up, too, wondering whether she had indeed heard a metallic clang from inside the wooden effigy, or whether she had simply imagined it. Then the stillness was broken by a series of shouts. All eyes looked to the south, where a group of horsemen were racing across the plain towards them. Their distinctive armour marked them out as Trojans, and at their head was the unmistakeable figure of Aeneas. Moments later they drew to a halt amid a cloud of brown dust that billowed forward to float around the hocks of the wooden horse. Aeneas leapt lightly from the back of his mount and, walking to the nearest of his riders, seized the bound and gagged man who had shared his horse and pulled him to the ground. The prisoner fell with a muffled grunt, but Aeneas dragged him back to his feet and pushed him towards Priam and Apheidas.

'My lord,' Aeneas began, acknowledging Priam with a low bow. 'Congratulations on your great victory. The Greek fleet has sailed and we found their camp completely deserted. All except for this man.'

Priam stared at the dishevelled figure. His face was half hidden behind the filthy rag that had been tied about his mouth, but the blood and bruises on his dirt-stained cheeks and forehead were clear to see. The man fixed his eyes firmly on the grass at Priam's feet, either too fearful or too stubborn to look at the old king.

'Who is he?'

'He refused to say, my lord.'

A flicker of impatience crossed Priam's face. 'Then did you and your men give him this beating?'

'No. He's exactly as when we found him, hiding in the ruins of one of the huts. Though we had to bind him so he wouldn't try to escape.'

Priam flicked his hand at the gag, which Aeneas hastily removed. As the strip of cloth fell to the ground, Astynome almost cried out in shock. The prisoner was the young Ithacan, Omeros.

'What's your name, lad?' Priam asked, addressing him in Greek.

Omeros did not respond.

'Answer the king!' Apheidas snapped, impatiently.

Omeros lifted his gaze to Priam's knees and opened his cracked and blooded lips.

'Omeros,' he rasped. 'An Ithacan.'

'One of Odysseus's men,' Apheidas said, leaning in towards Priam.

Priam ignored the obvious comment and told Idaeus to give the prisoner water. The herald did as he was commanded and Omeros drank the cooling liquid greedily.

'Where is the Greek fleet?' Priam demanded.

Again Omeros was reluctant to answer, provoking Apheidas to strike him across the face with the back of his hand. The blow reopened one of his cuts and left a fresh smear of bright red on his dirt-stained cheek.

'They've had enough. Gone home.'

'Just like that? After ten years of war?' Apheidas sneered. 'I'm sure that's what you'd *like* us to believe.'

Omeros merely shrugged and continued to stare at the ground.

'Why would they leave after all this time?' Priam asked. 'They stole the Palladium, the very thing that protected Troy for all these years – so why go now?'

Omeros shot an uncertain glance at Apheidas, then looked at Priam.

'Stealing the Palladium was the very thing that condemned them. They thought it'd bring them victory, but all it did was earn them Athena's wrath. They realised that when they tried to storm the walls and were repulsed again, just like in every previous attack over the past ten years. And if that wasn't evidence enough, the Palladium burst into flames three times – you don't have to be a seer to know that's a bad omen!'

'So where's the Palladium now?'

Omeros looked up at the horse.

'Up there. Inside the horse's head. Once they'd accepted they could no longer win the war, they built this thing to appease Athena and seek her blessing for the voyage home. No-one dared take the Palladium back to Greece with them, and they didn't want you to find it; so they hid it.'

Apheidas's eyes narrowed suspiciously.

'Why would you tell us that? In fact, why would Odysseus sail home to Ithaca leaving one of his men to be taken prisoner?'

'Because I'm no longer one of his men!' Omeros answered, angrily. He pulled at the rope that bound his hands behind his back, but to no avail. 'Damn it, if you're going to question me all day, at least take these bonds from my wrists.'

Priam nodded at Aeneas, who drew his dagger and slit the flax cord. Omeros shook his hands then rubbed them together, trying to encourage the blood to return to his veins. After a moment, he looked up at his Trojan interrogators and there was an embittered look in his eye.

'A while ago, I found out Odysseus had planted gold in Palamedes's tent, to implicate him as a traitor. They killed Palamedes for it, and ever since Odysseus has been afraid I might give away his dirty secret. So when the winds refused to blow and Calchas declared the fleet couldn't sail until the gods had been appeased with human blood, Odysseus saw his opportunity. He asked Calchas who had to die, and the old drunkard pointed at me – doubtless bribed beforehand by Odysseus. The Greeks dragged the horse at night to the top of the ridge where you found it this morning, then prepared to sacrifice me at dawn. They had to subdue me first – that's how I got these,' he indicated the cuts and bruises on his face, 'but before the sacrifice could begin, a gale sprang up and everyone ran for the ships. I escaped in the chaos as they torched the tents and huts and pushed the galleys out into the sea. Then I watched them sail away by the first light of dawn, following the coastline southward with the wind behind them.'

'What do you say now, Daughter?' Priam asked, turning to the sombre figure of Cassandra.

'He's a liar!' she hissed. 'The Palladium isn't inside the horse. Only death is in there – a plague of bronze that will wipe out the race of Troy. Burn it while you still can.'

Voices in the crowd cried out in protest, calling for Cassandra to be silent. The king returned his gaze to Omeros.

'My daughter is against you, though that would encourage most to decide in your favour. I sense Apheidas and others also remain sceptical, and their opinions are less easily dismissed. As for myself, I'm inclined to believe you, Omeros.'

'Thank you, my lord,' Omeros replied, kneeling.

'I only said I'm inclined to believe you,' Priam warned. 'There are still things about this horse that sit uneasily. Perhaps you can explain why the Greeks went to the effort of dragging it to the top of the ridge? And if they meant for us to accept it as a gift to be taken into the city, why did they make it too large for the gates?'

'Because Odysseus is a cunning man. He can anticipate how others think and creates his schemes to meet their expectations. The horse was brought here so that every person in Troy could see it, so that there would be a public debate about what to do with it.'

'What's it matter to the Greeks *what* we do with it?' Apheidas interrupted.

'Because this isn't just a gift to you or an offering to the gods – its head contains the Palladium, the key to Troy's safety, and the Greeks put it in there for a reason. They daren't destroy it, for fear of increasing Athena's wrath and making it impossible to ever return and resume the siege – which Agamemnon still has a mind to do. And the last thing the King of Men wants is for you to take the Palladium back inside the city walls and ensure Troy's invulnerability once more. That's why the horse was built too big for the gates. But if the *Trojans* destroy the Palladium, you'll bring a curse down on your own heads and guarantee a Greek victory if they come back. You see, Odysseus had calculated you would burn the wooden horse and the Palladium with it. He just hadn't accounted for me in his plans.'

As he spoke, a loud crash echoed across the valley. Every head turned towards the Scaean Gate, which was shrouded in dust. As the brown mist blew away in the wind, they could see that the large wooden portals had been removed from their hinges. Above the exposed archway, teams of men were standing around a hole in the parapet. On the ground below was an immense block of stone, the fall of which had caused the booming sound they had heard. Deiphobus had not delayed in carrying out his father's orders and was already dismantling the walls so that the horse could be taken inside the city.

'In the name of Apollo, stop them!' Cassandra wailed. 'Father, please believe me. There are *men* inside the horse. I have seen it!'

Astynome heard the words and turned to look up at the horse. Now she understood: Odysseus had hidden warriors inside the large wooden body, and among them was Eperitus. She looked at the faces all around her, staring up at the great effigy as it towered over them and pondering Cassandra's desperate warning. Surely they would see that they were being tricked, that Omeros and his story were just another part of Odysseus's scheme to smuggle armed men into the city – to have the Trojans themselves carry out his plan. Within moments they would be calling for firewood and torches from the city; the horse would be transformed into a blazing pyre, consuming the hopes of the Greeks – and her beloved Eperitus – with it. And Astynome was powerless to stop them.

Then the silence was broken – not by angry shouts, but a long, low laugh. Priam was staring at his daughter, with her wide eyes and torn black robes, and laughing. With his shoulders shaking, he laid his head back and laughed out loud. Idaeus joined him, then Omeros. The crowd followed, slowly at first but with growing mirth as the absurd idea of a horse full of soldiers took hold of them. Even Apheidas was infected by it, his amused smile broadening until he broke into billows of laughter, holding his hands to his sides.

'Take the horse into the city,' Priam ordered, still smiling.

Knowing Apollo's curse had defeated her again, Cassandra threw her hands over her ears and ran as fast as she could to the ford.

Chapter Thirty-Six
VOICES FROM HOME

E peritus was woken by a hand gently shaking his shoulder.
'Won't be long now,' he heard Odysseus's voice say in a
dry-throated whisper.

He opened his eyes to see the king's face leaning close, a blurred
grey oval in the almost complete blackness of the horse's belly. Many
others were with them, invisible in the darkness but filling Eperitus's
senses with the sound of their breathing and the sour odour of their
sweat. There was the ever-present smell of smoke, too, which still clung
to their clothing from the fires of the day before when they had put
the Greek camp to the torch. Odysseus patted his shoulder and leaned
back against the fir-planked wall, smiling reassuringly as if he were
back in the comfort of his own palace on Ithaca. But if he had meant
to encourage his captain, all he succeeded in doing was reminding him
that they were shut up inside the wooden horse and surrounded by
their enemies, awaiting the moment when they would enact the most
daring gamble of the whole war. Eperitus strained his senses, but the
city outside was silent and still, the celebrations finally over as its
people enjoyed the deep, wine-induced sleep of a nation at peace – a
treacherous, ephemeral peace that would soon be ripped apart by the
clamour of returning war.

Eperitus's stomach shifted nervously at the thought. He sat up and
stretched the stiffness out of his limbs. The hard wooden bench had
numbed his backside and his efforts to rub some life into each buttock
earned grumbled complaints from Sthenelaus on his left and Little Ajax
on his right. Looking around, he could just make out the faces of the
others who had been chosen for the mission. There were only twenty-
four of them – all that could fit in the cramped interior of the horse –
but they were the best warriors in the Greek army, hand-picked by

Odysseus and Menelaus for their courage and fighting skill. They were also the most high-ranking – every one a king, prince or commander – and if their mission failed and they were killed or captured it would mean total defeat for the Greeks. And yet victory could not be obtained without such risks. The grim-faced men inside the horse understood that; they also understood that victory would earn them immortal glory and a name that would live on long after their bodies had perished and their souls had gone down to Hades. It was this desire – the appeal of glory to every warrior – that Odysseus had used to ensure they would agree to his bold, reckless scheme.

Eperitus looked at the king's face – eyes closed, head back – and recalled the debate aboard the beached ship, when the full extent of his plans had been laid before the key members of the Council of Kings. All understood immediately that it would bring about the end of the conflict at a stroke: either Troy would fall in a single night, or the cream of the Greek army would be caught and wiped out. But when many baulked at so high a risk – most significantly Agamemnon – Odysseus had played on their weariness with the seemingly endless war and spiced his appeal with the promise of undying fame. His smooth, persuasive voice reminded them how they had set out from their homes expecting a quick victory bathed in the blood of Trojans and rewarded with a rich bounty of gold and slaves. Instead, they had endured ten years of siege warfare, deprived of the comforts of home and the love of their families. And though at first they had tried to ignore the omen from Zeus that the war would last a decade, he warned them not to forget it again now that the prophecy had come to the end of its course. *Now*, Odysseus said, was not the time to shy away from risks, but to seize them and gamble everything.

The debate was easily won, with Agamemnon and Nestor's doubts overruled by the sheer enthusiasm of Menelaus, Neoptolemus, Diomedes and many others. In the days that followed, Eperitus – the most gifted craftsman in the army – oversaw the building of the wooden horse while the rest of the Greeks threw themselves into making the fleet seaworthy again. All passage into or out of the camp was halted, to prevent spies informing the Trojans of what was happening. Finally, two days after the horse was finished, the winds sprang up again and the rest of Odysseus's scheme was put into motion. The camp was packed up in a hurry, and whatever could not be stowed aboard the hundreds of galleys was burnt. Meanwhile, the gates and part of the surrounding walls had been knocked down and the colossal horse wheeled out onto the plain. Under the command of Agamemnon and Nestor, the fleet then sailed the short distance to Tenedos and hid itself on the western flank of the island where it would not be seen from the shore. After nightfall, Omeros was left alone in the remains of the camp – waiting to be found by the Trojans the next morning – while teams of oxen had dragged the wooden horse to the ridge overlooking the Scamander. Here the beasts had been set free and the picked band of warriors had climbed up into the horse, their armour shrouded in cloth to stop it gleaming in the darkness or clanking inadvertently. Epeius came last, drawing the rope ladder up behind him. Though a renowned coward, he was included in the party because he was the only man who knew how to open or close the trap door, which he had designed to be invisible from the outside. The door shut with a click, and the longest day of Eperitus's life began.

It had been a day filled with discomfort, stiffness and boredom, sliced through by moments of intense fear and anxiety. Dawn had seen the arrival of Apheidas and Aeneas, and Eperitus's urge to leap out and face his father had only been checked by his self-discipline and the inner knowledge the night would bring other opportunities for revenge. Menelaus had been less restrained when Deiphobus had arrived with Helen in his chariot. He had not seen his wife so close in ten years and her beauty had lost none of its allure, but the sight of her with her new husband had him clawing at the hatch to get out. It had taken all the strength of Neoptolemus, Idomeneus and Diomedes to hold him down and keep him quiet.

But perhaps their greatest fear had come with the appearance of Cassandra, shrieking madly and calling for the horse to be burned. Eperitus had gripped the handle of his sword – there was no room for their spears within the belly of the horse – expecting to have to jump out and fight the throng of Trojans below. Then Astynome, his beloved Astynome, had stepped from the crowd and spoken out against the black-clad daughter of Priam, casting doubt upon her words of doom until the arrival of Omeros finally convinced the Trojans to accept the horse. After that, the towering effigy had been dragged across the fords and into the city through a breach the Trojans had made in their own wall. While Cassandra had walked alongside the horse, shouting in a strained voice that it was full of Greeks, the Trojan women laid a carpet of flowers in its path and the Trojan men sang songs of victory. And as evening approached and Troy was consumed with darkness, the people feasted and drank, letting the wine erase the memory of the hardships they had suffered as they danced arm in arm, circling the horse and trailing through the streets in long human chains until, eventually, drunkenness and exhausted sleep had taken them.

A curse in the darkness woke Eperitus from his thoughts.

'Damn this waiting! Where's Omeros? He should have been here by now.'

Odysseus opened an eye and turned it towards the source of the outburst.

'Keep your voice down, Epeius.'

'No I won't! I've had enough of being crammed inside this horse with no room to stand or stretch my legs –'

'Then perhaps you should have made it bigger,' Little Ajax growled.

'It's alright for a dwarf like you,' Epeius snapped. 'I'm twice your height and I've spent a day and a night with my knees tucked up under my chin. I want to get out before I go mad!'

Little Ajax gave a snarl and rose from the bench, but Eperitus placed a hand on his shoulder and pulled him back down. Odysseus leaned across and faced Epeius.

'We'll be out soon enough. Have patience.'

'What if Omeros has been found out?' Epeius asked. 'What if he's locked in some Trojan dungeon, or if he's already had his throat cut?'

Odysseus smiled at him. 'If he'd been found out, d'you think we'd still be waiting here in the darkness? They'd have made a burning pyre of us long before now. Besides, you should have some faith in the lad. You saw how he dealt with Priam earlier, convincing the old king that we wanted the Trojans to set the horse ablaze. Do you think that was an easy trick to pull off?'

Epeius shook his head. 'I suppose not.'

'Of course it wasn't! He's a born storyteller and he's got a level head – that's why I chose him for the task. And when he judges the time is right, he'll go up to the walls and set a torch on the parapet for the fleet to see. Once that's done, he'll come straight here and give us the signal to climb out.'

'He'd better not get himself caught,' Menestheus, the Athenian king, said.

'He won't,' Eperitus answered. He turned to the others, who were fully awake by now and leaning forward on their knees. 'It's Agamemnon I'm concerned about. It won't be easy sailing into the harbour at night and disembarking the army in complete darkness.'

There was a murmur of agreement.

'My brother'll be here on time,' Menelaus assured them, curtly. 'He may not have liked your plan, Odysseus, but he won't let us down.'

'Quiet!' Eperitus hissed in a whisper. 'Someone's coming.'

Silence fell as the warriors listened intently for what Eperitus's hearing had already picked up. Their eyes were pale orbs in the darkness as they exchanged tense glances. Then they heard it: the sound of voices – one male, one female – approaching the horse.

Eperitus twisted on the bench. Behind him was one of the holes that Epeius had drilled in the wood to keep the horse's occupants from suffocating. He pressed an eye to the small aperture and looked out on the scene below. The horse had been hauled halfway up the main thoroughfare from the Scaean Gate to Pergamos, and left at a broadening in the road where busy markets must once have been held in times of peace. Since Eperitus had last looked out in the late afternoon, the wide square had been cleared of the tents where hundreds of allied warriors had been bivouacked and a large, circular fire had been built by the wheeled hooves of the great horse, the embers of which still glowed hot and sent trails of smoke up into the night air. Around it were scores of feasting tables and long, low benches, many of which were lying overturned. The remaining tables were piled up with wooden platters – some empty and others still half-filled with staling food – and countless kraters and goblets. The ground in-between was littered with food, broken cups, items of clothing and even a few shoes – not to mention countless sleeping bodies – so that it looked more like the aftermath of a battle than a feast. Picking their way through all this as they walked down from the gates of the citadel were a man and a woman, followed by four female slaves. The man was tall and richly dressed in a pale, knee-length tunic and black double cloak, fastened at his left shoulder by a gleaming brooch. The woman was almost as tall and leaned unsteadily against the man's arm as they approached the horse. She wore a white chiton and her black hair lay in long, curling fronds across her shoulders.

'Who is it?' Sthenelaus hissed.

'Deiphobus,' Eperitus answered, glancing cautiously at Menelaus, 'and Helen.'

The Spartan's brow furrowed sharply. He leaned across and hauled Epeius away from his eyehole, pressing his face to the opening.

'I can't believe it's over,' Eperitus heard Helen say. He placed his eye back against the hole to see her standing below the horse and craning her neck to look up at it. 'It still doesn't seem possible that in the morning I can leave the city and go riding across the plains if I want to.'

'Believe it,' Deiphobus responded, snaking an arm about her waist. 'And the only escort you'll need is me at your side.'

'See how she doesn't brush his arm away!' Menelaus hissed.

No-one replied.

'But –' Helen raised a hand lazily towards the horse as she slumped drunkenly against Deiphobus. 'But why just leave? They've been here ten years, spreading slaughter and destruction, dying in their thousands, and then they simply decide to *go*? It doesn't make sense.'

'It does to me.'

Helen turned to Deiphobus, who was clearly sober.

'They weren't as strong as we assumed,' he explained. 'It's just as Apheidas says: the Greeks are a vicious people, but they lack stamina and courage. The years have worn away at their morale and now they've had enough. They've run off back to their wives and children.'

He draped his arm across her shoulders, but in a move that earned a grunt of approval from Menelaus, she stepped forward from his half-embrace and placed her hands on her hips, looking up at the horse.

'What about the things Cassandra said?'

Deiphobus shrugged his shoulders indifferently. 'My sister says a lot of things, and nothing at all of any worth.'

Helen features dropped into a mournful grimace, mimicking Cassandra's look of permanent woe. 'But there are *men* inside the horse,' she wailed in perfect imitation of her sister-in-law. 'I've seen it!'

Deiphobus gave a derisive snort. Helen flitted around him like a spectre, then stepped forward and laid a hand on the upper arch of one of the horse's wheels, so that Eperitus was barely able to see her through the narrow aperture.

'I quite like the idea. Can you imagine it, Deiphobus? The wooden horse, full of Greek chieftains listening to us at this very moment?'

Deiphobus laughed and gave a dismissive flick of his hand, but looked up at the horse anyway and narrowed his eyes slightly.

'Who do you think would be inside?' Helen continued. She began circling the horse now, slipping from Eperitus's sight and her voice fading a little as she moved around the other side. 'Which warriors would they hide in its belly?'

'Open the hatch, Epeius,' Menelaus demanded. 'Let's see the look on her face when she sees *me* jump out.'

'Quiet!' Neoptolemus said, raising his fingertips almost to Menelaus's mouth.

'This is a silly game,' Deiphobus said. 'Cassandra's full of the most ridiculous fantasies, dressing them up as oracles of doom. The other morning she was running around the palace screaming that a woman in black was going to kill her with an axe. I told her she must have been looking at herself in the mirror!'

'Do you think Agamemnon would be in there?' Helen persisted.

'Never,' Deiphobus laughed, conceding that he would have to play along. 'They wouldn't risk the leader of their army.'

'Yes, you're right. Besides, Agamemnon would never put himself in danger if he could order somebody else to do it for him.'

'That's true,' Little Ajax whispered.

'What about my husband, Menelaus?'

'He isn't your husband any more. I am. And if he *was* up there, do you think he'd be hanging around listening to us play your absurd game?' Deiphobus looked up at the horse. 'Are you in there, Menelaus? Don't you want to come out and save the woman who used to be your wife? Aren't you going to rescue her from my kisses?'

He grabbed Helen as she completed her circuit of the horse and tipped her back in one arm, kissing her on the mouth. His free hand moved over her breasts, squeezing each in turn.

'By all the –!' Menelaus began, springing back from the eyehole with a thunderous look on his red face.

Before he could say any more, Diomedes's hand closed over his mouth and Teucer and Philoctetes, the two archers, took a firm hold of his arms.

Helen stood and pushed Deiphobus away.

'I'm being serious. If not Menelaus, then what about Diomedes?

'Why would Diomedes be so stupid as to enter the city inside a giant horse?' Deiphobus asked, sounding slightly exasperated. 'You saw how close we came to burning it this morning. I'll tell you where Diomedes is – sailing back to Argos to see his wife again for the first time in a decade.'

'Aegialeia,' Helen said, smiling as an idea struck her. She laid a finger on the tip of her nose and looked down thoughtfully for a moment, before approaching the horse again. 'Oh husband! Are you up there?'

Diomedes released Menelaus's mouth and snapped his head round in the direction of the voice.

'Aegialeia?' he whispered.

He crawled to the eyehole that Menelaus had vacated and looked out.

'Don't be a fool,' Eperitus rebuked him. 'It's Helen.'

'Diomedes?' Helen continued, flawlessly recreating the voice of the Argive queen, whom she had met several times when married to Menelaus. 'Have you missed me?'

Deiphobus laughed at her genius for mimicry. The illusion broken, Diomedes slumped back onto the bench and was quiet.

Helen began to circle the horse once more, grinning as she looked up at the tall structure and occasionally pausing to run her fingertips over its wooden legs.

'Are you up there, Idomeneus?' she called, copying the Cretan's wife's sing-song voice. 'My bed was lonely without you, at least for the first year. Then I got bored and found other men to fill it. Now I'd rather you didn't come back at all.'

Eperitus turned and saw Idomeneus's face stern and tight-lipped in the shadows.

'And where have you been, Sthenelaus?' came another voice, harsh and nasal. 'Helping yourself to Trojan slave girls, I've no doubt! Well, the war won't last forever, and when it's over I'll be here waiting for you.'

Deiphobus's laughter was followed by Helen's this time, while Sthenelaus sucked at his teeth and shook his head.

'I'd rather the war went on for another ten years than go back to her,' he muttered.

Then another voice was pitched up towards the horse, causing Eperitus to freeze and glance across at Odysseus.

'I'm waiting, too,' it said. 'When are you coming back to me, my love?'

'Somebody has to stop her!' Odysseus hissed, balling his fists up on his knees.

'You know it's not Penelope,' Eperitus told him.

'It doesn't matter –'

'Odysseus, my love! Do you miss me like I miss you? Don't you want to kiss my pale breasts again, and feel my soft thighs wrapped around you?'

Eperitus pushed his hand over Odysseus's mouth, stifling the cry that was on his lips and forcing him back against the inner wall of the horse.

'*It's not Penelope!*'

Odysseus knocked his hand away and took a deep breath, turning his face aside so that Eperitus could not see the anguish in his eyes.

'That's enough,' they heard Deiphobus say. 'Come on, Helen. Let's go home so I can taste *your* breasts with *my* lips.'

There was a peel of feminine laughter, followed by silence and then more laughter, receding this time as Deiphobus and Helen retraced their steps back towards Pergamos.

Chapter Thirty-Seven
THE GATE FALLS

The men inside the horse were quiet for a while, barely able to look each other in the eye. Eperitus glanced at Odysseus, but his chin was on his chest and his gaze firmly fixed on his sandalled feet. Then the silence was broken by a loud rapping on the legs of the horse, which carried up through the wood and was magnified sharply within the small space where the warriors were huddled.

'My lords! Are you in there?'

Eperitus sighed with relief. It was Omeros.

'At last,' said Neoptolemus, slipping his red-plumed, golden helmet onto his head and fastening the cheek guards beneath his chin. 'I only wish my father were here with me now, to claim the glory that should have been his.'

'And Great Ajax, too,' said Teucer, clutching at his bow. The nervous twitch that had once defined him had faded after the death of his half-brother, and now he sat calmly with his face set in a determined stare. 'He would have relished this moment.'

Odysseus shook his head. 'Neither would have entered Troy in the belly of a wooden horse. They hated trickery and would only have walked through the gates on a carpet of fallen enemies. But the fact you're here, Neoptolemus, shows you've already surpassed your father's qualities. Unlike him, you know a war like this can't be won by strength and honour alone. Now, Epeius, open the door and let's set about our task.'

Epeius's cowardly instincts had brought him out in a glistening sweat now the long wait was over, but while the two dozen warriors about him removed the sacking from their armour and made ready for battle, he wiped his brow and probed the wooden floor with his fingers. There was a click and the trap door swung downward on its

305

hinges, flooding the interior of the horse with a red glow from the dying fire below. Eperitus picked up his grandfather's shield and, swinging it over his back, was first at the hatch. He stared down and saw Omeros looking back up at him.

'The way's clear,' his squire called in a low voice.

Eperitus kicked the rolled-up rope ladder down through the hole and began his descent, jumping the last part and landing beside Omeros. He looked around at the still-sleeping Trojans, draped over or around the feasting tables, then up at the cloudy sky, pressing closely down on the walls and towers of Pergamos further up the slope. His limbs and back were stiff and the soles of his feet tingled as the blood struggled to return to them, but he drove the discomfort from his mind and drew his sword from its scabbard.

A moment later, Odysseus was with them, followed rapidly by Neoptolemus, Menelaus and Diomedes.

'Is the signal in place?' Odysseus asked.

'And can you be sure the fleet saw it?' Menelaus added.

'The torch is on the walls, my lords, just as you ordered,' Omeros replied, 'but it was too dark to see if there were any ships in the harbour. If they're there, though, they'll have seen the signal.'

'What about guards?' asked Eperitus. 'Did you see any patrols?'

'None. Not a single man – they're all in a drunken sleep, completely convinced we've given up and gone.'

'You did well,' Odysseus said, patting Omeros's shoulder. 'I couldn't have done any better myself.'

Eperitus gave his squire a wink and Omeros bowed his head to hide the broad grin on his face.

'Everybody's out,' Diomedes announced. 'Now it's time we went about our business. All it needs is one Trojan to wake and give the alarm –'

'We'll do everything as I explained before,' Odysseus said. 'Diomedes: you, Little Ajax and Idomeneus take half our number down to the Scaean Gate to let the army in. Menelaus, Neoptolemus and I will take the rest and secure the gates to the citadel.'

'And what about these?' Little Ajax demanded, sweeping his sword in a menacing arc over the sleeping Trojans. 'Do you plan to just let them go on sleeping, ready to wake and bear arms against us? I say we cut their throats and rid ourselves of the bastards here and now.'

Eperitus looked at his king, who twice before had cut the throats of groups of sleeping warriors, preferring the opportunity of a defenceless enemy over notions of honour. On one of those occasions, the fate of Ithaca had depended on his actions; on the other he had murdered his victims for the sake of a team of prize horses. This time, though – to Eperitus's approval – Odysseus shook his head.

'We only kill those who resist us – the night's going to be vicious enough without cold-blooded murder. Besides, we haven't the time to waste. We need to go now.'

Diomedes gave a nod and signalled for Little Ajax, Teucer and the others in his party to follow him. They set off at a trot down the main street, their accoutrements jangling lightly as they headed for the dim outline of the city walls and the tower that guarded the Scaean Gate. Odysseus signalled to Omeros.

'Go with them, lad, and find Eurybates. Remind him to keep a firm grip on my Ithacans. They've had a hard war and even the best of them will be tempted to excess, but I want them to stay disciplined. Now go.'

Omeros set off and Eperitus laid a hand on Odysseus's shoulder.

'We need to go, too,' he urged.

Menelaus was already running up towards Pergamos, closely followed by the others. Only Neoptolemus remained, beckoning with his drawn sword for the two Ithacans to follow. They weaved a path towards him through the sleeping Trojans, then all three ran to catch up with the rest of the party. It was not long before they were approaching the sloping walls of the citadel and the imposing tower that guarded the gates. Menelaus slowed to a halt and crouched in the shadows of a nearby house, signalling for the rest to do the same. Neoptolemus, Odysseus and Eperitus joined him.

'I'd forgotten how ugly their gods are,' Menelaus whispered, pointing to the six crude statuettes that stood on plinths before the tower. He turned to Odysseus. 'You know the city better than the rest of us. Isn't the gate in the shadows, to the right of the tower?'

Odysseus nodded and looked up at the battlements. There were no figures pacing the walls or faces peering down at them over the parapets. All was silent.

'They won't have left it unguarded, not even tonight, but the last thing they'll be expecting is a dozen fully armed Greeks. I suggest we sling our shields on our backs, sheath our swords and walk into Pergamos.'

Before they could question him, he was moving out of the shadows towards the tower. Not wanting to let his king take the risk alone, Eperitus was the first to follow, with Menelaus, Neoptolemus and the others close behind. Just as Odysseus had predicted, the gates were not unguarded: two men sat on stools to the left of the archway, their spears sloped against their shoulders, while two others stood opposite them, leaning against the wall with their heads bowed sleepily. The wooden gates were held open by two large blocks of stone, and all four guards were quiet, half asleep, only stirring to life as they saw the band of warriors approach.

'No entry after midnight, brothers. You know that,' said one of the soldiers, levering himself away from the wall with his elbow. 'Curfew still applies, even in peacetime.'

He laughed quietly at his own humour, though his laughter quickly died away when he saw the men were not slowing down.

'I said –'

As one, Odysseus and Eperitus drew their swords, closely followed by Menelaus and Neoptolemus. Eperitus sprang forward, pushing the point of his blade into the first guard's chest. It sliced through his heart and passed out of his back, causing his legs to buckle and his body to fall backwards, almost pulling Eperitus with him. He placed his weight on his front foot and held on to the hilt, so that the momentum of the dead man's torso pulled it free of the blade. Scuffles and grunts indicated the demise of the other guards and when Eperitus turned it was to see their bodies lying in pools of their own blood.

'Menestheus, check the guardroom,' Odysseus said, pointing through the archway.

The Athenian king nodded and led a group of warriors into the shadows. Eperitus's hearing picked up the sound of blades drawn and muffled grunts, but the lack of any other noise indicated the Trojans within the guardroom had barely had the chance to wake before their souls were released from their bodies.

'Now what?' Neoptolemus asked.

'We wait here and hold the gates until the rest of the army arrive,' Odysseus replied.

'Not me. I'm going to find my wife.'

Menelaus finished wiping his blade on the cloak of the guard he had killed, then stood and peered into the shadowy archway that led into the citadel. Odysseus side-stepped into his path, shaking his head.

'You can't go to the palace alone. It's too dangerous. Wait for your brother to arrive.'

'I mean to find her, Odysseus, and you aren't going to stop me. I've waited too long for this.'

'Then be patient a little longer –'

Menelaus was not interested. He shouldered his way past Odysseus and then through Menestheus and the other Greeks as they emerged from the archway.

'You'll get yourself killed and then this whole war will have been for nothing,' Odysseus called after him.

'The gods will protect me,' Menelaus replied with a growl.

Eperitus laid a hand on Odysseus's shoulder. 'We have to go with him.'

'I promised Agamemnon I'd wait here until he arrived.'

'Neoptolemus can hold the gates,' Eperitus urged. He looked at Achilles's son, who replied with a curt nod. '*We* need to keep Menelaus safe.'

Odysseus hesitated a moment longer before agreeing.

'You're right, of course. But it's not Menelaus's safety we should be worried about – it's Helen's when he finds her. Come on, then, let's go after him.'

'Look at all these throats, just waiting to be cut. And we're tiptoeing around them as if they were mere babies.'

'Keep your voice down, Ajax,' Diomedes whispered, staring over his shoulder at the Locrian. 'Once the gates are open you can spill as much blood as you like, but not before.'

They were picking their way through scores of Trojan warriors, who had made their beds on the main thoroughfare around a large, makeshift fire. The flames had died away but the red glow of the embers lit up the huddled shapes of the nearest, revealing bearded faces that had put behind them the horrors of war and were at peace. Some shared their blankets with wives, slaves or prostitutes, whose smooth faces were framed by tumbles of dark hair. These were the people who had resisted the Greeks so valiantly and for so long,

Diomedes thought, and soon their ten-year struggle would be over. As he had climbed out of the belly of the horse, his sword arm had been eager to go to work – more so because Helen's mocking words had filled him with an urgent, paranoid desire to get home and reassure himself of his wife's fidelity while he had been away. But as he saw his sleeping enemies and considered the ignoble end that was approaching them, he was moved to an unusual pity. Though he hated them with a passion for prolonging the siege with their bitter resistance, he had also learned to respect them. They did not deserve to die in their sleep or just startled into wakefulness, fooled by the ruse of a clever trickster. To Diomedes's mind, slaughter in the darkness lacked the glory of a battle under the blazing sun, in which Troy's walls were scaled or her gates forced by an army of proud victors. But that army had died with Achilles and Great Ajax. The survivors would do anything to see Troy fall – Diomedes included – even if their own honour fell with it.

Diomedes stepped on an outstretched hand, unable to prevent his weight crushing the Trojan's knuckles against the hard stone beneath. The man groaned and pulled his arm away. Diomedes's sword was at his throat in an instant, waiting for the eyes to flicker open and see the dozen armed men standing about him. Instead, the man turned over and draped his arm across the woman at his side.

'Come on,' Diomedes hissed to the others.

They navigated their way free of the remaining bodies and looked at the dark mass of the walls, just a short way off now. The dense ceiling of cloud acted like a shroud, choking the city streets in blackness and making it impossible to see whether there were any soldiers on the Scaean Gate or the tower above. Even after a night of drunken victory celebrations it was unlikely there would be no guards at all, so Diomedes decided to approach with caution. He signalled for Philoctetes and Teucer to join him, then, telling the others to wait, led the two archers down to the gates. They crept from doorway to doorway until they reached the corner of a mud hovel, from which they could see the tall wooden portals and the guard tower that had repulsed every attack that had ever been thrown at them. The battlements above the gates had been removed stone by stone – just as Odysseus had said they would be if the horse was to be dragged into the city – leaving a wide, ugly gap in the walls. The gates were firmly shut and barred, though, and in the shadows beneath the tower stood four guards armed with helmets, shields and spears.

'You see them?' Diomedes asked.

His companions nodded.

'We have to take them quietly. If just one of them raises the alarm, the rest of the guard will empty out of the tower and prevent us taking the gates. And if they wake the rest of the city, we'll never be able to cut our way out again.'

'We understand,' said Philoctetes, sliding an arrow from his quiver and fitting it to Heracles's horn bow. 'We shoot a man each, then draw another arrow, aim and shoot again before the remaining guards realise what's happening.'

'And if we miss with either shot,' Teucer added, 'we alert the Trojans, get ourselves massacred and lose the war.'

Diomedes nodded and gave an apologetic shrug. Teucer grinned at him, then knelt, drew two arrows and pushed one into the ground. The other he fitted to his bow, pulling it back to his cheek and aiming along its long black shaft.

'Back right,' he whispered.

'Back left,' Philoctetes answered, 'then front left. Now!'

The bowstrings hummed and Diomedes saw the two men closest to the gate jerk and fall. His heart beat fast and his throat thickened as he watched the remaining guards turn in surprise, then run towards their comrades. The bows hummed in unison a second time and the last two Trojans fell on top of the two who had died only moments before them.

'Shots worthy of Apollo himself,' Diomedes commented with relief, patting Philoctetes and Teucer on their shoulders. 'Now stay here while I fetch the others. And shoot anyone who approaches the gates.'

He stood to leave, but a hissed warning from Philoctetes brought him back into the shadows. Once again, both bows sounded. Diomedes stared about in confusion, then caught sight of a body falling from the summit of the tower. It turned once in midair before hitting the ground with a crunch where the other corpses already lay. The Argive king scanned the tower and the broad parapets for more guards, but could see none. Then, with a quick nod of gratitude to the watchful archers, he turned again and headed back to where Little Ajax and the others were waiting. They saw him coming and went to meet him. Together they ran down to the gates, passing the humped shapes of many sleeping Trojans who would never now see the light of dawn. They passed Philoctetes and Teucer, still poised with arrows fitted, and sprinted the final stretch to the gates, as if afraid a company of warriors might leap out at the last moment and block their way. But no-one saw them as they jumped the pile of bodies and reached the wooden doors; no-one heard as they lifted away the bar and let it fall with a crash onto the cobblestones; and no-one cried out as they hauled the heavy portals back on their hinges to reveal the dark landscape beyond. And as they peered out into the gloom, no-one was there to meet them.

'Where are they?' Omeros asked. 'Perhaps they didn't see the signal. By all the gods, they must still be in the ships!'

Diomedes stared out at the land between the walls and the River Scamander, where the only feature was the sacred oak beneath which Achilles had fought and killed Hector. Had that really only happened in the spring, he thought, momentarily distracted. Was it now only the eighth month of the year? And where was the army, now that victory was so close? Had they missed the signal and, believing the occupants of the horse lost, set their sails towards Greece?

'Agamemnon! Where are you?' Little Ajax called. 'The gates are open – what are you waiting for?'

There was desperation in the short, brutal warrior's voice that made it carry out into the void. It filled Diomedes with the sudden fear he would rouse any nearby Trojans, and quickly he raised the point of his sword to Ajax's throat.

'Quiet, damn you!' he hissed. 'Are you trying to wake every soldier in Troy?'

In a deft move, Little Ajax twisted away from Diomedes's blade and brought his own weapon up to meet it with a ringing clash. Then, all around them, the darkness began to shift. Black figures rose up from the ground, first in their scores, then in their hundreds, as if the souls of the dead were rising from the pits of Hades. Diomedes and Little Ajax forgot their quarrel and stepped back as the army of wraiths closed about them from the plain. Slowly, their pale faces and limbs became clearer, and one by one they slipped the black cloths from their shields and breastplates so that the metal and leather shone with a dull lustre in the darkness. Last of all they raised the points of their spears or drew their swords with a metallic slither, forming a wall of bronze about the open gates. The Greek army had arrived, and the sleeping city lay exposed before them.

Two figures approached from the massed ranks, the plumes on their helmets waving gently in the soft night breeze.

'It worked! It actually worked,' declared Agamemnon, with muted triumph. 'Zeus be praised!'

'And Odysseus, too,' Diomedes reminded him. 'His brains have succeeded where the might of Achilles and Great Ajax failed.'

'We haven't succeeded yet,' said Nestor, standing at the King of Men's side. 'There'll be much bloodshed before this battle's over.'

'But it's the *last* battle,' said Agamemnon. He turned towards the thousands of waiting soldiers and raised his spear above his head. 'Troy is ours! Victory is ours! But it shall not be an empty one. I'll not have the city sacked and its population scattered, so they can return and rebuild it when we've gone. I'll not see the shadow of its towers fall across the Aegean again, to be a thorn in the side of future generations of Greeks. No, it must be destroyed. Put it to the torch. Throw down its walls and gates. Don't suffer even one stone to remain on another. Destroy its flesh and blood, too. Kill every man, boy and infant you come across. And when you have shown *them* no mercy, do whatever you like with their women. Those are my only commands; now see that you carry them out to the full.'

His words were met with a shout and the clashing of weapons against shields. He turned on his heel and strode into the city, his blood-red cloak billowing out behind him. As he passed between the gates, a dozen sleepy Trojans ran out of a door in the side of the tower, only to be slaughtered and trampled over by the swarm of invaders following on the heels of the king of Mycenae. The Scaean Gate had fallen. The annihilation of Troy had begun.

Chapter Thirty-Eight

INSIDE THE PALACE

A eneas's eyes flickered open. He lifted his head slowly from the table, where it had been laying in the crook of his arm, and squinted out at the dark, still market square. Sleeping bodies lay here and there amid the wreckage of overturned benches, empty wineskins and broken kraters. Nothing moved and the only noise was the sound of mingled snores drifting up into the night air. And yet something had woken him; some deeper instinct was warning him that things were not as they should be. Having long ago learned to listen to his intuitions, he forced himself to sit up and feel for his sword. There were many who had left their weapons behind, refusing to bring them to a celebration marking the end of the siege, but his hung reassuringly at his side.

He lifted his legs over the bench and got up. Steadying himself against the table, he fought the thumping of the wine inside his head and took a second look around. Everything was quiet, calm, peaceful, as if the war had happened a generation ago and they had merely been commemorating it. Then his gaze fell on the wooden horse, standing tall and menacing in the centre of the square. Here, Aeneas sensed, was the source of his disquiet. It stood up to its hocks in garlands, which the womenfolk had plucked from the meadows around the Scamander. Offerings of food, too, had been piled all around it in honour of Athena and the other gods who had brought victory so unexpectedly to Troy. The horse had not moved; it had not changed; and in the darkness he almost missed the small detail that was to save his life. But something lifted his eyes to the Greek characters inscribed in its flank, and it was then he noticed some of the letters were missing. No, not missing – they had been blacked out. Aeneas blinked and took a few paces towards the giant effigy. And then he saw that the letters were not blacked out, but that a piece of the horse's side had been removed, revealing a dark interior from which a ladder of knotted rope was dangling.

Aeneas felt his flesh go cold. His eyes widened and his fingers closed tightly around the hilt of his sword. Now he understood and the truth filled him with sudden, overwhelming terror. The horse had contained men – who and how many, he could not guess – and those men would soon be opening the city gates for the rest of the Greek army, which would have sailed into the bay under cover of darkness. In an instant the whole plan was clear before him. Zeus had weighed the Greeks and Trojans in his scales and they had come down in favour of the Greeks.

The sound of raised voices drifted up from the Scaean Gate. He turned to face them, feeling his heart race in his chest. Then he heard a scream and knew there was nothing he could do now to save Troy from its fate. In the brief space of time that followed, he sifted the options that were open to him and understood what he had to do. He looked down at the figures lying around him and kicked one of them awake. The soldier stirred, reluctantly, then grabbed at the foot that was beating against his ribs.

'What do you think you're –?'

'Shut up, man. The Greeks have returned: they're in the city now. Wake as many warriors as you can and find whatever weapons are to hand. Do you understand?'

The man frowned, rubbing his eyes and cheeks, then gave a nod.

'Where are you going?' he called after Aeneas as he ran towards Pergamos.

Aeneas ignored him. He had thought of heading to the palace and warning Priam and Deiphobus, but the Greeks were certain to have sent men to take the citadel gates and guard them. And that left him only one choice, the choice that his heart would have chosen anyway. His father, his wife and his infant son were staying in the home of Antenor, the elder, and his wife Theano, the priestess of Athena. Troy was lost, but Aeneas could still save his family.

Odysseus and Eperitus ran through the archway and into Pergamos.

'Menelaus, wait!'

'Go back,' the Spartan answered. 'My mind's made up.'

He had reached the foot of the broad ramp that led up to the next tier of the citadel, but despite his words seemed reluctant to go any further. His sword hung idly from his hand and he was staring up at the poplars that lined the road ahead as if they were giant sentinels, threatening to attack if he placed even one foot on the neatly laid cobbles.

'Ours' too. We've decided to come with you.'

Menelaus turned to face the Ithacan king.

'I don't need your help, Odysseus.'

'Yes you do. *I* know where Helen's quarters are and unless I show you the way you'll waste valuable time searching the palace to find her. Right now, Agamemnon and the rest of the army are streaming in through the Scaean Gate. Soon the sounds of battle are going to carry up here and alert the royal guard that something's wrong. And unless you find her straight away, Deiphobus is going to put Helen in his chariot and take her away to safety.'

As he finished speaking, a distant shout of alarm rose into the air and was cut short. Menelaus threw an anxious glance up the ramp, then turned to Odysseus.

'Very well, come with me, but don't try to get in the way when I find my wife, or I swear by all the gods you'll regret it.'

Odysseus turned to Eperitus, placing his hands on his upper arms.

'And now our paths must diverge, old friend. The night will be dangerous and bloody and I wish we could face it together, but the gods have set us different tasks to complete. My way lies with Menelaus, but you have to find Astynome and keep her safe. And if you can, you must face your father.'

'My place is to guard you.'

'I can look after myself well enough, and unless you'd rather I relieve you as captain of my guard then you'd better start obeying my orders. But I promise you this, Eperitus: somewhere beyond the fire and smoke, when Troy's in ruin and her streets are piled high with the dead, we'll meet again. Now, go and save the woman you love.'

The two men embraced, then Eperitus turned and ran into one of the side streets, where he was instantly absorbed by the dense shadows.

'Come on then,' Menelaus snarled, impatiently.

A breath of wind brought with it the faint clatter of bronze from the lower city, accompanied by the dull murmuring of angry voices contending with each other. Driven by a renewed urgency, Odysseus and Menelaus sprinted up the ramp to the second tier of Pergamos. An awe-inspiring press of two and three-storeyed mansions loomed out of the darkness on every side, but there was no time to admire the great buildings that had stood for so long and were now doomed for destruction. They ran on towards the second ramp, where the temple of Zeus lay to their right and the equally impressive temple of Athena to their left. Odysseus felt a pang of regret and doubt as he recalled his recent encounter there with the goddess.

'Who's that?' demanded a voice ahead of them.

Odysseus had almost forgotten the guards who kept a constant vigil at the foot of the ramp that led up to the palace courtyard. Fortunately, Menelaus was not so slow.

'The Greeks have entered the city!' he answered without halting. 'We need to warn the king.'

Four soldiers appeared from the shadows, fully armed and alert. They looked at each other in confusion, too shocked by the news to consider that the men running towards them might be enemies. By the time they saw Menelaus and Odysseus raising their swords, it was too late. Menelaus plunged his weapon into his first victim's chest, the sharpened point forcing its way through his scaled armour and finding his heart. Odysseus's sword skimmed over the second man's shoulder and sliced through his throat, toppling him backwards as he clasped both hands about the fatal wound. The remaining warriors fumbled for their spears, but were not quick enough. One fell headless to the cobblestones, while the other folded over the point of Odysseus's blade. It took a matter of moments for the attackers to ensure the guards were dead before continuing up the ramp to the third tier.

The wide courtyard before them was empty, but Odysseus placed an arresting hand on Menelaus's chest while he scoured the shadows beneath the palace walls for more guards. Behind them, the clamour of destruction from the lower city was growing and here and there the low clouds were beginning to glow orange as one house after another was put to the torch.

'There's not much time,' Menelaus said, staring back over his shoulder. 'We need to find my wife now.'

'There's a servants' entrance over on the left,' Odysseus replied, pointing away from the high muralled walls of the main palace to an unadorned, single-storeyed wing set back from the rest of the building. 'I can find my way to her quarters once we're inside.'

He ran across the broad courtyard, kicking up spumes of the soft earth as he went. Menelaus followed close on his heels and together they reached the shadow of the building just as the main doors of the palace swung open and a handful of armed men came running out. They stopped sharply and began speaking in hurried voices, pointing to the orange clouds above the lower city.

'That's Deiphobus,' Menelaus hissed, gripping his sword and taking a step toward the courtyard.

Odysseus pulled him back.

'There'll be time to deal with him later, but while he's distracted we should find Helen and take her to safety.'

Hugging the shadows, they reached the servant's entrance and pushed it open. Torches flickered in the passageway beyond, but there was no-one to be seen. Knowing time was slipping away from them, Odysseus led a weaving path through the narrow corridors of the building, passing open doorways that gave fleeting hints at their contents: a pungent whiff of root vegetables and herbs; the reek of fish; a heady scent of wine; the sweet aroma of bread. They entered a broader passage that angled to the right and soon led them to the foot of a flight of stairs. Odysseus took the steps three at a time, not caring who or what might be waiting above, and ran on through more deserted corridors where there were fewer torches and the smells coming from the open doors were of human bodies, accompanied by the sounds of snoring. They reached a door guarded by a sleeping sentinel, whose throat Menelaus paused to slice open with his sword before running on in Odysseus's wake.

Then they came to a turn in the passage that was bathed with the glow of newly lit torches. Odysseus crouched low and signalled for Menelaus to do the same.

'Is her bedroom near?' Menelaus whispered.

'Just around this corner. But listen, someone's speaking; if Helen's there, she's not alone.'

At that moment, a door opened and the muffled voices became clear.

'I don't know if it's the whole Greek army, but we can't take any risks. We heard the fighting and saw the flames from the courtyard, so I'm going to take you somewhere safe before it's too late.'

'Deiphobus!' Menelaus hissed.

Before Odysseus could stop him, the Spartan king had pulled the shield from his back and was running around the corner. Odysseus swore and followed as quickly as he could, almost colliding with Menelaus as he turned into the broad, well-lit corridor. Just a few paces away, standing before the open door to Helen's bedroom, were Deiphobus, two of Helen's maids and two members of the royal guard. Their faces wore looks of astonishment as they gaped at the two gore-spattered Greeks. For a heartbeat Menelaus and Odysseus stared back at them in silence, hesitating at the unexpected sight of the armed warriors. Into this moment of anxious stillness stepped Helen, dressed in a gauzy white chiton with her black hair tied up behind her head, as if she had not yet been to bed. She carried a black cloak over her arm, which slipped to the floor as she set eyes upon her first husband.

'Menelaus,' she said, barely breathing his name.

Chapter Thirty-Nine
HELEN & MENELAUS

G et back!' Deiphobus ordered, snapping to his senses and pushing
Helen into the bedroom. 'You two, do your duty!'

The guardsmen lowered the points of their spears and advanced
side by side down the corridor. Behind them, the maids screamed and
ran after Deiphobus, only to have the door slammed shut in their faces.
They turned and fled, just as Menelaus knocked aside one of the spear
points with his shield and stepped inside the guard of its owner, sinking
his sword into the man's unprotected groin. He cried out in agony and
lurched sideways into the second Trojan, who tried to push him away
with his elbow. Seeing his chance, Odysseus rushed forward and
lunged at him. He stepped back to avoid the point of Odysseus's sword,
but caught his heel on his dying comrade and fell in a heap. Odysseus
finished him quickly.

'Come on!' Menelaus called, leaping over their fallen enemies.

He kicked open the door and crashed into the bedroom. Odysseus
followed, his heart pounding hard against his chest. In the centre of
the room was a large bed. White curtains billowed inward from a
window behind it, ushering in the savoury whiff of smoke and the pink
glow of fire from the lower city. On the other side of the bed was
Deiphobus with Helen held firmly in his arms. Two more of Helen's
maids stood in an open doorway at the back of the wide chamber –
which Odysseus knew led to Helen's bathroom – their beautiful faces
blighted by terror. But these details were of little concern compared to
the four other guardsmen whom Deiphobus had brought with him to
escort his wife to safety, and who were standing ready with their spears
gripped tightly in both hands and their shields on their arms.

Menelaus stared at Helen, his face an angry mask that hid emotions
Odysseus could only guess at. Helen looked back at him, almost too

afraid to hold his gaze but also conscious that to look away would be an admission of guilt before her avenging husband. She must have known that Menelaus's sudden appearance inside the palace meant a Greek victory, and that whatever happened now her life was balanced on the edge of his blade. Belatedly, she began to struggle against Deiphobus's grip, sending looks of helpless longing toward her first husband and trying to ignore the knowing presence of Odysseus.

Deiphobus nodded at his guards. Cautiously they edged forward, searching with experienced eyes for a gap that would invite the points of their spears into a killing thrust. But Menelaus and Odysseus were too battle-hardened to make foolish mistakes and braced themselves for their own chance to strike and kill. Odysseus risked opening his shield a little and was rewarded with a premature lunge from one of his opponents. He stepped aside so that the spear passed between his body and his shield, then hacked down with his blade to hew off the Trojan's left hand. The man's weapon fell with a clatter and he stepped back, holding the stump of his wrist into his armpit. His companion knocked him to one side with his shoulder and ran shouting at Odysseus, who stepped away and lashed out with the rim of his shield, forcing the man to duck and turn with his back to the door.

Menelaus quickly tired of his enemies' probing jabs and with a bellow of rage leapt at them. One spear point caught fast in his shield, almost pushing him into the path of the second weapon, which glanced off his ribcage but failed to penetrate the armour. In his fury, the Spartan slashed at the face of his first foe and felled him, before turning on his heel and sweeping the other man's head from his shoulders. Seeing this, Odysseus's remaining opponent tossed his spear aside and fled through the open doorway.

The Greeks now turned back to face Deiphobus and Helen. The remaining soldier, still clutching his maimed limb, staggered across the beautifully adorned bedroom, splashing the animal pelts that lined the floor with large drops of blood. He lurched towards the window in his confusion and fell unconscious at Helen's feet. Deiphobus released his wife – who knelt down beside the fallen soldier – and stepped forward, drawing his sword as he advanced.

'Stay back, Odysseus,' Menelaus warned. 'This one dies by my hand and mine alone.'

'You'll not find me as easy as the others,' Deiphobus responded in Greek.

Menelaus's lips curled back in a snarl, tinged with joy at the prospect of killing Helen's latest husband. Then, as Deiphobus prepared to fight, Helen stood up and closed behind him. The Trojan prince stiffened and thrust out his chest, his face suddenly strained. A line of blood appeared at the corner of his mouth, then with a choke burst out over his chin.

Odysseus had seen Helen draw the sword from the fallen guard's belt, but only guessed her intentions at the last moment, springing forward with his palm held out in an arresting motion. His warrior's sensibilities, so brutalised after ten years of war, told him it was not right for one so beautiful, so outwardly pure as Helen to sink to the level of murder. But he was too late. As Deiphobus slipped to the floor and rolled onto his back – as if to snatch a final glance at her face – the bloody weapon in her hand and the red stains on her white dress were evidence of her deed. Why though? Odysseus wondered. Out of revenge for a forced marriage? Or as a token of repentance before her returning husband, in the hope of saving her own life?

Menelaus looked down at the lifeless form of Deiphobus, then at the woman who had killed him, the woman for whose sake so many men had died. Their eyes met and for a long moment there was no rage or bitterness in Menelaus's gaze, only fascination as he reacquainted himself with the face he had once loved so well, and for which he had crossed the Aegean with the greatest fleet the world had ever seen. Helen looked back at the father of her children, a man who, as her husband, had only ever treated her with kindness and respect; a man she had never hated, and yet whom she had never loved. And to Odysseus's shrewd mind the old familiarity between the two was still there, as if – for a brief space – the infidelity, war and years apart from each other had never happened. Then, as the Ithacan had expected, the recognition of those dividing forces stole into their gaze, reawakening their more immediate emotions and pulling them back to the present. For Helen, it was a flicker of guilt, followed by a more dominant fear – fear of the man she had betrayed, and who was no longer separated from her by the walls, armies and princes of Troy. For Menelaus, seeing her shame and her fear brought his righteous anger rushing back. Tears rolled in rapid, heavy drops down his cheeks: tears he had never shed for the thousands who had suffered for the sake of his love, but which came forth now as he remembered the pain she had inflicted on him. And it was a pain that demanded retribution.

He leapt towards her, his sword flashing red. Helen screamed, but Odysseus had anticipated Menelaus's reaction and threw his arms about the Spartan's chest, pulling him back.

'Control your anger! We haven't fought for ten years just so you can murder the woman we came to save.'

'Let me go!' Menelaus spat, desperately trying to throw off Odysseus's bear-like grip.

'Not until you've calmed down.'

'Menelaus,' Helen said, her voice soft but commanding.

Menelaus ceased struggling and looked up.

'Husband,' she continued. 'Listen to Odysseus. Have you been through so much, just to kill me? Have you suffered for all these years just to rip open my flesh with your sword and bathe in my blood? Have thousands died just to slake your lust for vengeance? Such an empty victory! Or can something be retrieved from all this destruction?'

Odysseus slipped his arms from about Menelaus's chest and eased the sword from his fingertips. Menelaus did not move.

'I wanted you back,' he replied. 'That's why I came after you. I've thought of little else since we first landed on these shores.'

'And now you have me.'

'Do I, Helen?' Menelaus retorted. 'Do I have my wife back, or – as it seems to me now we are face-to-face again – am I simply stealing another man's woman, nothing more than a slave to tend to my needs and sleep with me, hiding her hatred beneath a bowed head? If that's the case, then we'll both be better off if I kill you now.'

Helen dropped the sword that had murdered Deiphobus and held her bloodstained hands imploringly towards Menelaus.

'Don't let it all be in vain. We were man and wife once; we can be again, and not without love, as you fear. Tell him, Odysseus. Tell him how I begged you to take me back with you to the Greek camp, so that I could be with my rightful husband again.'

Odysseus remembered how Helen had pleaded with him to take her from Troy, even offering him her body if he would return her to Menelaus and free her from the confines of the city walls and forced marriage to Deiphobus. He also recalled his debt to her, for not giving him away to the Trojan guards when he was at her mercy.

'It's true, Menelaus, and if she hadn't insisted on bringing Pleisthenes it might have been possible. And look there. Is that the act of a woman in love, to murder her husband in cold blood?'

'That poor soul?' Menelaus said. 'Even I can see she didn't love him. But Deiphobus isn't my concern – Paris is. The man who entered my house as a guest and left a thief, surrendering his honour for the sake of my wife.' He turned his eyes on Helen. 'Last year I might have believed you still loved me, that this whole war had a true purpose. Then I faced Paris on the battlefield and he told me the truth: that you fell in love with him in Sparta; that you came to Troy not as a captive but of your own free will. Is that true, Helen?'

Menelaus's tone was threatening, and yet there was doubt in it, too. And hope.

Helen looked down at the bloodstained furs.

'Why dwell on the events of a decade ago? The only thing that matters is here and now.'

'No! Our lives are founded in the past. If you betrayed me then you can do it again, and I would rather kill you now than have that.'

Helen paused, then raised her eyes to his, fixing his gaze.

'I never loved Paris,' she lied. Her features were firm, but Odysseus saw the glint of a tear in the corner of her eye. 'I never loved him, Menelaus. He took me from you against my will, brought me here and forced me to marry him. I would never have left my children, or you, for another.'

'Yet you came to love him,' Menelaus countered. 'You shared his bed willingly, happily. You were lovers.'

Helen's tears were flowing now and as her eyes flickered towards Odysseus he saw shame in them, knowing he knew she was lying.

'I never loved him,' she sobbed. 'His touch repulsed me, and though he forced himself upon me I never gave myself willingly.'

'I don't believe you,' Menelaus insisted. 'You enjoyed being mounted by him!'

There was no conviction in his words now. The last of his anger was submitting to his desire for her, a desire that revealed itself by his talk of Paris and Helen's lovemaking. Helen must have realised this and seen that the contest was entering a realm where she had the dominant power. She took a few paces towards him and fell to her knees.

'My body has always been yours, Menelaus,' she said, seizing the front of her chiton and tearing it open, 'and it will be yours again.'

A splintering crash came from somewhere within the depths of the palace, followed by a woman's scream. Menelaus glanced over his shoulder, then back down at Helen. The sight of her perfect face and her bared breasts were almost enough for him. And yet he still refused to surrender to his need for her.

'Swear it, Helen. Swear by the name of Aphrodite that you never loved Paris. Swear he took you from our home against your will.' With a swift movement, he pulled a dagger from his belt and held the point to her throat. 'Swear it, or by Ares's sword I will slice your beautiful head from your shoulders and throw it into the flames of Troy!'

'Menelaus, give me the dagger.' Odysseus's sword was pressed against the Spartan's ribs. 'Helen saw through my disguise when I came to steal the Palladium, but she didn't betray me to the Trojans. She even drugged the temple guards and showed me a way to leave the city unnoticed. Without her Troy would never have fallen, and if that doesn't convince you of her loyalty to you then I don't know what will. But I also owe her my life, and if you don't take that blade from her throat then I'll run you through. Do you understand me?'

'All I want is her oath, sworn in the name of Aphrodite,' Menelaus hissed, without removing his eyes from Helen or his dagger from her neck.

More screams came from the corridors behind them. Then Helen spoke, with her eyes closed and her voice trembling.

'I swear it, Menelaus. As Aphrodite is my witness, I never loved anyone but you.'

Menelaus withdrew the blade and tossed it into a corner of the room. Dropping to his knees, he wrapped his arms around his wife and drew her clumsily into his chest. He pressed his face into her hair, the tears falling heavily from his eyes again as he breathed in lungfuls of her perfume.

'Then you're mine again, at last, and this cursed war is truly over. Let's find Pleisthenes and go home. To Sparta.'

Chapter Forty
LOVE & VENGEANCE

The streets of Pergamos were confusing in a night without moon or stars, lit only by the reflected orange glow from the fires that were springing up in the lower city, but it was not long before Eperitus found himself emerging from the shadows opposite the temple of Apollo. His father's two-storeyed house was beside it, and after a quick glance at the dark doorways and windows of the surrounding buildings, Eperitus crossed to the modest portico with its twin columns standing like sentinels, one on either side.

His heart beat faster as he laid his palms against the wooden doors and paused. For a whole night and day in the cramped discomfort of the wooden horse he had pondered this moment and what he would do when it came. Sitting on the hard bench with his head in his hands, he had thought about Astynome and all they had been through together. Despite her betrayal, he knew she loved him and that he still loved her. That was something worth fighting for, something much greater than the cold, selfish motivations of glory that had given his life meaning before. It was why Odysseus had let him go. The king knew the value of love, and that Eperitus would need to protect Astynome from the army of vengeful Greeks that would soon be rampaging through the citadel.

But if Eperitus wanted nothing more than to sail back with Astynome to Ithaca, where Agamemnon, Apheidas and the walls of Troy would never be able to separate them again, he knew that even then he could not find satisfaction until he had faced his father for one last time. Unlike his lust for glory, he could not so quickly abandon his need for revenge. Apheidas had caused too much destruction in his life for him to simply turn his back and walk away. What was more, if he was to enjoy the future in peace with Astynome he had first to rid himself of the shadow of his past. He was sure Odysseus had known that, too.

He leaned his weight against the wooden doors, which were unbarred and swung open easily. Inside was the main hall, dark but for the red glow of the fire that seemed to pulsate like a heart at its centre. Eperitus shut the doors quietly behind him and waited, letting his supernatural senses expand into the cavernous black chamber. The light from the hearth did not reach beyond the four pillars that surrounded it, but his keen eyes could pick out the erect shapes of several chairs, a number of long tables pushed against the walls, and the faded outlines of the murals on the plaster above them. Through the smell of burning wood and ashes, he could discern the lingering aromas of bread, roast meat and wine from an earlier meal, mingling with other smells from deeper within the house. The air in the hall was still, other than the slight updraft as the smoke from the hearth was drawn through the hole in the apex of the ceiling, and the only sounds were the crackle of the fire and the creaking of wooden beams as they settled in the cooler night air. And the faint, restrained breathing of the other person in the room.

Eperitus drew his sword.

'Come out of the shadows,' he ordered, speaking in the Trojan tongue.

A figure rose up from one of the chairs against the wall to his left and walked towards him.

'Eperitus!'

Astynome's black hair was tied up behind her head and even in the faint light from the hearth Eperitus was able to recognise the familiar features of the face he loved so much. Slipping his sword back into its sheath, he moved forward and welcomed her into his arms. She brushed her cheek against his, then sank her head upon his shoulder, as if weary from their time apart. He raised a hand to her nape and pushed his fingertips into her hairline, enjoying the warmth of her skin and the softness of her hair. There was a clean, fresh aroma about her that sent his mind back to the times they had shared a bed, long before any darkness had come between them.

She looked up at him with her large, brown eyes, and he responded by pressing his lips to hers.

'I expected to have to find you and wake you,' he said.

'I knew you were coming,' she replied, indicating the cloak she was wearing. 'The night you stole the Palladium, Odysseus told me that if a wooden horse entered Troy the war would end and I would be reunited with you. I didn't understand at the time, and even less so when I saw that wheeled monster being dragged towards the city – I think the gods confounded us all so we wouldn't guess its true purpose – but when Cassandra spoke I realised there were men hidden inside the horse. And I knew you were one of them.'

'We'd all be dead if you hadn't spoken up against her.'

She shrugged. 'Well, here you are. What happens now?'

'The army should have sailed into the bay under cover of darkness. Even as we speak the Scaean Gate is being opened to let them in. It's the end of the war, Astynome, and the end of Troy. Agamemnon won't suffer anything of the city to remain, or its people.'

'It was inevitable,' Astynome said, shaking her head. 'Troy could not stand forever, not against the will of Zeus. And yet I wish it didn't have to end like this, with such ignominy – a great city murdered in its sleep.'

'There was no other way, but at least it means we can be together again. That's why I'm here – to keep you safe until it's all over, then take you back with me to Ithaca. If you still want to come?'

Astynome smiled. 'Of course I do. My life's nothing without you, Eperitus. But you're not just here for me, are you.'

'I gave Palamedes my word I would keep Clymene safe if Troy was ever sacked.'

'I mean Apheidas.'

Eperitus held her face and tenderly brushed her cheeks with his thumbs.

'I can't leave without avenging his crimes.'

'Honour and vengeance! The two things that have kept men killing each other since the creation of the world.'

'You forget love.'

'At least love can also stay a man's hand!' Astynome retorted. Then her eyes softened again and she glanced down at his armoured chest. 'Clymene's already in her room waiting – I told her to be ready to flee the city – but *must* you risk everything to face Apheidas? I know when you were his prisoner I said I would help you take your revenge, but now I'm not so certain. Does killing a man really solve anything? Will murdering your own father right the wrongs he has committed? It seems to me the best way to defeat Apheidas is to be everything he is not, to be loving where he is hateful, to be selfless where he is ambitious. And that's the kind of man you are, Eperitus – it's why I fell in love with you. But if you seek him out and avenge his crimes in blood, you're taking the path he would take. Instead of defeating him, you'll *become* him. If you want to be free of his shadow, then leave him to his fate and walk away from this place.'

Her words were sacrilege to a warrior, whose code demanded that the merest slight had to be avenged in blood. And yet they held a challenge he could not ignore. Did he want to kill his father and inherit his legacy of hatred? Or could he turn away, even now when revenge was finally within his grasp, and take a different path?

'A woman wouldn't understand,' said another voice from the shadows on the opposite side of the hall. 'A man who runs from his responsibilities is only half a man, doomed to live life with his head hung low and his spirit in shadow. Isn't that so, Son?'

Eperitus spun round to see a man and a woman step into the circle of firelight. The tall figure of his father was unmistakable. He carried a spear in one hand and a shield in the other, and the red glow from the embers played menacingly on his scaled cuirass. It took a moment longer to recognise the woman as Clymene, her shoulders stooped and her chin on her chest. Eperitus slipped his grandfather's shield from his back and took its weight on his left arm, while slowly drawing his sword from its sheath. It seemed his decision had been made for him.

'Father,' he said. 'At least you've saved me the trouble of looking for you.'

'And I thought Astynome might have talked you into running away. But what were you planning, Son? A knife in my sleep? That seems to be the Greek way of doing things.'

'No, you can be sure I'd have woken you first. I wouldn't want your ghost to slip off to Hades without knowing who it was that took your life.'

'Ah, that must be the Trojan in you, Son.'

Eperitus spat. 'I've rejected that part of my inheritance, just like my grandfather did when he made Greece his home. It's a shame you didn't follow his example.'

'And become a skulking coward, sneaking into cities hidden inside a wooden horse?'

Eperitus raised an eyebrow.

'If you knew, why didn't you burn it when you had the chance?'

'I didn't know,' Apheidas admitted with a shrug. 'I *suspected* something was amiss with the horse, but when Cassandra started screaming that there were men inside the idea of it seemed ridiculous. And that was the work of the gods, I'm sure of it. Then, after the celebrations were over, Clymene here woke me to say that Astynome was planning to flee, and when I looked out my window I could see flames in the lower city and hear cries. That was when the truth became clear to me.'

'Clymene!' Astynome said, her tone both accusative and dismayed. 'How could you betray me? I was trying to help you.'

Clymene raised her pained face to look at her friend.

'I'm sorry, Astynome, but Apheidas is my master and the Greeks are our enemies. When you said we needed to get out of the city before it was too late, I knew it meant *they* were coming. But I don't *want* them to come! They murdered my son in cold blood, and if I can do anything to save Troy from them then I will. And I have.'

'You silly woman!' Astynome replied. 'Troy is doomed, and you've thrown away your only hope of escape.'

'And you think you're just going to walk out of the city unscathed?' Apheidas mocked. 'At least Clymene has shown loyalty, whereas you will die a traitor!'

Eperitus moved Astynome behind him and walked towards the hearth.

'No-one is going to die except you, Father.'

'So you think. I overheard you'd sworn to protect Clymene, but merely taking an oath doesn't mean it's going to be fulfilled. Let me demonstrate.'

Apheidas turned towards Clymene and with a quick thrust pushed the point of his spear through her chest and out her back. Astynome sprang forward with a cry of protest, but Clymene was already dead, her body toppling back into the hearth. The flames leapt up to welcome her and a blaze of orange light illuminated her laughing murderer.

'See, Eperitus? There's one oath you'll never be able to fulfil. Now, let's see whether you can keep your other promise – to kill me.'

Apheidas tossed the spear up and caught it with his upturned hand. In the same movement, he pulled it back and hurled it at his son. It split the air with a hiss, passing a finger's breadth to the right of Eperitus's neck.

'Get back, Astynome!' Eperitus shouted. 'Get back *now*!'

He ran at his father and hewed the air where a moment before he had been standing, but the older man had already judged the fall of the weapon and jumped back into the shadows. Drawing his own sword, he leant forward on his front foot and drove the point at his son's exposed midriff. Eperitus turned and blocked the thrust with his shield, following the movement with an arcing sweep of his blade. Apheidas slipped behind a pillar and the bronze edge drew sparks as it bit into the stone.

Eperitus charged him again and their weapons met, the loud scraping of the blades echoing back from the walls as they bent into each other. They locked eyes, then with a grunt Eperitus pushed his father back into the shadows.

'You've still not got it in you to kill me, Son.'

Eperitus looked at his father's sneering face and felt a surge of hatred. Then he remembered Astynome's words and wondered whether she was right, that there was something of Apheidas's anger in himself. Was he looking at a reflection of what he could become? The thought subdued his fury and he stepped back.

The hiss and pop of the fire was accompanied now by the stench of burning flesh, a smell all too familiar from the many funeral pyres Eperitus had witnessed over the years of the war. He saw his father move to the right, then realised Astynome had ignored his orders and was standing close by. Guessing Apheidas's intentions, he ran across to protect her, just as his father dashed out of the darkness. The red glint of a blade was followed by a scream. Apheidas reeled away, clutching at the side of his face where the point of his son's sword had opened the skin. Eperitus instinctively lifted his hand to touch the scar on his forehead, which Apheidas had given him in the temple of Artemis at Lyrnessus several weeks before.

'Stay back, Astynome! Get out of the house and find somewhere safe to hide until this is over.'

'I'm staying with you,' she said, her voice resolute. 'Haven't you noticed the clamour outside? The Greeks are already in the citadel, so I'd rather die here with you than be raped and killed out there.'

Before Eperitus could reply, Apheidas turned and ran towards a side door, shouldering it open and letting in the pungent smells of cold night air and vegetation. As if to confirm Astynome's fears, the sounds of screaming and the clash of weapons could be clearly heard in the near distance.

'Let him go,' Astynome said, as Apheidas ran into the square garden that was visible beyond the open doorway. 'He can't get out of Troy alive.'

'He can,' Eperitus answered. 'He's too much of a survivor. I have to finish him now, while I have the chance.'

'Then didn't my words mean anything to you earlier? Do you want to become like him?'

'I'll never let that happen.'

'Then think of me. If he kills you, he'll surely kill me too. Even if he doesn't, I'll be captured and taken back to Greece as another man's slave, forced to serve his every need and left to dream of what could have been between us. I want to be *your* wife and lover, Eperitus, the mother of *your* children. Is facing up to your father worth losing that?'

Eperitus hesitated, beset by doubt. Had he become so selfish in his pursuit of Apheidas that he was prepared to risk Astynome's safety? Was he so driven by his hatred of his father that it surpassed his love for her? Yet he had sought revenge for too many years now, and the fear of losing his opportunity quickly overcame the intellectual and emotional arguments that had suddenly emerged against it. He shook his head.

'I have to face him, Astynome. Forgive me.'

He ran through the doorway into the garden, dark but for the light of a single torch in a bracket on the wall. It took a moment for his senses to adjust to the open surroundings, trying to spot his father in the pillared cloisters that surrounded the courtyard, or among the shrubs and fruit trees that filled it. But the night breeze blowing through the foliage made it impossible to distinguish any other movement, while the rustling of leaves disguised all other sounds, except for the constant hiss emanating from the snake pit at the garden's centre. Eperitus gave an involuntary shudder and moved forward.

He spotted the glint of a blade from the corner of his eye and whirled to meet it, just as Astynome cried out in warning from the doorway behind. Eperitus stopped the blow with the middle of his sword, but was sent reeling backwards. He caught his heel and fell.

With a victorious grin across his face, Apheidas ran out of his hiding place, his sword raised in both hands above his head. Without thinking, Eperitus rocked back and kicked out with all the force he could muster, catching his father in the stomach. He fell, crushing some of the low shrubs that lined the path that led to the snake pit. Eperitus was up in an instant, but Apheidas was already on his feet and raising his shield to counter the sweep of his son's sword. A series of blows were exchanged, each one delivered with deadly accuracy and blocked with instinctive skill, until eventually the two men reached the gaping pit and stood back from each other, sweat-covered and breathing heavily.

'Neither of us can win, lad,' Apheidas gasped. 'Why don't you give this up and let me take my chances out there in the streets? You can try to deny the blood that's in your veins, but I'm still your father and it's an offence against the gods for you to try and kill me.'

'*You* are an offence against the gods,' Eperitus replied. 'If I let you go, you'll only blight the lives of others, usurping power and murdering innocent people like Arceisius and Clymene. By killing you, I'll be *honouring* the gods.'

He rushed forward again, catching Apheidas off guard and knocking his sword from his hand so that it skittered across the paved edge of the pit. Apheidas lifted his shield in desperation, blocking the thrust that would have skewered his groin and deflecting it into his thigh. He shouted with pain, but as Eperitus raised his sword for the killing blow, Apheidas found the strength to lash out with the rim of his shield and catch him on the side of the head, sending him spinning backwards onto the flagstones.

Eperitus fought the blackness that threatened to consume him, calling on his hatred to push himself back up from the floor and find his feet. His head was dull with pain and as he touched the side of his face he could feel the blood where the lip of Apheidas's shield had gashed the skin. Then his vision cleared and he saw his father standing at the edge of the snake pit with Astynome held before him. A burning torch lay on the ground, which she must have taken from the bracket by the door.

'I seem to remember we've been in this position before,' Apheidas mocked.

Eperitus recalled the temple of Thymbrean Apollo, when his father had used Astynome as a hostage to ensure his escape, knowing Eperitus would not risk seeing her hurt.

'He's unarmed,' Astynome shouted.

Apheidas clapped his hand over her mouth.

'I don't need a weapon. One twist of my arm and her neck will break. Do you understand?'

Eperitus nodded, slowly. 'Just release her and I'll let you go. You have my word.'

'You're not very good at keeping your promises, though, are you? And if you think I believe you're just going to forget everything I've done and let me walk out of here, then you're a bigger fool than I am. But there's another way to solve this little dilemma. I've heard it said that for a man to conquer his fears he has to face them. Shall we see if it's true?'

A smile spread across his face as with a resigned gesture he pushed Astynome into the pit. Her scream echoed briefly from the walls and was suddenly silenced. Shocked, Eperitus ran to the edge and stared down into the Stygian blackness, while his father ran limping to another door on the opposite side of the courtyard. Eperitus turned, part of his mind telling him that Apheidas was escaping, but knowing full well that to pursue him was to condemn Astynome to death. And so he turned back to the gaping hole at his feet and, almost as if his actions were being controlled by someone other than himself, he threw his grandfather's shield onto his back and reached for the torch Astynome had let fall on the flagstones. Tossing it into the black void, he prayed to Athena to protect Astynome, then jumped.

Chapter Forty-One
AT THE TEMPLE OF ZEUS

Odysseus could hear the sounds of chaos long before he and Menelaus – with Helen, Pleisthenes and the remaining maids trailing behind – had found their way back to the servants' entrance. The high-pitched screams of women penetrated the palace walls clearly, while the deep-throated shouts of hundreds of men formed a low roar in the background. The clatter of weapons could be heard, too, chattering away like angry birds as Trojan warriors tried to resist the overwhelming tide of the victorious Greeks. Then, as Odysseus reached the door and pushed it open, they saw the night sky ablaze before them, flames and smoke pouring up from Troy as its buildings burned with terrifying, glorious ferocity. Rain clouds pressed low over the city, bathed orange and scarlet by the fires below, and the warm night air crackled with the sound of fiery destruction.

Odysseus shielded his eyes against the heat and light, then, drawing his sword, turned to Menelaus.

'Keep the others close. There are men out there who'll gladly murder us just to get at the women.'

'They can try,' Menelaus growled.

Behind him, Helen stepped out into the night with Pleisthenes at her side. The lad had not said a word to his father since they had burst into his room, even when the Spartan king had taken him in his arms with tears in his eyes and spoken to him in the strange Greek language he barely remembered from his early childhood. Instead, he had pulled away and moved to his mother's side, staring at Menelaus as if he were his enemy. Now, arm in arm, Helen and Pleisthenes stared at the burning sky with silent awe. The maids followed them from the palace and immediately began to wail in anguish at the sight before them.

'Helen, shut them up for all our sakes,' Odysseus pleaded.

She spoke to them in a low voice and they fell quiet. Odysseus looked out at the broad courtyard, which had been so peaceful a short while before. Now it was strewn with the bodies of men and women, while on the opposite side a remnant of the Trojan royal guard fought valiantly against a much larger company of Greeks. In a corner, a man lay on a naked woman, pushing aggressively into her. The woman flapped limply with each movement, and for a horrible moment Odysseus suspected she might be dead.

'Let's go,' Menelaus said.

They ran to the top of the ramp that led down to the middle tier of the citadel. A group of four Greeks ran up the slope towards them, brandishing their swords.

'Stand aside!' Menelaus commanded.

The brutal grins dropped from their smoke-stained faces and they parted before him, though with obvious reluctance as they stared greedily at the women he was escorting. The streets below were teeming with soldiers. Some were fighting their way into the two-storeyed houses at the same time as others were trying to leave with the plunder they had found. This consisted of anything they could lay their hands on, from silver cups to fine dresses or skins of wine. More than once, Odysseus saw men whose arms were laden with loot cut down before they could defend themselves, and their goods taken from their dead bodies. In other houses, people were leaping from upper windows as flames devoured the ground floor, only for the men to be put to the sword and the women to be dragged off by packs of soldiers and raped.

'Look!' a voice rang out. 'Women!'

A group of soldiers ran towards them, intent on taking Helen and her maids for themselves. Menelaus did not bother to order them back, killing the first with a swift stroke and sinking his sword into the stomach of the second. This only made the others angrier and Odysseus and Menelaus were forced to kill or wound four more before the rest retreated.

'By all the gods, this is chaos!' Menelaus exclaimed. 'It's worse than a pitched battle.'

'What did you expect?' Odysseus shouted over the clamour. 'Come on: we need to find some of our own Ithacans or Spartans if we're going to get Helen and your son to safety. Let's head to the gates.'

They found their way down to the lower tier of Pergamos, where to their relief the gates were protected by a disciplined company of Myrmidons. Their commander was Peisandros, who stepped out as they approached and held up his hand.

'No prisoners or loot beyond this gate, Agamemnon's orders. Take them into the barrack room for fair distribution later.'

'You can tell my brother that Helen of Sparta is no man's prisoner,' Menelaus answered. 'Neither are my son or any of these maids.'

Peisandros stared wide-eyed at the blood-caked faces of the two kings, then with a shout of joy seized each man's hand in turn and shook it.

'My lords! We feared you were dead. There've been all sorts of rumours –'

'Rumours haunt every battle,' Odysseus chided him with a smile. 'I've been killed at least a dozen times during this war. And a veteran like you should know better than to listen to such nonsense.'

'True enough,' Peisandros agreed, his gaze wandering to Helen. 'So you've found her. And no less beautiful than the last time I saw her, all those years ago in Sparta.'

'More beautiful,' Menelaus corrected him. 'Now, go and pick twenty of your best men to escort us back to the ships.'

'Yes, my lord,' Peisandros replied, shooting a last glance at Helen before striding off to carry out his orders.

'Now you've found yourselves a guard, Menelaus, I'm going back into the citadel,' Odysseus said.

'Are you mad?' Helen asked, a look of genuine concern on her face. Odysseus shook his head.

'Eperitus is somewhere up there. I won't abandon him to be mistaken for a Trojan by a pack of victory-drunk Greeks.'

Menelaus took his hand in both of his.

'Thank you, Odysseus. I doubt things would have turned out as they have without your help.'

Helen released her hold of Pleisthenes and stepped forward.

'Menelaus is too frugal in his praise,' she said, embracing the Ithacan king closely. 'We owe you everything.'

'Can I send a few of Peisandros's men with you?' Menelaus offered.

'No need – it'll be less dangerous without Helen and her maids. But there is one thing you can do for me.'

'Name it.'

'You remember Antenor, the Trojan elder who was our host when we came to the city before the siege started?'

'Of course.'

'His house is close to the citadel walls, a little to the right beyond the gates – you'll remember it when you see it. If he and his family are still alive, take them down to the ships with you. He was a good man and doesn't deserve to be slaughtered with the rest.'

'Few do, if you ask me,' Menelaus replied, 'but I'll do as you wish. May Athena go with you, Odysseus.'

Odysseus nodded, though the Spartan's words were a painful reminder that the goddess had abandoned him. He turned and ran back into the anarchy of the citadel. The mayhem had, if anything, increased. Bodies were everywhere, many stripped of clothing, others left like bundles of rumpled linen, barely recognisable as human beings. Odysseus had seen more battles than he could remember, but witnessing the slaughter of armed soldiers was poor preparation for the sight of old men, women and children lying murdered in the streets. He came across a dead woman, naked but for a single sandal, her outstretched hand still clutching the arm of a trampled infant. Many others lay where they had been stabbed, with lifeless eyes staring up at the blood-coloured clouds above. There were some, though, whose bodies had been hewn horribly by several blades. The scene sickened him and he thought of his beloved Penelope and little Telemachus – only ten years old – and how they might look dead on the streets of Ithaca. Vulnerable Ithaca. The fact he had left his home and family unprotected for so long suddenly tore at him, filling him with surprising panic.

A scream interrupted his thoughts and a half-naked girl ran from a nearby doorway. Her sun-darkened skin marked her out as a slave, but beneath the dishevelled hair and the bleeding lip Odysseus could see she was beautiful. Five men ran out of the house after her, the first still clutching a piece of the girl's dress in his fist. He also carried the marks of her fingernails on his red jowls.

'Come back here, you whore!' he shouted, dashing after her as she ran to the foot of the ramp that led up to the middle tier of the citadel. 'We haven't finished with you yet.'

'Eurylochus!' Odysseus shouted angrily, recognising his cousin. Two of the others he also knew to be Ithacans, though they were the kind of soldiers he was not proud to think of as his countrymen. The other two were Taphian mercenaries who had arrived earlier in the summer with the last batch of reinforcements from Troy. 'Leave her alone! Why aren't you with the rest of the army?'

The five men paused and half turned at the authority in Odysseus's voice, but there was no shame in their drunken faces as they stared back at their king. Indeed, the Taphians eyed him with distinct rebellion in their eyes, as if they would happily have struck him down there and then.

'What army?' Eurylochus replied. 'There is no army, just packs of soldiers getting their own back on the bastards who've kept us from our homes for ten years.'

'She's getting away!' one of the others shouted ruefully, as the girl ran up the ramp and disappeared.

Odysseus felt his temper snap.

'Get back into the city and find as many Ithacans as you can!' he shouted, red-faced with anger as he advanced on them. 'Start restoring order, damn you. And if you lay hands on another woman without my permission, I'll see you hanged for it in the morning. Do you understand?'

Eurylochus scowled at him and the others showed an open reluctance to do as they were ordered. One of the Taphians circled to Odysseus's unshielded right, while the other clutched the handle of his sword and began easing the blade from its sheath.

'Put it away, Selagos,' Eurylochus hissed at him. 'Let's go find the rest of our countrymen.'

He spat on the flagstones as a last, defiant gesture, then slunk off reluctantly towards the gates to the lower city, followed by his cronies. But as Odysseus ran up the ramp to the middle tier of the citadel – hoping to find the girl and take her under his protection – he saw them turn aside down one of the narrow streets, doubtless hunting for more victims. The girl was nowhere to be seen when Odysseus reached the top of the slope, and after a fruitless search among the nearest alleys he knew she was gone, perhaps already snatched up by another group of soldiers. Suddenly weary, he stumbled into a doorway and leaned with his back against the wall. He had barely calmed his breathing again when a fierce clash of weaponry erupted from nearby. Five men in Trojan armour came sprinting around the corner of a house. Their leader was splendidly armoured and Odysseus recognised him as one of Priam's few remaining sons; the others were members of the royal guard. Their weapons were red with gore and exhaustion was written in their every movement as they ran towards the temple of Zeus, farther up the street. Odysseus had hardly noticed the large, richly decorated building until that point, but as the men lumbered towards it he realised that they were seeking sanctuary inside, desperately hoping that the gods would protect them. As he looked at the edifice, he noticed for the first time that there was a ring of Greek soldiers standing about it. For a moment he was mystified; then he realised that others must have sought refuge there, and so far the victorious invaders had maintained enough self-discipline to respect the sanctity of the temple, preferring to set a watch over it and keep anyone from leaving or entering.

A number of Greeks now moved to block the advance of the handful of Trojans. At the same moment, another group of Greek soldiery came running around the same corner the Trojans had first appeared from. Neoptolemus was at their head, unmistakeable in his father's god-made armour.

'There he is!' Neoptolemus shouted. 'After him.'

Priam's son turned at the sound of Neoptolemus's voice, knowing that his route to the temple of Zeus was blocked and that he would have to face Achilles's ferocious son in battle. Taking a spear from one his companions, he launched it into the pack of pursuing Greeks. The throw was straight and powerful, but Neoptolemus raised his magnificent shield and knocked it aside with contempt. With a hateful shout the two sides ran at each other, their shields crashing and weapons ringing loudly. Odysseus stood up, trying to see more of the uneven struggle. Strangely, he felt himself hoping the Trojans would give a good account of themselves, or at least make a break for the temple. But the fight was over almost immediately, with Neoptolemus pushing his way out of the crowd and bellowing triumphantly, the severed head of Priam's son held aloft in his hand.

A despairing cry tore through the night air as he showed his trophy to the baying soldiers. Odysseus looked at the pillared entrance to the temple, where an old man stood with his fists raised to the heavens. He was surrounded by half a dozen crying women, several of them pulling at the man's cloak in an attempt to keep him within the confines of the temple. Their efforts were in vain: the man pushed them away and staggered down the broad steps towards the towering statue of Zeus that fronted the building.

Without his black wig and face powder, Priam was only recognisable to Odysseus by his great height and the wailing figure of Hecabe following him from the temple. The old king ignored his wife's pleading and stooped to pick up a discarded spear. That such a frail being was able to lift the weapon was amazing, and as he raised it above his shoulder and called to Neoptolemus the young warrior merely laughed and tossed Priam the head of his son.

'What are you waiting for, you old fool?' he goaded, throwing his arms open and standing with his legs apart on the flagstones. 'Avenge your son's death.'

'Priam, no!' Odysseus shouted, guessing what was about to happen and running out from the doorway.

If Priam heard him, he paid no attention and hurled the spear with all his remaining strength. The throw was pathetic, skittering across the floor to be stopped by Neoptolemus's sandalled foot. The Myrmidon prince's mocking features were instantly transformed. Curling back his lip, he sprinted towards the king of Troy, his sword raised high above his head. Priam turned and staggered back to the temple, sprawling over the steps as Neoptolemus caught up with him. Odysseus barged his way through the crowd of black-clad Myrmidons and called out.

'Stop! Neoptolemus, stop!'

Neoptolemus was now standing astride Priam on the steps. He turned to see Odysseus running towards him, then with a scornful grin reached down to seize Priam's thinning locks of grey hair. Pulling the old man's head back, he lifted his blade and brought it down with a savage blow, slicing through the throat. The head came away and swung from his hand, dripping trails of blood over Neoptolemus's legs and feet. For a brief instant silence pressed down on the scene. The king of Troy was dead. The Trojan people's cause was finished. This was the moment that ended the war.

Then screams broke the stillness. The women gathered at the top of the steps – Priam's surviving daughters – cried out in horror at the murder of their father and fled back into the temple. Odysseus slumped back against the plinth of the statue of Zeus, while behind him the Myrmidons and the other Greeks gave a victorious shout and rushed towards the holy sanctuary.

'Come on,' Neoptolemus encouraged them. 'Agamemnon ordered that no stone was to be left standing on another. Tear this place down; take what you want, including the women – you've earned it. Then burn it to the ground!'

Odysseus watched Hecabe drag herself to her feet, only to be knocked down again by the stampeding soldiers. A spearman paused beside her, stooped down and proceeded to tear at the old woman's clothing. Odysseus kicked him onto his back and pressed the point of his sword against his throat.

'Leave her alone,' he hissed.

The Myrmidon stared back at him angrily, then dragged himself back on his elbows and pushed the weapon aside.

'Your welcome to the old hag,' he replied with a sneer, before leaping to his feet and running into the temple.

Screams were now emanating from the open doorway. Odysseus looked up wearily and saw Neoptolemus still standing on the steps, wiping his blade on Priam's cloak. The Ithacan fought to control his anger before walking up to Achilles's son.

'You've earned your father's armour tonight, Neoptolemus,' he began. 'Achilles was a savage man, but I never thought I'd see his brutality outdone.'

Neoptolemus laughed at his contempt.

'Wasn't this what you brought me here to do, Odysseus? To fulfil the oracle and end the royal line of Troy? Then don't complain if I choose to accomplish my destiny with as much cruelty and ruthlessness as is necessary.'

'The royal line isn't ended yet,' Odysseus told him, then turned his back on the prince and walked over to Hecabe.

'Come with me,' he said, helping her to her feet. 'I'll keep you safe.'

Chapter Forty-Two
THE SNAKE PIT

Eperitus's feet hit the earthen floor where the flames of the torch had cleared a circle among the writhing mass of snakes. His legs buckled beneath him and he fell onto his front, only to feel a searing pain shoot through his arm. His first thought was that he had been bitten, but as he rolled away he felt the heat of the torch and realised he had been burned. He lay there for two or three heartbeats, listening with horror to the hiss of the snakes all around him, then pushed himself up onto his haunches.

His fingers closed about the stem of the torch and he swung it round in an arc. It fluttered briefly and blazed up again, revealing a sight that filled him with revulsion. A sea of serpentine bodies surrounded him, squirming and thrashing as they retreated from the flame. Dozens of heads rose up, exposing pink, ribbed mouths with fangs that glistened in the torchlight. The sight of them made him nauseous, contracting his stomach muscles so tightly that he had to press his hand over his mouth to stop himself from vomiting. He swivelled on one foot and swept the torch in a circle about himself, forcing the snakes as far back as he could while he searched for Astynome among them. She was nowhere to be seen and for a horrifying moment he imagined her body had already been lost beneath the vile creatures. Despair gripped him, knowing that no-one could survive the venomous bite of even one snake, let alone so many.

It was the darkest moment he could remember since the murder of his daughter. He had been powerless, then, to stop Agamemnon from sacrificing Iphigenia to appease the gods, and now he had failed Astynome too. Apheidas had murdered her and deprived him of his only joy in life, his only hope for the future. A blackness descended on his heart. He looked around at the countless snakes surrounding him and pictured them crawling closer and closer, finally darting towards him and burying their fangs deep into his flesh. And when death had overcome him they would cover his body with theirs, just as somewhere in that wide pit they had already covered Astynome's. It seemed an ironic end – so different to the glorious death he had always expected – and yet he supposed it would be easy enough. He lowered the torch and watched as the serpents stopped retreating before it.

Then he heard a noise – small, almost lost among the constant, menacing hiss. A sob. Quickly, he raised the torch and held it in the direction of the sound. Another sob was followed by a low moan, and then he saw her, a black-robed figure lying on the steps above the deadly reach of the creatures below. Life and the desperate love of it came rushing back into Eperitus's veins.

'Astynome!'

He waved the torch in another circle about him, driving the snakes back again, but the torch was dying and he knew time was running out.

'Astynome, can you hear me?'

The crumpled figure groaned again and began to move. There was a squeal of pain followed by a sharp intake of breath, but she raised her head and looked at him groggily.

'Eperitus?'

'Yes, it's me. Are you badly hurt?'

'Gods!' she exclaimed, pushing herself up on her elbows. 'The snakes!'

'You're safe. You landed on the steps, but you might have broken something.'

'I think I've sprained my ankle. I don't know if it's broken, though.'

'Wait, I'll come to you.'

'But the snakes –'

'Don't move, Astynome.'

Eperitus looked down at the floor and the mass of legless, lipless creatures that carpeted it. The flame sputtered, its light already receding so that the hundreds of snakes became a single, glistening throng that coiled and slithered in the shadows all about him, their eyes momentarily reflecting the fire as he passed the torch this way and that. Again he felt his stomach muscles tighten and he had to fight the weakness in his limbs that forbade him to take the first step. Then he recalled Apheidas's words: that for a man to conquer his fears he had to face them. He thought, too, of what his father had told him about being bitten as a child, a traumatic memory that his mind had buried deep in his unconscious to leave only a fear and loathing of snakes behind. But the gods had protected him then and they would protect him now.

He took a step towards Astynome and the snakes retreated before his torch, though not as far as he would have liked. He threw a glance at the foot of the stairs, not wanting to take his eyes for more than a moment from the deadly reptiles that surrounded him. The steps were still five or six paces away, not nearly close enough to jump onto, and stopped half a man's height above the floor.

'The torch's going out,' Astynome warned, desperation entering her voice.

'Don't worry. I've got an idea.'

Ideas were more Odysseus's domain than his own, but fear had sharpened his mind and he knew there was but one chance to get out alive. He waved the torch again and took another step towards Astynome. The snakes moved back, but only a little. One unfortunate strike now might reach him. Quickly, he slipped his grandfather's shield from his back and let it lean against his shoulder, while with his free hand he untied the knot in its leather sling and loosened the excess. He pulled his dagger from his belt and cut the sling, winding one end tightly around his wrist.

'*Eperitus!*'

The torch fizzled and went out. He tossed it aside and threw the broad shield down onto the coiling, twisting brood before him. There was a sharp hiss and a snap from behind: one of the snakes had darted at him and missed. Eperitus jumped onto the shield, feeling the soft, spongy mass beneath the leather as he sprang off again and reached for the stairs. Somehow he found them, his ribs colliding painfully with the stone steps, despite his breastplate, as he clawed his way to safety. He sensed bodies striking at the air about his ankles and then he was up, safe, with Astynome sobbing as she tried frantically to haul his heavy bulk higher up the steps.

'It's alright,' he gasped. 'It's alright, I'm safe.'

'Have you been bitten?' she asked, the panic clear in her voice.

'No, no. I didn't feel anything.'

He lay on his back, looking up at the orange-hued clouds passing over the pit, and shuddered from head to foot. The convulsive shivering did not stop until Astynome lowered her face over his and kissed him.

'Thank you for coming after me,' she whispered.

He reached up and touched her cheek. 'I wouldn't have abandoned you. But next time I'll use the steps.'

She smiled and he sat up, feeling the tug of the leather strap around his wrist. Taking it in both hands, he pulled his grandfather's shield slowly from the pit, pausing only to make sure there were no snakes attached to it before knotting the two ends of the strap and slinging the shield onto his back once more. He bent down and lifted Astynome into his arms, then carried her back up to the garden above.

'Did Apheidas escape?'

'Yes,' he answered.

'I'm sorry I didn't stay back as you ordered. What are you going to do?'

'Take you somewhere safe,' he said, lowering her onto a stone bench and kneeling before her. 'Which ankle is it?'

'That one. Ouch! Be careful.'

'I don't think it's broken, but I doubt you'll be able to walk on it for a few days.'

'What about Apheidas? Are you going after him?'

'And leave you here? Listen to what's happening out there. Look at the sky, the smoke … They'll be looting this house and putting it to the torch before long and I *won't* abandon you to be raped and murdered. Your life is far more important to me than his death. I'm only sorry I didn't listen to you earlier.'

As he spoke, they heard crashes and shouts erupt from the hall.

'Where's that lead to?' Eperitus asked, picking Astynome up again and nodding towards the door that Apheidas had escaped through.

'An alley alongside the temple of Apollo.'

Eperitus crossed the garden as quickly as he could with Astynome in his arms and kicked open the door. To his right, the alley continued to the battlements and bent round to the right again, with a side entrance in the temple wall opposite. To the left he saw the small square he had crossed earlier to enter Apheidas's house and ran towards it. A body now lay face-down at its centre – an old man with a dagger protruding from his ribs. Astynome gasped at the sight and turned her face away.

'We'll see a lot more corpses before this night's over,' Eperitus said.

He ran on, following Astynome's directions as they headed for the gate to the lower city. Buildings were burning on all sides, throwing orange sparks and columns of black smoke into the air, while here and there groups of marauding soldiers shouldered open doors and ransacked houses at sword point. The screams from within declared the fate of the occupants. After they had seen the second body of a child, Astynome buried her face in Eperitus's shoulder and refused to look any more. Then a harsh call rang out and two Greeks blocked Eperitus's path.

'Give us the woman,' the first demanded. 'We'll pay for her. Look.'

He pointed to two other men, standing in a doorway surrounded by looted goods. One of them lifted a skin of wine in one hand and a copper bowl in the other.

'Not interested,' Eperitus replied, and made to move around them.

The second man stepped in front of him, blocking his way. He was tall and strong, and an axe hung loosely but menacingly from his right hand. Eperitus felt Astynome's arms tighten about him.

'It's a fair exchange,' the man said. 'We don't want to cheat a fellow Greek. And we don't want to *kill* a countryman, either, unless we have to.'

Eperitus took two steps back towards a nearby wall and lowered Astynome to her feet. She laid a hand against the wall for support.

'That's more like it,' the first man said.

The smile dropped from his face when Eperitus drew his sword. The man placed both hands about the haft of his axe and was hurriedly joined by his comrades from the doorway. Then a voice called out.

'Eperitus!'

Eperitus turned to see Omeros running towards him, accompanied by Antiphus and Polites. At the sight of the giant Ithacan and the bow in Antiphus's hand, Eperitus's assailants moved back and retrieved their trinkets, before slipping off into the shadows.

'Excellent timing, Omeros,' Eperitus greeted him. 'Truly excellent.'

He embraced each of the Ithacans in turn, elated to see friendly faces amid the chaos of Troy's demise.

'Is it like this everywhere?

Antiphus nodded. 'Worse in most places. Agamemnon ordered every male Trojan to be murdered and every building to be burned.

Diomedes, Idomeneus and a few of the others are trying to restore some order, but the whole army's been struck with madness.'

'Have you seen Odysseus?' Omeros asked. 'We've been looking for him.'

Eperitus felt sudden shame that he had not given a single thought to his king's safety since leaving him and Menelaus on their search for Helen.

'He was heading for the palace when we parted. I'll go see if he's still there.'

'We'll come with you,' Polites said.

'No. I want you to take Astynome back to the ships at once. Avoid danger and don't delay – I'm holding each of you responsible for her safety. And she's hurt her leg; you'll need to carry her, Polites.'

Polites nodded and before Astynome could protest, plucked her up in his broad arms as if she weighed no more than a child. Eperitus stroked her hair and kissed her.

'You'll be safe now – I trust these men with my life, and I know they won't let you be harmed.'

Astynome smiled at him.

'It's not me I'm worried about. It's you. Find Odysseus, but promise me you won't go hunting Apheidas. He still has a hold on you, Eperitus.'

'If you're looking for your father,' Omeros interrupted, mishearing their conversation, 'we saw him heading up the ramp towards the palace only a short while ago. He was limping, but he still cut down every man we saw stand in his way.'

'Eperitus,' Astynome urged. 'Promise me.'

'I promise he won't come between us again,' he answered, kissing her one last time before setting off at a run.

Chapter Forty-Three
THE RAPE OF CASSANDRA

'How do I find Apheidas's house?' Odysseus asked. 'Apheidas is dead,' Hecabe said. 'By now they'll all be dead.'

'Do you know where he lives?'

Odysseus looked at the old woman. Tears had traced clean lines down her smoke-stained cheeks and her grief for Priam had left her eyes devoid of life; and yet she had summoned the strength and courage to stand and follow Odysseus.

'Through there,' she answered, pointing down the nearest street.

It was filled with figures moving to and fro, their identities hidden by the flames and smoke that filled the narrow thoroughfare. As they watched, a wall of one of the burning buildings collapsed and fell down into the street, burying several people and sending up a cloud of dust to mingle with the smoke. The screams of the injured followed it.

'Is there another way?'

'Why does it matter? Even Apheidas can't have survived *this*, and by now his house will be just another smoking ruin.'

'My friend went there. I need to know he's safe.'

'Of course you must,' the old woman sighed. 'Forgive me. You can go around by the city walls.'

Odysseus took the Trojan queen's hand and led her through the relentless anarchy towards the high battlements that ran behind Pergamos. Seeing Hecabe's age, none of the pillaging soldiers tried to stop them as they picked their way between the dead and dying. Another building collapsed ahead of them in a cascade of fiery debris. Odysseus waited a moment, then raising his hand before his eyes forged through the dust cloud that had billowed up from the ruins like a wraith. Hecabe followed, choking loudly. A figure lurched towards them through the haze, but Odysseus knocked it aside with his shield.

The scream indicated it was a woman.

'Come on,' he said to Hecabe, his voice rasping from the dryness in his throat.

They staggered on down the street, grey from the dust and ash, and reached the steps that led up to the ramparts. Odysseus placed a foot on the first step, but Hecabe held back.

'Not up there,' she said. 'Down here.' She pointed to a shadow-filled alley that ran between two houses to their left. 'It leads to the temple of Apollo, next to Apheidas's house.'

Odysseus peered cautiously into the alley. Everything was silent and black, but as he stared he thought he saw a movement, the faintest glimmer of polished metal in the gloom. Pushing Hecabe behind him, he drew his sword.

'Who's there?'

He was answered by a roar of anger. A figure dashed at him from the darkness, a blade gleaming in its hand. Odysseus raised his shield, blocking the thrust aimed at his head. He replied with a low sweep of his sword that was met by his attacker's shield. They swapped more blows and in the confusion Odysseus could hear the man breathing heavily as he manoeuvred for advantage, guessing he was already at the end of his strength. With a grunt, the man swept Odysseus's sword aside with his half-moon shield and followed by driving his sword at the Ithacan's throat. It was a skilful attack and might have succeeded, if the arm that delivered it was not already weakened and sluggish. Skipping aside, Odysseus kicked out at his exposed flank and caught the man in the stomach. He cried out in pain and staggered back against the nearest house, the sword falling from his hand. The next instant, Odysseus had him pinned to the wall with the edge of his weapon pressing against the man's neck.

'Who are you? Greek or Trojan?'

'He's my son,' answered a voice from further down the alley. 'Aeneas, prince of the Dardanians. I am King Anchises.'

'Aeneas?' Odysseus said with surprise, peering closer at the grimed and bloody face of the man who had attacked him.

'Kill me if you have to,' Aeneas replied, his voice weak with exhaustion. 'You'll succeed where many have failed and gain your share of glory from it. But spare my father and son, I beg you. And if you're willing, see them safe to Dardanus and you'll be rewarded with greater riches than you will find among the pickings of Troy.'

Odysseus lowered his sword.

'I don't want your blood, Aeneas. Tell Anchises and your son to come out into the street. I won't harm them.'

Aeneas spoke in the Trojan tongue and his father, a man as old as Priam but more bent with age, emerged from the alleyway. He was followed by a small boy of perhaps three or four years, who stared at Odysseus with eyes that had already seen immeasurable horrors. Odysseus stepped back from Aeneas and studied him in the fiery half-light reflected downward by the clouds. Judging by his bloodstained armour and the scars on his arms and legs, the Dardanian must already have fought in several battles that evening.

'Hecabe!' Aeneas said with delight, noticing the Trojan queen and moving forward to embrace her. 'Then ... then where's Priam?'

'Slain,' she answered. 'By Achilles's son. And where is Creusa? Where's your wife?'

'Your daughter is lost,' Aeneas answered, putting his hand to Hecabe's face as fresh tears fell from her eyes. He turned his stern gaze on Odysseus. 'So what *do* you intend to do with us?'

'You can't fight your way out, not in your state. But if you surrender, then you, your father and your son will be put to death.'

'Even little Ascanius?'

Odysseus nodded. 'Agamemnon's orders are that every male is to be slaughtered, but I've had enough of his slaughter. I'm willing to help you escape, Aeneas, and I know a secret way out.'

Aeneas looked at his father and son. The boy stared back at him with blank eyes, but Anchises slumped back against the nearest wall.

'I've had enough, Son. Let me die here – I'll only burden you.'

Aeneas shook his head, and, weak though he was, bent down and lifted his father onto his back.

'Lead the way, Odysseus.'

The Ithacan nodded and led them up the steps to the battlements. A few bodies littered the ramparts, but no living soul stood in their way. To the east, the sky was beginning to lighten with the first hint of dawn, while below them to the west the great bay was filled with the sleek, black shapes of the Greek fleet, illuminated by the flames rising from the city. Signalling for the others to stay close, Odysseus followed the course of the walls to the place Helen had showed him only a few nights before.

'This is your only hope,' he said, indicating the hole through which he had escaped with the Palladium. 'It doesn't smell pleasant, but it's only a short drop to the rock shelf below and from there you'll be able to find your way to cover on the banks of the Simöeis. You should go, too, Hecabe.'

The old woman shook her head.

'I won't add to Aeneas's load. Besides, I can't leave without knowing whether any of my sons or daughters have survived. I will remain with you and let the gods decide my fate.'

Aeneas lowered his father from his back and peered down the hole in the alcove that acted as a latrine for the guards. He wrinkled his nose at the smell, then looked back at the burning city and listened to the shouts and screams still rising from it.

'It's better than going back into that nightmare,' he said. 'But I have one question before we part, Odysseus. We've been enemies for ten years, and if we'd met on the plains you would have done your best to kill me, and I you. So why are you helping me now?'

'I've been responsible for the deaths of too many brave men already,' Odysseus replied, 'and not all of them honourably. It was because of me that Great Ajax killed himself. I've contrived the deaths of others, too, just to shorten this war and be able to go home. Worst of all, I've even dared to defy the gods so I can see my family again. These things must be atoned for, Aeneas, and maybe by helping you I'm taking the first step on a long journey back to virtue. Perhaps you will plant a new Troy – here in the ruins of the old or somewhere far away, but one that will last a thousand years and with a people that will preserve the honour of their ancestors. I don't think that would be a bad thing. But now you must go, before the sun rises and exposes you to unwanted eyes.'

Cassandra lay between the feet of the statue of Athena, where the Palladium had once rested before the Greeks had stolen it. She was curled up in a ball, crying like a child as the sounds of murder and rape echoed around her from the walls of the temple. All night she had lain there, hiding from the drunken taunts of the Trojan revellers and yet fearing the moment when their celebrations would end and the belly of the great horse would open. And there she had remained, even when the dreaded clamour of destruction began to slowly filter through the closed doors of the temple. What else could she do? Her instincts had told her to run and hide, but her inner-vision told her there was no point. The thing that was destined to happen to her would happen here – Apollo's prophetic gift had revealed it to her in all its horrific detail. There had been a time when she had tried to change the course of her visions, but the outcomes were always the same. Exactly as she had pictured them through the dark prism of her second sight.

And so she had waited, trembling with fear and stiff with the hard coldness of the stone. She had flinched when the doors of the temple had burst open and women and their crying children had come flocking inside, and yet she had not moved. And none had seemed to notice her, a small bundle of black clothing at the foot of Athena's statue. Perhaps they had thought her dead, or more likely they had not cared for anything other than what their own fate would be. They soon found out. The crash of bronze from the portico, the shouts of dying men – a fight more ferocious than any on the battlefields of the previous ten years, as Trojans fought in defence of their families. The awful chattering of weapons had entered the temple, and from some of the female screams that followed Cassandra knew they had taken their own lives rather than be captured. And now, with the Trojan men overwhelmed, came the sounds of what it meant to be captured. Boys put to the sword. Girls screaming as their mothers and older sisters were brought down beneath packs of laughing soldiers. The sound of clothes being torn, men grunting and women sobbing. And then, at last, the thing she had foreseen happened.

Rough hands grabbed her and turned her over. A brutal, bearded face with a broken nose and merciless eyes – the face of the man the Greeks called Little Ajax. The large brown snake coiled around his shoulders hissed at her hatefully. Then the man's mouth opened in a wide, lascivious grin from which unintelligible words came spilling over her. She looked away, knowing what would follow. The slap was far harder and much more painful than her vision had allowed her to guess at. It made her cry again, sobbing hysterically as she remembered what came next. Fingers curled about the neckline of her dress, slowly to make sure of the grip, then pulled hard. She felt the material tighten around the back of her neck before it tore, and then there was more pain as his fingernails scraped across her chest and broke the skin. He kept on ripping the soft, weak cloth, exposing her breasts to the cold air of the temple, revealing her stomach and pubic hair. She closed her legs tightly, pointlessly, and stared up at the smoke-stained ceiling where the faint outline of gold-painted stars still gleamed, the only stars visible that night. The man spoke again, urgently and harshly – the voice of a man used to being obeyed. But she did not obey and this time he punched her, filling her head with a ringing pain that vied against the pain of her knees being forced apart and the man pushing himself between them. He fumbled and she shut her eyes, more fearful now than at any other time in her life. Then he was inside her, hurting her, and fresh tears pumped down her cheeks, trickling into her ears and hair as she prayed and prayed and prayed for release. Even though she had foreseen that no release would come.

When it was over and, laughing, he had gone, she lay and listened, not even bothering to cover her nakedness. She had done it often as a child: lying still and attuning her ears to the sounds of the night. The fighting was almost over, but in the absence of resistance the destruction of the city was only now coming into its fullness. In the temple, she could still hear the women being raped, although their distressed protests had grown weaker. And then she felt something change – a new presence her earlier vision had not extended to. Men were entering the temple, but these were not a violent rabble: they were cool-headed and disciplined. For a moment she thought they might be Trojans, victors who had driven the Greeks out of the city and were restoring order. The sound of swords being drawn and the desperate cries of the rapists as they were executed gave her hope, such warming hope that she dared not turn and look in case it was destroyed. Then she heard commands, Greek commands, and her hope was conquered by returning fear. At least before she had been given foreknowledge of what would happen to her, down to the last, cruel detail of what Little Ajax would do to her. But this was different. She no longer knew what was coming, only that it was not her death. *That* she had already foreseen.

More commands, followed by running feet. A helmeted face stared down at her, then she was being lifted by strong arms and carried across the temple floor. Her head lolled, catching glimpses of the aftermath of the desecration that she had heard so vividly: a dead soldier slumped against a pillar; two little boys lying in pools of blood; a naked woman, dragging herself on her hands and knees over the flagstones. Then she was being lowered to her feet, forced to stand despite the weakness in her limbs, and not caring that the torn remains of her dress hung like parted curtains, revealing her nudity.

She saw a man before her. There were several men, but he was the one her eyes focussed on. He had long brown hair that had a red sheen in the torchlight, a neatly tended beard and a handsome but mature face with cold blue eyes. His breastplate was a rich working of gold, blue enamel and tin, with a pure white tunic beneath and a red cloak about his shoulders. As she looked at him, trying to remember where she had seen his face before, he removed the cloak and swept it around her to cover her nakedness. His eyes bored into her, strangely fascinated.

'Who are you?' he asked, speaking in the Trojan tongue.

She looked up at him but could not muster the strength to answer. Another man stepped up to the Greek's shoulder – an old man with a grey beard and a wise face – and whispered Cassandra's name in his ear. She heard Priam's name uttered alongside it and knew the old warrior was stating her royal lineage.

'You remind me –' the first man began, before faltering and shaking his head with a smile. 'You remind me of my wife, but as she was when I first fell in love with her. That was many years ago.'

'I'm no man's wife, sir, and not destined to be.'

Cassandra folded the cloak tighter about her tired, abused body. The wool was warm and soft, but its vivid redness threw her mind back to the newest vision to haunt her dreams. She was in an unfamiliar room, looking down at herself sprawled on a rich bed covered in blood – her blood. In the next room was a naked man lying dead in a blood-filled bath, while a vengeful woman stood over him with an axe. That man, she realised with a sudden shock, was standing before her now.

'Who says you will not be married?' he asked.

'The lord Apollo.'

'Ah, a god,' he said, reaching out and running a lock of her hair between his fingers. 'Well, I am King Agamemnon and I am releasing you from his service –'

'You misunderstand me, sir –'

'And you fascinate me, Cassandra. You will come back to Mycenae with me as a gift for Clytaemnestra, my wife. Or, if you please me, as her replacement.'

Cassandra backed away and shook her head. Mycenae – that was the unfamiliar place in her vision, the place of her death.

'She will kill you, my lord. She will kill us both.'

A frown flickered across Agamemnon's brow, a momentary concern before the curse of Apollo smoothed it away with a smile.

'You're traumatised, and no wonder,' he said, looking around at the defilement of the temple. He stepped forward and took her into his arms. 'This has been a difficult night, but you have nothing to fear now. You'll be safe with me.'

Chapter Forty-Four
AMBITION'S END

Burning buildings were beginning to collapse now as Eperitus picked his way through the rubble-strewn streets of Pergamos towards the palace. After watching his father push Astynome into the pit of snakes and then make his escape, he had given up any hope of avenging his crimes. Strangely, though, the concept of him going unpunished was less bitter than he had imagined it would be. His relief that Astynome had survived was so overwhelming that, in comparison, the thought of killing Apheidas and wiping away the stain from his family's honour seemed almost unimportant. Her words, too, had affected him. Her belief that the best way to defeat Apheidas was to be all the things he was not, and that to seek revenge was to become more like him, had struck deeper than he expected. Perhaps he feared keeping his father's legacy of hatred and anger alive. After all, other families had carried the curse of their forefathers through generation after generation, just as Agamemnon and Menelaus were still suffering from the offences of their great-grandfather, Tantalus. The only hope of throwing off such a curse was to break the cycle of retribution. More than that, he was aware that with Astynome he had something to live for. The young warrior who had been exiled from Alybas all those years before, without a home, family or friends, no longer existed. He was older and stronger now, with a new homeland and new loyalties. The things that had driven his younger self – to see his family's honour restored – had at last been superseded, if not fulfilled. And for a short while he had convinced himself they did not matter any more.

Then, when Omeros told him they had seen Apheidas, he realised he had been wrong. He had to go after him. Whether he wanted to take a final opportunity for revenge – despite everything Astynome had warned him against – or simply hoped to find his father's body, he could not yet say. Only he knew he had to see the matter to its conclusion.

The ramp to the palace was scattered with the dead and dying. The courtyard above was also covered with corpses, including many Trojan soldiers who had made their last stand there. Now all was still and silent, but for the flames roaring from the upper windows of the once-beautiful building. Then a familiar voice called his name and he turned to see Odysseus running across from the steps that led up to the battlements, followed by Hecabe.

'Thank the gods you're alive,' Odysseus exclaimed, embracing his captain. 'But where's Astynome? Didn't you find her?'

'She's safe. And Helen?'

Odysseus nodded and briefly summarised the things he had seen and done since they had parted.

'And now we need to gather the army back together and restore discipline. Even if Agamemnon has ordered every male to be slain, I won't have my Ithacans take any more part in it. And I intend to make sure there's at least one functional part of this army that can offer protection to the women of Troy.'

He glanced at Hecabe, but the old woman understood little or nothing of his Greek.

'My father's in the palace,' Eperitus announced awkwardly, aware that he was asking to neglect his duty as captain of Odysseus's guard.

'Then we'd better deal with him first,' Odysseus replied.

The destruction inside the palace had left it almost unrecognisable, causing Hecabe to wail aloud as her grief was renewed. The plastered walls, many of which had boasted intricate and colourful murals, were now stained by smoke or splashed with blood. Doors had been kicked from their hinges and every room ransacked, leaving behind a mess of dead bodies, smashed furniture and torn hangings. Here and there the debris had been piled up and set alight using torches ripped from their brackets, choking corridors with smoke as the fearsome flames consumed everything within their reach. Covering their faces with the corners of their cloaks, Eperitus, Odysseus and Hecabe pushed on towards the great hall, where Eperitus's instincts told him they would find his father.

They soon found the antechamber where Eperitus and Odysseus had once awaited an audience with King Priam, in the days before the war. The raging fires had not yet reached this part of the palace, and as they pushed open the large wooden doors they found the throne room in semi-darkness, lit only by the dying glow of the rectangular hearth at its centre.

'Wait here,' Odysseus whispered to Hecabe as he and Eperitus clutched their swords and advanced into the gloom.

A row of black columns stood either side of the hearth, drawing the gaze naturally towards the dais at the far end of the great hall. On it was a tall throne cut from a single piece of rock and lined with thick furs. A large man sat on the throne with his elbows propped on his knees and his forehead resting in his hands as he gazed down at the floor. He could almost have been asleep, so still was he, and though he wore no crown his battle-scarred armour and the sword balanced across his lap made him look like a king from Troy's legendary past. The prostrate forms of dead men lay all around him. A few were old – some of Priam's counsellors, who must have sought refuge in the great hall and then fought to protect their master's throne. The rest were soldiers, a mixture of Trojans and Greeks. Whether they had died fighting each other or had been killed by the man on the throne was unclear, but Eperitus guessed Apheidas had bought his new throne in blood.

'So this is where your ambitions have brought you, Father,' he said. 'The last king of a doomed city, with no crown and only dead men to bow down before you.'

'At least I had ambitions, Son,' Apheidas replied, lifting his head slowly. 'Unlike you, ever a slave to the commands of others. Now *that's* the Trojan in you.'

'Better to serve a real king than to become a mockery of one.'

Apheidas shook his head and a tired smile filtered across his face.

'You're right, of course. And now I suppose you've come to murder me and usurp my mock throne. That was always *your* driving ambition, wasn't it – to kill me and restore your precious honour? Well, I won't resist. My leg's finally given up, you see,' he said, patting the thigh Eperitus had wounded earlier. 'Here I am, king of Troy at last, and even my own body won't do what I want it to.'

He lowered his face into his hands again and to Eperitus's shock began to cry, his heavy shoulders shaking with the force of his sobs.

'Perhaps I should have been more like my father – more like you – a loyal servant, knowing my limitations instead of aiming at things forbidden by the gods. And what have I gained? Your brothers died serving my ambitions and I drove you away, earning your hatred in place of your love. So come and get it over with. Send my miserable ghost down to Hades's halls, where at least I'll be able to forget the mess I made while I was alive.' He took the sword from his lap and tossed it across the hall. 'Kill me Eperitus; I won't fight you any more.'

Eperitus looked at his father as he lay with his head back against the throne, inviting death. It was a moment he had hankered after for twenty years, but now it was here he no longer wanted it. He would not be his father's executioner and inherit his legacy of hatred. Astynome had saved him from that.

Apheidas sensed his reluctance.

'Kill me, damn it! I murdered Pandion and your friend, didn't I? I killed Astynome, damn it – do you care so little for her that you can't even avenge her death!'

'She isn't dead – you failed in that, too. But you *did* bring dishonour on our family and you murdered my friend, Arceisius. Crimes that have to be paid for.'

Eperitus's fingertips touched the dagger in his belt, the ornate blade that Odysseus had given to him when they had first met. He tugged it free and walked around the long hearth to where his father sat. Apheidas eyed the knife in his son's hands, then leaned back again and exposed his throat.

'Do it,' he rasped through clenched teeth.

'You do it,' Eperitus replied, and tossed the blade onto his lap.

Apheidas flinched at its touch, then with shaking hands picked it up and held it before himself. Eperitus stepped back, even now not trusting his father. He turned to look at Odysseus, uncertain, seeking the reassurance of his king, and in that moment Apheidas let out a groan. Eperitus's head flicked back to see the dagger embedded in his heart, his dying hands slowly peeling away from its hilt. Then his head lolled onto his chest and he was dead.

After a while, Odysseus walked around the hearth and put a hand on his friend's shoulder.

'Time to move on.'

Eperitus nodded. Slipping his grandfather's shield from his back, he dropped it at Apheidas's feet then turned and followed Odysseus out of the great hall.

Chapter Forty-Five
AT THE SHIPS

P enelope stood beneath the thatched canopy of the lookout post on top of Mount Neriton and gazed at the ocean of cloud that had covered the world. In the distance the mountainous peaks of the mainland pierced the layered vapour like the spines of an ancient monster, while at the furthest edge of creation the chariot of the sun had burst free of the haze and was riding up into the pale skies. Before long, its fierce heat would drive away the low-lying fog and leave land and sea naked before its gaze. For now, though, the air remained damp and chill and the breeze on the mountain top found its way into Penelope's mist-soaked clothing, forcing her to pull her cloak tighter about herself.

She had come here to be alone and think over the news of the evening before. Whenever she felt her emotions threatening to expose her inner weaknesses, she would climb the steep flanks of Mount Neriton and dismiss the elderly lookout; and when she had conquered herself and could once more put on the calm, controlled mask of a queen, she would go back down to the palace to face whatever her duties required of her that day, whether they be as simple as buying food in the marketplace or as daunting as facing Eupeithes in the Kerosia. This morning, though, the lookout must have seen the thick fog and decided to wait before climbing up to his post, and his absence made the place seem lonelier than ever. It was as if every living soul had been taken from the world and she was the only person left.

She walked to the edge of the flat, grassy space where the lookout post was sited. Far below her, through the white, churning vapours, she could hear the waves of the Ionian Sea crashing against the rocky skirts of Ithaca, carrying on the war that had been fought since the beginning of time. She looked down at what was visible of the stony slope before it was swallowed by the fog, and tried to picture the invisible cliffs below and the green sea as it frothed about the tumble of jagged boulders. Ten more years would pass, the Pythoness had confirmed, before Ithaca's king would find his way home. Mentor, Antinous and the twenty warriors who had sailed with them to Mount Parnassus had returned the evening before, repeating the priestess's cryptic verses and the interpretation given by her attendant. Mentor had announced the oracle before the Kerosia, while Antinous had sulked in his seat and looks of shocked dismay settled on the faces of Eupeithes, Oenops and Polyctor. Penelope had felt an initial burst of relief, as if tight bonds had suddenly been released from about her chest, but what small joy she felt was brief. Eupeithes's rise to power had been cut short, and though he remained dangerous Penelope knew he would rather sit out the ten years than risk civil war against the royal guard – who were firmly loyal to their king and queen – and the people of Ithaca. But if she had gained time, what, ultimately, did that matter if the oracle was true? What did anything matter if another ten years had to pass before Odysseus came home again?

She wedged the toe of her sandal beneath a small rock and flicked it into the milky haze below. Her whole body seemed to ache with desire for her husband. She wanted nothing more than for him to return and lift the weight of the kingdom from her slender shoulders, and then to take her to their bed and make love to her. Ten years had been almost insufferable without his touch; ten more would be impossible. Her breathing became suddenly thicker and she laid a hand on her chest, trying to calm the panic that was taking hold of her. Odysseus had said a man could overcome his fate, she reminded herself, and she had to have faith in him for that. That would be the hope that carried her through – that and Telemachus. For even if the Pythoness's vision came true, Penelope was still the mother of Odysseus's son. For his sake she would carry on as Ithaca's implacable queen, fighting for the kingdom that one day he would inherit – unless, of course, Odysseus never returned and she was forced to honour her agreement with Eupeithes. Then she would have to choose a new husband to become king ahead of Telemachus.

She hated herself for taking such a risk, but knew it had been the only way to placate Eupeithes's ambitions. Now his insistence on a new king had been checked and he was in no position to stir up rebellion.

Their agreement had also allowed Penelope to send a messenger to Sparta, telling Halitherses to bring Telemachus back home as her son was no longer under serious threat. All the same, after the Kerosia she had confronted the fat merchant beneath the portico of the great hall and told him that if anything did happen to Telemachus, she would hold him responsible. What was more, Odysseus would too when he eventually returned. Something in Eupeithes's expression had made her think he did not believe Odysseus *would* return, but he said nothing and Penelope knew he had understood her message.

She wiped away a tear, angrily crushing it out of existence. Her son was returning, she reminded herself. Telemachus's presence would be enough to keep her going. And yet, if she had to endure a further decade without Odysseus, where would she get the strength from? His long absence had already drained away Anticleia's will to live; his mother had been ailing for a long time now, and Laertes believed the news from the oracle would be the death of her. Penelope snuffed out another tear and glared down at the cloying mists that fenced her in on the lonely hilltop.

'Good morning, Mistress.'

She turned, in surprise, to see the grey head and long grey beard of the lookout a few paces away. Conscious of her tears, she looked away again.

'Good morning.'

'If you want I should go back down for a while, then just you say so.'

'No, no. I was just going anyway.'

The old man ventured a little closer.

'The fog's clearing, my lady. It's often thickest just before the dawn, but it doesn't last forever. Look south and you can already see the sun on the waves.'

Penelope followed the line of the old man's outstretched arm and saw the glint of golden light riding the Ionian Sea around the island of Zacynthos, the southernmost point of Odysseus's kingdom. The sight of a sail made her catch her breath, but in the same excited instant she had already realised it was nothing more than a fishing vessel. But she knew the lookout was right: the fog would not last forever, and one day the sail on the water would belong to the galley that brought her husband home again.

The clouds remained, threatening rain yet refusing to weep for the destruction of Troy. Like the stone lid of a sarcophagus, they continued to press down claustrophobically over the whole of Ilium and to the far horizon of the Aegean. The bright light of morning was stifled to a dull gloom, and the Greeks emerging from the insanity of the night were left reflecting on their crimes and debauched excesses.

When a summons arrived calling for Odysseus to attend the Council of Kings at the Scaean Gate, Eperitus asked, and was given, leave to return to the ships and check on Astynome's welfare. He passed the heaped booty being stacked in orderly piles on the plain between the walls and the bay, for later distribution among the victorious army, and looked for the familiar, blue-beaked galleys of the small Ithacan fleet. With a thousand vessels beached or anchored in the hoof-shaped harbour it took him a while, but eventually he was greeted by the calls of a skeleton crew as he approached the gangplanks that had been angled down onto the sand. To his surprise, every man was clean-shaven, making them hard to recognise without the beards they had worn for so many years.

'The oath's been fulfilled,' Eurybates explained, seeing Eperitus's curious look as he helped him up the last part of the gangplank and onto the deck. He stroked his jaw uncertainly, unfamiliar with its smoothness. 'Troy's in ruins and Helen's back with Menelaus, so we're free to shave and cut our hair again.'

'I suppose we are,' Eperitus replied. 'But *all* of you? Most of you had beards before the war, and I thought Polites was born with one.'

'I wanted a change,' Polites defended himself.

'Have you seen Odysseus?' asked Antiphus, approaching from the stern with Omeros at his side.

Antiphus's hairless face was gaunt and bony, but Omeros's baby cheeks looked much more natural without the desperate, downy growth that had covered them for the past few months.

'The king's alive and well. Where's Astynome?'

The others all looked at the stern, where a young, helmeted soldier was leaning back against the rear of the ship with his elbows on the rail. As Eperitus stared at him, trying to picture his grubby, smoke-stained face with a beard, the soldier removed his helmet and shook out his long black hair. It was Astynome.

Eperitus left his comrades and hastened to the rear of the galley, where he was met with a warm embrace and a long kiss. When he finally pulled his lips away from hers, he looked down in amazement at her leather breastplate, the greaves about her shins and the short sword hanging from a scabbard in her belt. Astynome stood back and opened her arms so that he could admire her more fully.

'I had to strap my chest down with bands of cloth before I could get the armour to fit,' she explained, tapping her fingers on the cuirass, 'and this sword's beginning to weigh me down a bit, but other than that I could almost be an Ithacan. Don't you agree?'

'You lack one important thing: a sprig of the chelonion flower – the badge we Ithacans wear to remind us of our homeland. Here.' He took the fragment that remained of his own chelonion from his belt and tucked it into hers. 'Now you're an Ithacan warrior. And a more brutal, fearsome figure I've never seen before.'

Her grimed face broke with a smile and she slapped his breastplate playfully, before allowing him to take her into his arms and kiss her again.

'So, are you going to tell me why you're dressed as a soldier? Especially as a Greek, your despised enemies.'

'Omeros's idea, after Agamemnon's men started searching the ships for plunder and captured Trojans.'

'On what grounds?' Eperitus asked, a hint of anger in his voice.

'For fair redistribution,' she replied, raising her eyebrows questioningly. 'I wanted to dress as a slave, but Omeros said they were even taking women who'd been with the army for years, unless they could prove otherwise.'

Eperitus laughed. '*Now*, I understand. They shaved their beards so that you wouldn't stand out. See how much they love you already?'

'Me? Not me, Eperitus – you! They love you as much as they do their own king. It's clear from the way they talk about you both – and fret about you when you're not here. They protected me because I'm *your* woman, not for any gallant notions of defending an escapee from Troy.'

He gave a dismissive shrug to hide his embarrassment and turned away to look at the still-burning city with its columns of black smoke driven at angles by the westerly wind.

'Did you go after your father?' she asked, cautiously.

'Yes.'

She put her arm about his waist and kissed his shoulder. 'I knew you wouldn't listen to me.'

'You're wrong.'

'Oh? Then did he escape?'

'He's dead. He took his own life. Right up until I entered his house last night, I'd always thought I would be the one to kill him. Then it all changed. The gods had other plans, I suppose. It's strange, but now he's gone I wish he hadn't died in such an ignoble way. For all his wicked, misguided ambitions, he was a great warrior – the greatest I've ever had to fight. The only satisfaction I take from the whole thing is that I didn't have to kill him myself.'

'I'm glad you didn't.'

He kissed her forehead.

'It's strange, though. I should be happy that he's dead, but instead I just feel … *empty*. Now the war's over and he's gone, I'm not sure what lies ahead any more. For the first time since he exiled me from Alybas and gave me a purpose in life, my future's suddenly uncertain again.'

'So like a man,' Astynome smiled, shaking her head. 'You spend years not knowing whether today's going to be your last one on earth, then the moment the danger's removed and your life is safe again you feel lost, as if your whole reason for existence has been taken away. Well, it hasn't. You have me and together we will make a home on Ithaca and populate half the island with our children. That'll keep you occupied!'

He laughed and brushed his fingertips over the small but distinct cleft in her chin, admiring the beauty that layers of smoke and dirt could not hide.

'It sounds like a good way to stay busy. And perhaps,' he whispered, with a glance towards the rest of the crew, sitting on the benches and chatting, 'we'll be able to make a start before the fleet sails.'

He kissed her and raised a hand to touch her breast, only to find the hardened leather of her borrowed cuirass. She laughed, her mouth so close he could feel the brush of her breath on his lips. Then her smile faded and she pulled back, looking down at his chest and frowning.

'But your need for vengeance hasn't been satisfied yet, has it? Your father's dead, but –'

'But Agamemnon still lives,' he finished. 'I know.'

'So what will you do?'

'It's hard for a warrior to accept injustice, especially when done to someone he loves. What would you do if a man murdered your daughter?'

'I'm a woman, not a warrior. I would weep for the child, and eventually I would start again. You must do the same, Eperitus. You know you cannot face Agamemnon – if you do you will die – but if you swallow your hatred for him then you can have another daughter with me. Reclaim the life he took from you; don't let him prevent you from being a father a second time. And then be the parent your own father was not. Don't you see you have the power to destroy everything, or to make everything right again?'

Her words had a feminine logic, full of hope and the desire to renew and nurture life. Eperitus sighed.

'Even if I had a chance to kill Agamemnon, I couldn't take it,' he said, turning to lean his forearms on the bow rail and look again at the ruins of Troy. 'I swore to Clytaemnestra I would not, so I have to be satisfied that she will repay him for his crimes. And yet I wish I could just do *something*.'

Astynome joined him, resting her head against his shoulder. Together they watched the teams of men working at every point of the walls, dismantling the battlements stone by stone and sending the huge blocks tumbling to the ground below. Progress was slow, but already the great defences had lost their sense of order and uniformity, taking on a frayed look as if the seas had risen up and smoothed away their edges. The perfection that the gods had made was being destroyed by men in an act of sacrilegious vandalism. From the streets behind the walls came the hiss of fire and the occasional crash of yet another building succumbing to the flames. These sounds were dominated, though, by the incessant beating of hammer and pick, as those structures that the fires were not bringing down were made unusable by the hands of the Greek army, its tight discipline restored now after its fanatical rampage of the night before. Other soldiers were still busy carrying out the plunder from the city and placing it in carefully arranged heaps outside the walls, marching back and forth in lines like ants.

'So ends Troy,' Astynome sighed.

'As long as the stones remain, the city can be rebuilt,' Eperitus replied.

'But who will build it? With every male dead, who will come back and restore Troy to anything like her former glory? And look! There's another. They've been doing it all morning!'

She squeezed her eyes shut and pressed her face against his armoured chest. Eperitus looked and saw two men on top of one of the towers, holding a small boy between them. The boy struggled when he understood why they had taken him up to the battlements, then the men pitched him over the broken parapet and his body was dashed to death on the stones below. Only then did Eperitus see the other boys, scores of them, lying all along the circuit of the walls in the strange, confused poses of bodies from which the energy of life had departed.

'Savages,' he whispered, vehemently. 'This is Agamemnon's work!'

'I suppose this is the price we Trojans have to pay for our defiance,' Astynome said. 'Perhaps if we hadn't fought so hard we would have been shown more mercy. Perhaps not, I don't know. Maybe all great civilisations have to end like this, otherwise we might rise up to challenge the gods themselves.'

Eperitus put his arm around her and pulled her closer, cursing the armour that stopped him feeling the warmth of her body against his.

'Do you wish things had turned out differently?'

'This destruction saddens me, and I'm sad I will never see my father again or return to Chryse. But also I'm happy. This is the past – that burning, crumbling city over there is the past – but you are the future. I have you and we have life, and we will bring more life into this world. The war's over and we're together. That's something to be hopeful about, isn't it?'

'It is,' he answered, before kissing her on the cheek and standing upright. 'And now I had better find Odysseus again. He gave me permission to see that you were alright, but he also wanted me to find him at the Council of Kings once I'd spoken with you. Do I have *your* permission to leave?'

Astynome smiled and nodded. Eperitus left the way he had come, stealing a last glance at her as he negotiated the precarious gangplank to the sand below.

Chapter Forty-Six
THE LAST KING OF TROY

The Council of Kings were seated in a wide double-circle before the Scaean Gate, partly beneath the shade of the sacred oak tree where Achilles had killed Hector. A handful of Agamemnon's bodyguard kept watch over the commanders of the army, though there were no enemies left alive in Ilium to do them harm. The only remaining Trojans now were women, and as Eperitus approached the assembly he noticed several standing beneath a canopy a few paces away from the Council, their hands bound with rope. Hecabe, Cassandra and Andromache – Hector's wife – were among them, looking grief-stricken and dishevelled, and Eperitus realised these were the remainder of Troy's royal household. To his surprise he saw Helen there, too, though unlike the others her clothes were fresh and her face and hair clean. Her chin was held defiantly high, but her eyes were fixed on the broken stones at the foot of the city walls where the Greeks were still busily hurling down the parapets that had withstood them for so long. Eperitus followed her gaze and saw the body of a small child among the rubble by the gates, where he had been thrown to his death. Eperitus turned his eyes away and headed towards the noisy ring of men.

Food was being served as he joined the Council, allowing him to slip in unnoticed and take his place next to Odysseus. A slave brought him a krater of wine and a plate of roast meat, fresh from the sacrifices the kings had made earlier that morning to thank the gods for their great victory. He had passed the place of slaughter on his way up from the ships: a dozen gore-drenched altars built of stones from the walls of Troy, the ground around them soaked dark with the blood of the hundreds of beasts that had been slain. Large numbers of men were still busy cutting up the carcasses, roasting the different parts of the animals, tending the fires and doling out the meat onto platters. The stench of the blood and the hammering of cleavers had reminded Eperitus of battle.

'Where were you?' Odysseus asked, leaning towards Eperitus as he folded a slice of meat in a piece of bread and prepared to put it in his mouth. 'The Council's nearly finished.'

'Already? I thought it'd take all day.'

'No. Everyone's in a hurry to get on with things and go home. Can't you sense it? There isn't a man here who doesn't want to finish the business of tearing down the walls, distributing the plunder and setting off.'

Eperitus put the food in his mouth and looked about at the battle-worn kings, princes and captains of the army, eating, drinking and talking among themselves as they waited for the debate to resume. This was probably the last time he would see any of them, he realised, now that the great expedition that had brought them together was finally over. Agamemnon, as ever, sat at the head of the circle. Eperitus eyed him coldly: the feelings of hatred he had stifled for so long were now gaining strength again, and the thought he would sail off to continue his life at Mycenae was galling. With difficulty, he pulled his gaze away and turned it to the other members of the Council. Nestor and Menelaus were on either side of the King of Men, while a pair of Mycenaean soldiers stood guard over the three of them, dressed in their impressive but outdated ceremonial armour. All the other great names were there, too: Diomedes, flanked by his faithful companions, Sthenelaus and Euryalus; Neoptolemus, wearing his father's splendid armour as he sat beside Peisandros; Philoctetes and Teucer, the two greatest archers in the army and now firm friends; Little Ajax; Idomeneus of Crete; Menestheus of Athens; and all the other noble warriors who had braved the dangers of the Trojan horse, to their eternal glory.

'And you, old friend?' Eperitus asked. 'You must be keen to haul up the anchor stones and set sail? To get back to Penelope and Telemachus.'

Odysseus could not hide a grin at the thought, but his eyes were less certain.

'The heart's eager, but the mind is afraid,' he replied. 'My whole body's crying out to hold Penelope again and to embrace my boy for the first time since he was a baby. And yet the idea terrifies me, too. What if Penelope doesn't love me any more? What if Telemachus hates me for abandoning him at such a young age? I would in his place – wouldn't you?'

The doubt in his intelligent, green eyes was genuine, but Eperitus laughed it off and threw an arm about his shoulder.

'Stop worrying. Remember the message Penelope sent with Omeros? Didn't she say she was desperate for you to return, and that Telemachus is longing for his father? When we finally sail back into that tiny little harbour, it's going to be the greatest homecoming in the whole of Greece. And,' he added, with a hint of solemnity, 'don't forget she said that Eupeithes is threatening his old tricks again. The sooner we get back, the sooner we can deal with him and his cronies.'

Odysseus simply nodded and turned his attention back to the other kings. A soldier had arrived and was handing Agamemnon a large clay tablet marked with tightly packed symbols. The king showed it to Nestor and they discussed its contents in hushed voices. Eperitus tipped out a slop of wine in libation to the gods and raised the krater to his lips.

'So, what did I miss?' he asked.

'There were some heated arguments about how the plunder should be shared –'

'Nine-tenths to Agamemnon and the scraps to be divided equally between the rest of us?' Eperitus asked, sceptically.

'Surprisingly, no,' Odysseus answered. 'He wanted a full half, but that received a lot of complaints and he backed down without much of a fight. Perhaps he's content with the destruction of Troy and the knowledge the Aegean will be controlled by Mycenae from now on. Either way, he agreed everything should be split equally, depending on the number of ships each king brought with him.'

Eperitus raised his eyebrows. 'And the captives?'

'The same, to be decided by lot. Except for the high-ranking women, that is. They were brought before the assembly and allotted by Agamemnon – Cassandra to himself, Hecabe to me, Andromache to Neoptolemus, Helen to Menelaus –'

'Why Helen?' Eperitus asked, glancing back over his shoulder at where the women stood. 'I saw her with the others as I came up from the ships, but she can hardly be thought of as a *prisoner*.'

'Agamemnon insisted, much to his brother's distaste. I think he's always known she left Sparta willingly, and this is his way of punishing her for that – by parading her like a common captive and letting her know what he really thinks of her. But she didn't play along with him. If Agamemnon was expecting humility, he got nothing but defiance. You saw she was still wearing a Trojan dress – despite the fact Menelaus has kept a chest of her old clothes on his galley for the past ten years – and that her hair was plaited in the Trojan style? She even had the nerve to address the Council in the Trojan tongue, as if to say she thought of herself as a Trojan and never wanted to be rescued in the first place.'

Agamemnon seemed to be concluding his conversation with Nestor and had taken his golden staff in both hands. Guessing the debate would resume again soon, Eperitus took a final swallow of his wine and handed the empty krater to a slave.

'What did Menelaus think to that?' he asked in a hushed voice as the other conversations began to die down

'I think he enjoyed seeing Agamemnon embarrassed,' Odysseus whispered. 'After all, whatever his brother does to Helen now, he does to Menelaus also. And I don't know what has passed between Helen and Menelaus since last night, but I think they've come to an understanding with each other about the past. They know their marriage has to work, if only because of the price that has been paid to win Helen back again. So if she wants to play games and put Agamemnon in his place, then Menelaus seems happy to go along with it. He knows she'll still be going back to Sparta with him.'

'Now I almost wish I'd been here to witness it – at least, to see Agamemnon's face.'

Agamemnon rose from his seat, his golden staff in his hand, and walked out to the centre of the Council. The last few conversations trailed away and all eyes now focussed on the King of Men.

'I've received the full tally of all items retrieved from Troy,' he announced, 'classed by type – gold, silver, copper, bronze, wood, wool, silk and so on – and measured by weight. The total weight of each item will be divided by the number of ships in the fleet, of which there are one thousand, one hundred and eighty-seven. Each –'

'My lord!'

The shout rang out from the Scaean Gate, from where a Mycenaean soldier was running towards the Council. He was not one of Agamemnon's bodyguard, though the quality of his armour indicated he was a lesser noble.

'My lord Agamemnon,' he panted.

'What is it?' Agamemnon replied coldly.

'We've found the boy you were looking for. Hector's son.'

'*Astyanax*?' the king asked. 'You're certain? Then bring him here at once.'

The guard signalled to a group of soldiers by the gate. They parted and a single man came forward carrying an infant boy in his arms. A scream pierced the hush that had spread across the Council and Andromache ran out from beneath the canopy where the Trojan women stood, followed closely by Helen.

'Keep them back!' Agamemnon ordered.

Two guardsmen threw down their spears and caught hold of the women, pinning their arms to their sides and pushing them back towards the canopy. Menelaus stepped forward angrily, but Nestor restrained him with a hand on his shoulder. In the same moment, the circle of kings parted and the soldier carrying Astyanax entered. He placed the boy down in the middle and left again, following his officer back to the gates. Astyanax, barely old enough to sit up, looked around at the faces of the Greek commanders, showing no signs of fear. He even produced a smile at the familiar sight of armed men.

'So,' Agamemnon announced, 'Hector's son has been found. Behold, men of Greece, the last king of Troy sits before you!' There was a ripple of uncertain laughter as Agamemnon stooped to lift the child onto his arm, the sceptre still balanced in his other hand. 'Your mother swore by all the gods that you were dead, boy, though I knew she was lying – women have no sense of honour, after all. And now we've found you, we have to decide what to do with you, don't we? Or, more to the point, *who* will do it.'

'Leave him alone!' Helen screamed.

Agamemnon ignored her, bouncing the boy playfully on his arm while looking about at the members of the Council. Eperitus glanced across at Andromache, who was on her knees with her face in her hands, being comforted by Helen. He knew how she felt, having watched helplessly as the King of Men had murdered his own daughter. For he already knew what Agamemnon intended to do with Astyanax, and the thought of it as he looked at Hector's son – so similar in looks to his valiant father – filled him with horror. And a sudden determination to stop it.

'It's obvious what should happen to the boy,' crowed a familiar, but unexpected voice.

A stooped figure cloaked in black with the hood pulled over his face rose from the outer ring of chairs and pushed his way into the centre circle. Agamemnon offered him the staff, and as he took it the man flicked back his hood to reveal his bald head and thin, pale face. His dark eyes stared about at the Greeks and there was madness in them.

'He has to die,' Calchas finished his statement. 'If he lives he will grow up to rebuild Troy and avenge the death of his father.'

'But who will kill the child, Calchas?' Diomedes called out. 'Will you?'

Calchas scowled at the Argive king.

'Thus speaks the man whose father failed to defeat Thebes, leaving his son to finish the task. Do you want your children to endure another war like this one, Diomedes, just because you don't have the ruthless courage to expunge your enemies? Scorn my words if you wish, but unless you want a new Troy to rise from the ashes then Astyanax must die!'

Calchas thrust the staff back into Agamemnon's hand and returned to his seat, letting his doom-filled words settle on the Council.

'I say kill the boy,' Little Ajax grunted.

His words were met by a smattering of nods and murmurs of agreement.

'Too many Greeks have died because of Troy, my own son among them,' said Nestor. 'Astyanax must die. We have no choice.'

Neoptolemus stood up and pointed with a snarl at the child in Agamemnon's arms.

'Kill him and be done with it!'

Others stood now, angrily voicing their support in an attempt to drown out the wailing of the Trojan women. Eperitus saw the smile on Agamemnon's face, and before he knew what he was doing he stood up.

'No. He's just a child. Give him to me and I'll bring him up as my own son.'

Silence fell on the assembly and every eye turned on Eperitus. In an instant, Odysseus was standing beside him with his hand on his arm.

'What do you think you're doing?' he hissed.

'Trying to save the boy,' Eperitus replied, his voice low but filled with determination. 'And if you allow this murder to go ahead, Odysseus, you're just as bad as they are.'

Odysseus looked into his eyes and bit on his lip, unable to reply. Then Agamemnon put the child back down in the dry grass and stared at Eperitus with an icy gaze.

'You heard the Council,' he said. 'The boy has to die. There's no debate on the matter, Eperitus; it's already decided.'

'I'll not stand by and watch you murder this child in cold blood, just like you did Iphigenia!'

He saw the shocked reaction on the faces of the Council, who seemed to collectively sit up and suck in breath. But his only thought now was for Astyanax: if he could at least fight for the boy, he might make up in some small way for his failure to save his own daughter. He fixed his stare on the Mycenaean king, whose usually aloof façade had given way to a look of intense hatred.

'Then your desire is granted,' Agamemnon seethed. 'You will not *stand by* and watch him killed. *You will be the one to kill him!*'

'Never,' Eperitus snapped.

'I *order* you to do it!'

Eperitus spat on the ground and drew his sword. Several of the kings reached for the hilts of their own weapons, while the guards behind Nestor and Menelaus raised their spears and aimed them nervously at the Ithacan. Then, seizing the long tail of hair behind his neck, Eperitus sawed through it and tossed it at Agamemnon's feet.

'I don't answer to you any more, Agamemnon. None of us do. The oath we took has been fulfilled and you're no longer the King of Men. You're just the king of Mycenae now, and I'm *not* a Mycenaean!'

'Eperitus is right, he doesn't have to follow your orders any more,' Diomedes said. Then, slipping a dagger from his belt, he sawed off the long mane of hair that had not been cut since the start of the war and flung it onto the dirt. 'And neither do I.'

Agamemnon was speechless with rage and his fury only seemed to increase as one by one the other kings, princes and captains who formed the Council began cutting away the tails from the back of their own heads and throwing them into the circle. When, at last, Menelaus and Nestor did the same, he finally realised that his hegemony over the Greeks had ended.

'This doesn't change the boy's fate,' he said. 'You, the Council, decided that he should die, not me alone. And if none of you has the courage to do it, then I will throw him from the walls myself.'

Eperitus stepped forward to protest again, but Odysseus pulled him back to his seat.

'Agamemnon's right. The decision was taken by the whole Council; you can't defend the boy against all the kings of Greece.'

'Give Astyanax to me,' Neoptolemus announced before Eperitus could react. 'If he's going to grow up to avenge his father, then as Achilles's son I'm the one who stands to lose the most if he lives. Besides, Andromache is my woman now; I don't want her pining for a bastard child when she'll be bearing sons for me.'

'And do you think she would ever forgive you for killing him, Neoptolemus?' asked Odysseus. 'More likely she'll put a knife into you when you're sleeping. No, *I'll* kill the boy.'

Eperitus watched incredulously as his king crossed the circle and picked up the small child, wrapping his faded purple cloak about him.

'Odysseus, no!' he said, rushing forward and seizing his forearm. '*What are you doing?*'

Suddenly Odysseus's face transformed with rage and he shoved his captain hard in the chest, sending him staggering backwards to collapse between Little Ajax and Teucer. He tried to get up again, but the two men held him fast.

'I'm a father,' Odysseus said, tight-lipped as he faced the Council. 'This is not something I do with pride; I do it with shame. But I'll do it because it has to be done – not for you, Agamemnon, nor the Council, but for the future of Greece.'

He pushed his way out of the ring of commanders and walked slowly towards the Scaean Gate, turning once to stare back accusingly at the members of the Council. They looked away guiltily and Agamemnon picked up the tablet from where he had put it down in the grass.

'We have unfinished business,' he said, looking down at the markings on the tablet. 'Yes, here we are. The weight of gold found in Troy was –'

His words faded into the background as Eperitus tried to see Odysseus through the ring of seated men, but Little Ajax and Teucer kept him pinned between them. They would not let him go, he realised, until Odysseus had reappeared on the walls and thrown Astyanax down to his death. Quickly his mind scanned back over what had happened, wondering if there was anything he had not understood, some statement that could justify Odysseus killing a child. But there was nothing, nothing at all. He felt numb, unable to comprehend what was happening. Once again, he was lying helpless while a child he had tried to protect was murdered.

A woman's scream shook the Council from its half-hearted dissection of the plunder list. All heads turned to the walls, then higher still to the top of the tower that protected the Scaean Gate. There stood Odysseus, Astyanax held high above his head. The child's white clothes blew in the westerly wind, and then with a howl of anger Odysseus hurled him down to perish on the stones below.

Chapter Forty-Seven
THE DEAD CHILD

Shaking off Teucer and Little Ajax, Eperitus sprang to his feet and ran from the shocked assembly towards the gates. The child's body lay among the wreckage of stone beneath the tower, his head dashed in but with surprisingly little blood spattered over the huge blocks on which he had fallen.

'Wait!'

Eperitus turned to see Peisandros's stocky physique sprinting towards him.

'What are you going to do?' the Myrmidon commander asked as he caught up with him. 'I mean, if you're going to confront Odysseus about this, then give me that sword first.'

'We're old friends, Peisandros,' Eperitus replied. 'You know me better than that by now.'

'Angry men have been known to do rash things.'

Eperitus shook his head, but handed Peisandros his sword anyway. 'I just want to know *why*. Why *would* he do that?'

Peisandros stared down at Astyanax's body. 'I don't know, but I'm coming with you.'

They ran through the gate and entered the doorway that led into the dark interior of the tower. Eperitus's eyes adjusted quickly and spotted the wooden ladder ascending to the next floor. The two men climbed it but found the room above empty except for a pile of spears in one corner and shields stacked against the foot of the wall. A dusty shaft of grey light fed into the gloom from a hatchway above and without hesitation Eperitus continued climbing. He reached the top of the tower and saw Odysseus standing against the parapet, looking out at the smoking ruins of Troy. As he clambered through the narrow square in the wooden floor, half-followed by Peisandros, Odysseus

looked at them both and raised a finger to his lips. The angry words
that Eperitus had been about to hurl at his king fell dead.

'Are you alone?' Odysseus asked them.

They nodded, mystified, and then Odysseus leaned across and
tipped the stack of shields forward to reveal Astyanax, alive and smiling
at them. Peisandros almost fell back through the hatch.

'But –' Eperitus said. 'But –'

'You saw me throw him from the walls?'

Peisandros rushed back to the opposite wall and looked down at
the body still on the stones below.

'Come back from there, you fool,' Odysseus ordered. 'Do you want
the Council to see you?'

'But how's it possible?'

Odysseus raised his eyebrows. 'Most things are possible, with a little
deception. After you tried to save Astyanax, Eperitus, I remembered
there was the body of an infant on the rocks by the gate – he was
thrown down from the walls just as the Council was convening this
morning. When I took Astyanax through the gate, I simply picked the
boy's corpse up as I went past. Once inside the tower, I swapped
Astyanax's princely garments for the plain sackcloth the dead child was
wearing, then threw him down from the top of the tower. The head
was already a mess, but I'm hoping nobody will look too closely at the
body. The hardest part was carrying them both up the ladder –
Astyanax under my cloak, and the other dangling by his ankle.'

Peisandros knelt by the child and offered him a thick, dirty finger.
Astyanax took it and pulled, laughing at the Myrmidon.

'So what are you going to do with him?' Eperitus asked. 'You can't
leave him here. He'll just be found and thrown from the walls anyway.
And if the Council find out –'

'I didn't have time to think about that,' Odysseus confessed, 'but I
think I have the answer now.'

'Oh?'

'You, Peisandros. Neoptolemus is your leader and Astyanax's
mother has been allotted to him.'

'So?'

'So you smuggle the boy on board with you and take him back to
Phthia. There're plenty of soldiers doing the same with other Trojan
boys; I've seen it – they haven't the heart to throw them from the walls,

so they're disguising them as girls and taking them back to Greece. You can do the same and bring Astyanax up among your own family.'

'*What*?'

'And make sure you tell Andromache that her boy is safe, so she can watch him grow up from a distance. But Astyanax is never to know his true identity, you understand?'

'Well, of course, but –'

'That's settled then,' Odysseus smiled. 'You've always been a good man, Peisandros. I'll make sure you get a little extra from the plunder, too. Just to help you feed the additional mouth when you get home, naturally.'

'Naturally,' Peisandros sighed.

Astyanax tugged at his finger and giggled, causing the Myrmidon to laugh out loud, despite himself.

As they walked back to the ships at the end of the day, with the sun already melting into the distant edge of the Aegean, Eperitus turned to his king.

'You took a big risk for the sake of that child. A child you've never even seen before, and the son of your enemy.'

'I hold no enmity towards Hector,' Odysseus replied. 'He was just a man fighting for his homeland, and now his soul is in Hades where it can't harm any more Greeks. If I took a risk, it wasn't for Astyanax's sake.'

'Then whose?'

Odysseus smiled at him.

'Yours. When I realised why you wanted to save the child – because you'd been unable to save Iphigenia, and because that failure has eaten away at you for ten years – I knew I had to help you. If I took a risk in doing what I did, then I did it for your sake Eperitus. Who else's?'

'Thank you,' Eperitus said, quietly.

They reached the Ithacan galleys, which were turning black against the crimson sunset.

'And now,' Odysseus said, looking up at the muddle of masts, cross spars and rigging, 'I suppose we had better think about going home.'

AUTHOR'S NOTE

Despite not appearing directly in *The Iliad* or *The Odyssey*, the story of the wooden horse is probably the most iconic and familiar of all the myths associated with the Trojan War. The idea of a simple trick succeeding where ten years of brute force had failed has an appeal that has stood the test of time. Naturally, there isn't a thread of historical evidence for the horse – after all, mythology is not history – though many have tried to interpret it in more realistic terms. Perhaps the most convincing is the suggestion, first put forward by the Romans, that the horse was a metaphor for an ancient siege tower. I preferred the courage and desperation of the original story, with the surviving heroes of the Greek army (except Agamemnon, of course) hiding in a wooden horse and hoping their enemies will take the bait.

The oracles that foretold the fall of Troy are less well-known. To the ancient Greeks the gods were as much a part of life as working, fighting, eating and sleeping. The fact that everything rested "in the lap of the gods", as Homer puts it, was unquestioned, so to have the outcome of the war depend on the fulfilment of divine prophecies was only natural. As ever, there are a variety of different versions of who predicted what and when, so I have chosen the ones that I believe best suit the story I'm trying to tell.

In the original myths, Helenus is a genuine seer whom the gods entrust with the final oracles that point to the fall of Troy. He even appears as a warrior, if only briefly, in *The Iliad*. But with two prophets already in the book – Calchas and Cassandra – and innumerable fighting men, I decided to rob him of these virtues and make him a charlatan instead. Though Odysseus was not sent to fetch the bone of Pelops, and the guardian of the tomb is entirely my own invention, he *was* sent to fetch Neoptolemus from Scyros and steal the Palladium from Troy. Disguised as a beggar, he entered the city, met Helen and gleaned important information from her before returning later with Diomedes and making away with the effigy.

Even with all the oracles fulfilled, Troy would not have fallen if Odysseus had not thought up the greatest military ruse of all time. This makes him the most effective hero of the whole siege and recognises that wars are ultimately won by brains rather than brawn. He also had the idea of leaving behind a man to persuade the Trojans the horse should be taken into the city rather than burnt on the plain. In the myths this job was done by Sinon and not by Omeros, who does not appear in any of the original tales.

One of the drawbacks of trying to condense such a vast collection of stories into a comparatively short narrative is that much has to be cut out. Regrettably, one such edit was the tale of Lacoön. Yet another Trojan seer, he protests the folly of bringing the wooden horse inside the city walls, but is cut short when Apollo sends two sea-serpents to crush him and his twin sons to death. The horrified Trojans take this as a sign that the horse is to be accepted, whatever their suspicions.

The horrific sack of Troy, with its widespread murder and rape, is typical of the end of any great siege where the victorious warriors take out their pent up anger on the city's population. Aeneas was one of the few males to escape – though *not* with the help of Odysseus – and according to the Romans his descendants later went on to found the city of Rome. Antenor and his family also escaped (*with* the help of Odysseus), but poor Astyanax did not. Some versions have the boy murdered by Neoptolemus, others by Odysseus. I have been kinder to both Astyanax and Odysseus in my account.

You will not find Eperitus in any of the myths. He, his love affair with Astynome (who appears in *The Iliad* as Chryseis) and his feud with his father are all inventions of my imagination. I wanted at least one major character whose fate, unlike those of Odysseus and the others, is entirely in my own hands!

And so the war is over, but not the adventure. In fact, the greatest chapter in the whole saga is just about to begin. As Odysseus turns toward home he is ignorant of the new challenges the Fates are lining up before him. From man-eating songstresses, seductive witches and one-eyed monsters, to the very depths of Hades, he must call on all his courage and wit if he is ever to return home to his beloved Penelope.